CARMEN SANDIEGO™

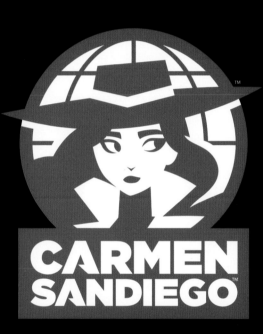

Based on the Netflix original series
teleplay by Greg Ernstrom

Etch is an imprint of Houghton Mifflin Harcourt Publishing Company.

hmhbooks.com

Designed by Jenny Goldstick and Stephanie Hays
The type was set in Proxima Nova.
The sound effect type was created by Jenny Goldstick.

ISBN: 978-0-358-45216-4 paper over board
ISBN: 978-0-358-45215-7 paperback

Manufactured in China
SCP 10 9 8 7 6 5 4 3 2 1
4500817397

CARMEN SANDIEGO™

THE NEED FOR SPEED CAPER

A GRAPHIC NOVEL

HOUGHTON MIFFLIN HARCOURT

BOSTON NEW YORK

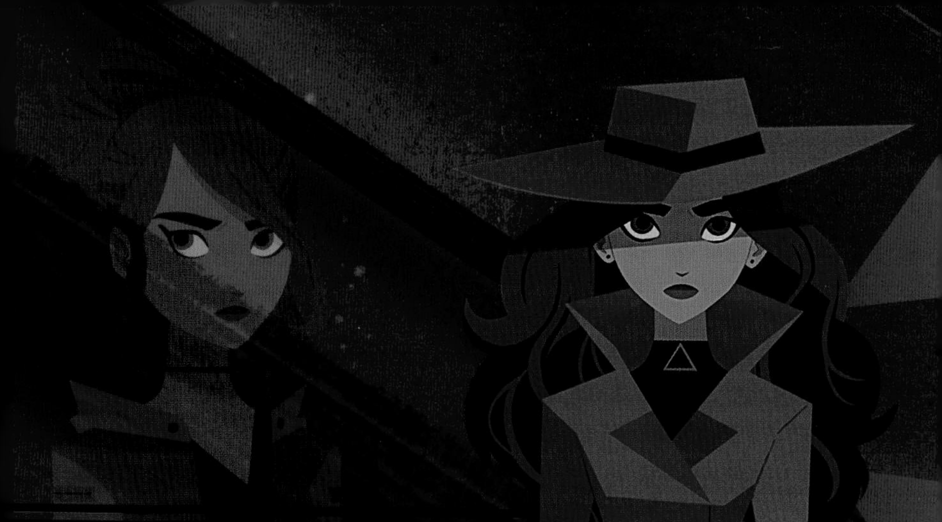

WHO IN THE WORLD IS
CARMEN SANDIEGO?

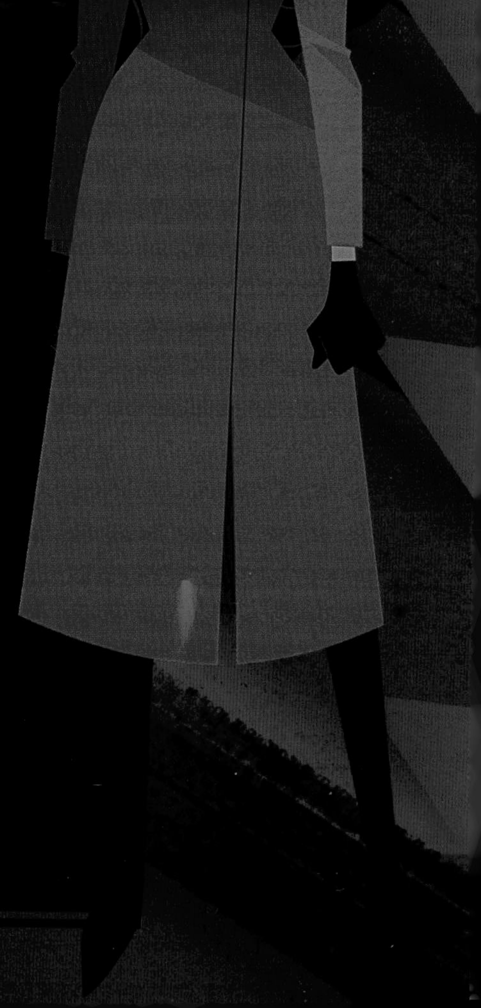

FORMERLY KNOWN AS:

Black Sheep

OCCUPATION:

International super thief, super sneak, expert fighter, gadget guru, mistress of disguise

ORIGIN:

Buenos Aires, Argentina

LAST SEEN:

San Diego, California

I was found as a baby in Argentina and brought to Vile Island, where I was raised as an orphan but I longed to set out and see the world.

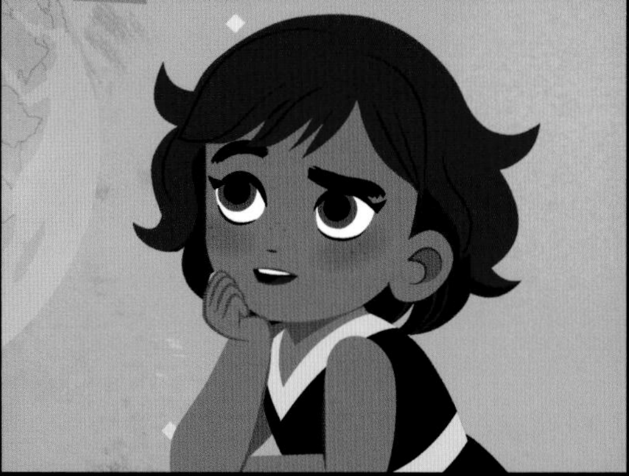

I couldn't wait to train at VILE's school for thieves. I wanted to become a VILE operative, traveling the world to steal precious goods.

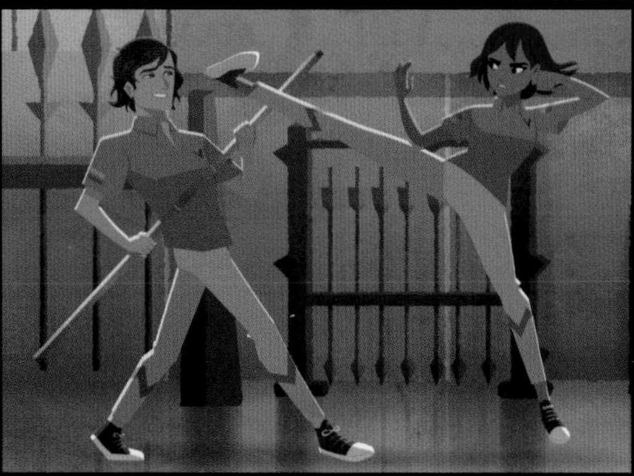

But I knew I had to escape after discovering what VILE really stands for: Villains' International League of Evil!

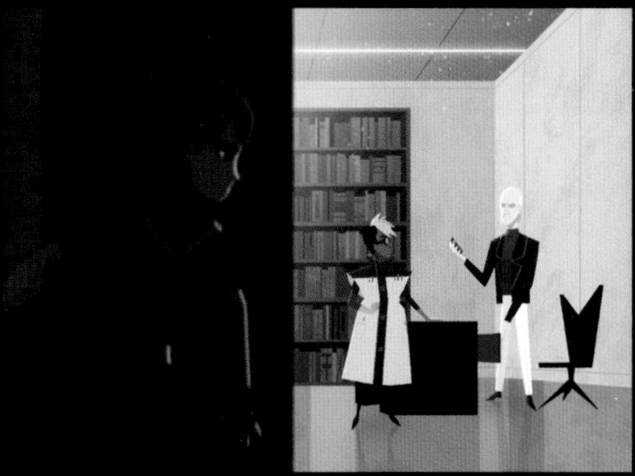

My new mission: securing the world's historic treasures from VILE.

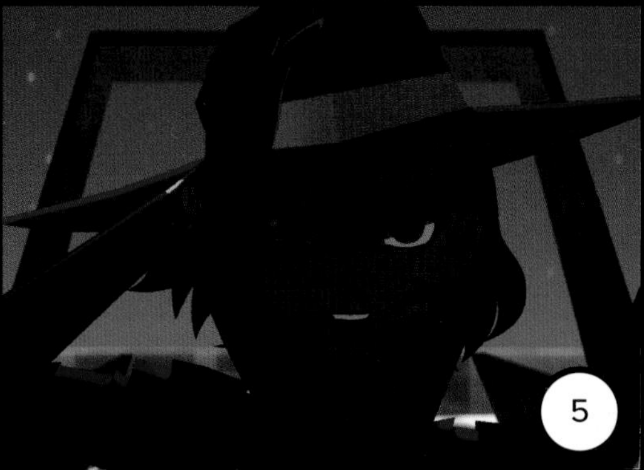

CARMEN'S CREW

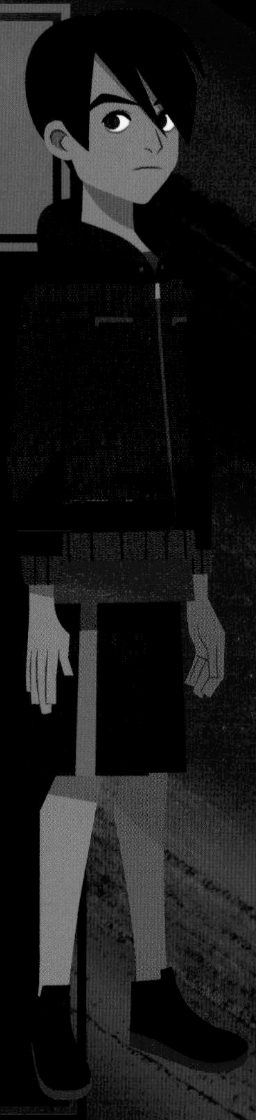

Player

White-hat hacker

BACKGROUND:

Player is a teenager from Niagara Falls, Canada. He met Carmen by hacking into her phone while she was still at VILE.

SKILLS:

- Learns everything about every place that Carmen goes to help guide her on capers
- Remotely deactivates security systems
- Scours the web for secret signs, coded messages, and hidden clues about VILE's next moves

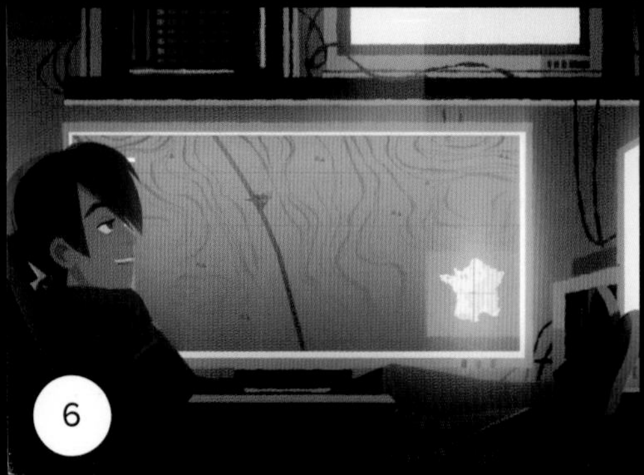

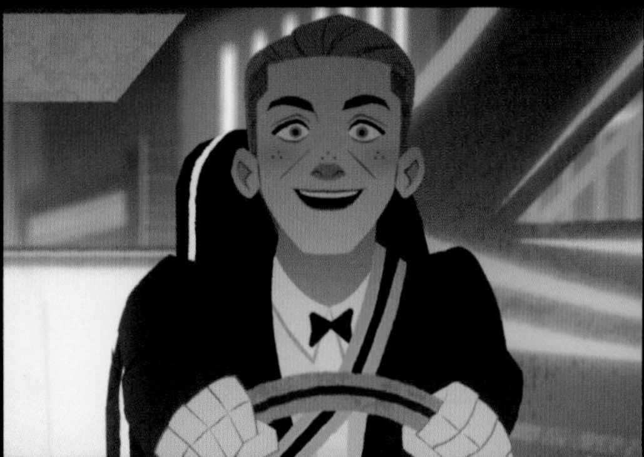

Ivy

Mechanic and tinkerer

SKILLS:

- Operates Carmen's gadgets and knows them like the back of her hand
- Great at fixing and making things
- Supremely loyal to Carmen

Zack

Driver

SKILLS:

- Great with cars, trucks, motorcycles, speedboats -- anything that goes fast
- Knows how to make a quick getaway
- Always hungry and eats almost anything...except for fish. BLECH!

BACKGROUND:

Ivy and Zack are street-kid siblings from Boston, Massachusetts, USA. They met Carmen when they were robbing the same donut shop, which was owned by VILE.

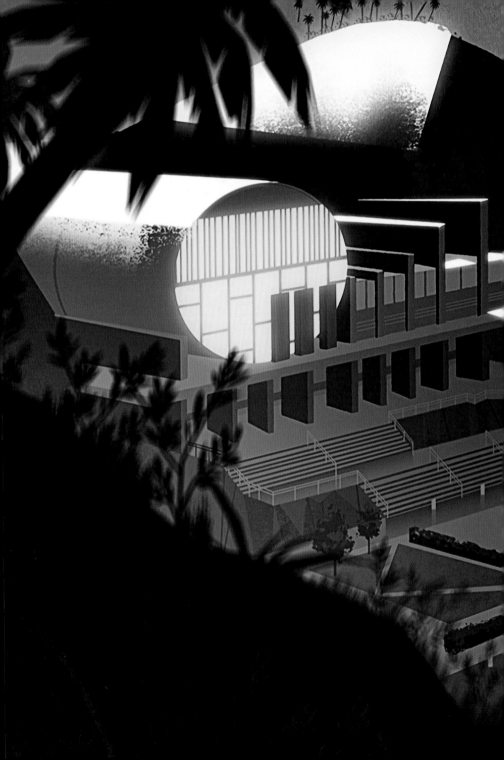

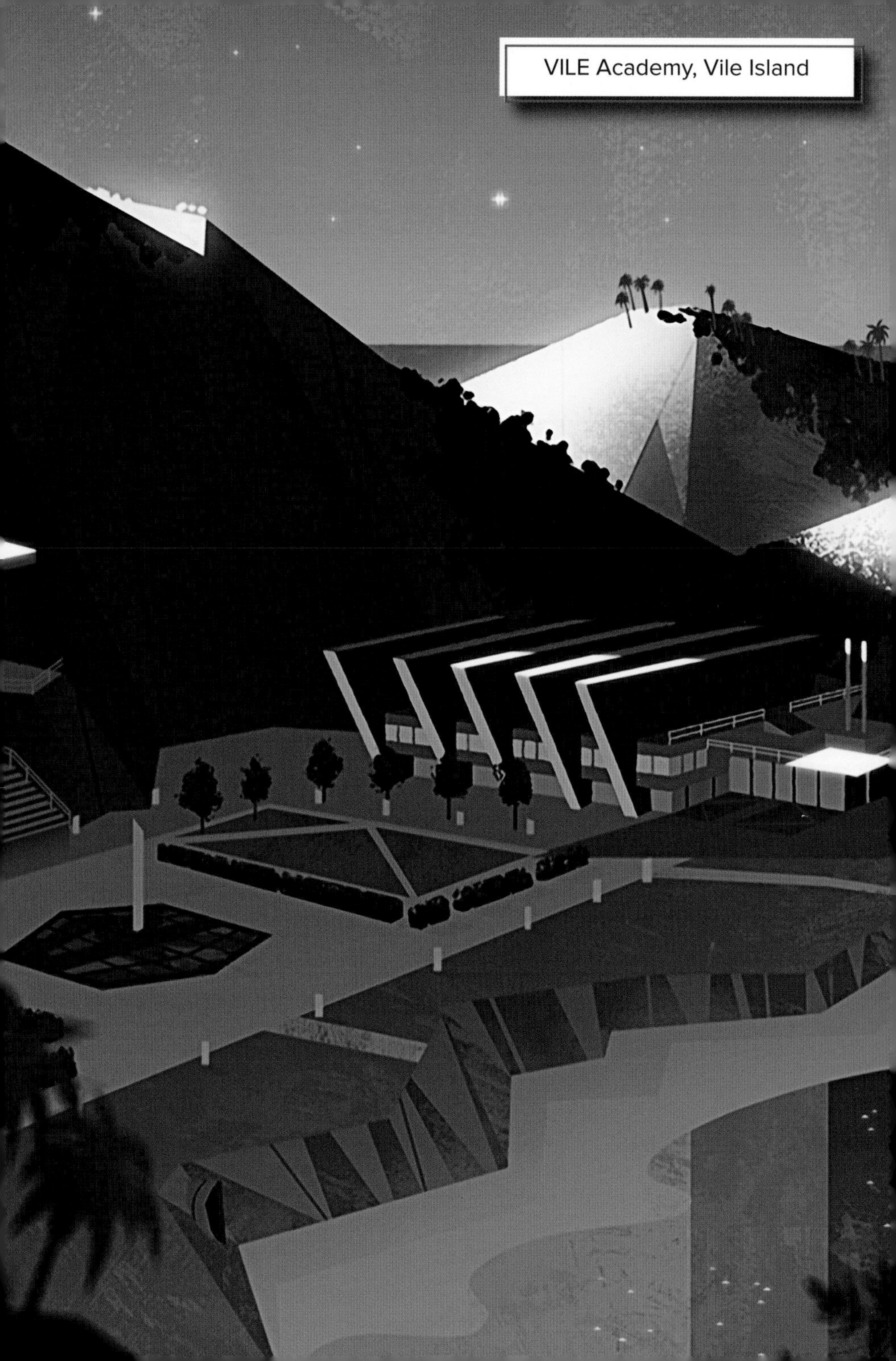
VILE Academy, Vile Island

VILE
Academy Instructors

Gunnar Maelstrom

A psychological genius, Maelstrom learns your weaknesses and twists your mind.

Countess Cleo

Cleo believes that ultimate wealth is ultimate power. She adores expensive everything.

Dr. Saira Bellum

Death rays, invisibility fabric, brain-wiping machines -- these are Bellum's favorite things.

Coach Brunt

Master of hand-to-hand combat, Brunt believes a butt-whooping is the solution to everything.

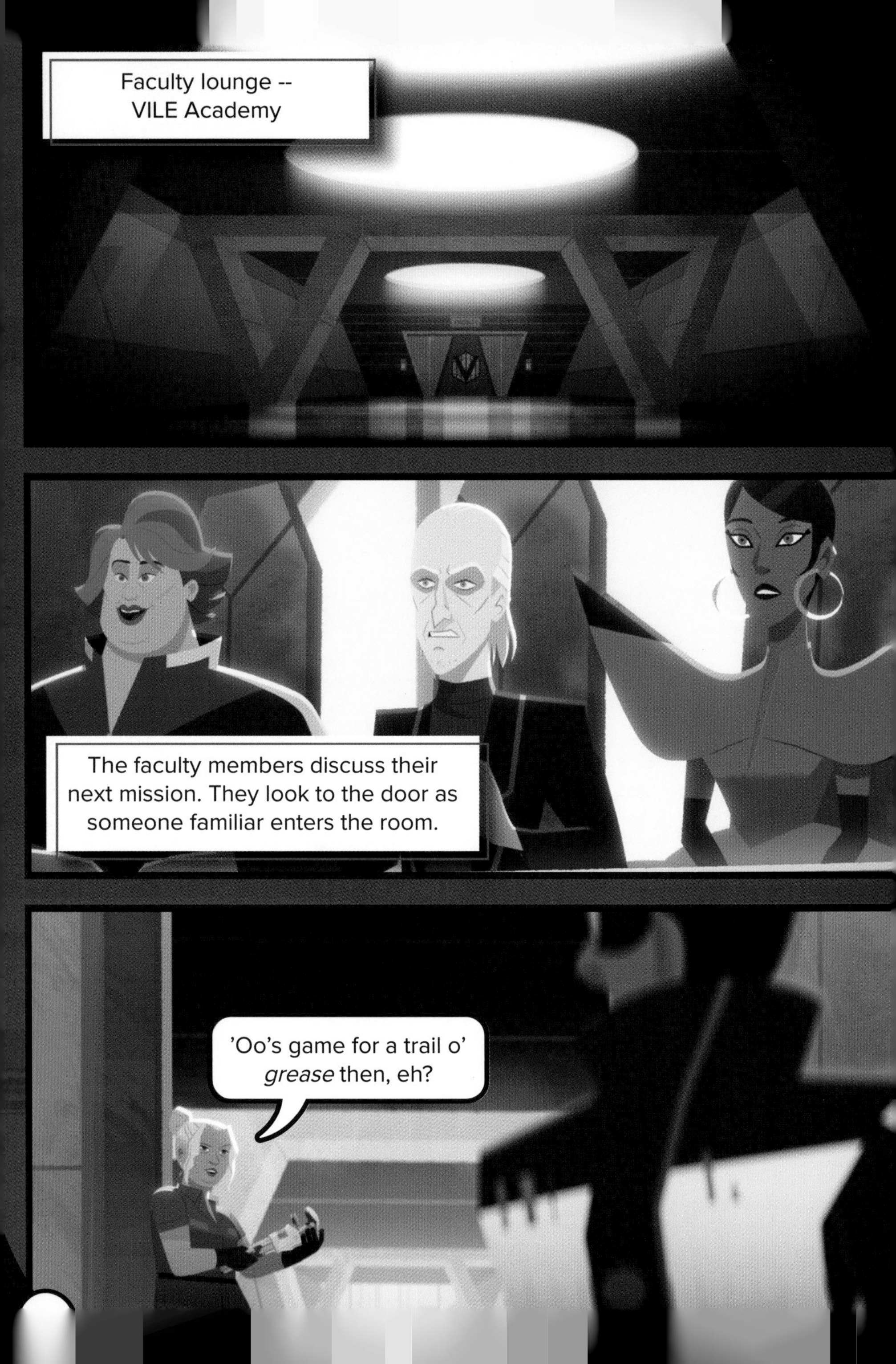
Faculty lounge -- VILE Academy
The faculty members discuss their next mission. They look to the door as someone familiar enters the room.
'Oo's game for a trail o' *grease* then, eh?

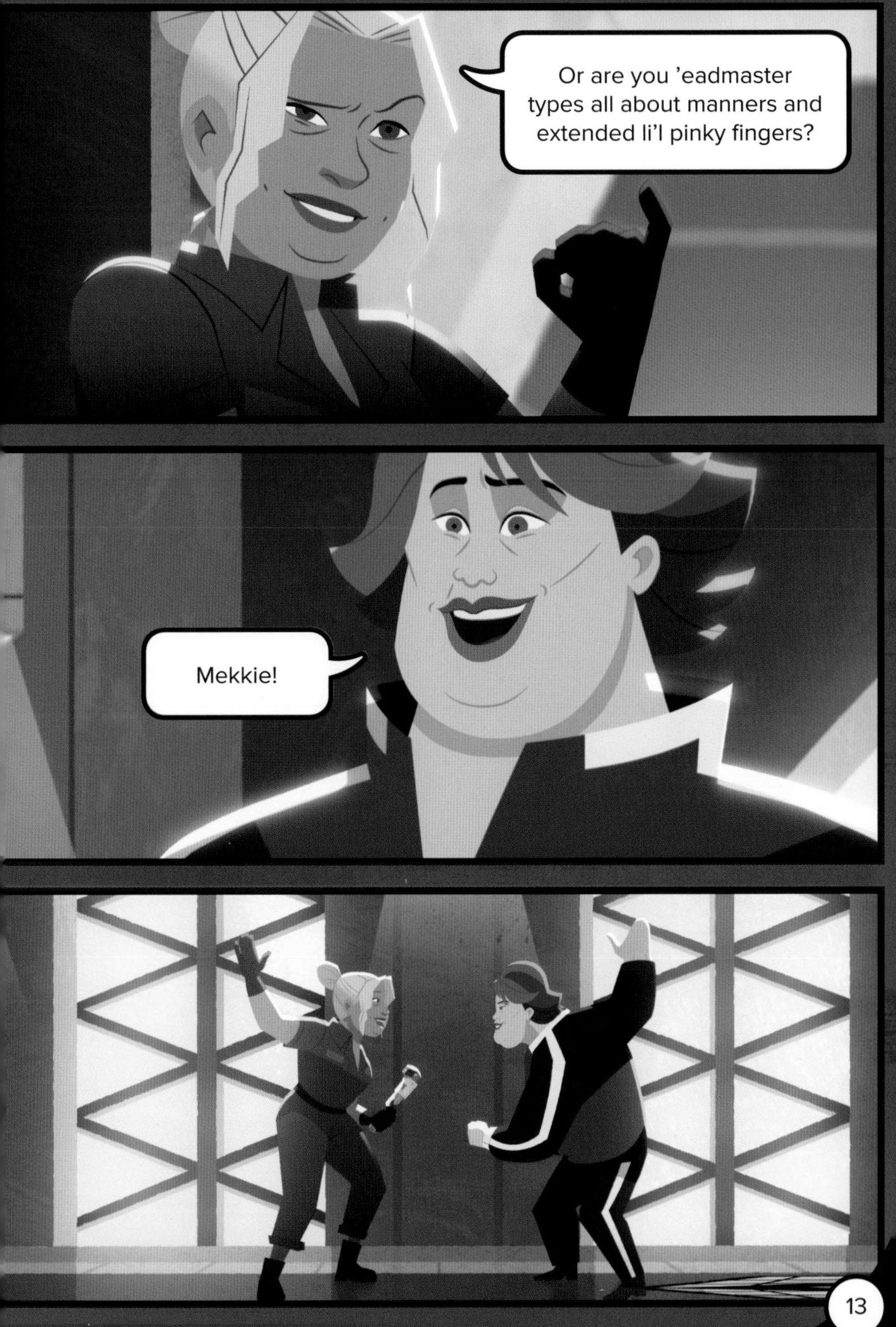
Or are you ’eadmaster types all about manners and extended li’l pinky fingers?
Mekkie!

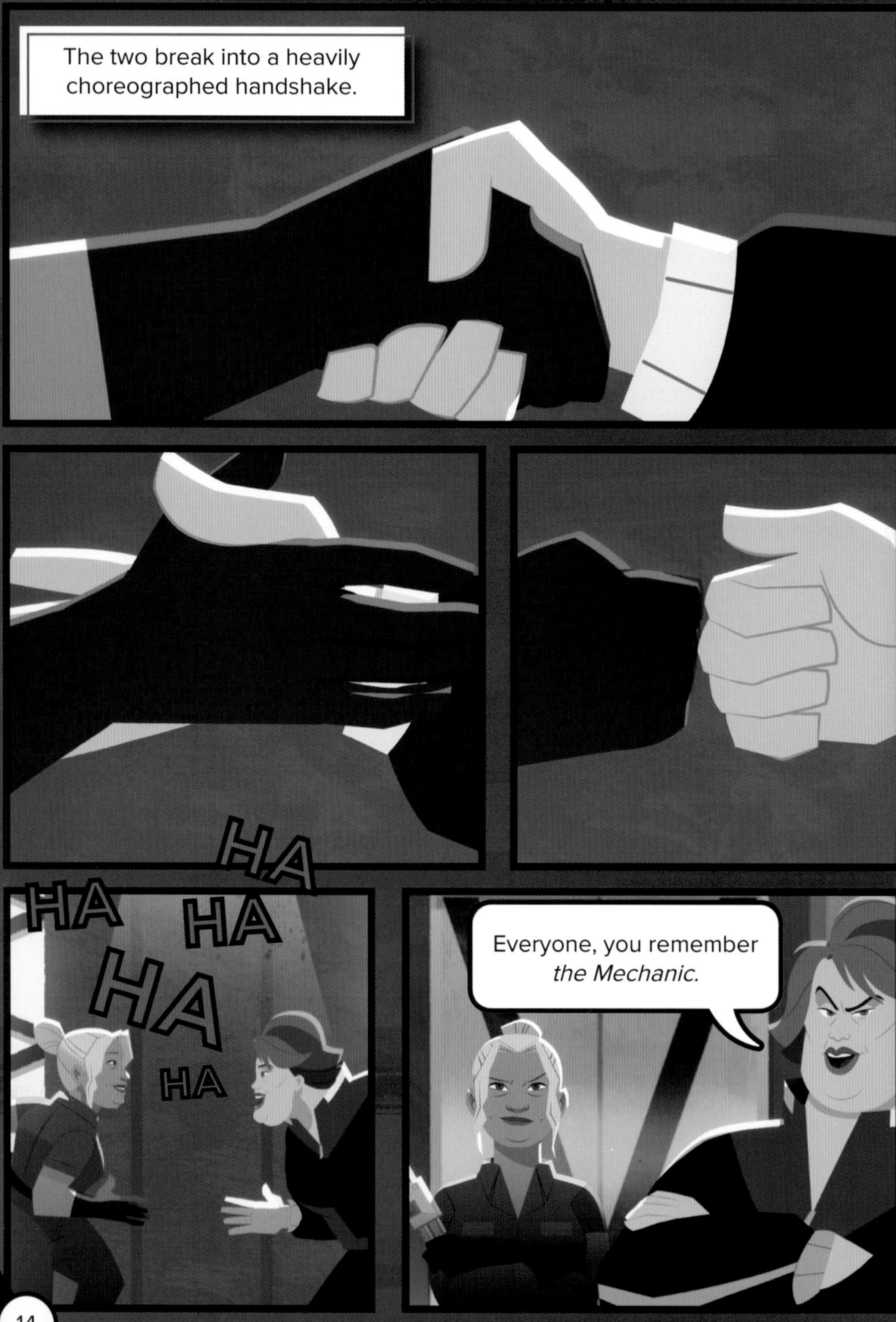
The two break into a heavily choreographed handshake.
HA
HA
HA
HA
HA
Everyone, you remember *the Mechanic.*

The Mechanic

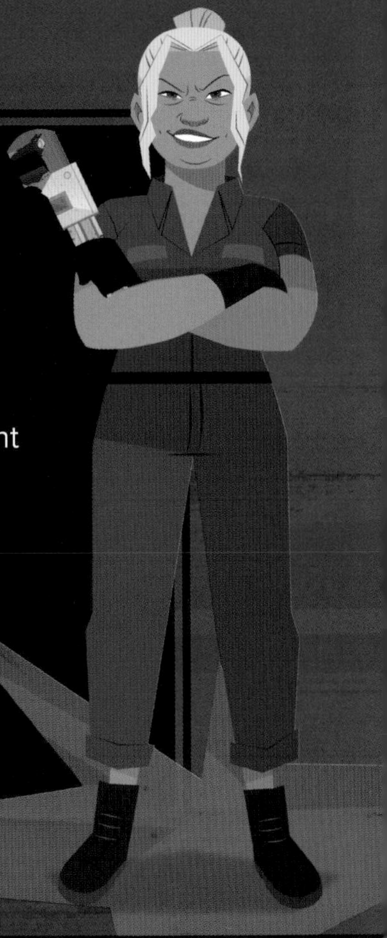

- Nickname: Mekkie
- Origin: East End, London, England
- Former teacher's pet of Coach Brunt
- Always works with her accomplice, the Driver
- Isn't afraid of getting her hands dirty

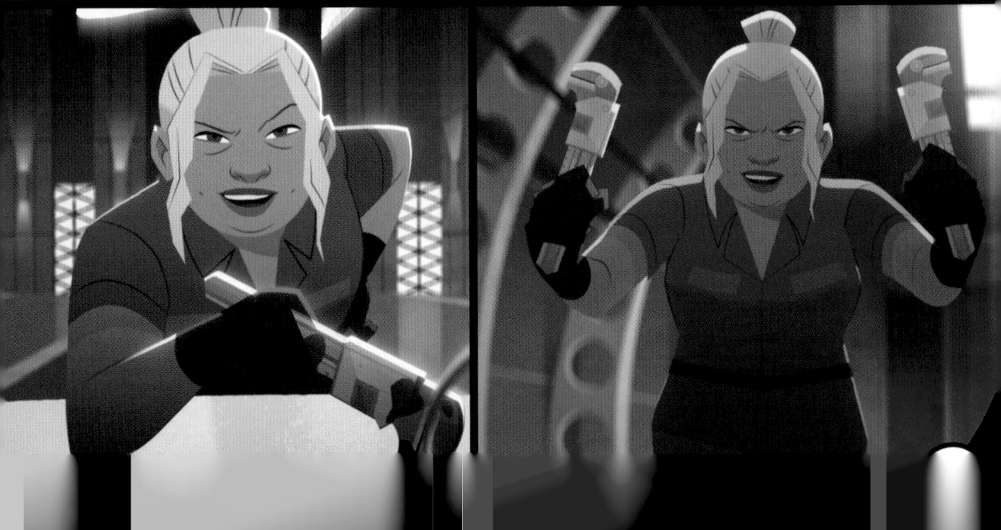

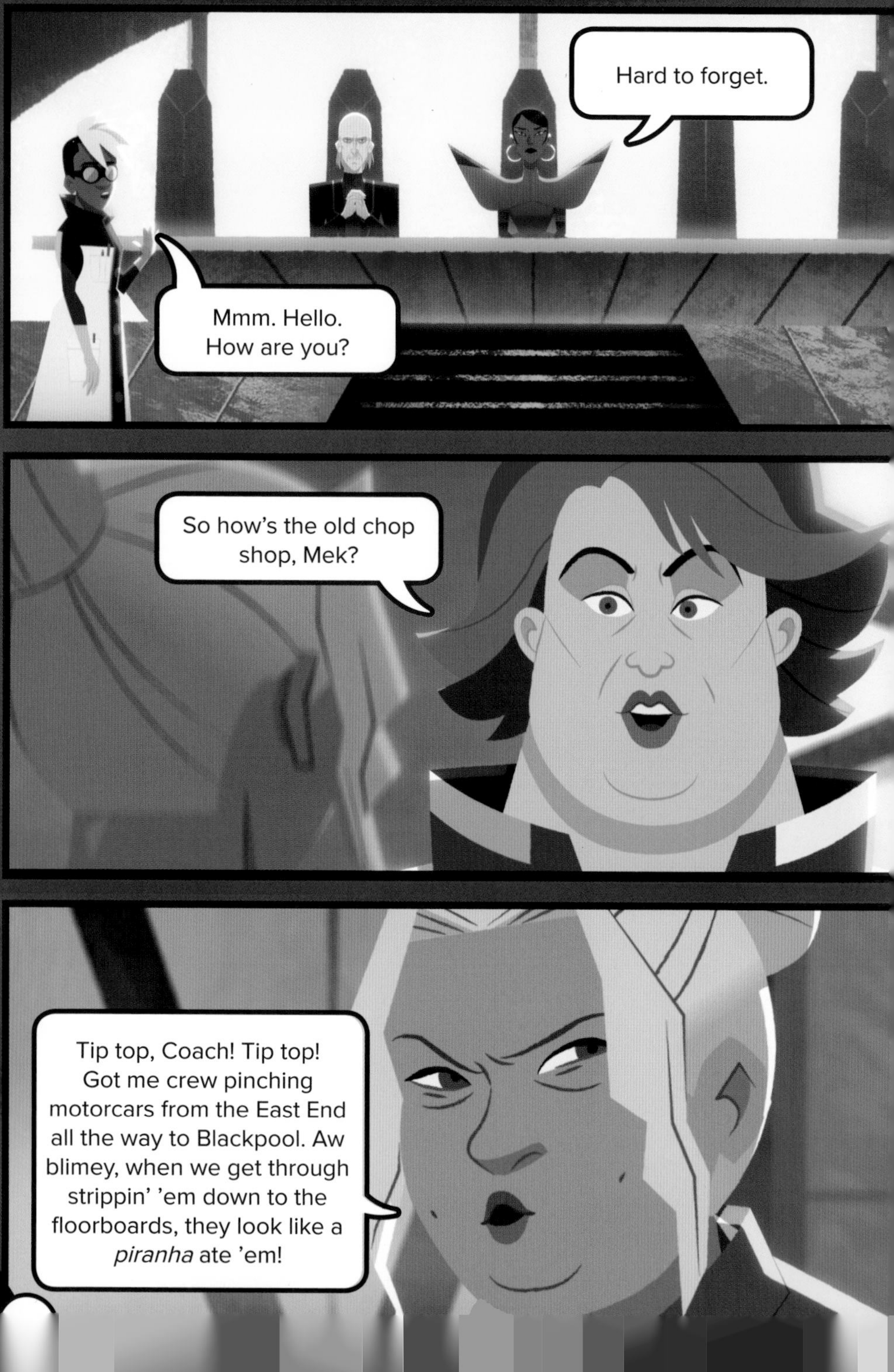

Hard to forget.
Mmm. Hello. How are you?
So how's the old chop shop, Mek?
Tip top, Coach! Tip top! Got me crew pinching motorcars from the East End all the way to Blackpool. Aw blimey, when we get through strippin' 'em down to the floorboards, they look like a *piranha* ate 'em!

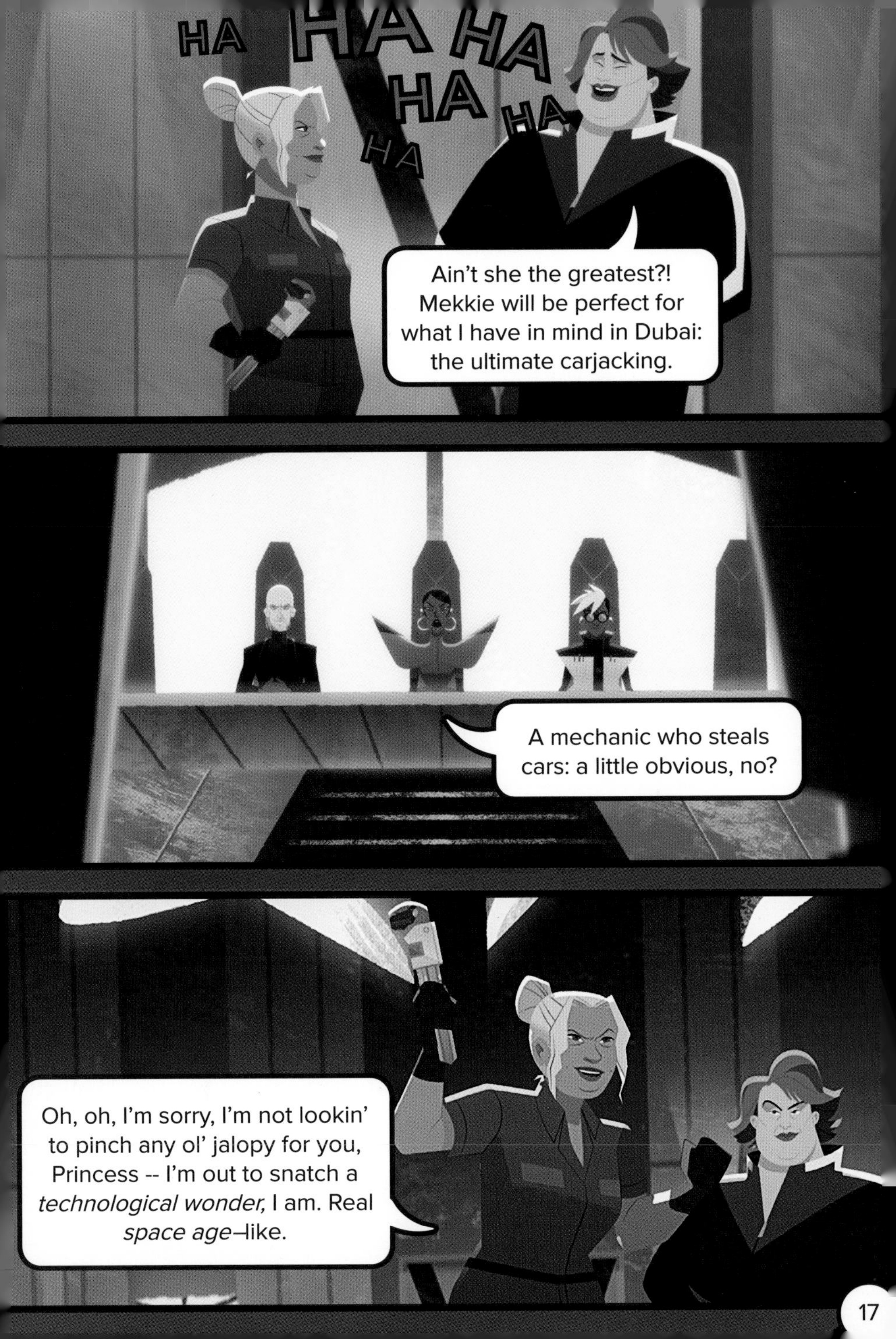
HA HA HA HA HA HA
Ain't she the greatest?! Mekkie will be perfect for what I have in mind in Dubai: the ultimate carjacking.
A mechanic who steals cars: a little obvious, no?
Oh, oh, I'm sorry, I'm not lookin' to pinch any ol' jalopy for you, Princess -- I'm out to snatch a *technological wonder,* I am. Real *space age*–like.

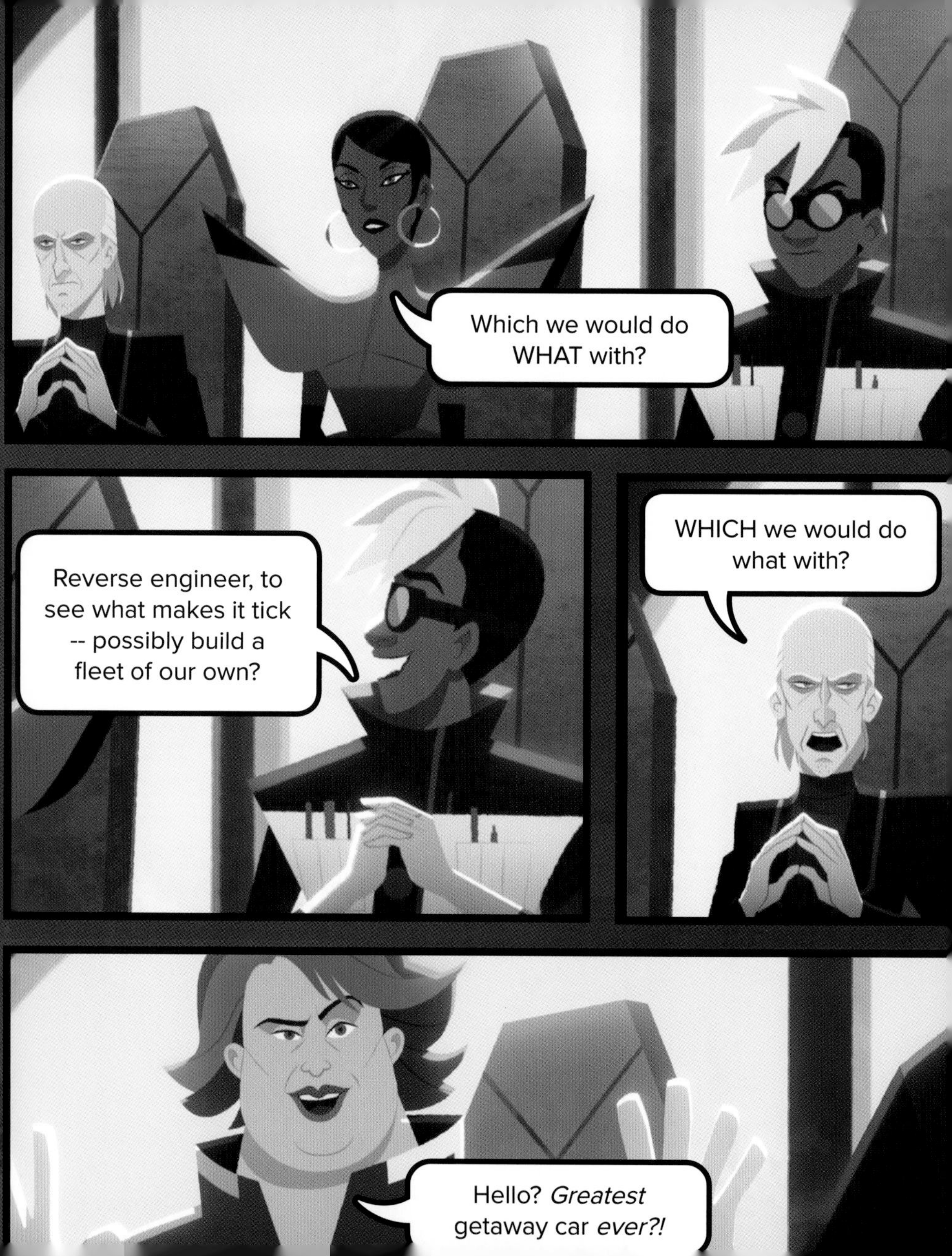
Which we would do WHAT with?
Reverse engineer, to see what makes it tick -- possibly build a fleet of our own?
WHICH we would do what with?
Hello? *Greatest* getaway car *ever?!*

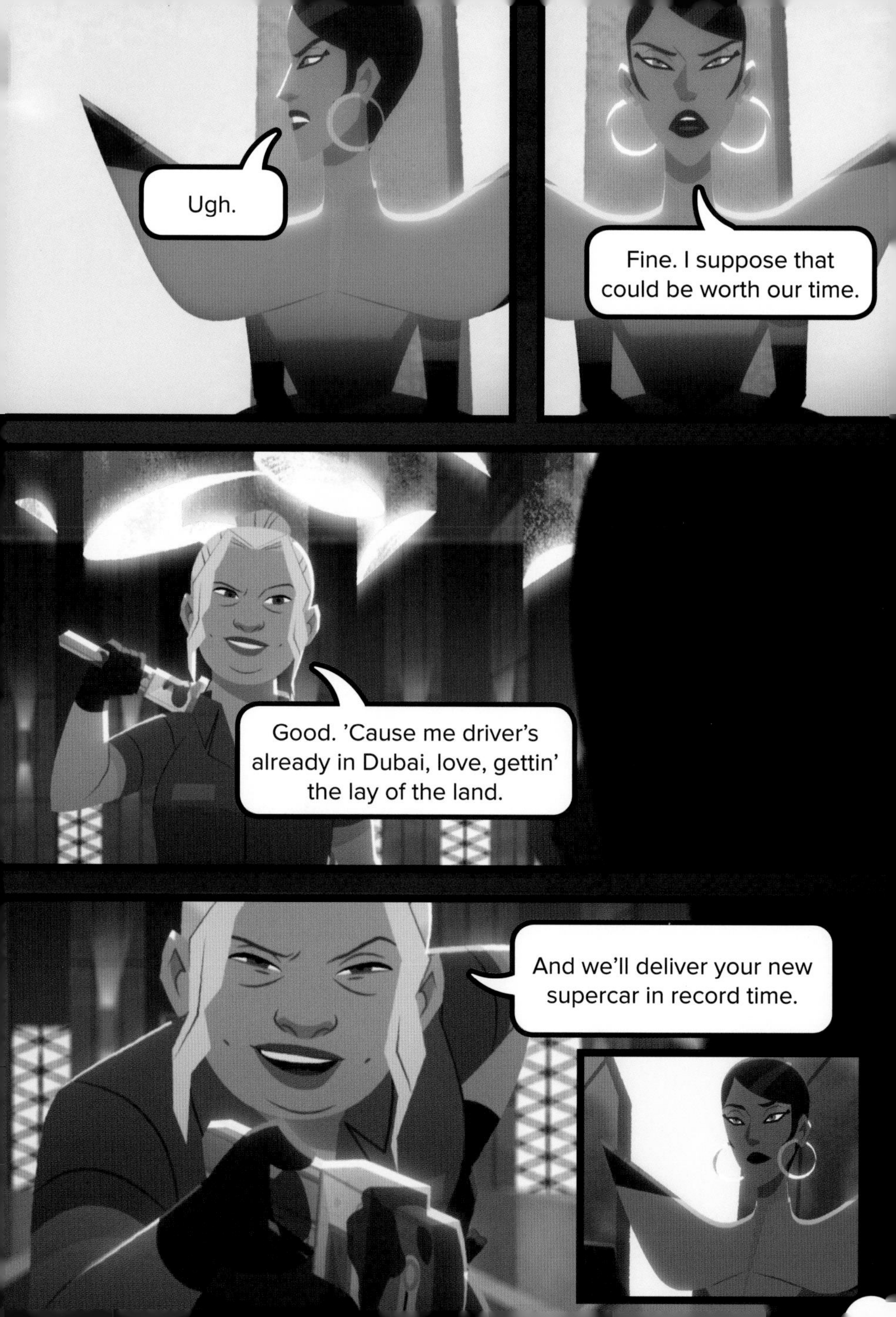
Ugh.
Fine. I suppose that could be worth our time.
Good. 'Cause me driver's already in Dubai, love, gettin' the lay of the land.
And we'll deliver your new supercar in record time.

Destination: Dubai, United Arab Emirates • ETA: 1800 hours

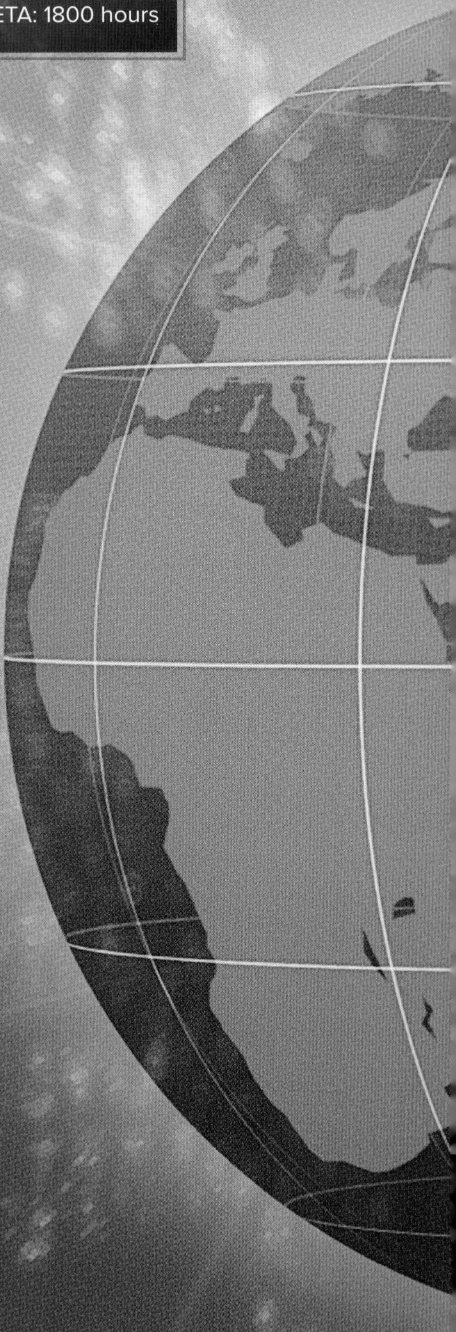

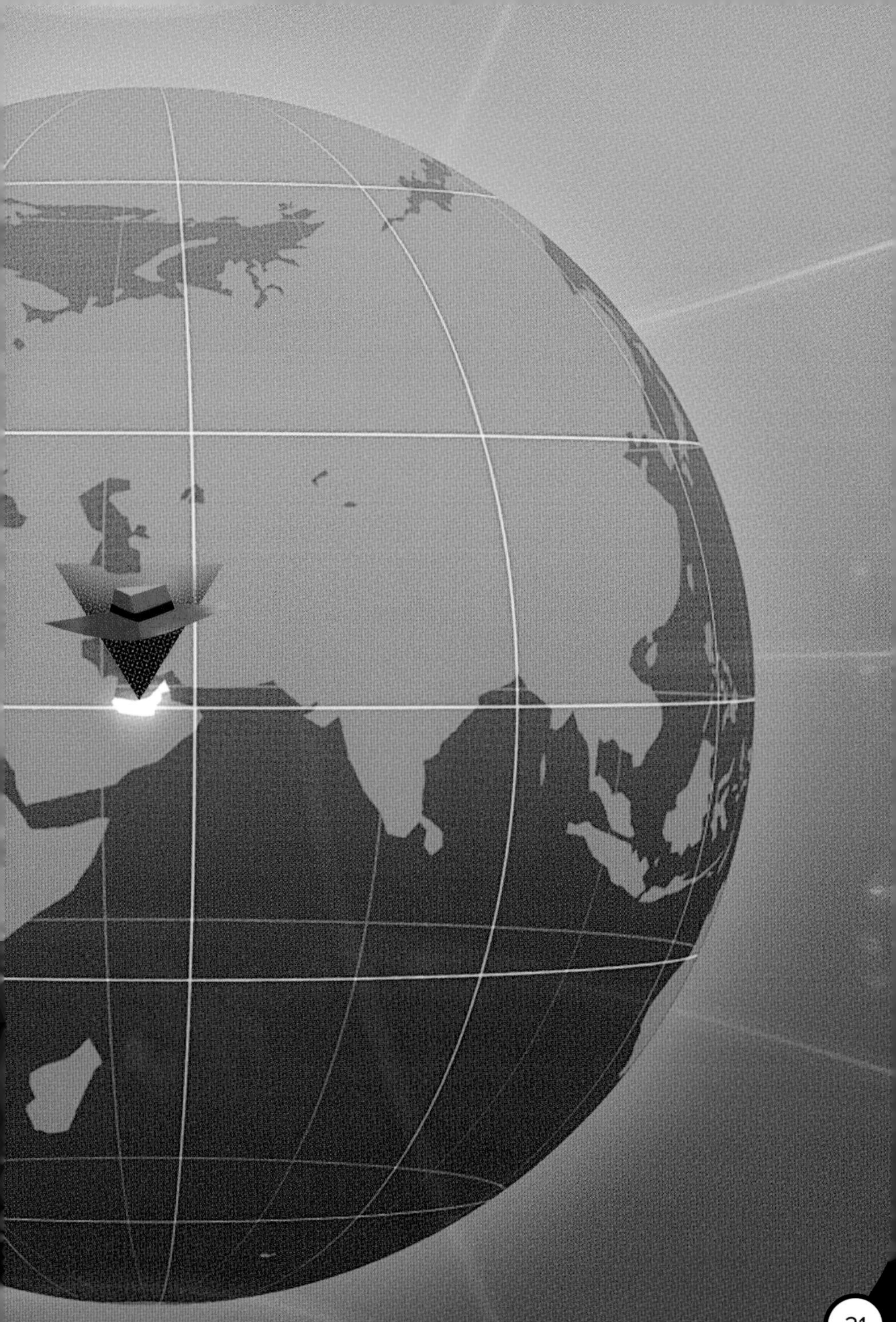

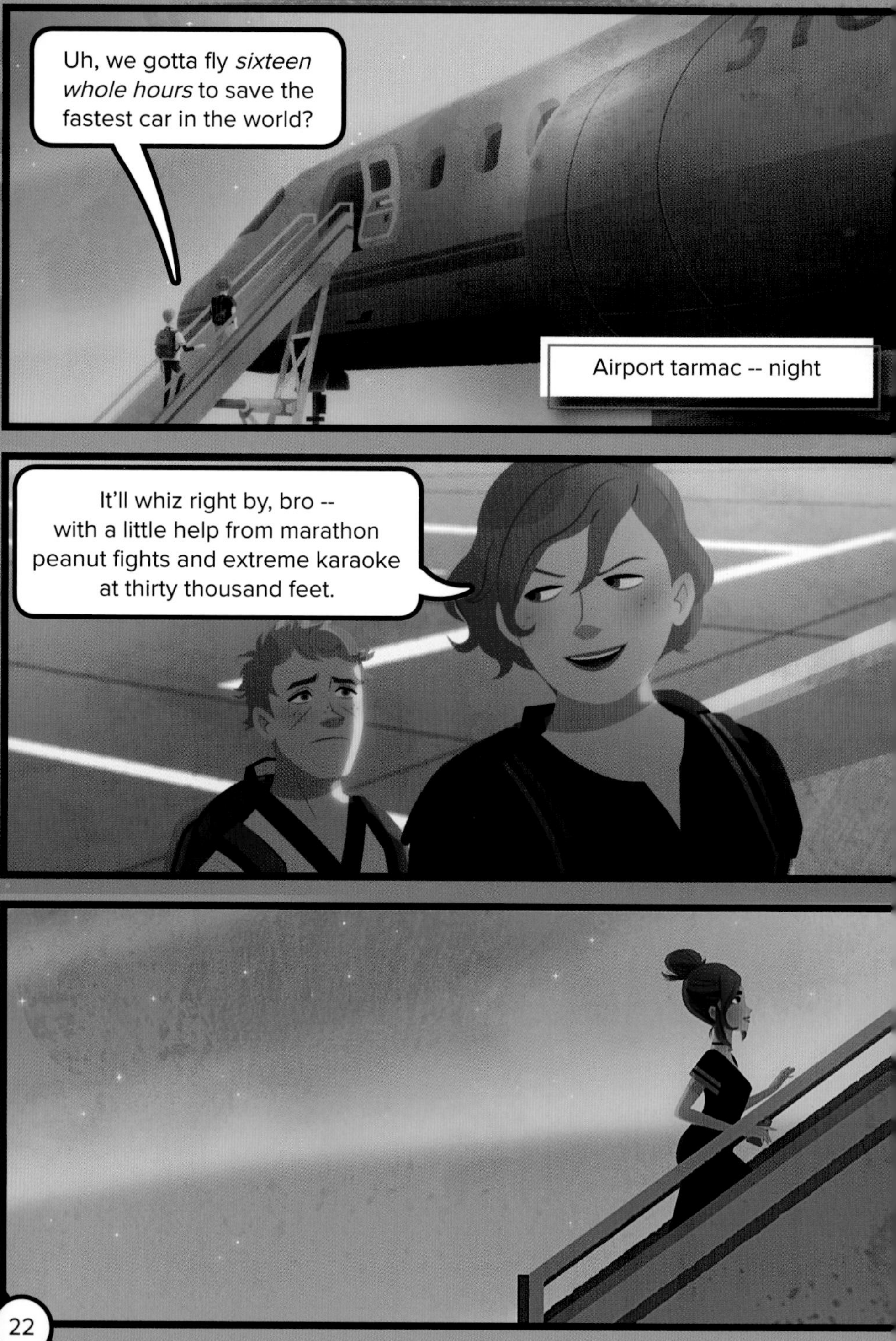
Uh, we gotta fly *sixteen whole hours* to save the fastest car in the world?
Airport tarmac -- night
It'll whiz right by, bro -- with a little help from marathon peanut fights and extreme karaoke at thirty thousand feet.

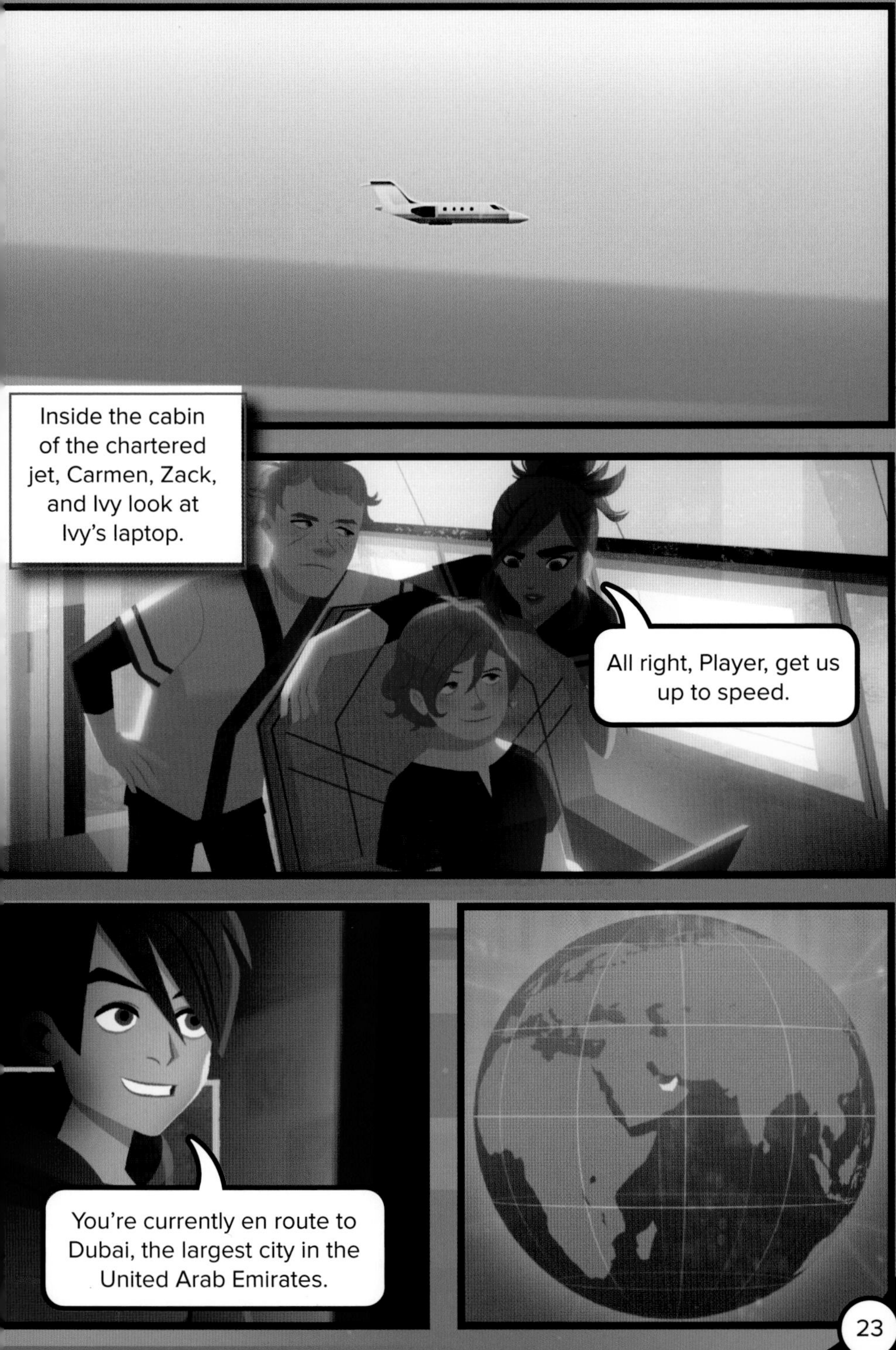
Inside the cabin of the chartered jet, Carmen, Zack, and Ivy look at Ivy's laptop.
All right, Player, get us up to speed.
You're currently en route to Dubai, the largest city in the United Arab Emirates.

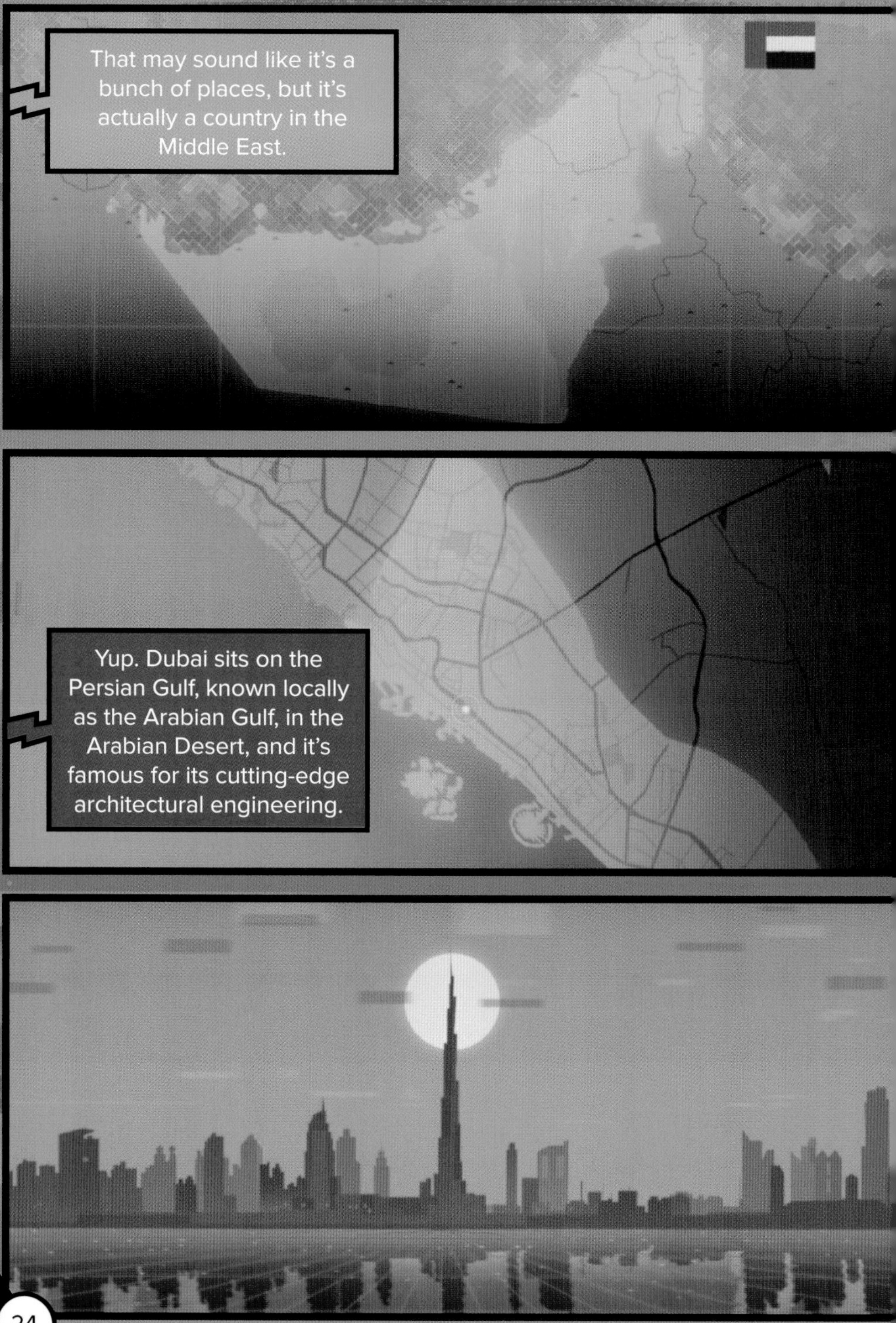
That may sound like it's a bunch of places, but it's actually a country in the Middle East.
Yup. Dubai sits on the Persian Gulf, known locally as the Arabian Gulf, in the Arabian Desert, and it's famous for its cutting-edge architectural engineering.

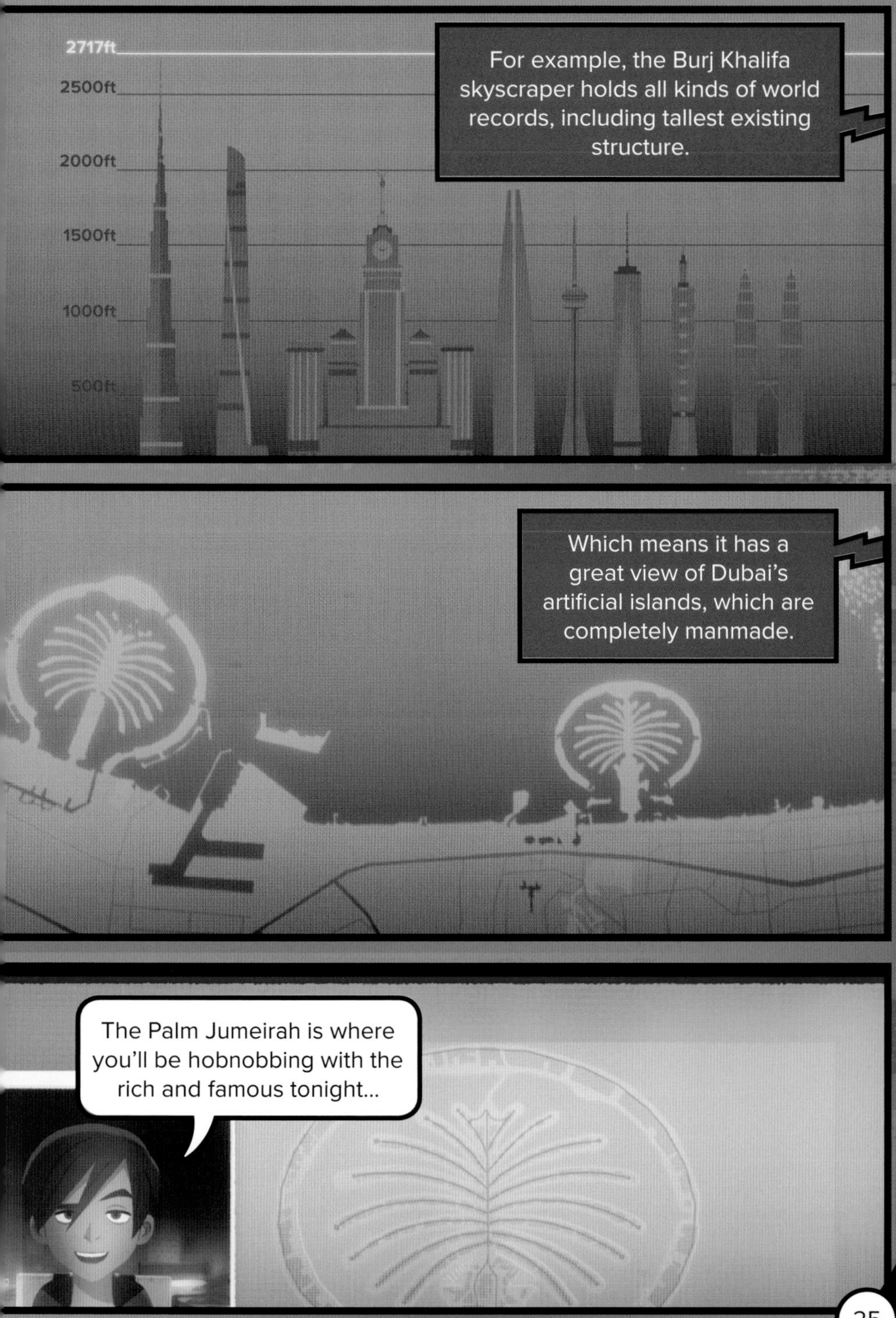
2717ft
2500ft
2000ft
1500ft
1000ft
500ft
For example, the Burj Khalifa skyscraper holds all kinds of world records, including tallest existing structure.
Which means it has a great view of Dubai's artificial islands, which are completely manmade.
The Palm Jumeirah is where you'll be hobnobbing with the rich and famous tonight...

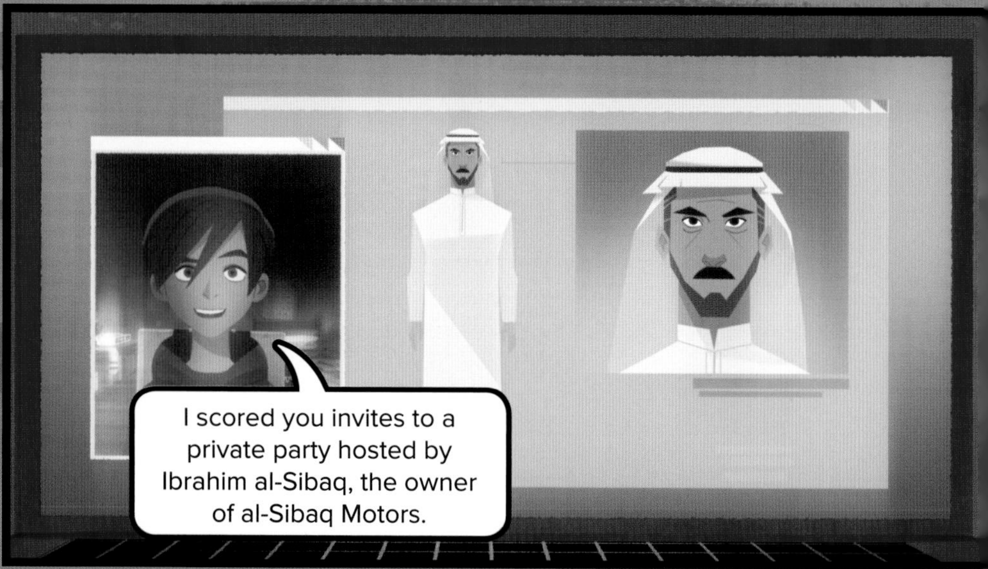

I scored you invites to a private party hosted by Ibrahim al-Sibaq, the owner of al-Sibaq Motors.

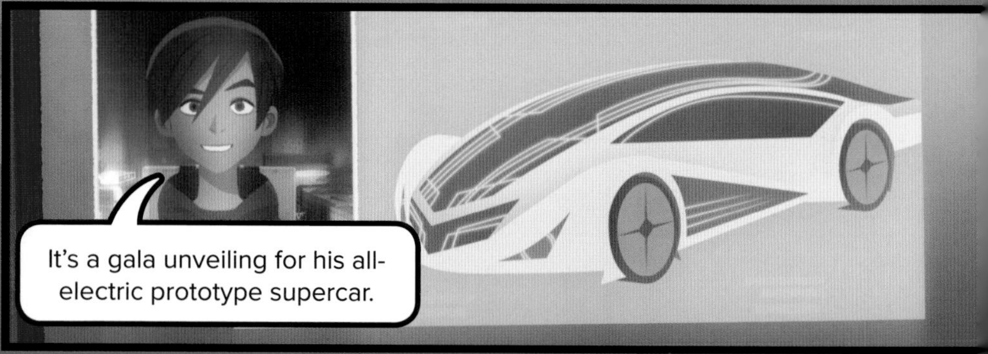

It's a gala unveiling for his all-electric prototype supercar.

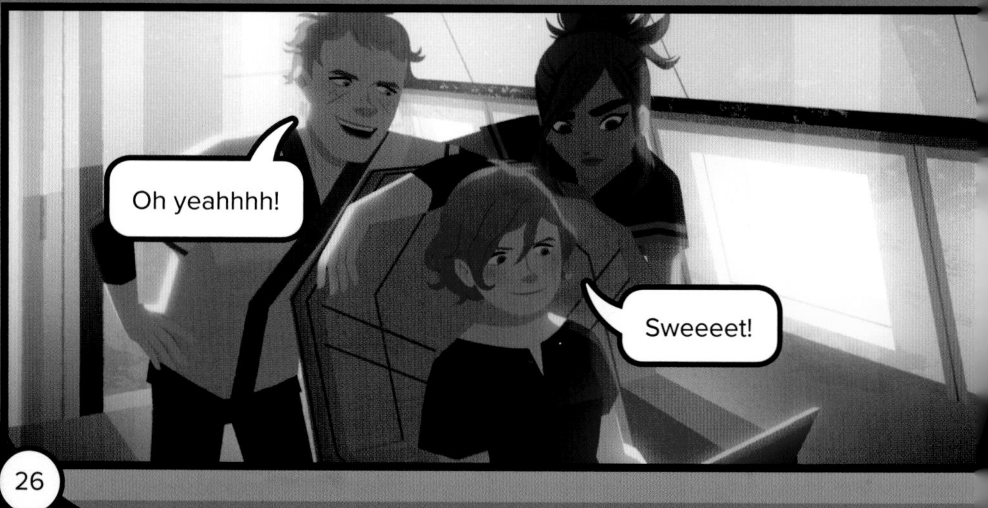

Oh yeahhhh!
Sweeeet!

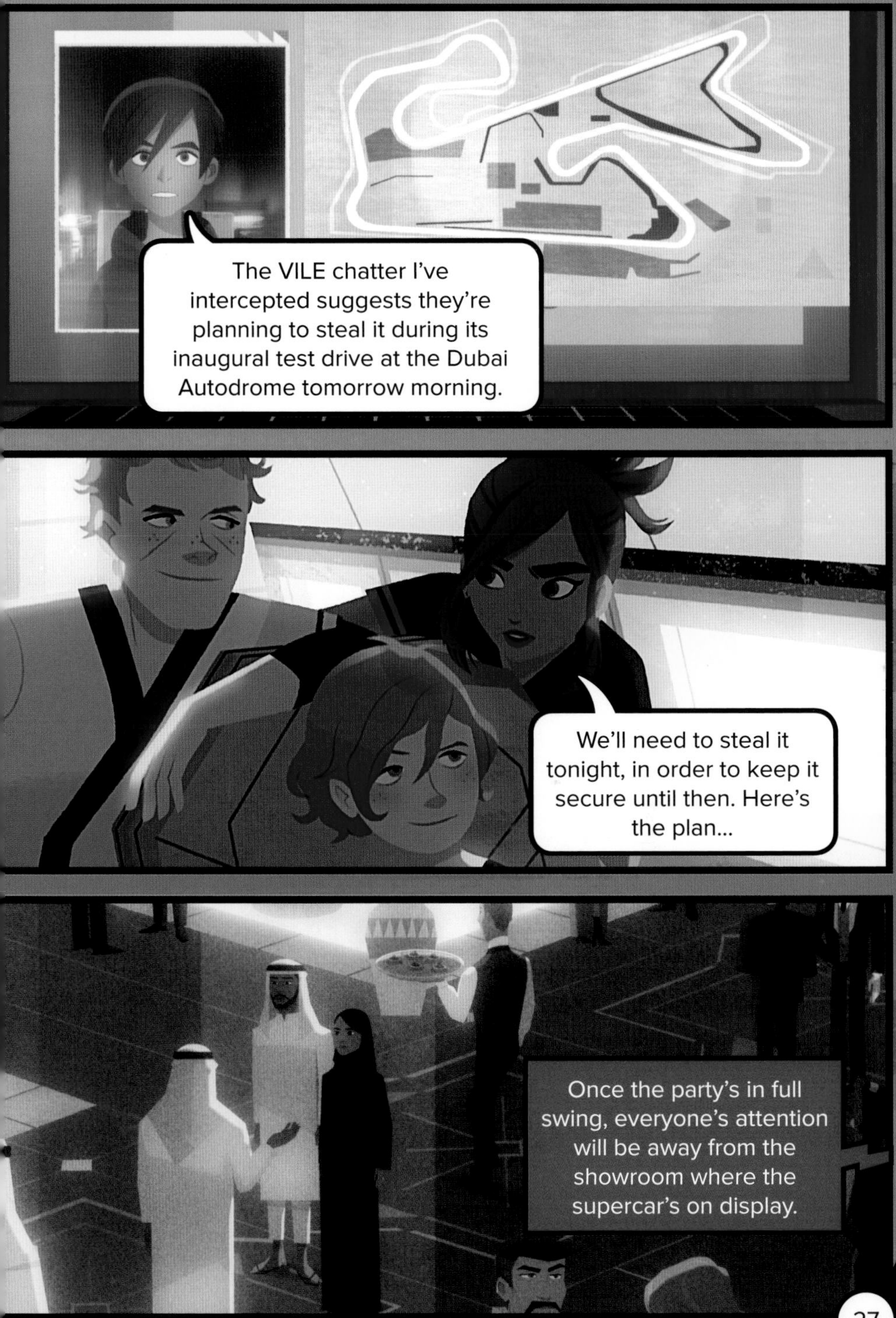

The VILE chatter I've intercepted suggests they're planning to steal it during its inaugural test drive at the Dubai Autodrome tomorrow morning.
We'll need to steal it tonight, in order to keep it secure until then. Here's the plan...
Once the party's in full swing, everyone's attention will be away from the showroom where the supercar's on display.

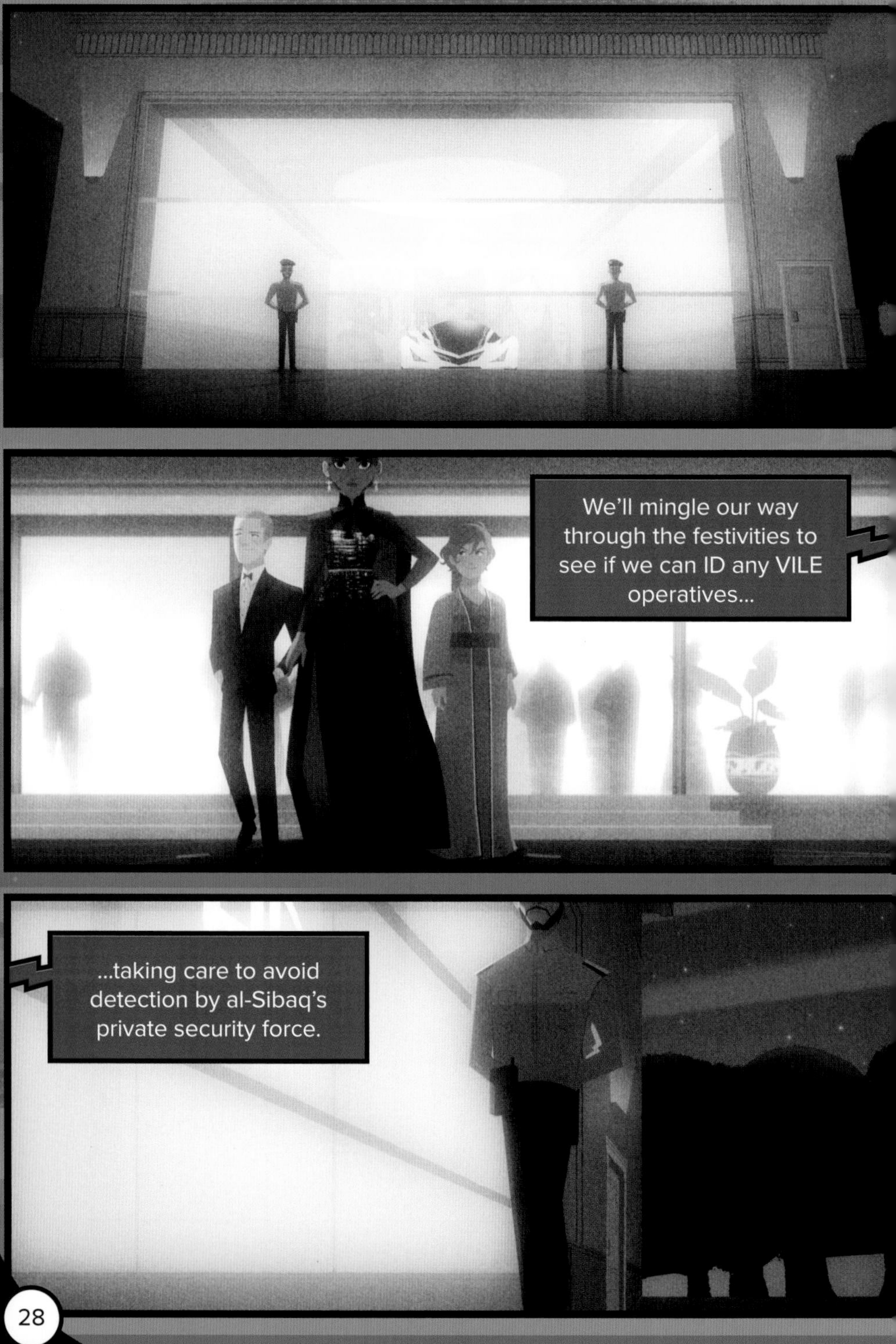

We'll mingle our way through the festivities to see if we can ID any VILE operatives...
...taking care to avoid detection by al-Sibaq's private security force.

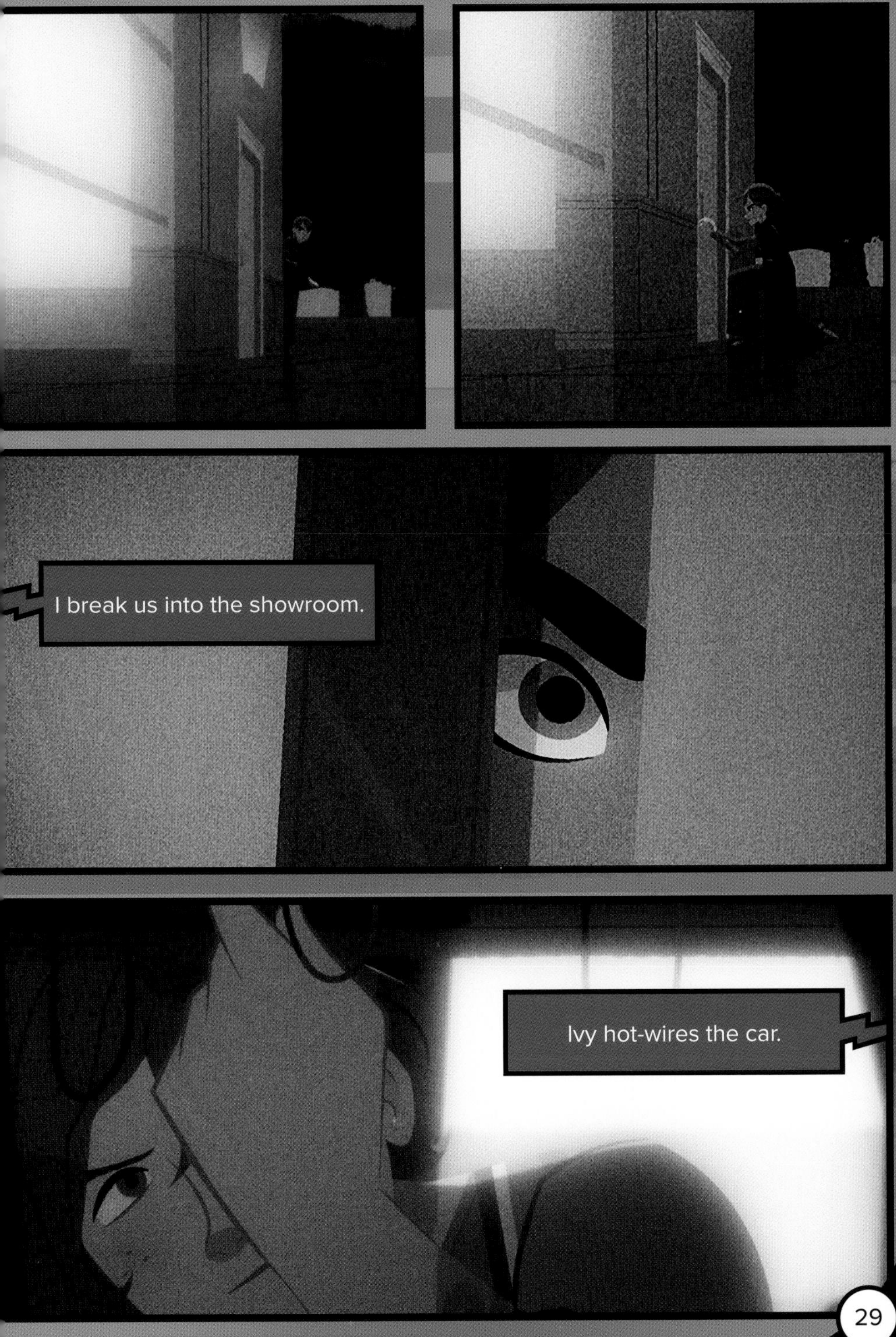
I break us into the showroom.
Ivy hot-wires the car.

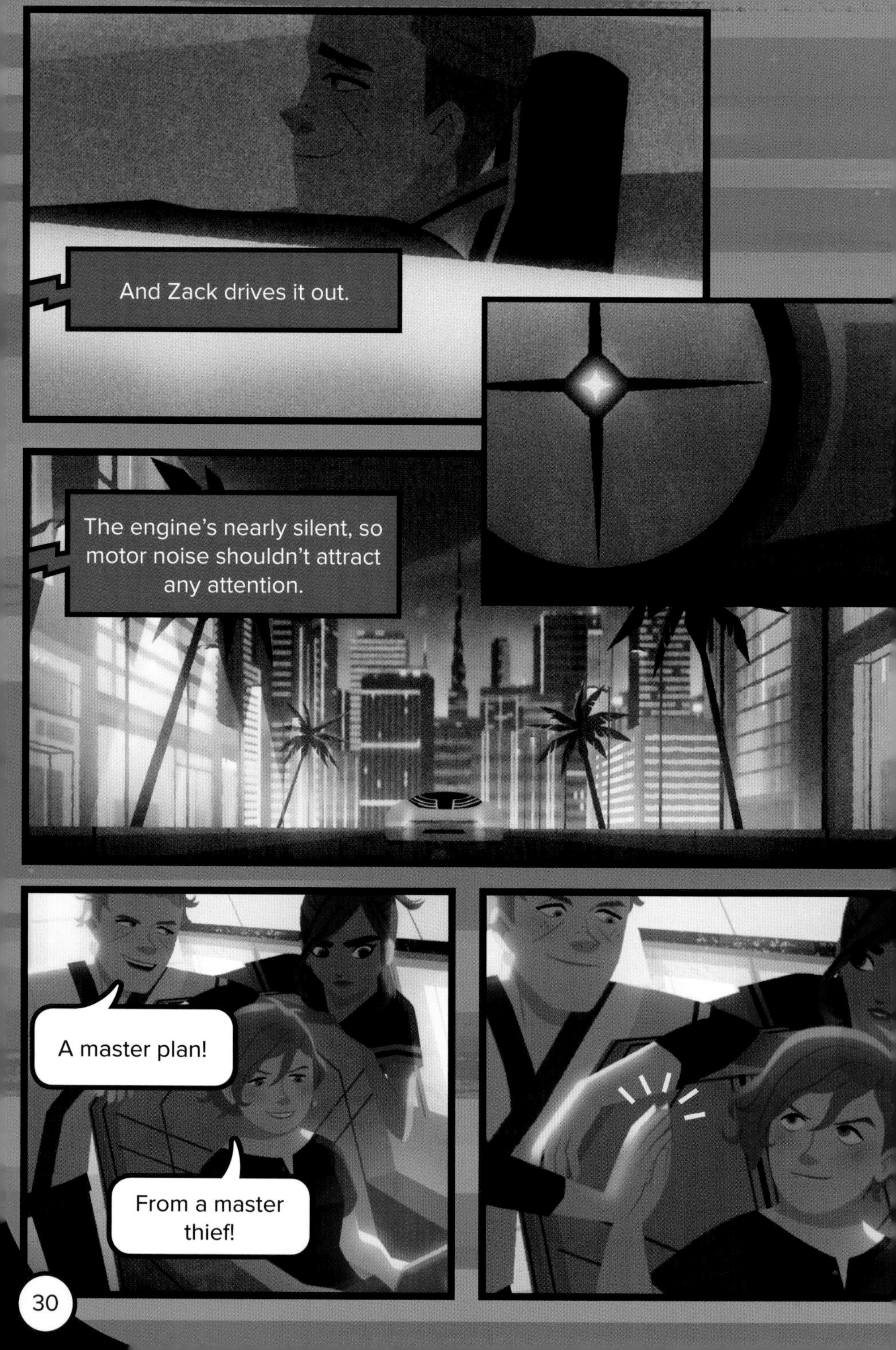
And Zack drives it out.
The engine's nearly silent, so motor noise shouldn't attract any attention.
A master plan!
From a master thief!

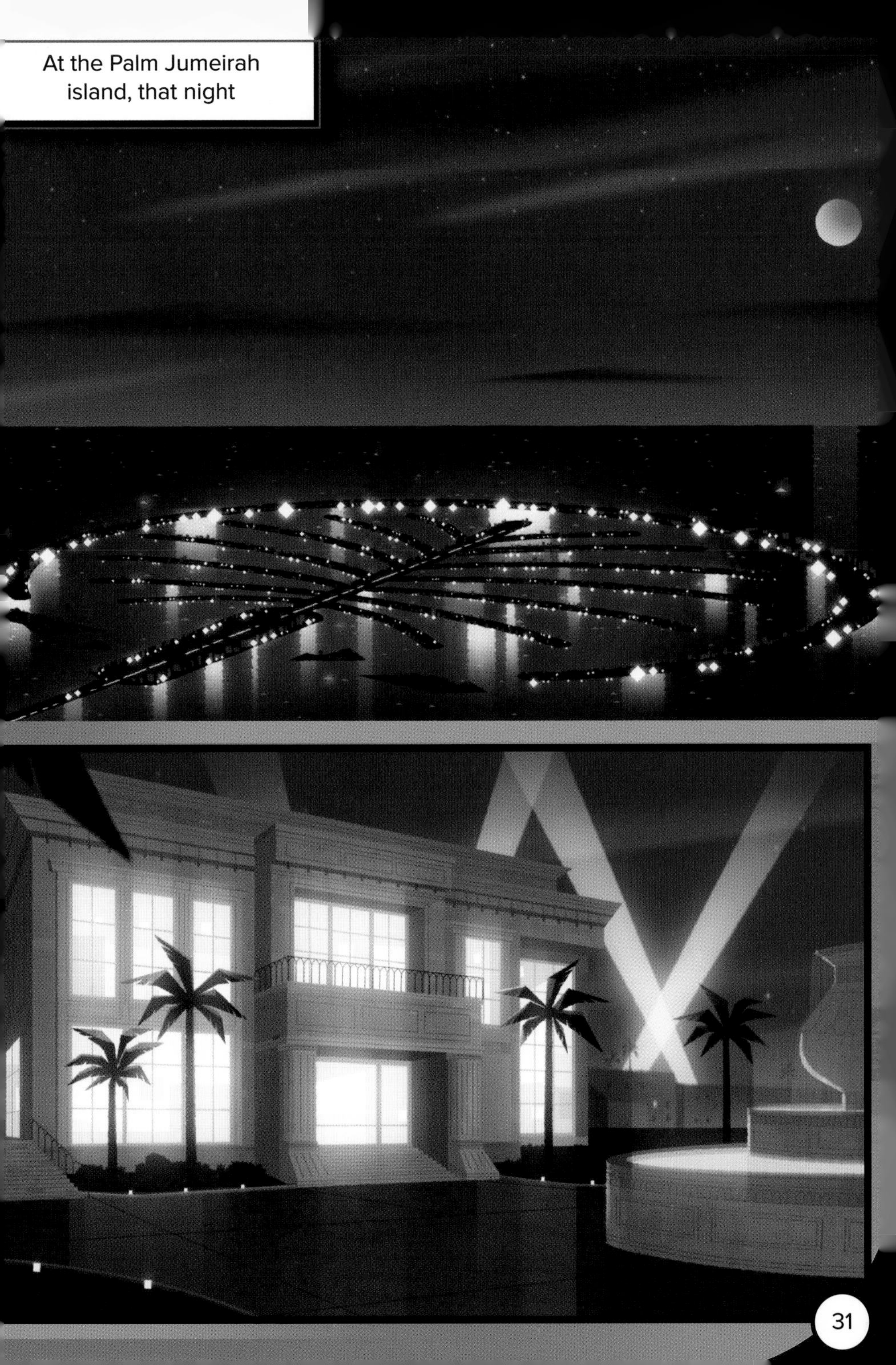
At the Palm Jumeirah island, that night

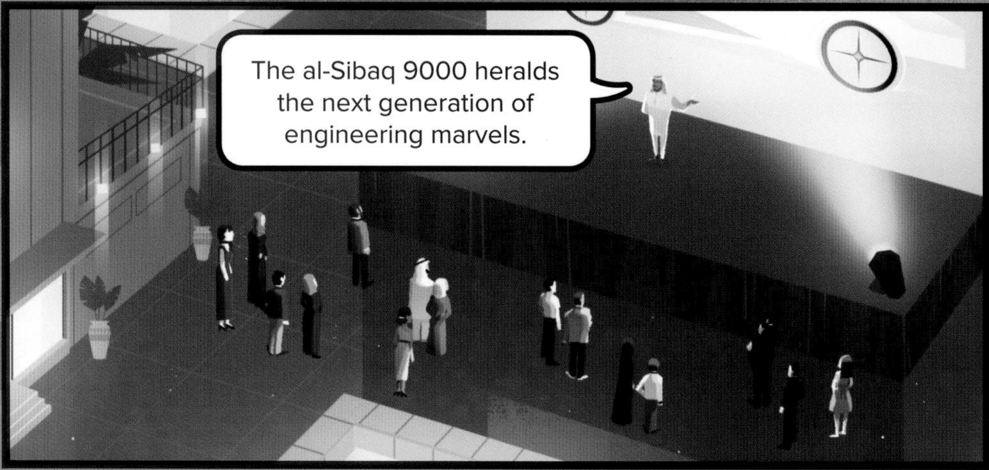
The al-Sibaq 9000 heralds the next generation of engineering marvels.

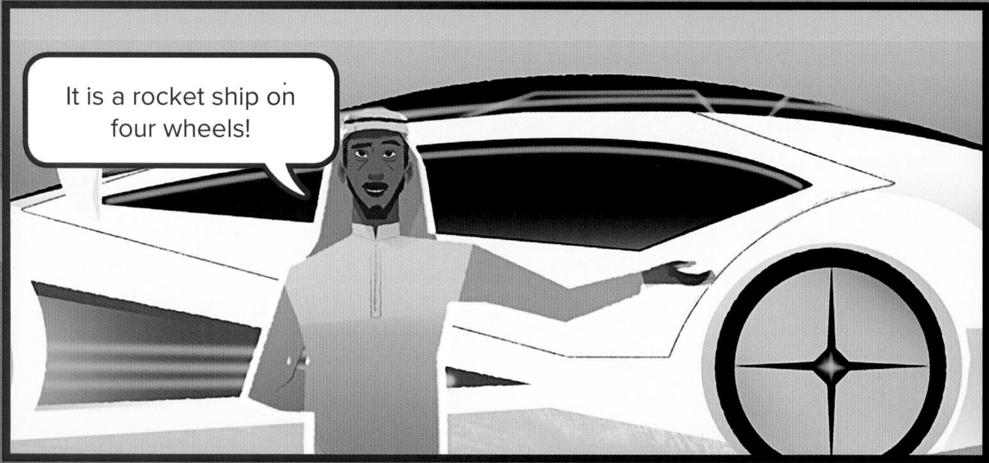
It is a rocket ship on four wheels!

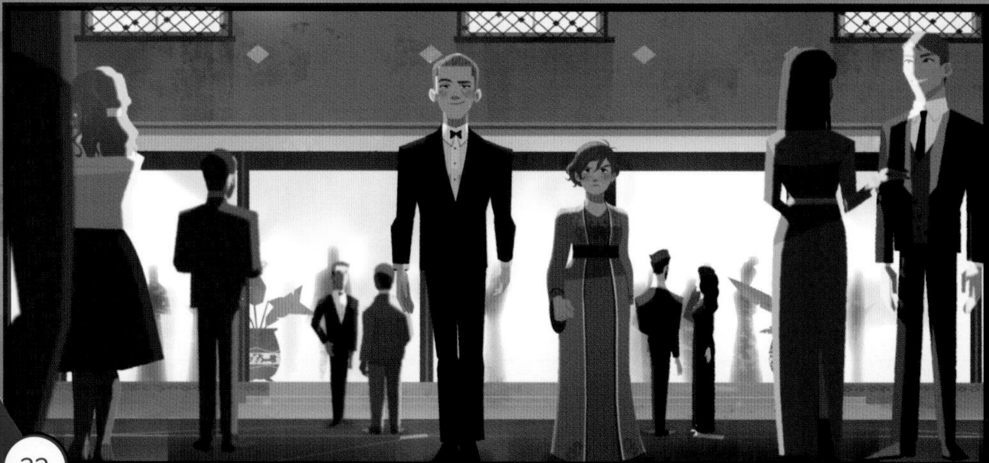

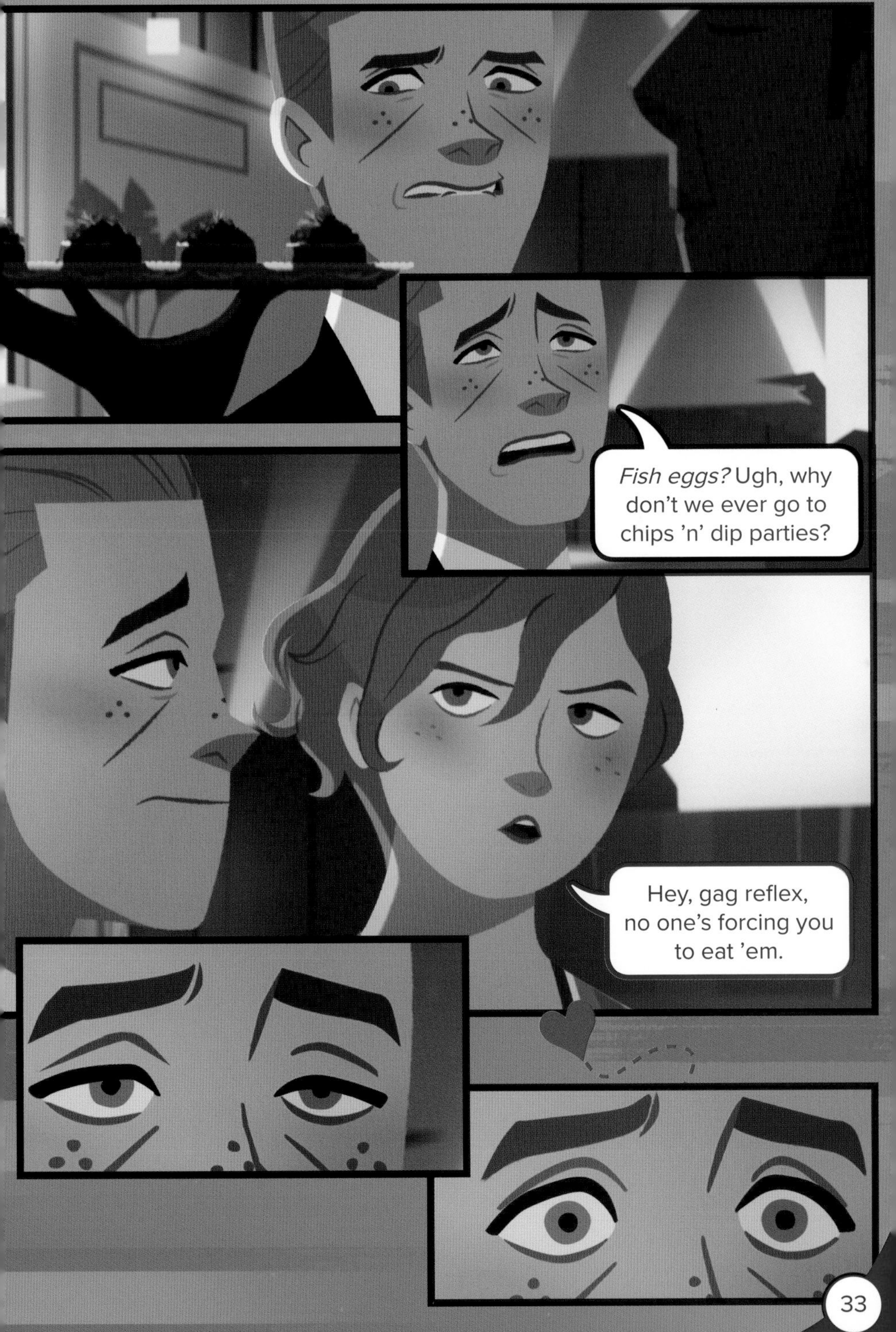

Fish eggs? Ugh, why don't we ever go to chips 'n' dip parties?
Hey, gag reflex, no one's forcing you to eat 'em.

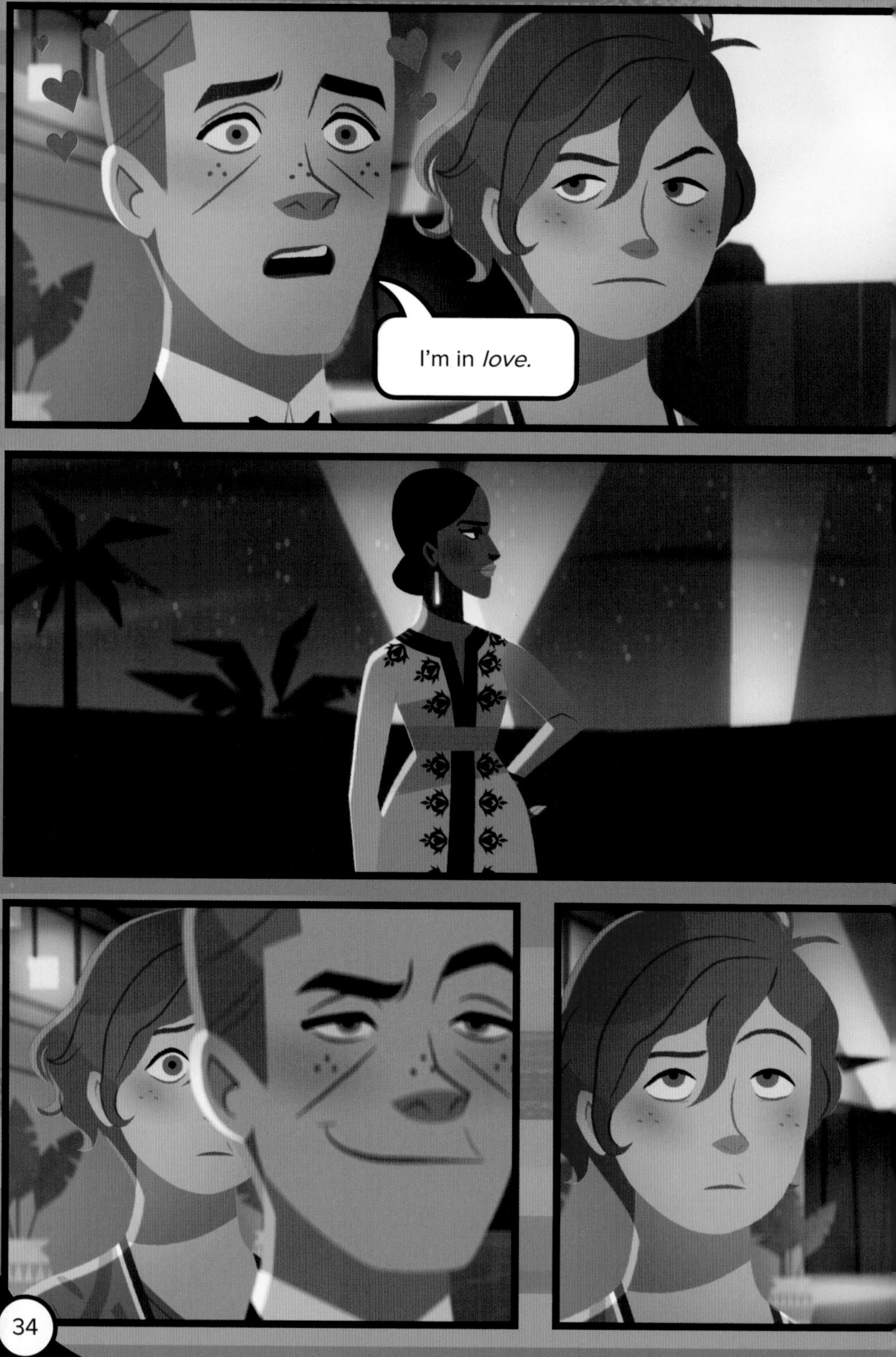
I'm in *love.*

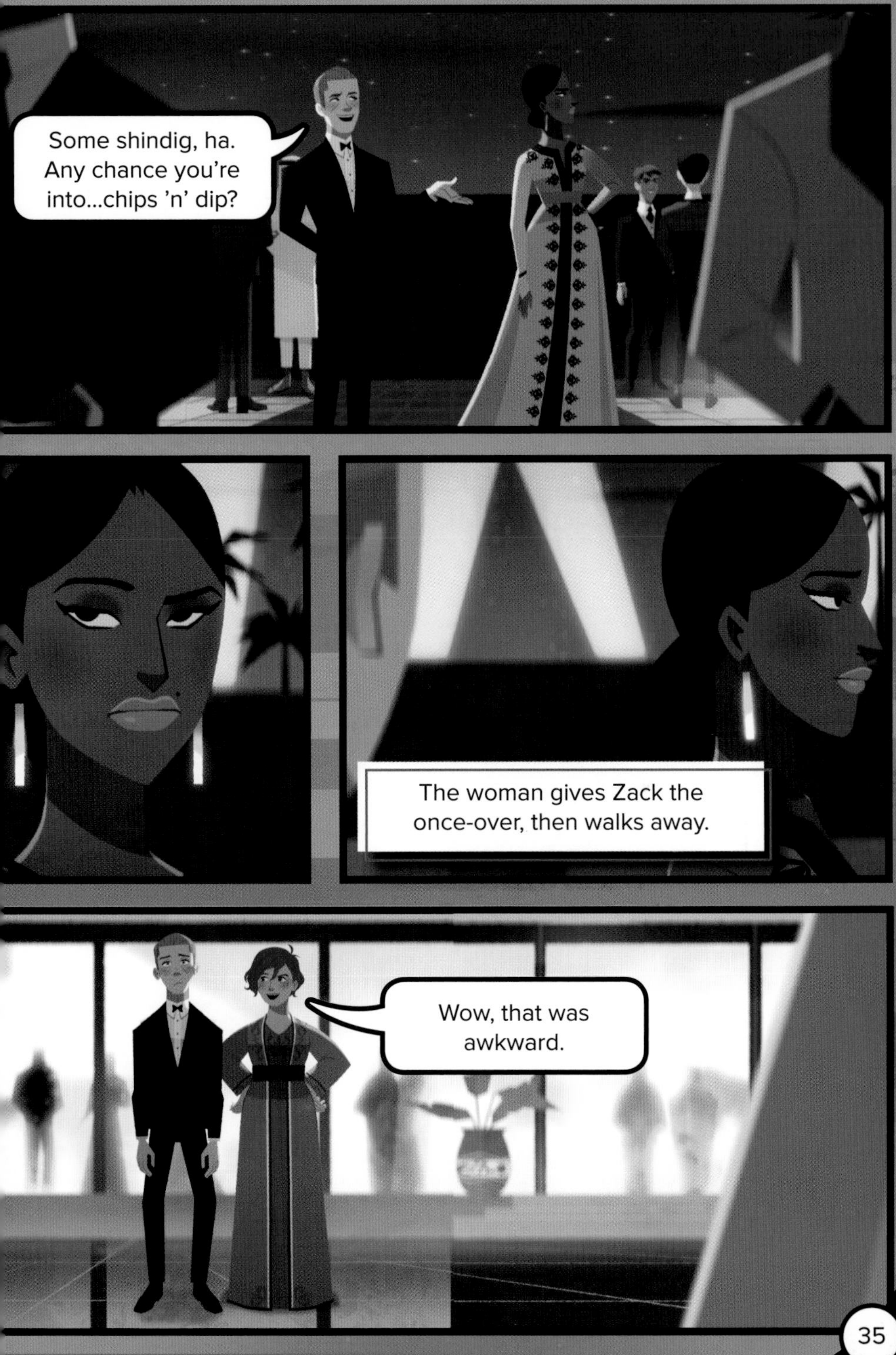
Some shindig, ha. Any chance you're into...chips 'n' dip?
The woman gives Zack the once-over, then walks away.
Wow, that was awkward.

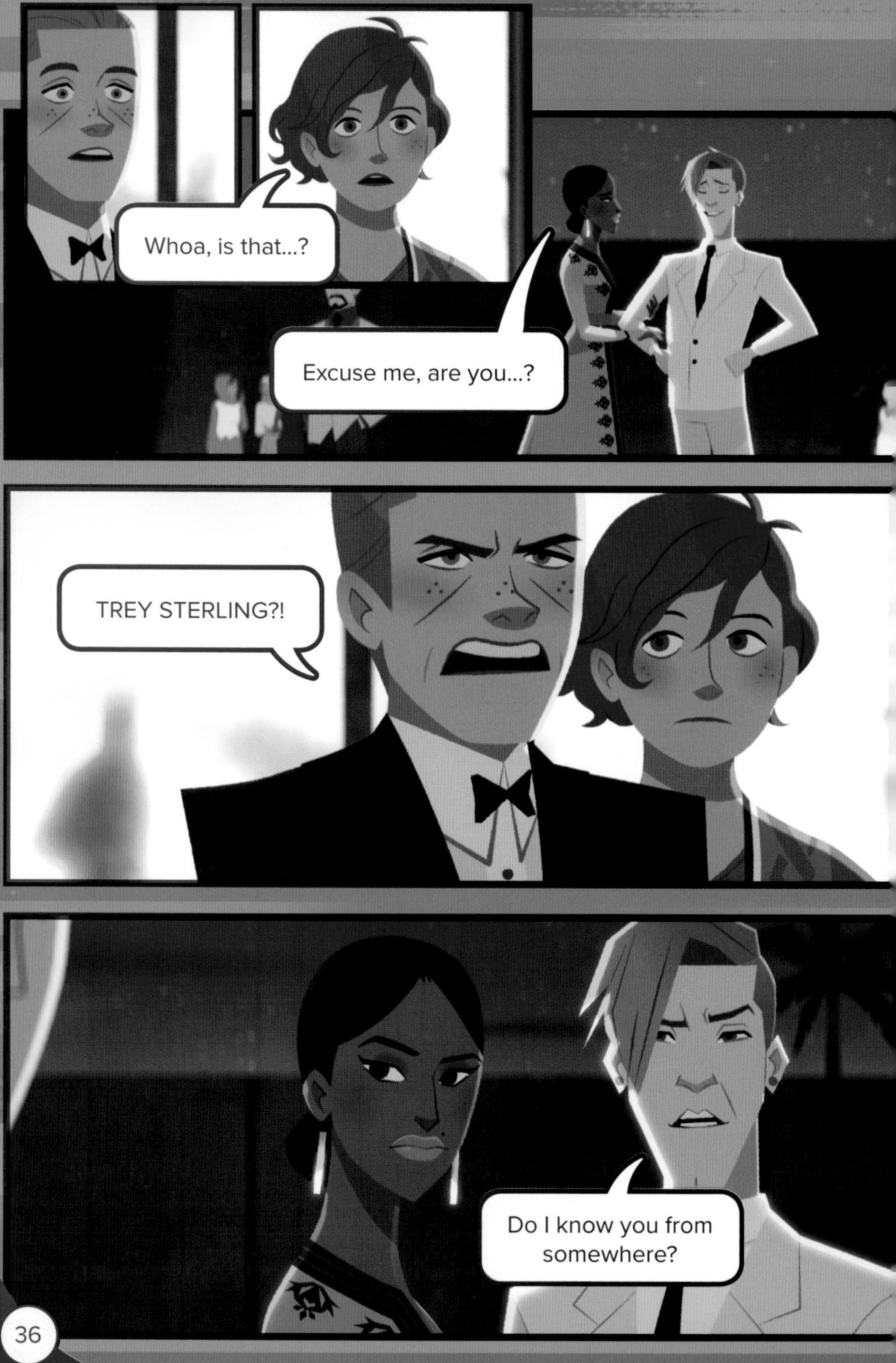
Whoa, is that...?
Excuse me, are you...?
TREY STERLING?!
Do I know you from somewhere?

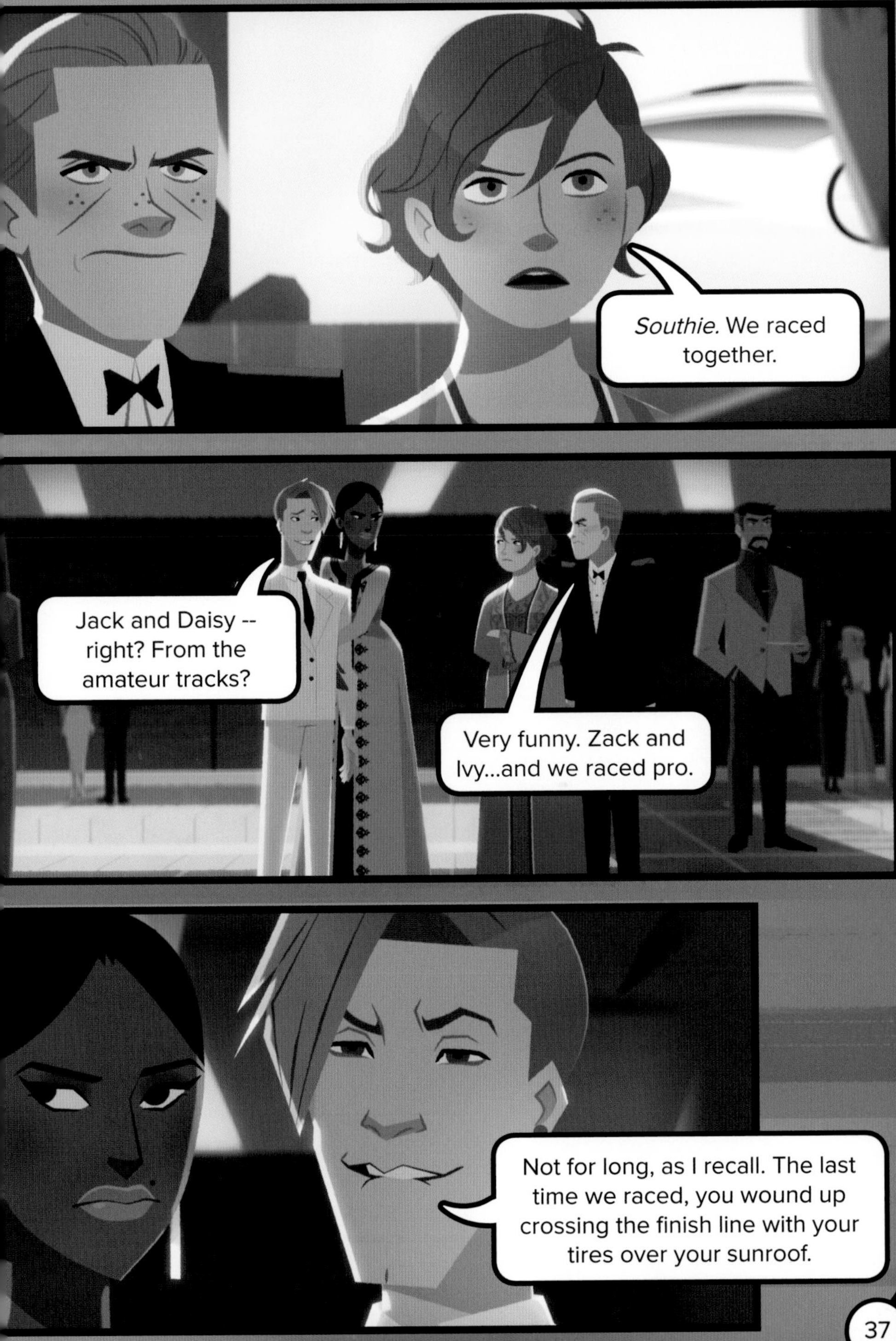
Southie. We raced together.
Jack and Daisy -- right? From the amateur tracks?
Very funny. Zack and Ivy...and we raced pro.
Not for long, as I recall. The last time we raced, you wound up crossing the finish line with your tires over your sunroof.

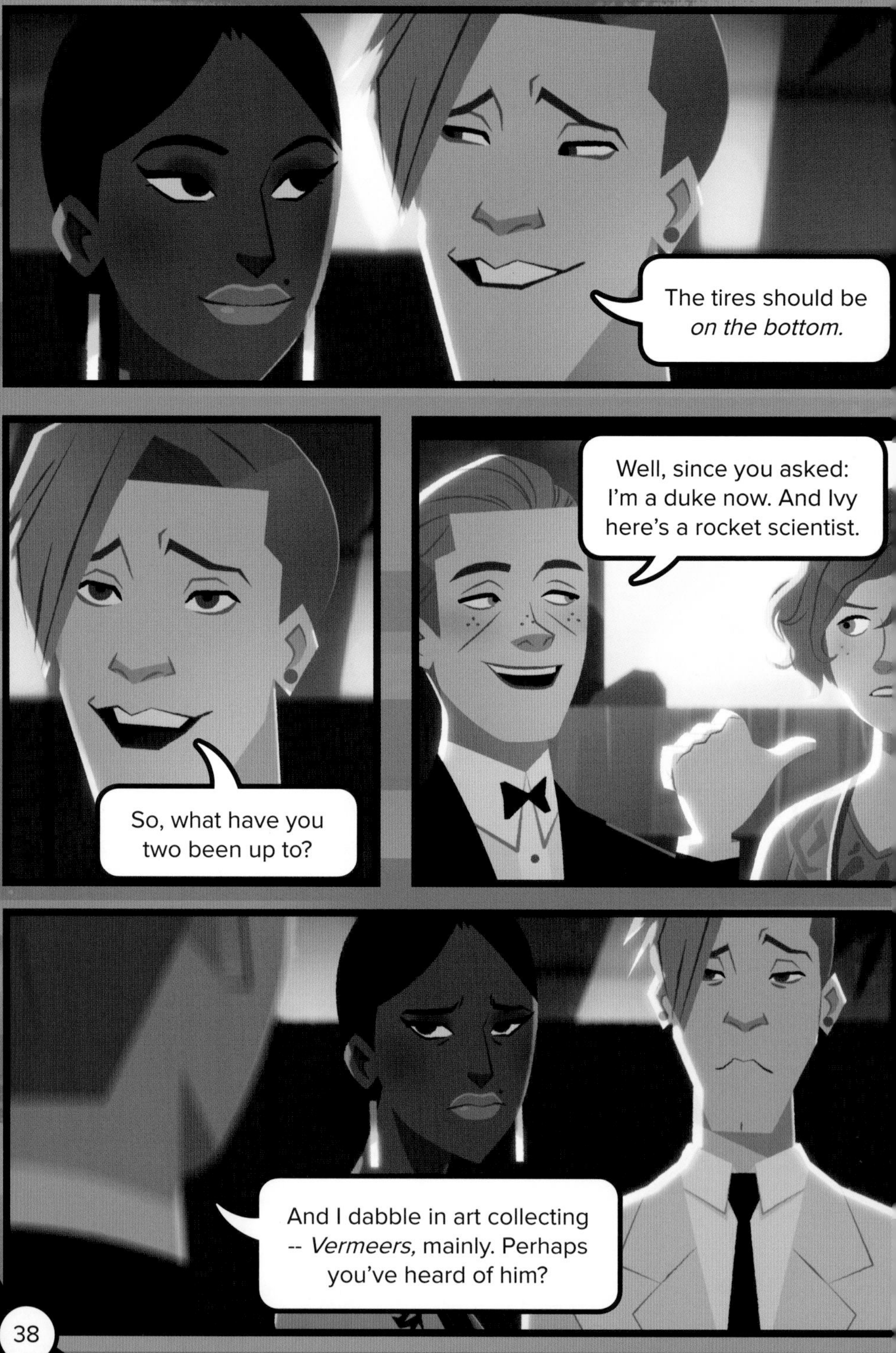
The tires should be *on the bottom.*
So, what have you two been up to?
Well, since you asked: I'm a duke now. And Ivy here's a rocket scientist.
And I dabble in art collecting -- *Vermeers,* mainly. Perhaps you've heard of him?

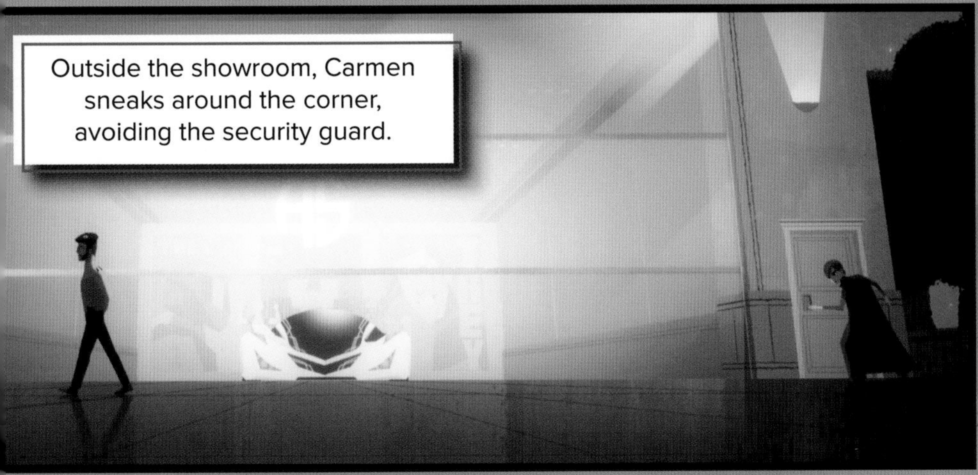
Outside the showroom, Carmen sneaks around the corner, avoiding the security guard.

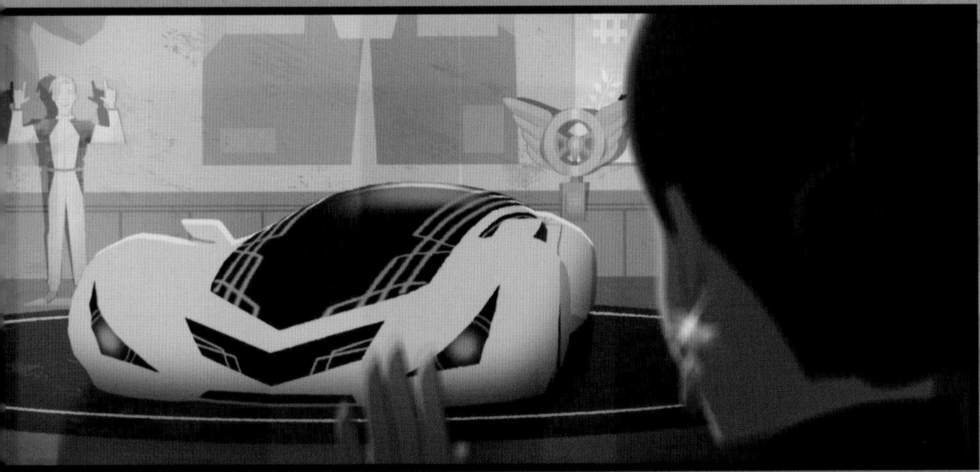

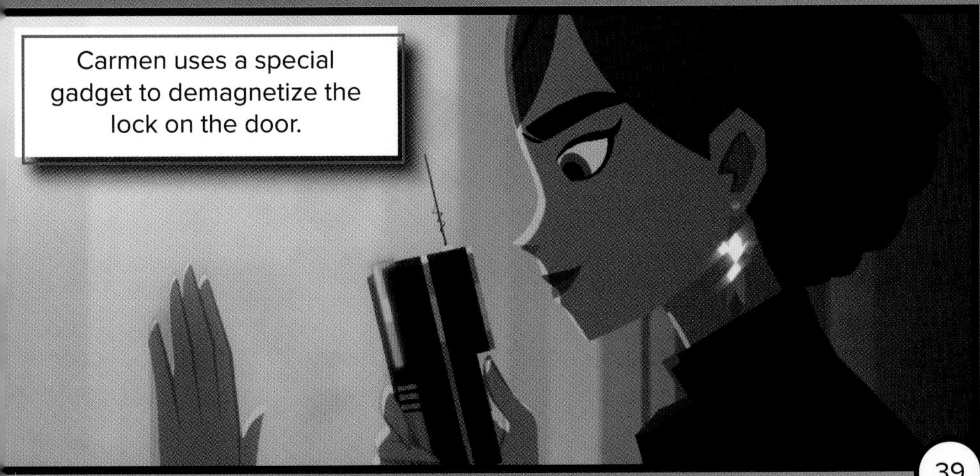
Carmen uses a special gadget to demagnetize the lock on the door.

click

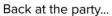
Back at the party...

C'mon, Zack, we have that "thing" we need to attend to?

Now, you two look familiar.

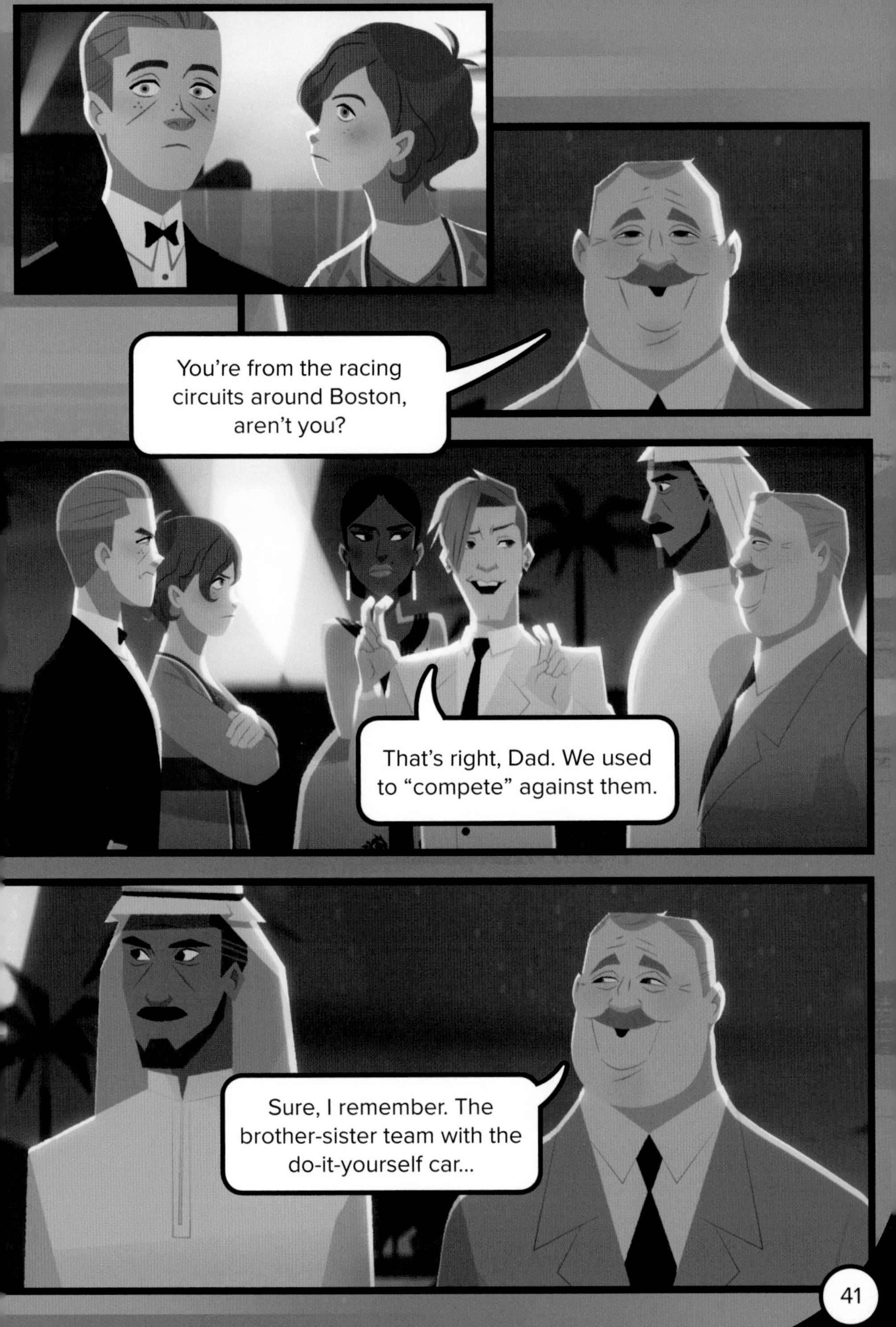
You're from the racing circuits around Boston, aren't you?
That's right, Dad. We used to "compete" against them.
Sure, I remember. The brother-sister team with the do-it-yourself car...

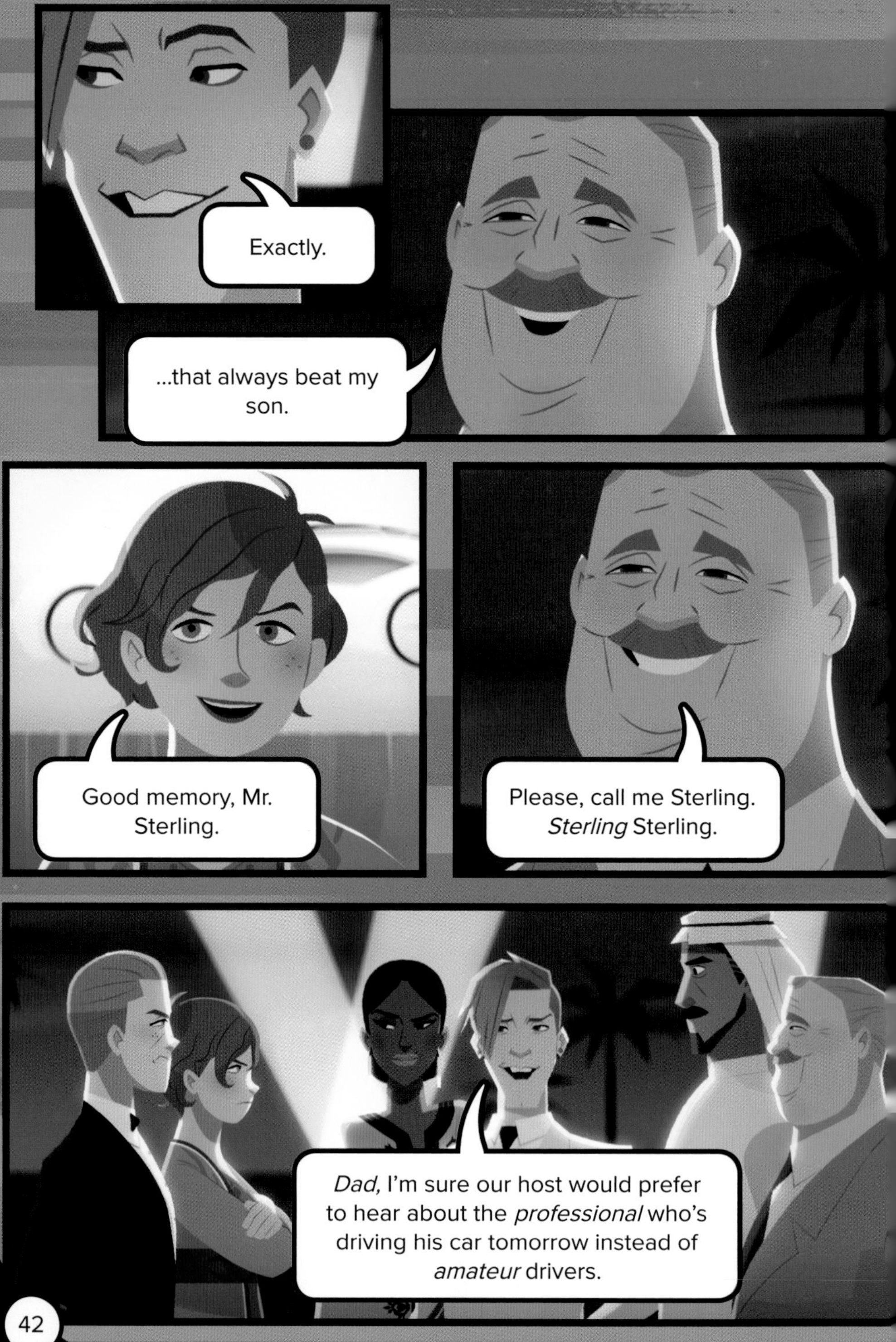
Exactly.
...that always beat my son.
Good memory, Mr. Sterling.
Please, call me Sterling. *Sterling* Sterling.
Dad, I'm sure our host would prefer to hear about the *professional* who's driving his car tomorrow instead of *amateur* drivers.

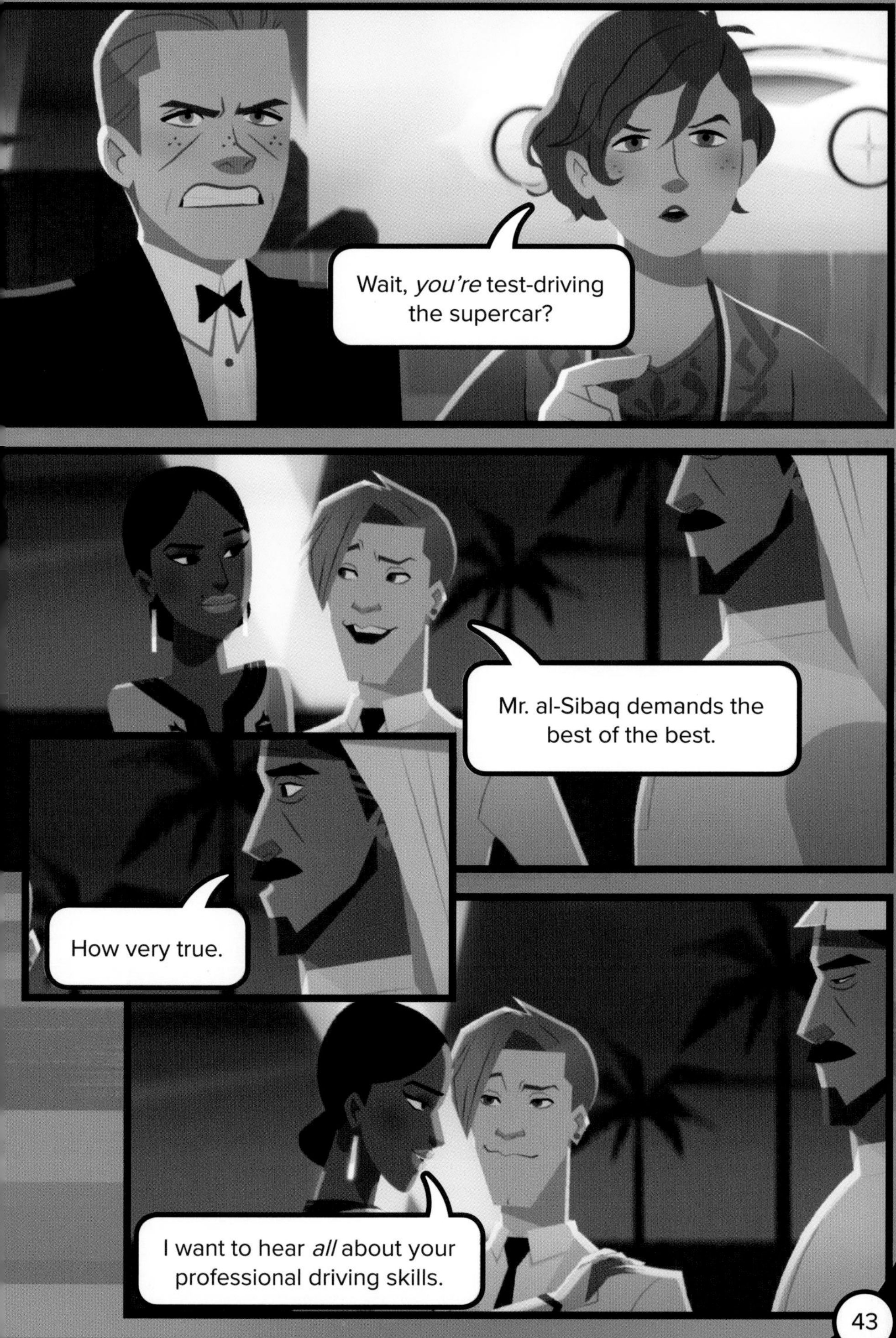
Wait, *you're* test-driving the supercar?
Mr. al-Sibaq demands the best of the best.
How very true.
I want to hear *all* about your professional driving skills.

The woman leads Trey away.

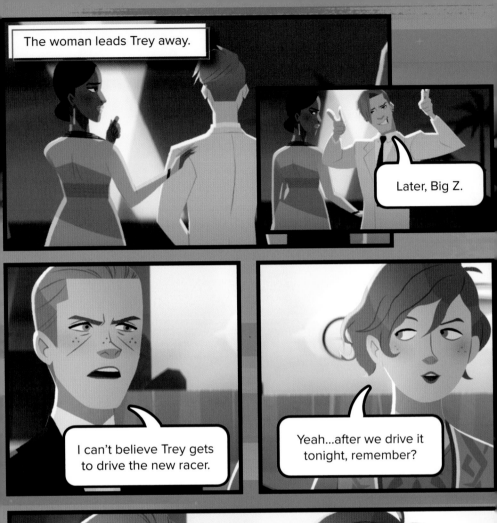

Later, Big Z.

I can't believe Trey gets to drive the new racer.

Yeah...after we drive it tonight, remember?

GASP!

Carmen!

We're late!

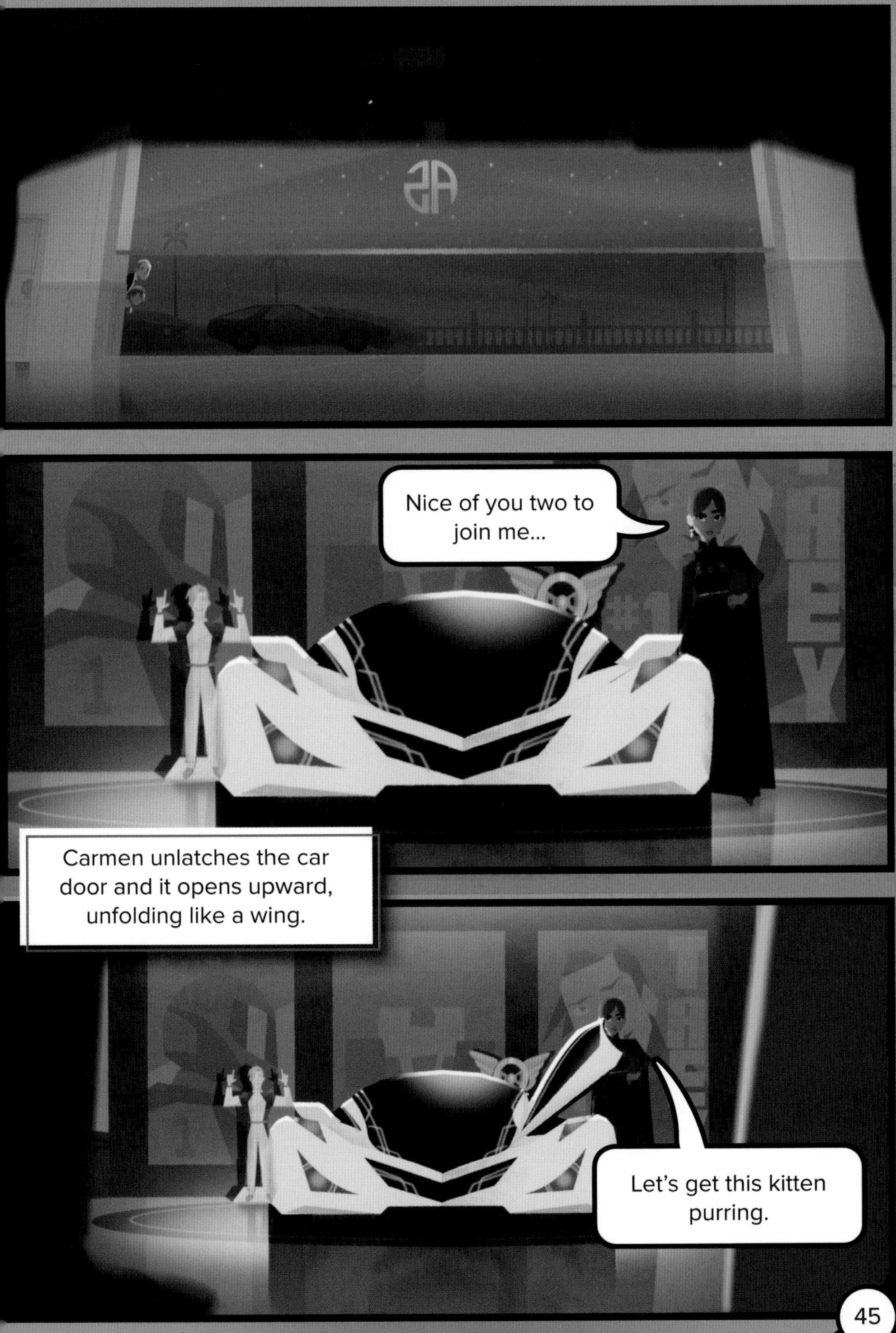
Nice of you two to join me...
Carmen unlatches the car door and it opens upward, unfolding like a wing.
Let's get this kitten purring.

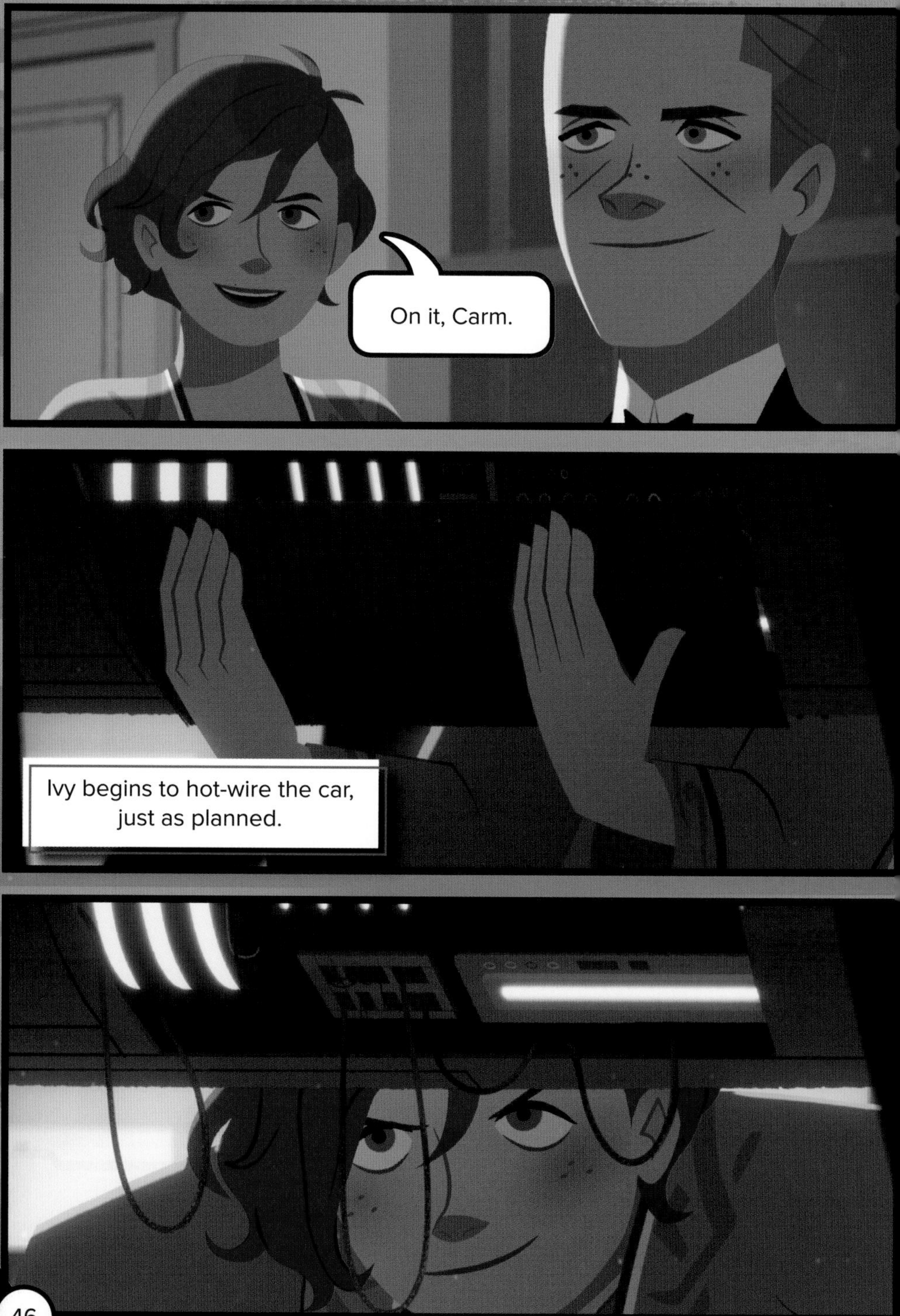
On it, Carm.
Ivy begins to hot-wire the car, just as planned.

What about you?

Two-seater. I brought my *own* getaway vehicle.

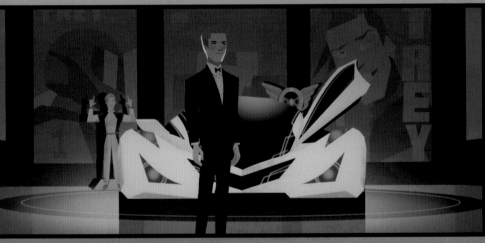

As the car begins to power up, Zack takes a look around the room.

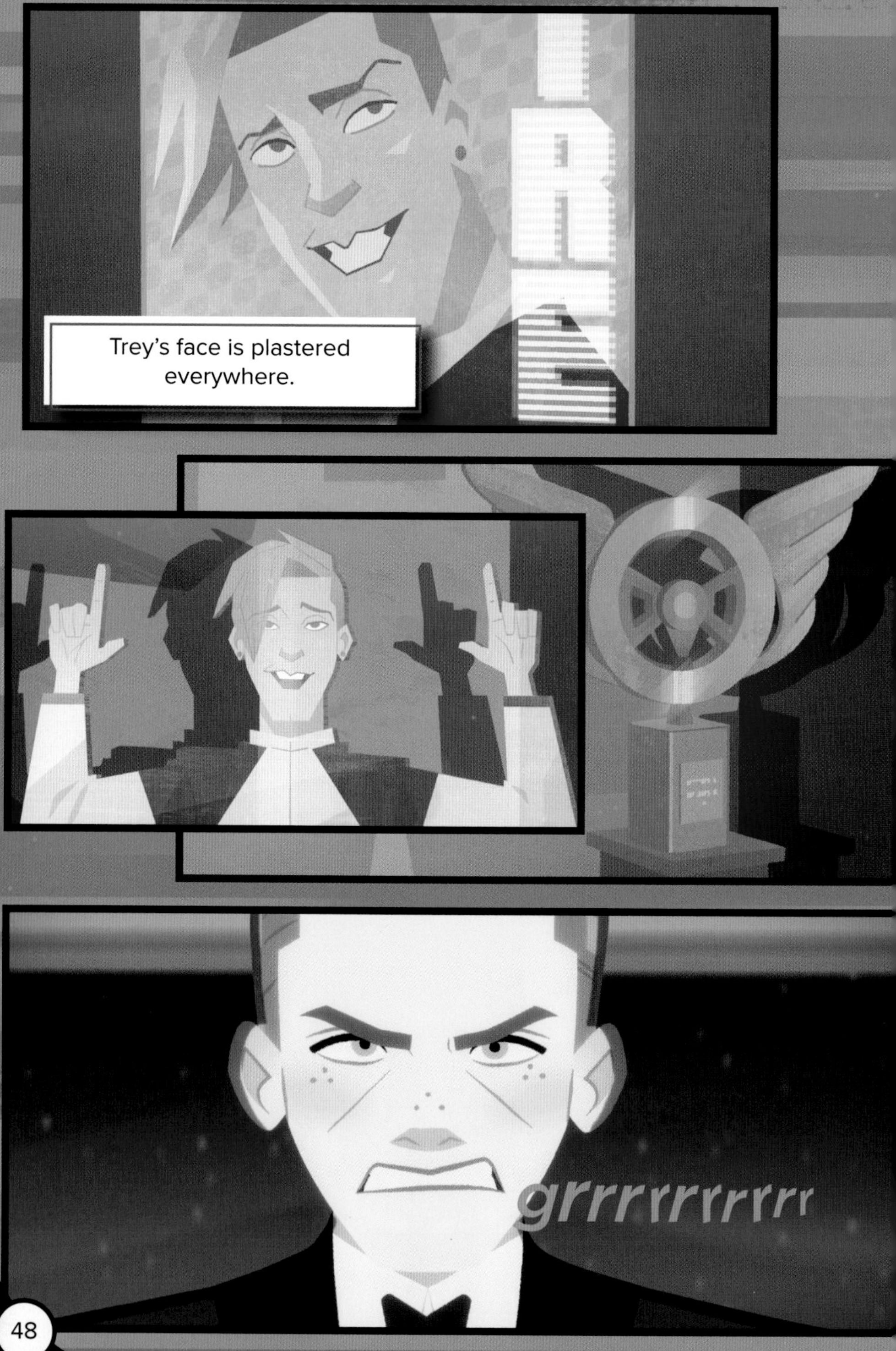
Trey's face is plastered everywhere.
grrrrrrrrr

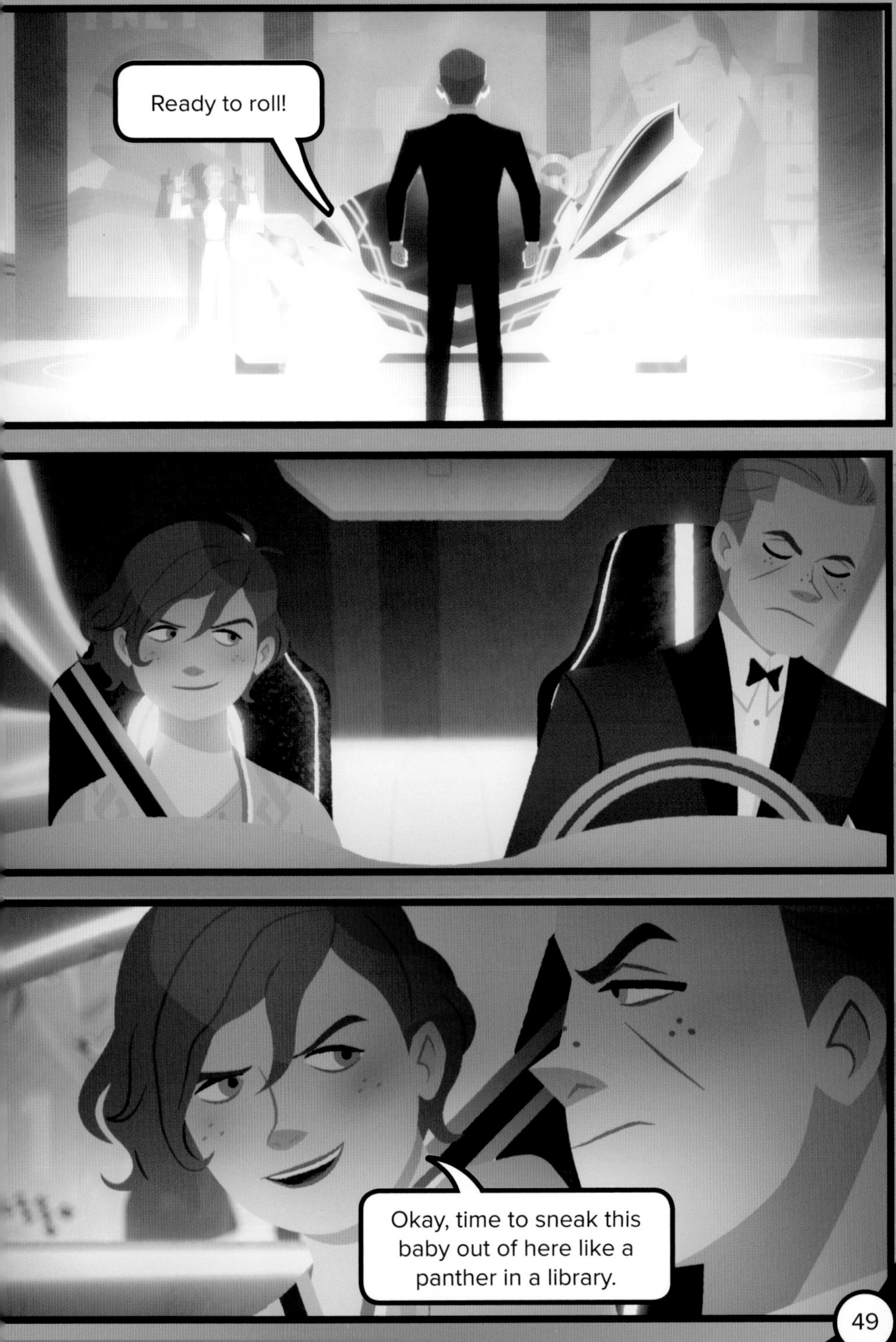
Ready to roll!
Okay, time to sneak this baby out of here like a panther in a library.

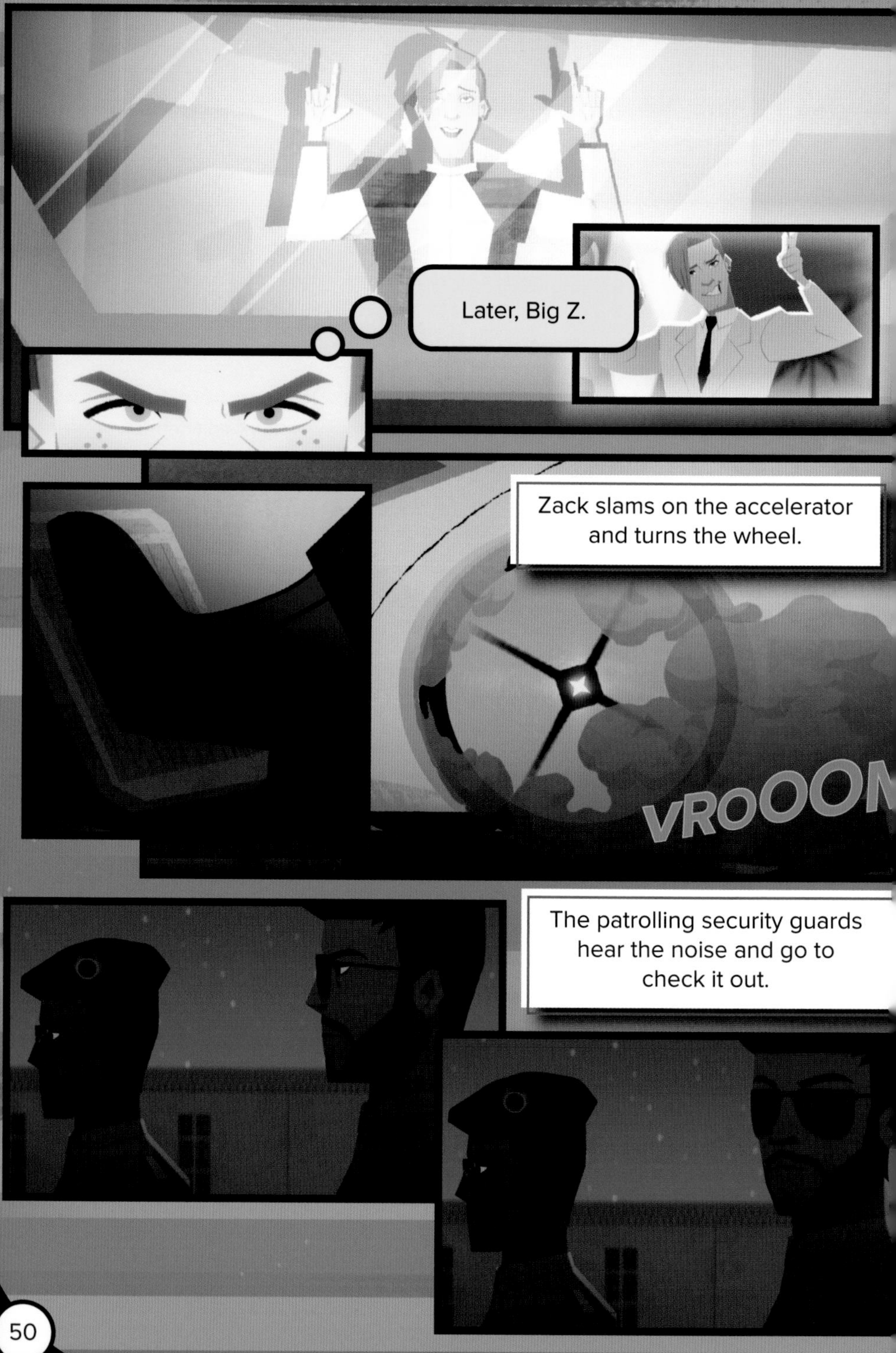

Later, Big Z.
Zack slams on the accelerator and turns the wheel.
VROOOM
The patrolling security guards hear the noise and go to check it out.

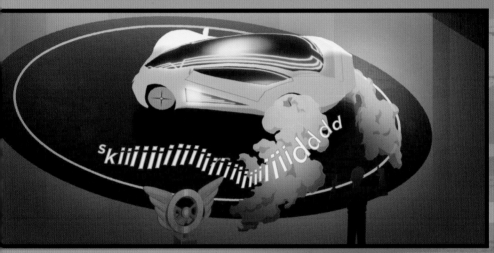

skiiiiiiiiiiiiiiiiiiiddd

screeeeeech

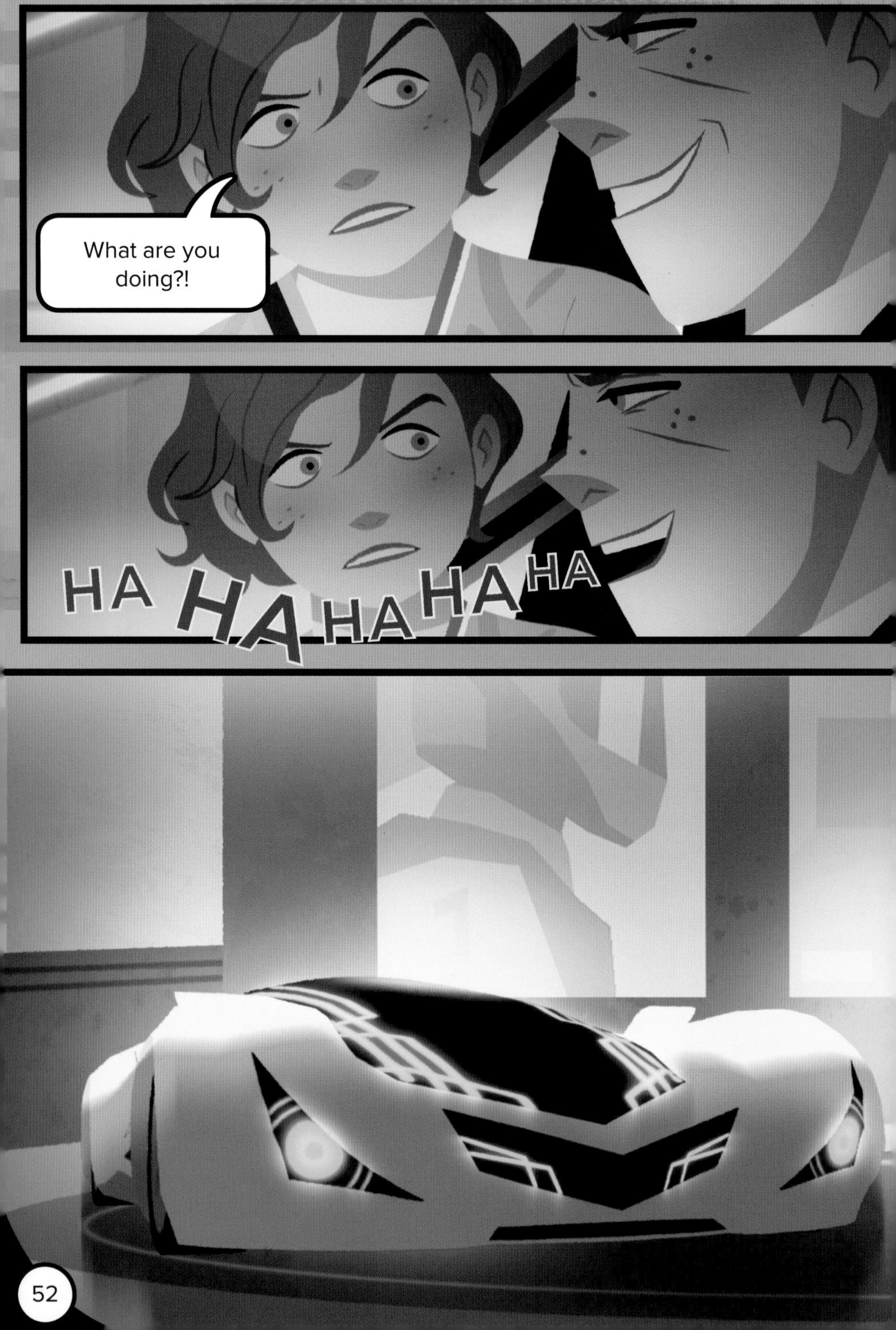
What are you doing?!
HA HA HA HA HA

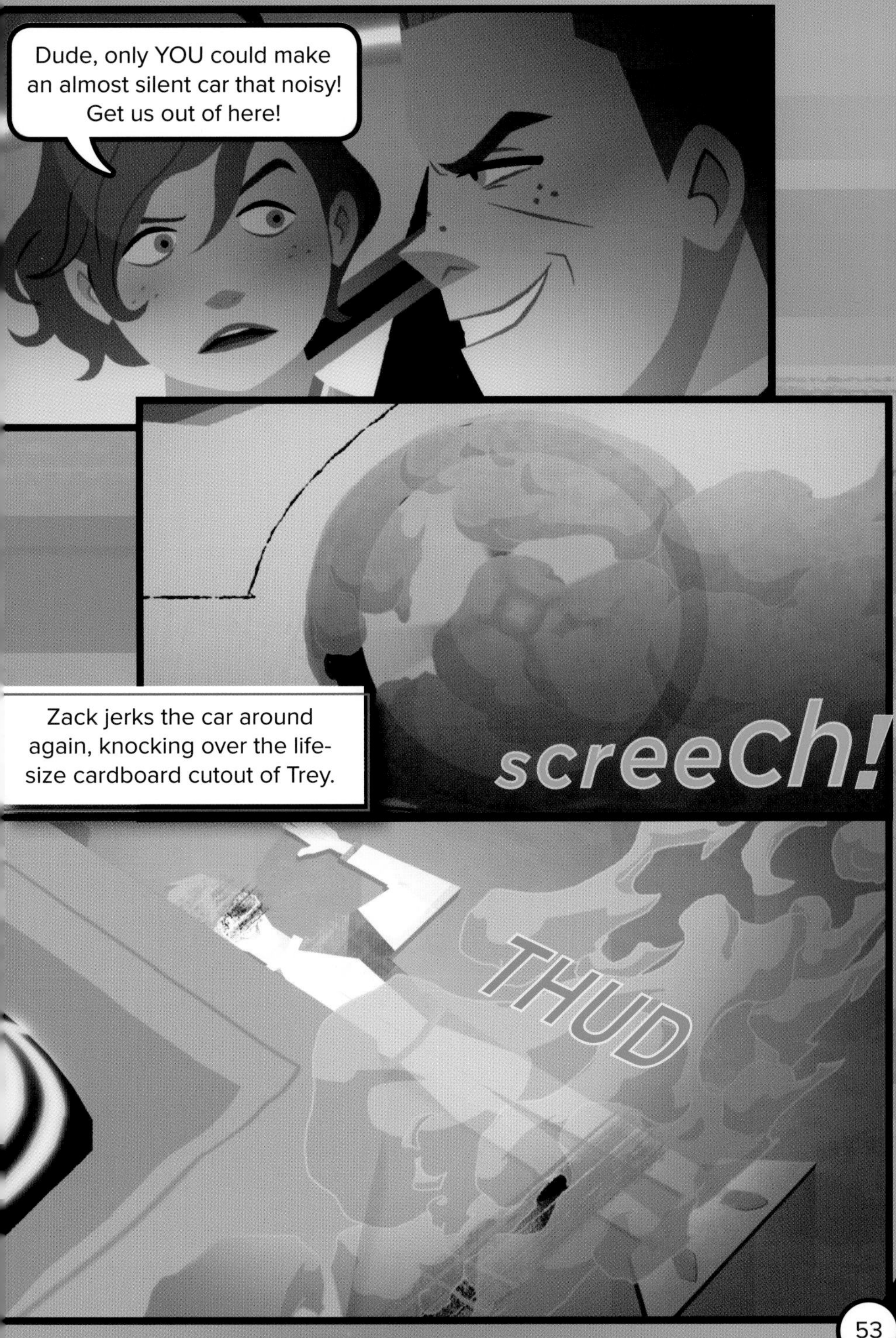
Dude, only YOU could make an almost silent car that noisy! Get us out of here!
Zack jerks the car around again, knocking over the life-size cardboard cutout of Trey.
screeCh!
THUD

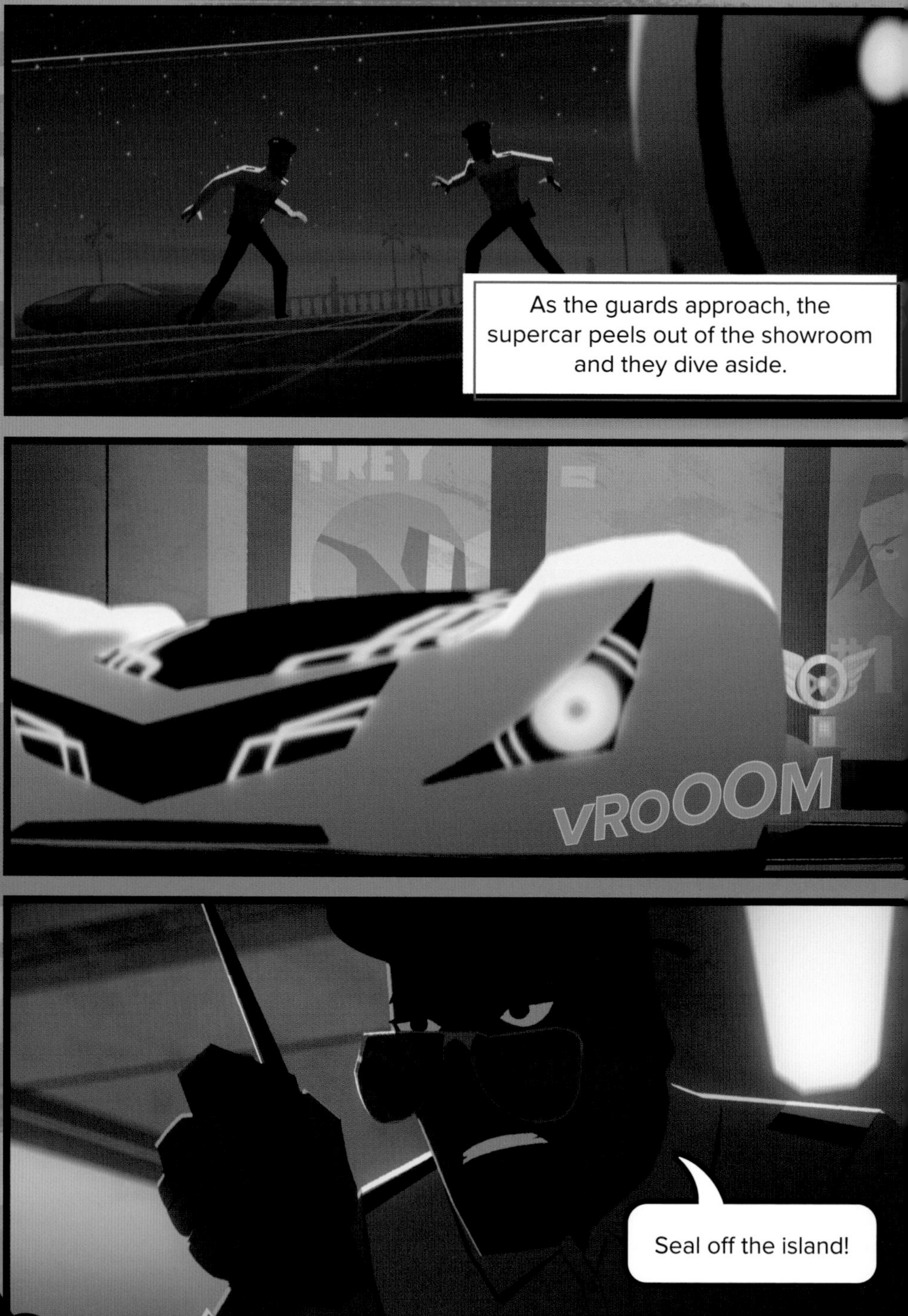
As the guards approach, the supercar peels out of the showroom and they dive aside.
VROOOM
Seal off the island!

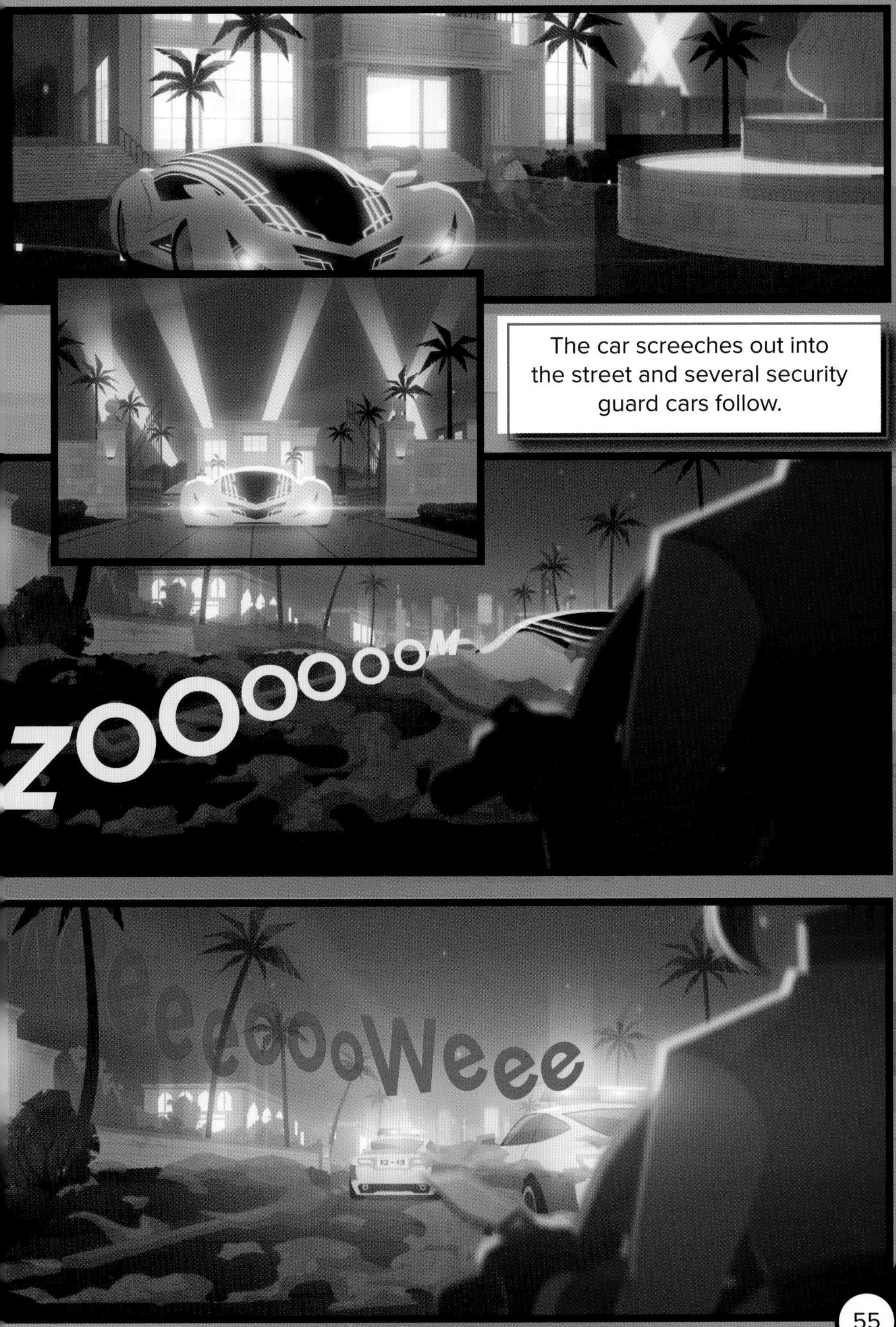
The car screeches out into the street and several security guard cars follow.
ZOOOOOOM
eeeoooWeee

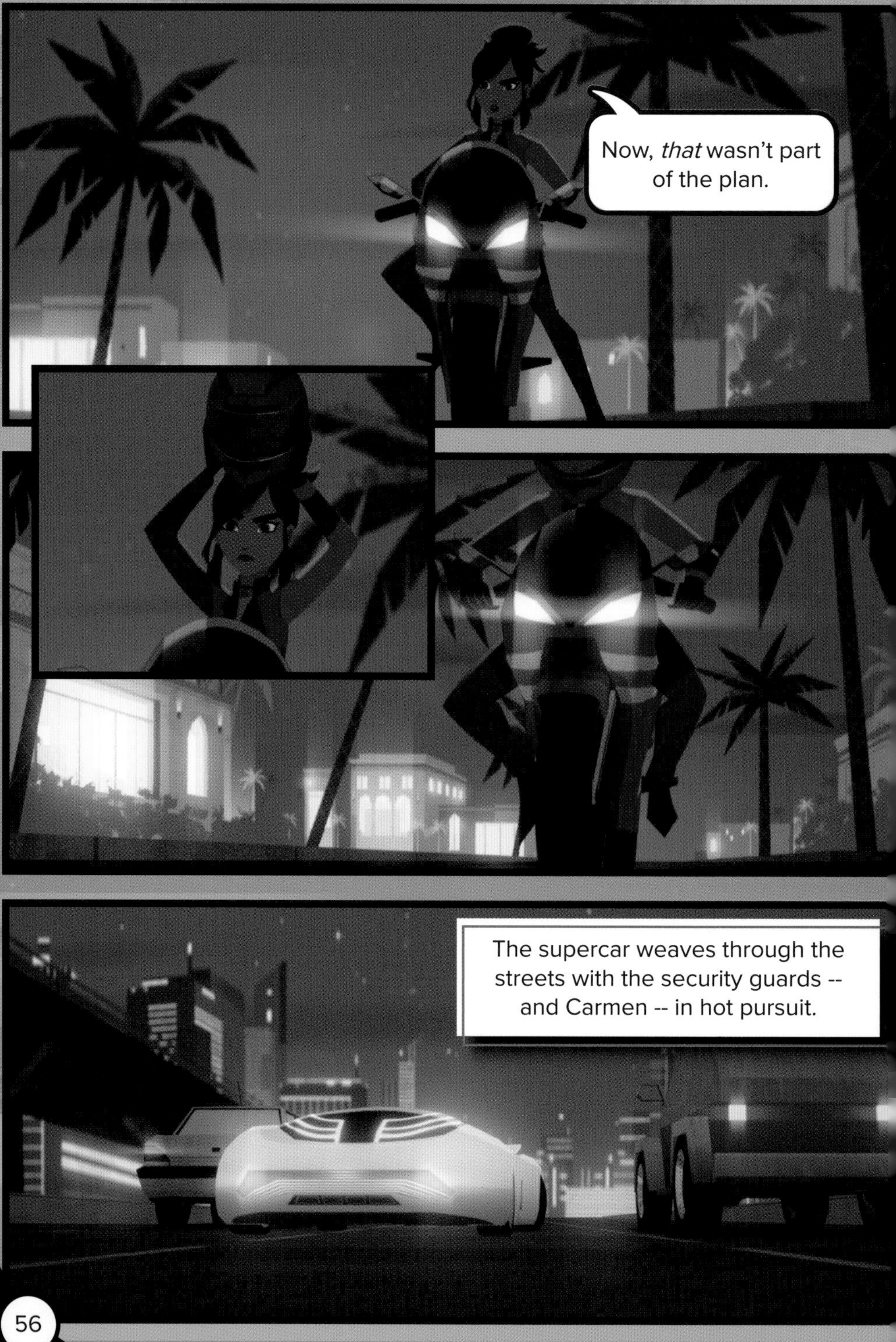
Now, *that* wasn't part of the plan.
The supercar weaves through the streets with the security guards -- and Carmen -- in hot pursuit.

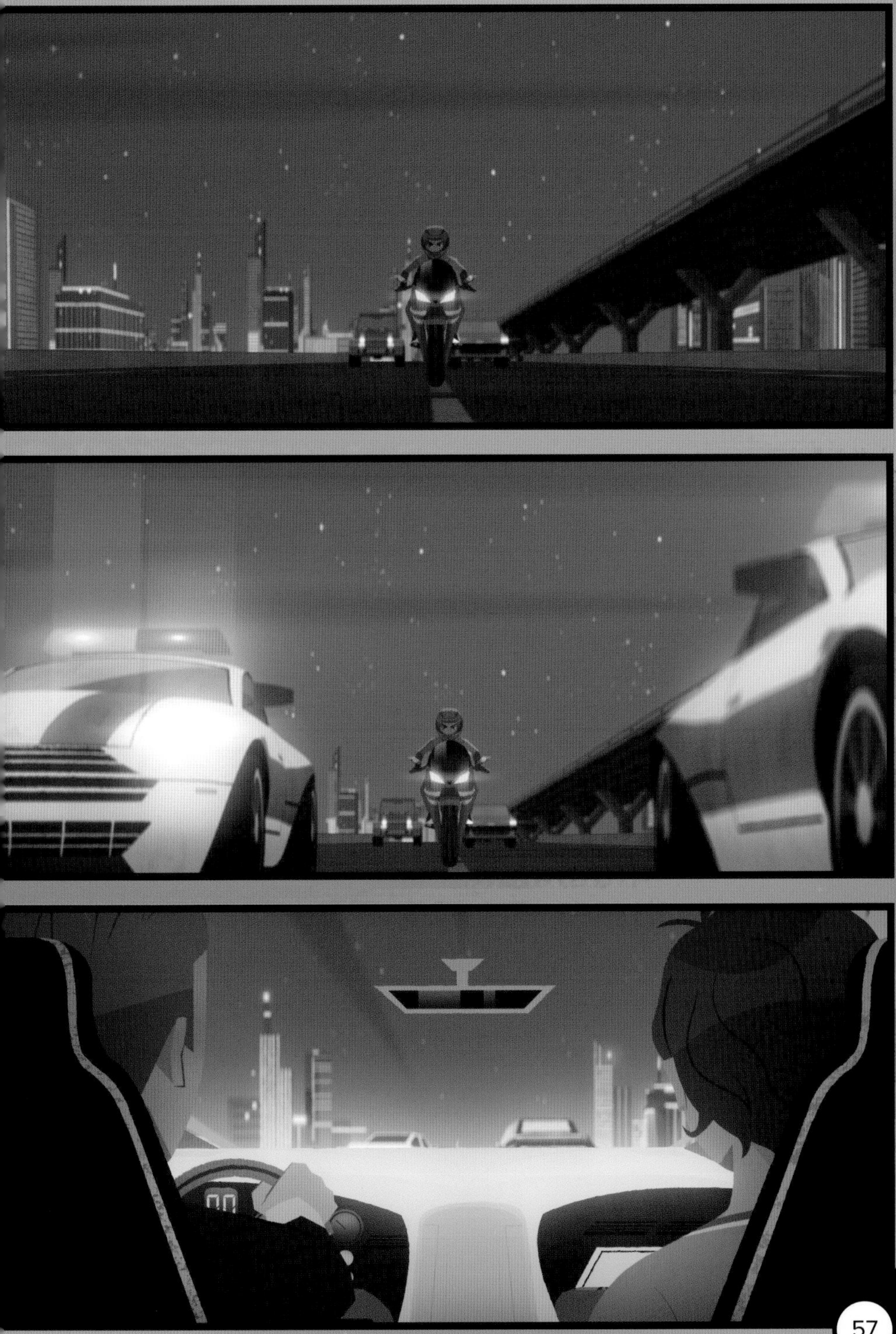

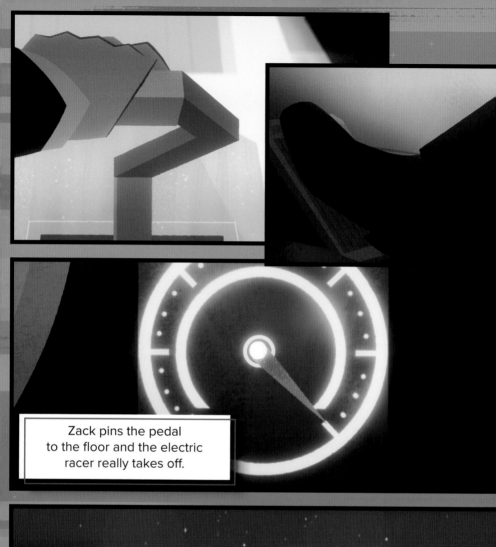

Zack pins the pedal to the floor and the electric racer really takes off.

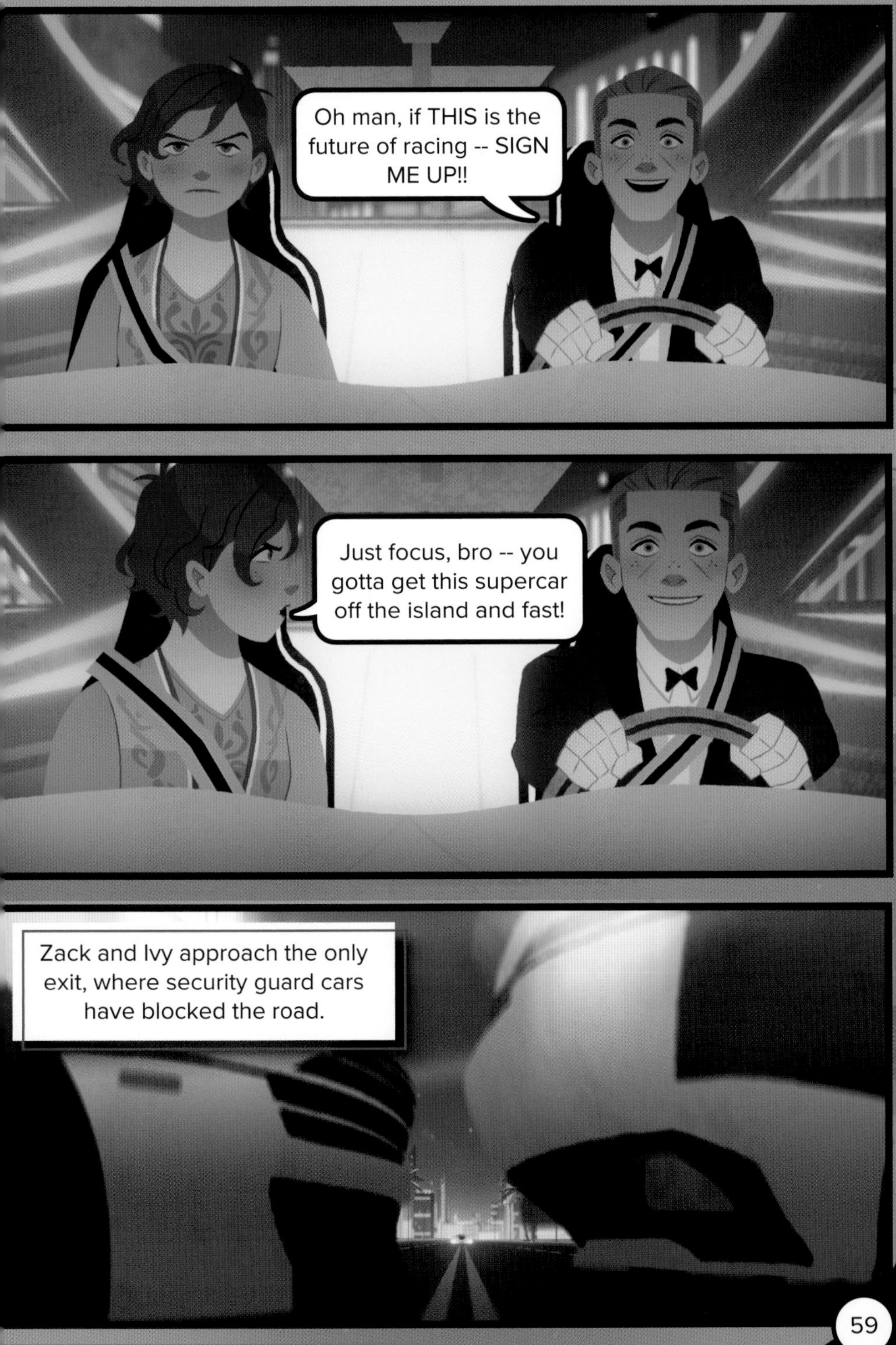
Oh man, if THIS is the future of racing -- SIGN ME UP!!
Just focus, bro -- you gotta get this supercar off the island and fast!
Zack and Ivy approach the only exit, where security guard cars have blocked the road.

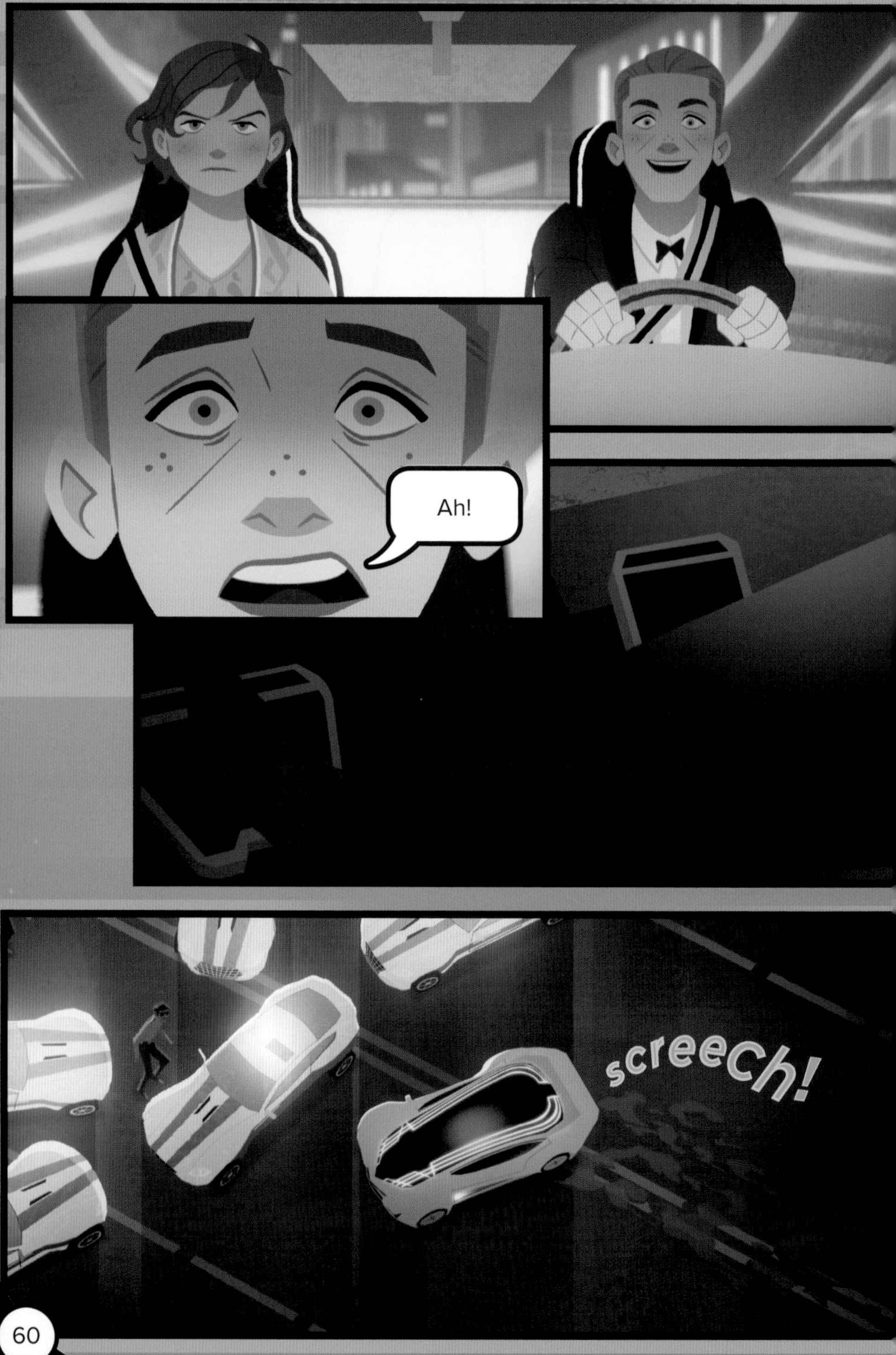
Ah!
screech!

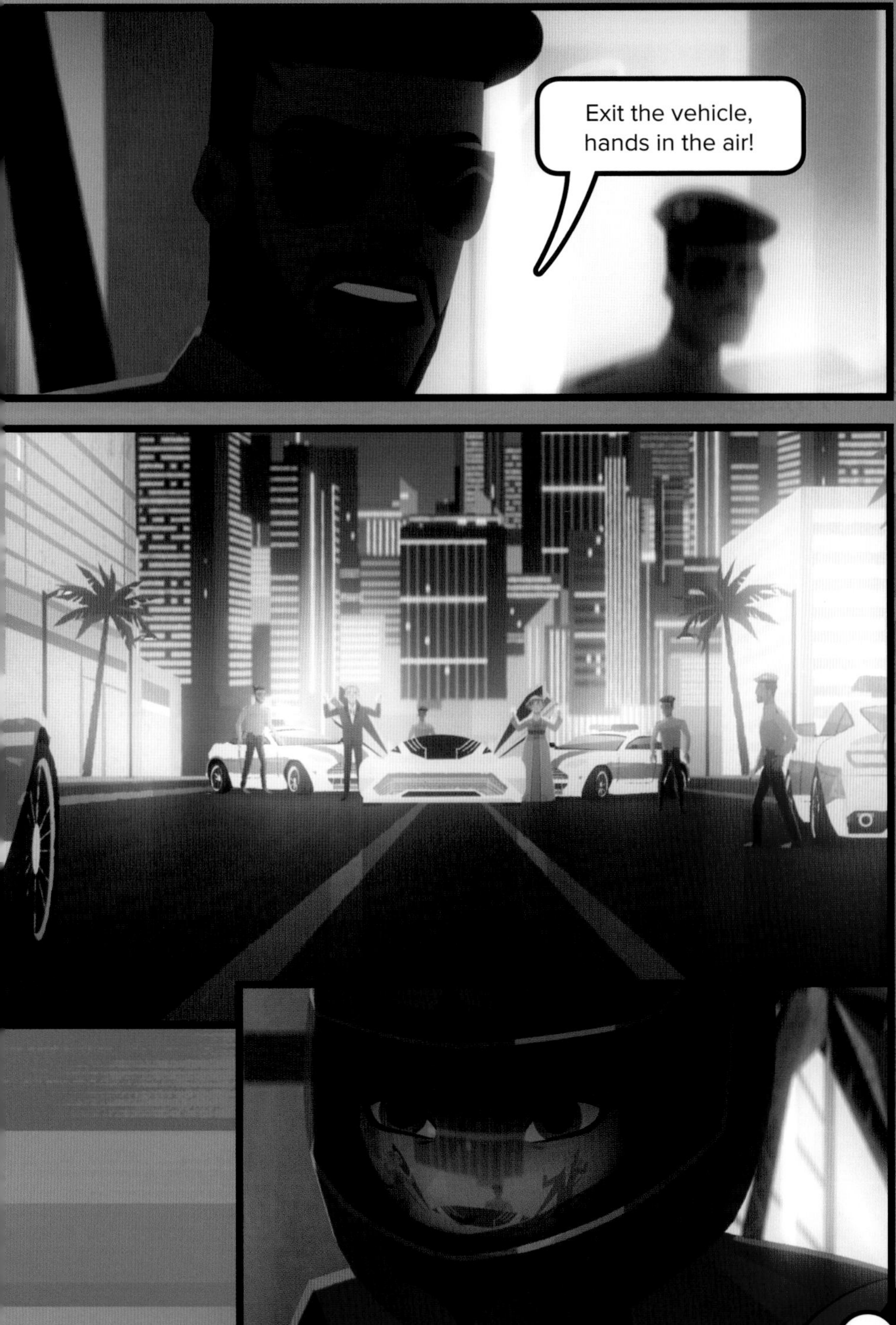
Exit the vehicle,
hands in the air!

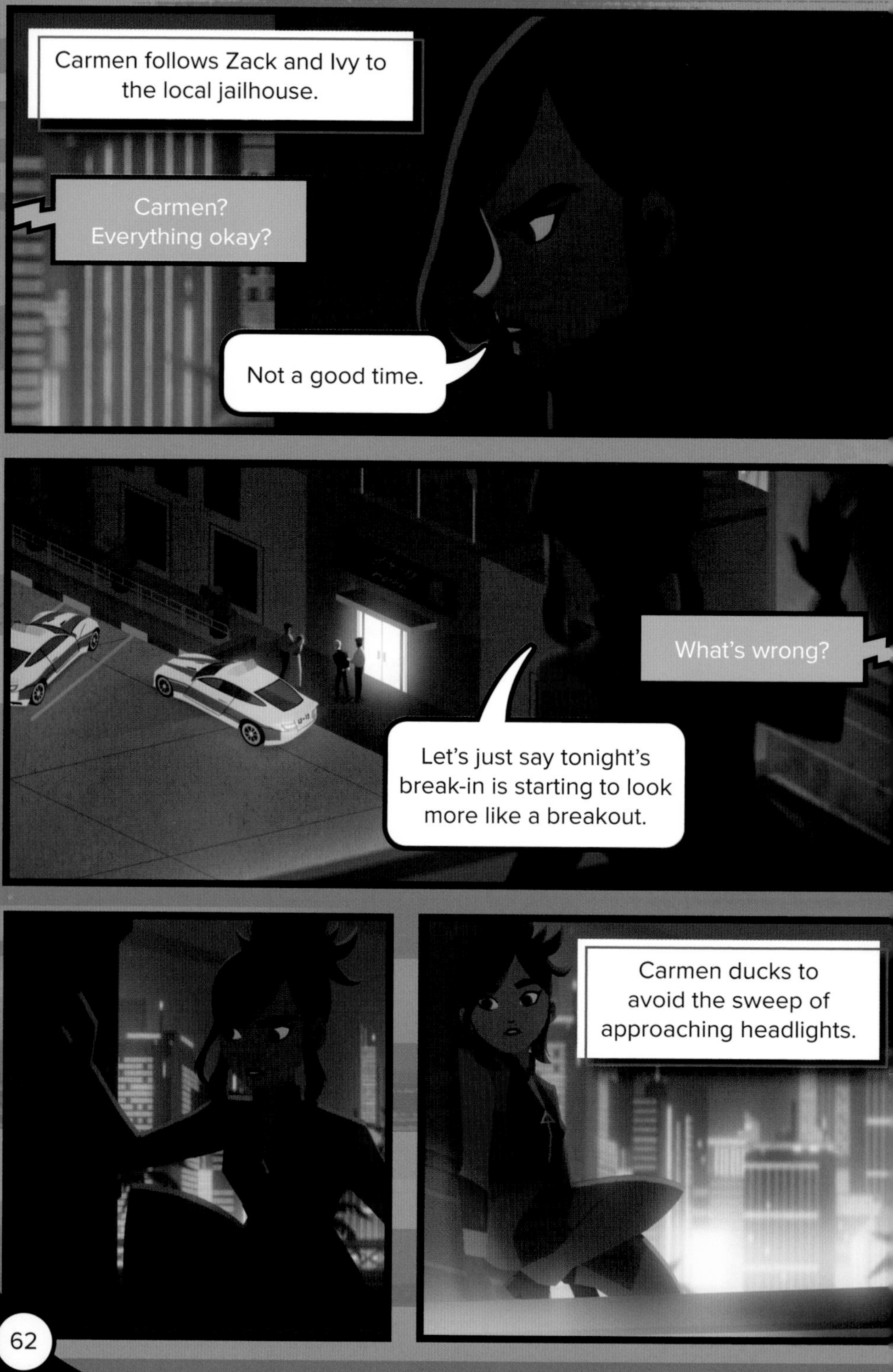
Carmen follows Zack and Ivy to the local jailhouse.
Carmen? Everything okay?
Not a good time.
What's wrong?
Let's just say tonight's break-in is starting to look more like a breakout.
Carmen ducks to avoid the sweep of approaching headlights.

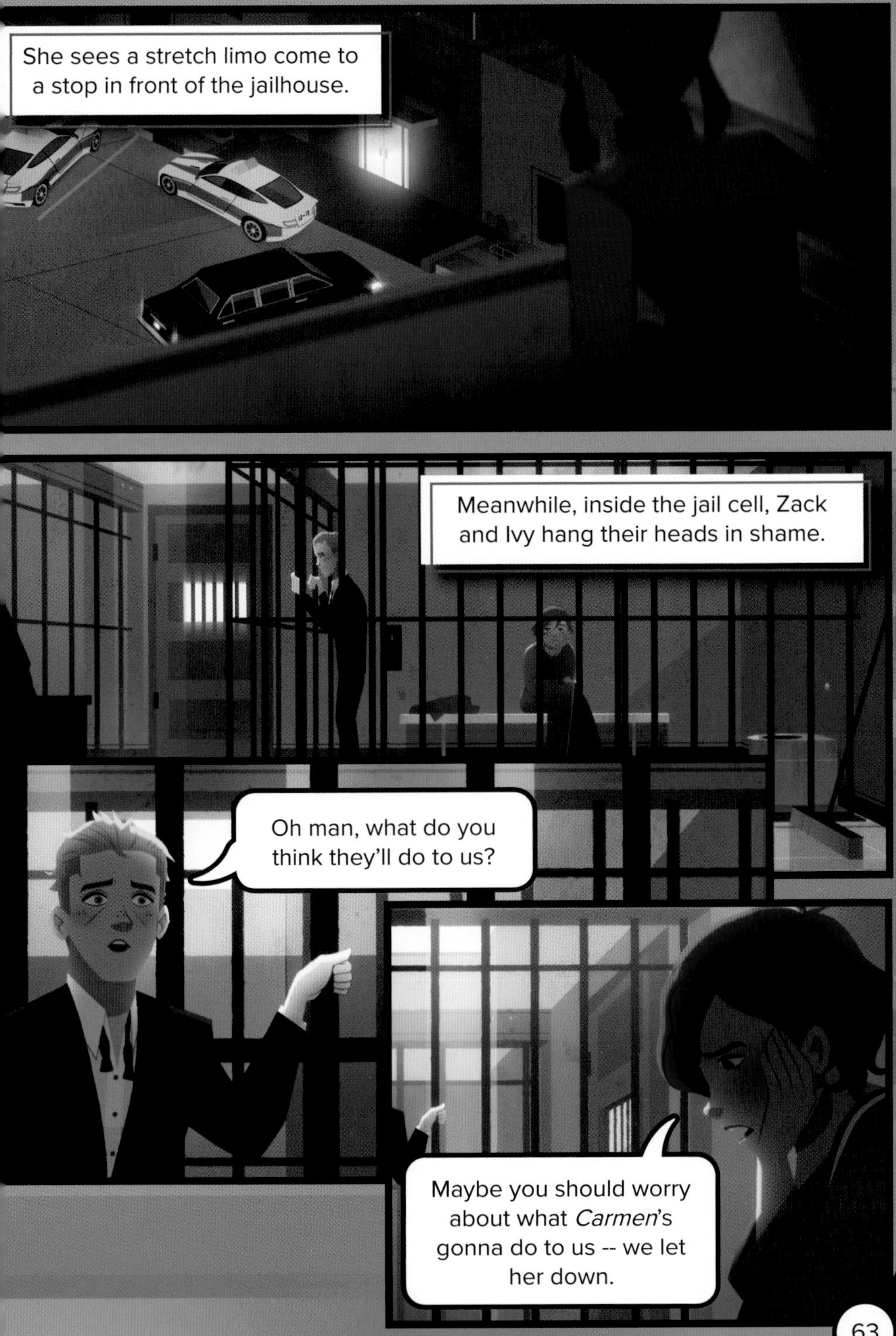
She sees a stretch limo come to a stop in front of the jailhouse.
Meanwhile, inside the jail cell, Zack and Ivy hang their heads in shame.
Oh man, what do you think they'll do to us?
Maybe you should worry about what *Carmen*'s gonna do to us -- we let her down.

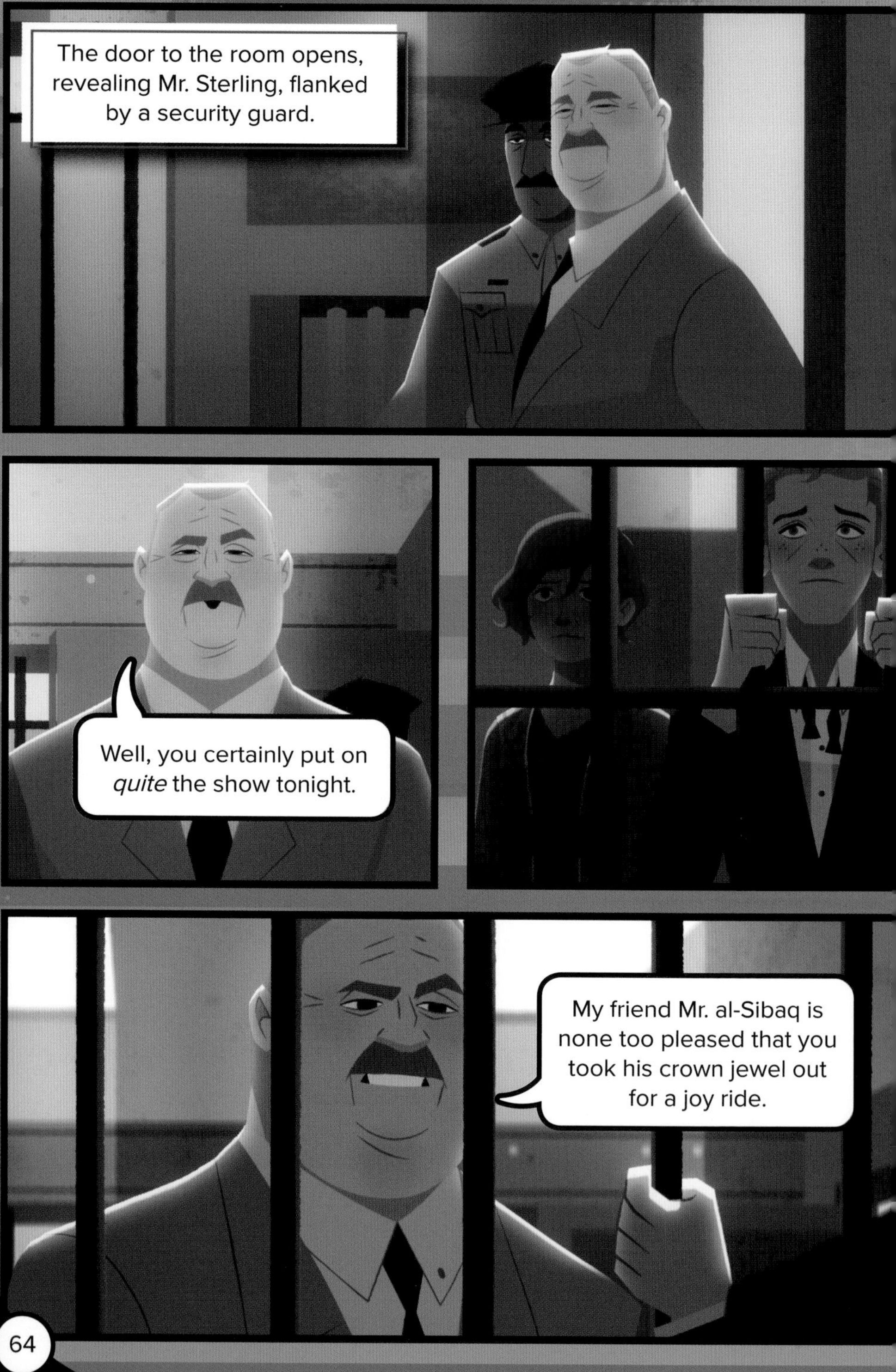
The door to the room opens, revealing Mr. Sterling, flanked by a security guard.
Well, you certainly put on *quite* the show tonight.
My friend Mr. al-Sibaq is none too pleased that you took his crown jewel out for a joy ride.

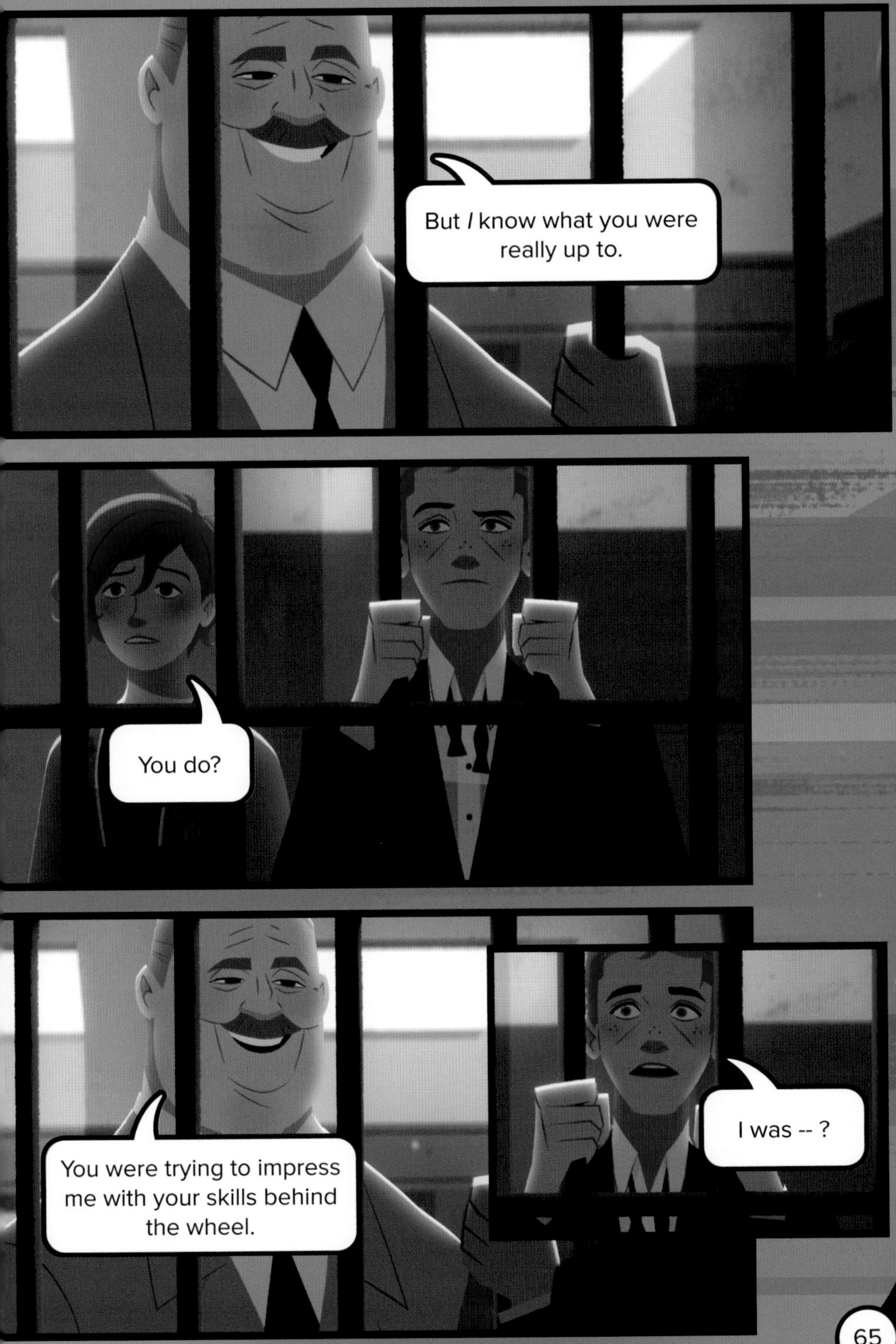
But *I* know what you were really up to.
You do?
You were trying to impress me with your skills behind the wheel.
I was -- ?

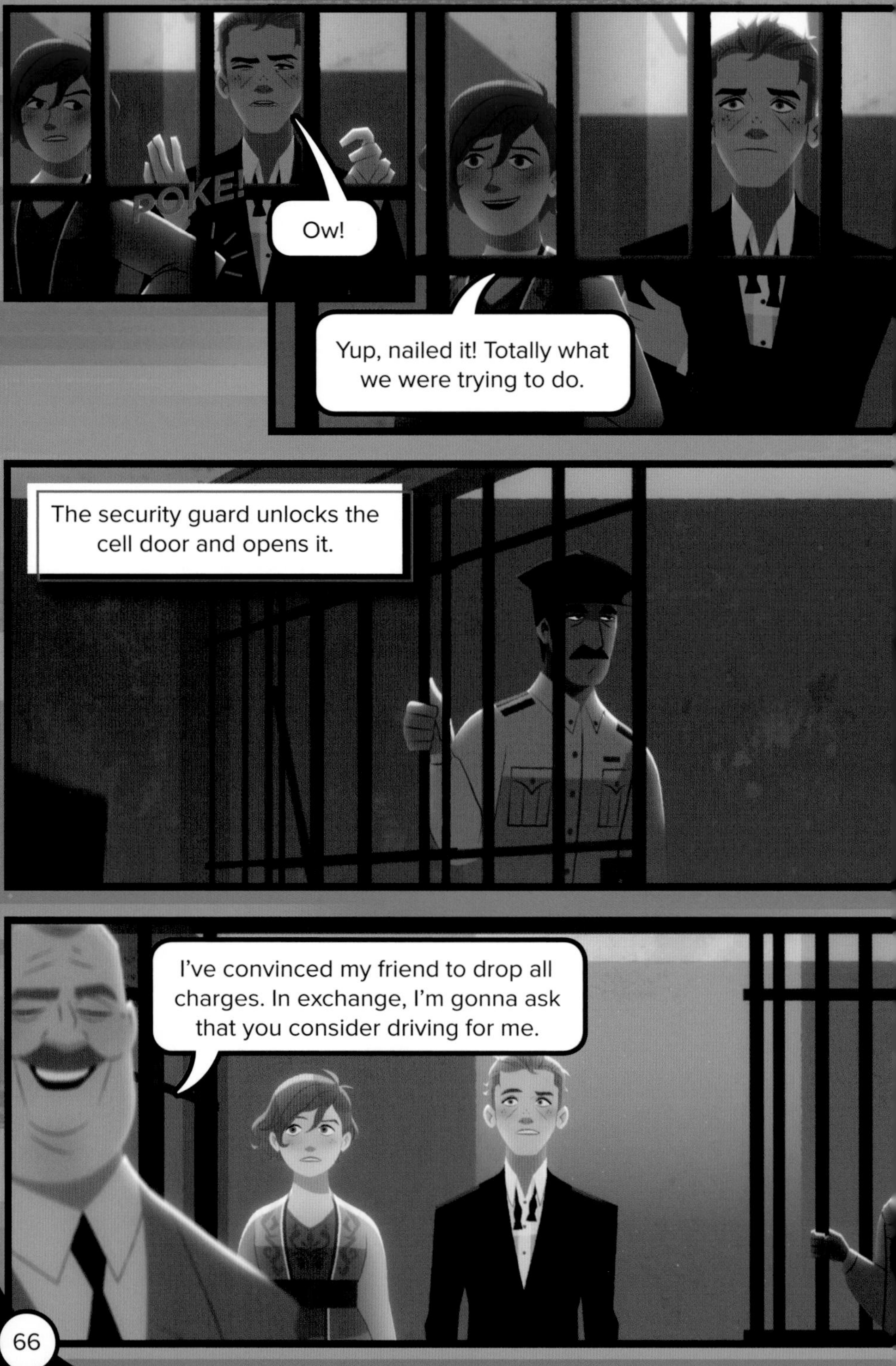

POKE!
Ow!
Yup, nailed it! Totally what we were trying to do.
The security guard unlocks the cell door and opens it.
I've convinced my friend to drop all charges. In exchange, I'm gonna ask that you consider driving for me.

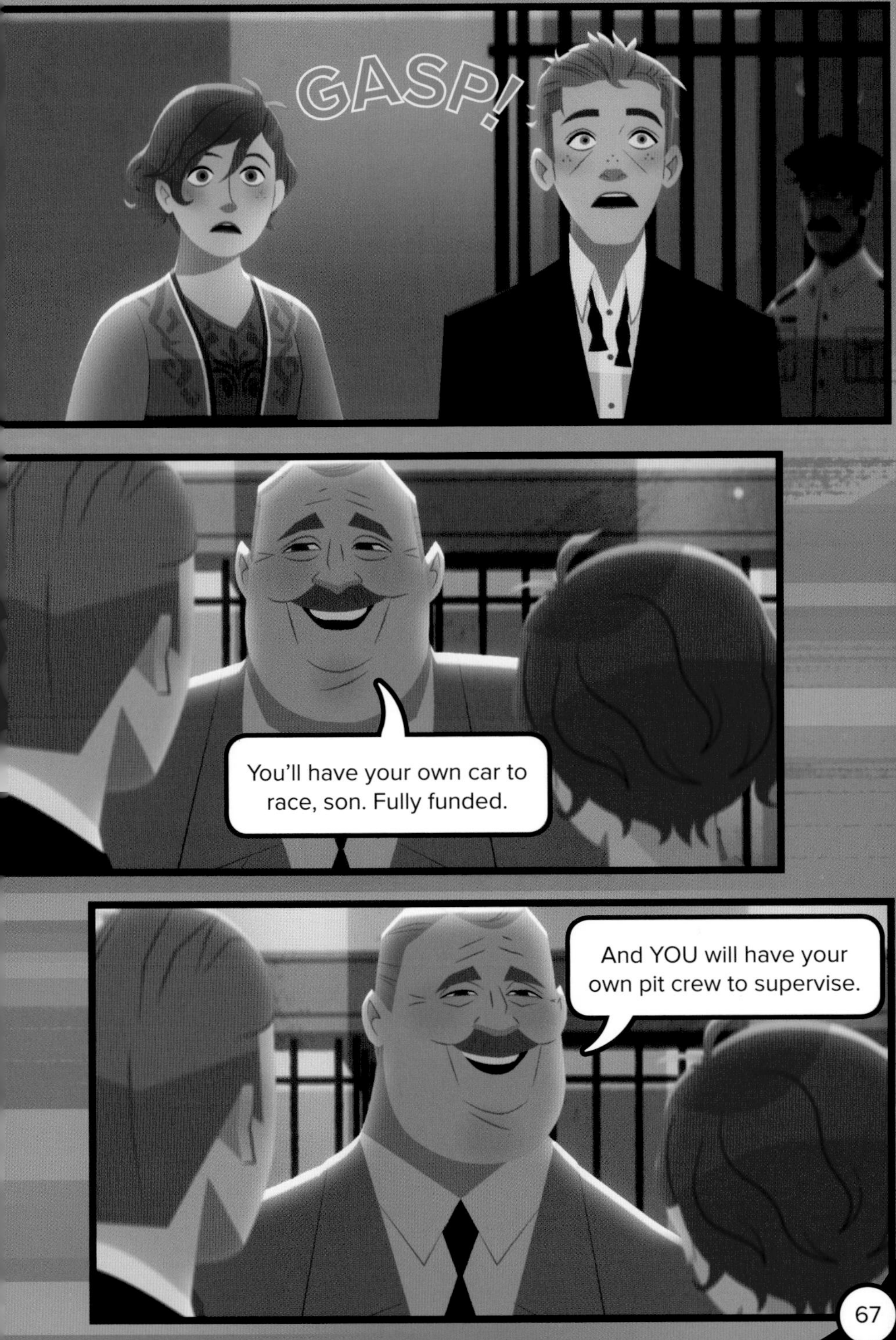
GASP!
You'll have your own car to race, son. Fully funded.
And YOU will have your own pit crew to supervise.

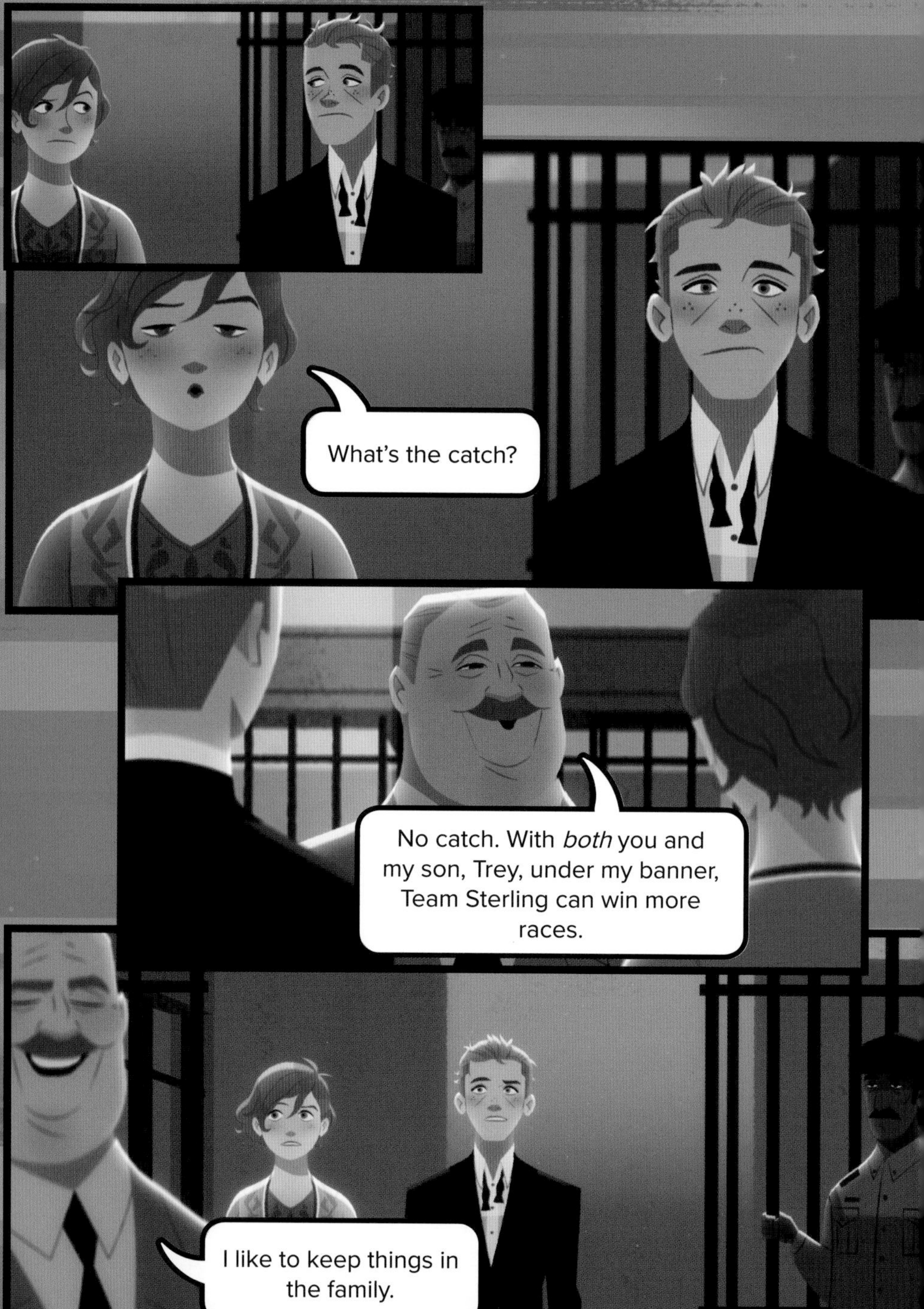
What's the catch?
No catch. With *both* you and my son, Trey, under my banner, Team Sterling can win more races.
I like to keep things in the family.

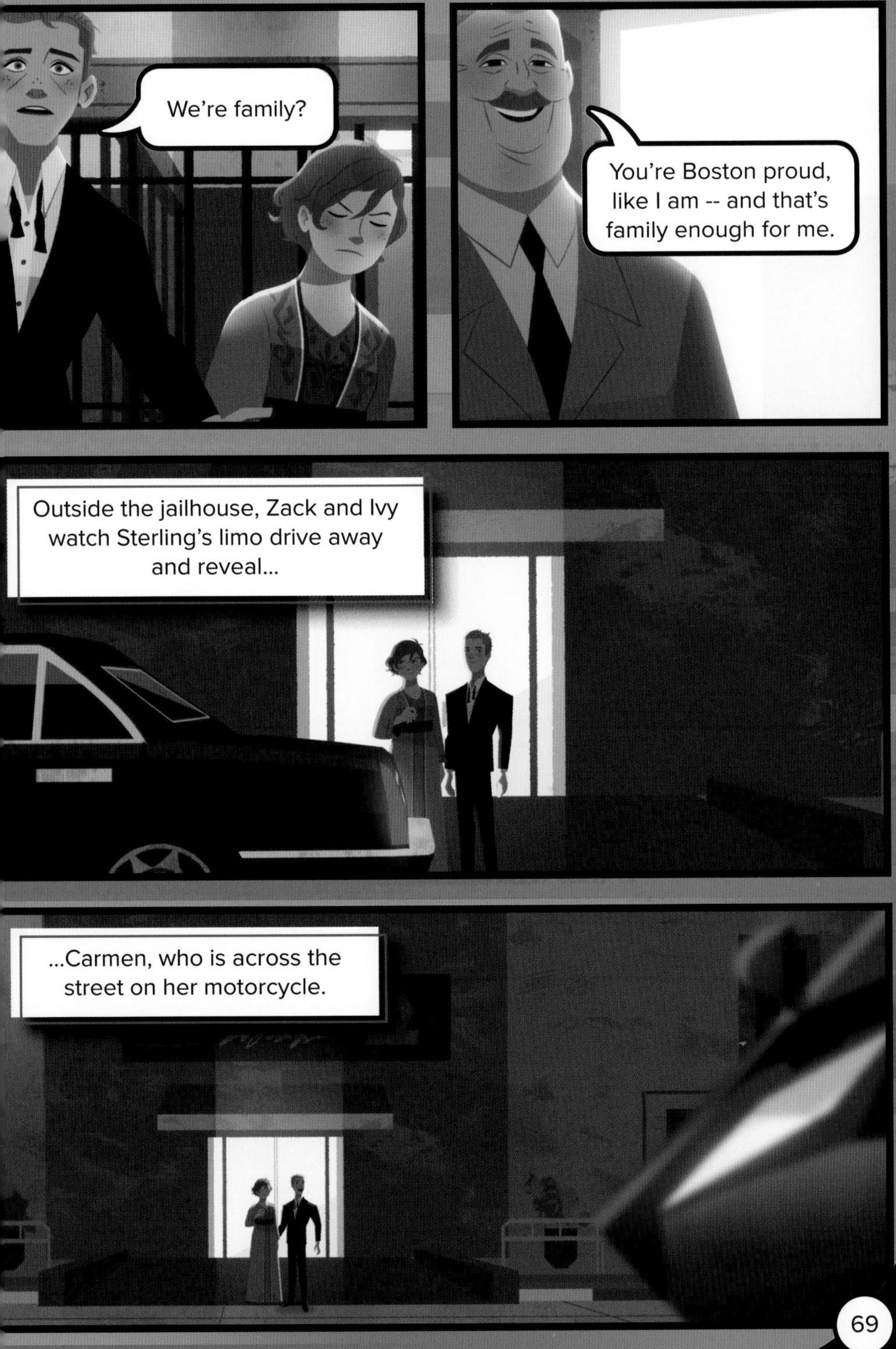
We're family?
You're Boston proud, like I am -- and that's family enough for me.
Outside the jailhouse, Zack and Ivy watch Sterling's limo drive away and reveal...
...Carmen, who is across the street on her motorcycle.

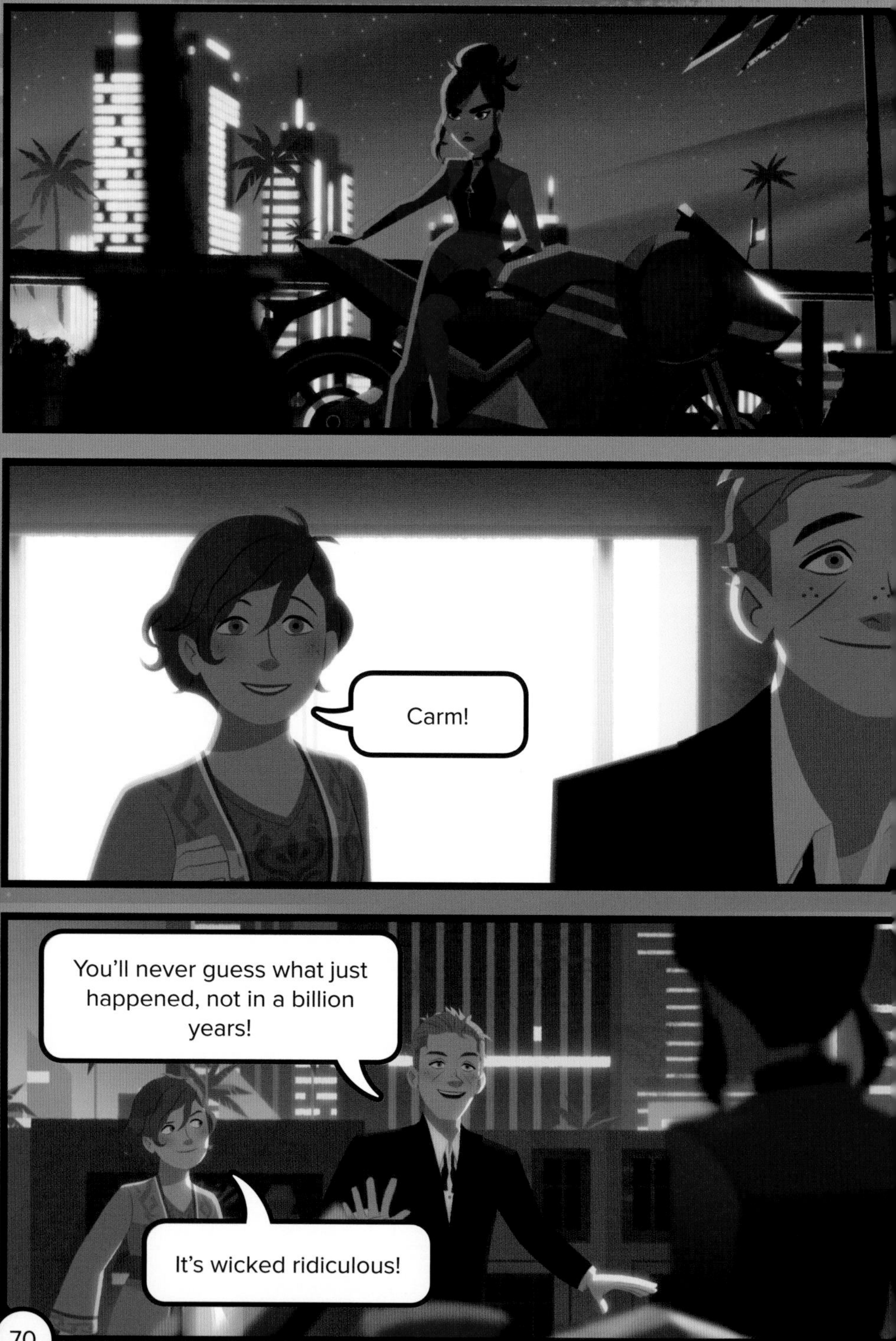
Carm!
You'll never guess what just happened, not in a billion years!
It's wicked ridiculous!

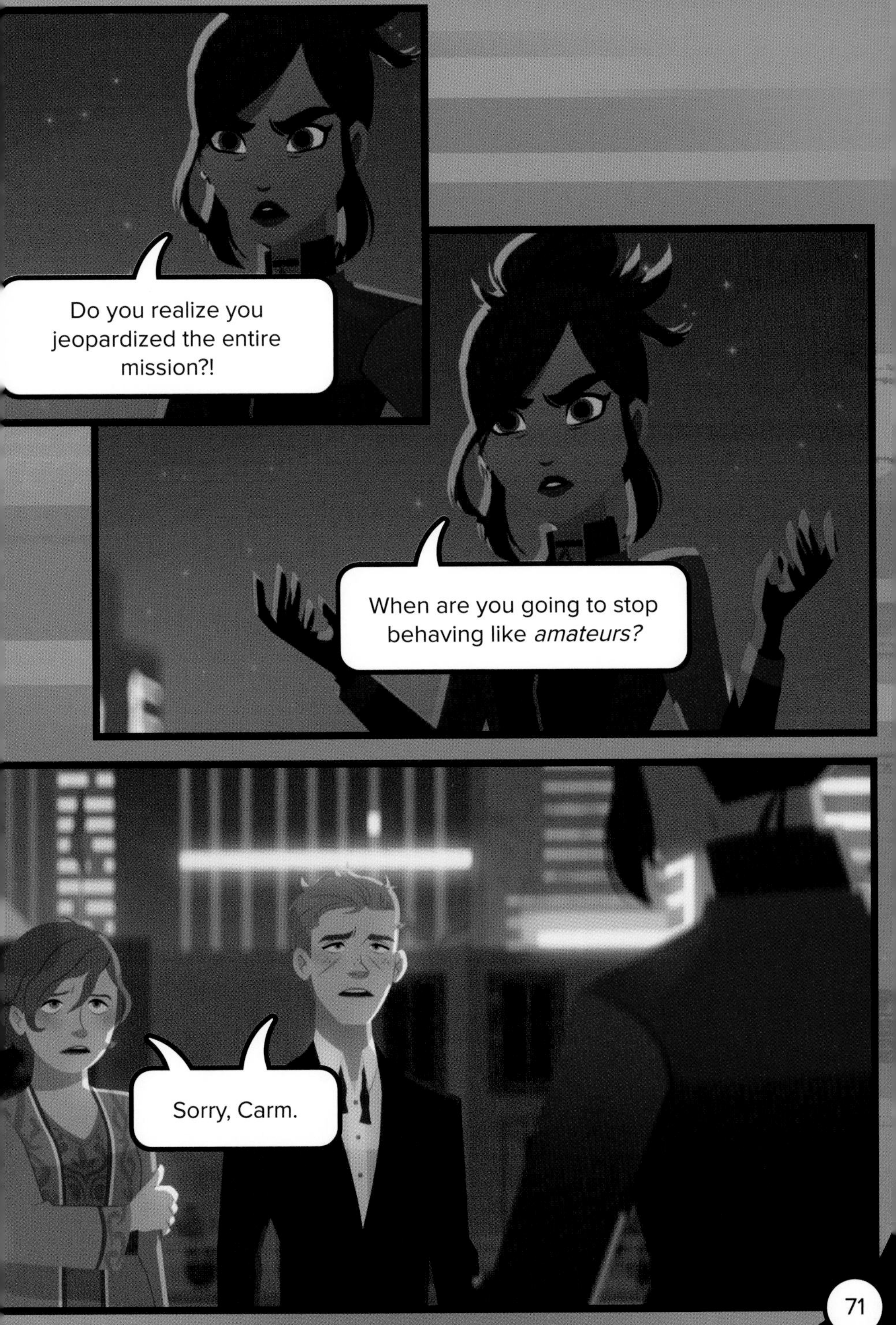
Do you realize you jeopardized the entire mission?!
When are you going to stop behaving like *amateurs?*
Sorry, Carm.

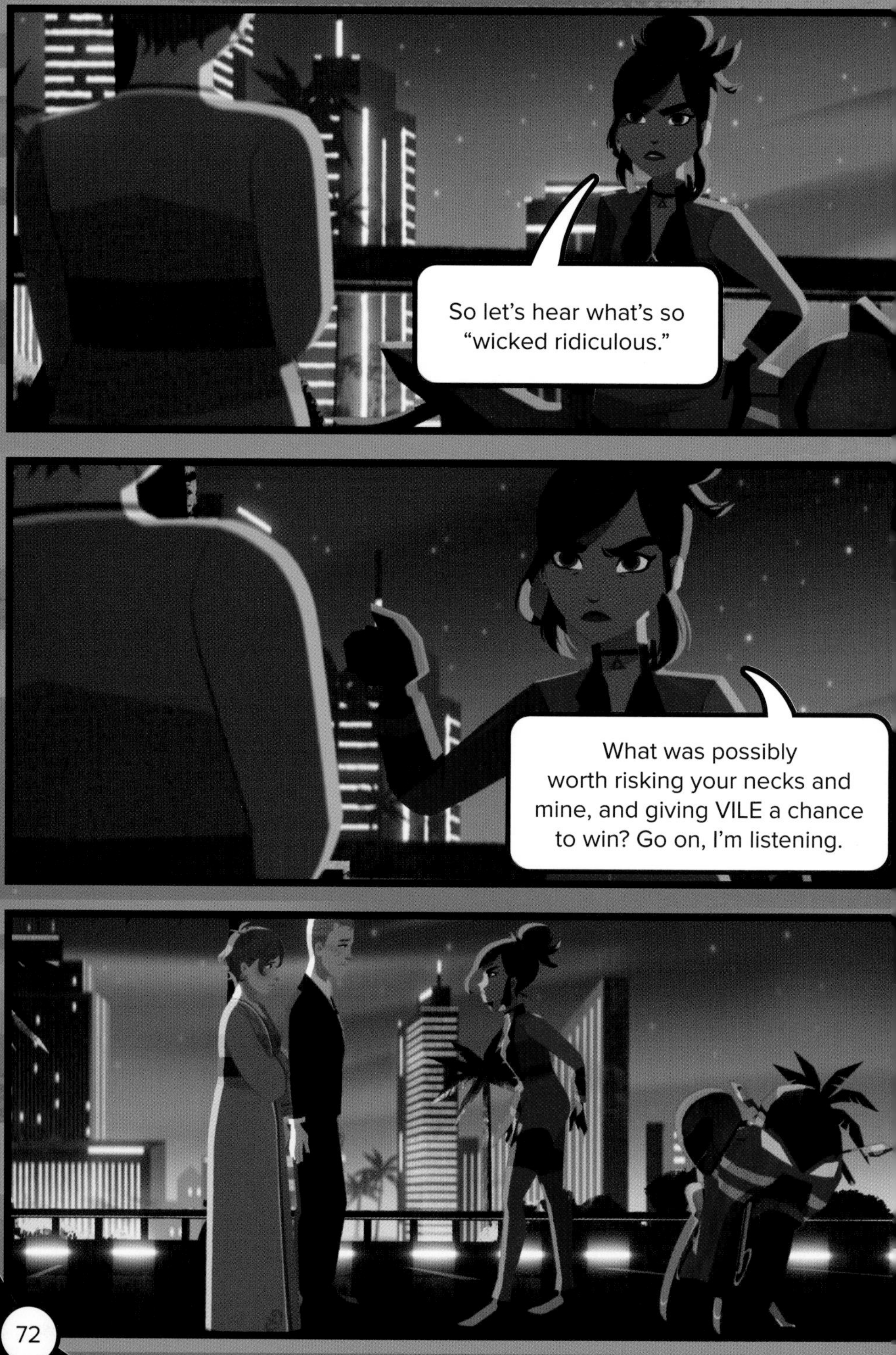
So let's hear what's so "wicked ridiculous."
What was possibly worth risking your necks and mine, and giving VILE a chance to win? Go on, I'm listening.

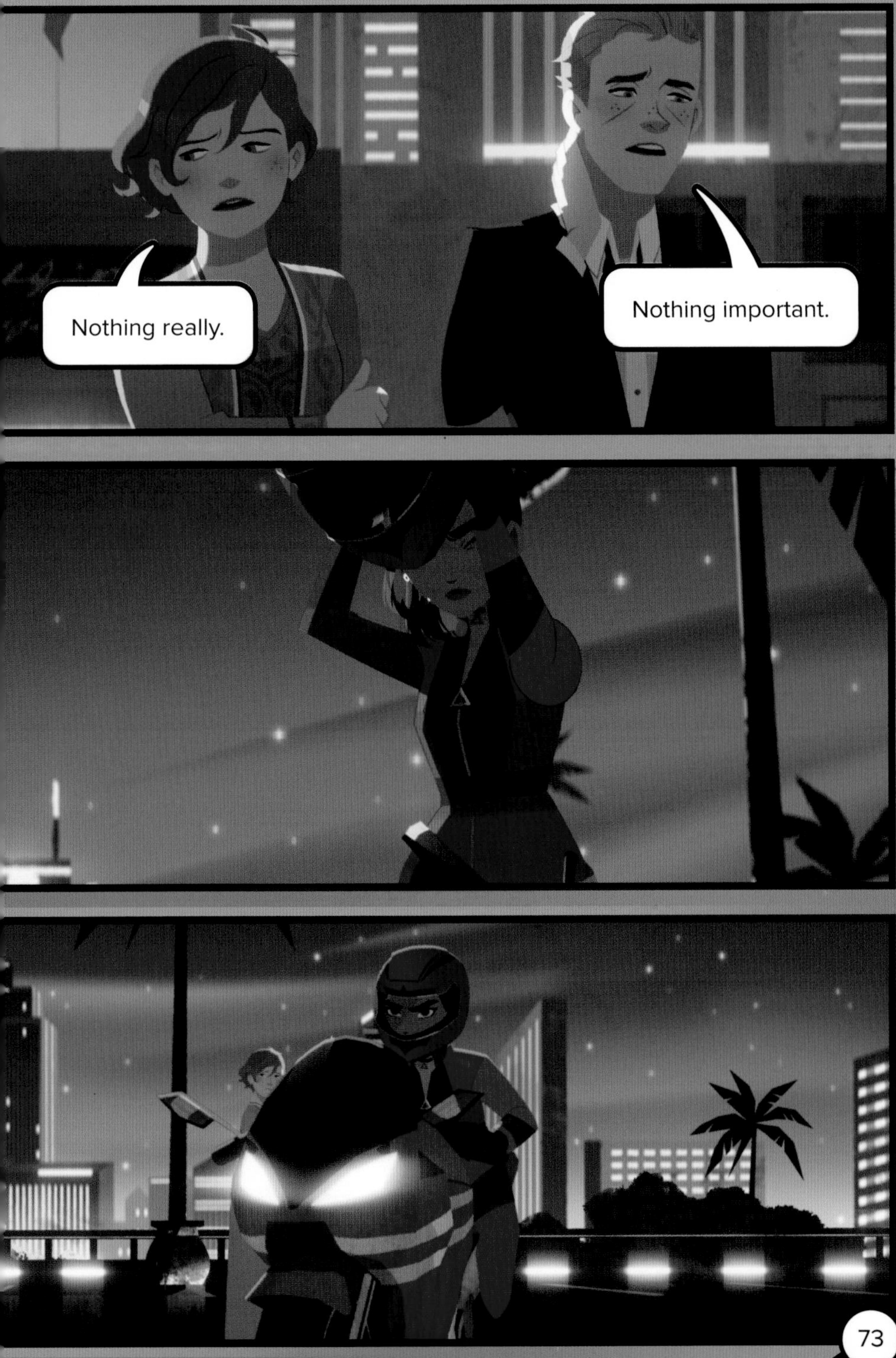
Nothing really.
Nothing important.

At the Dubai Autodrome,
the next morning

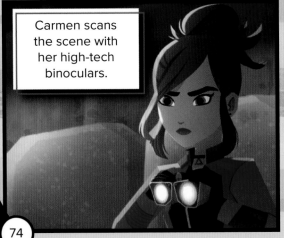

Carmen scans
the scene with
her high-tech
binoculars.

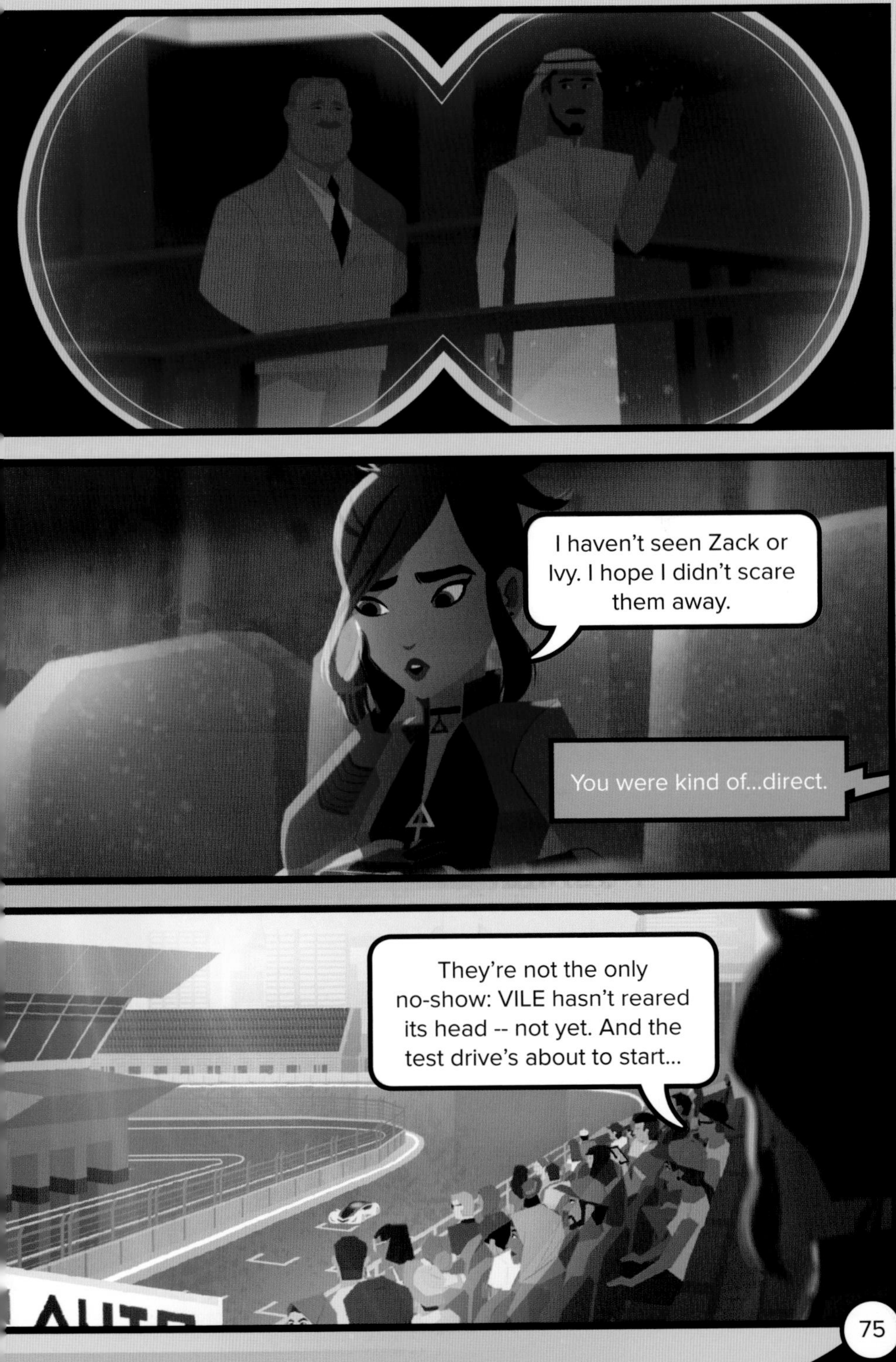
I haven't seen Zack or Ivy. I hope I didn't scare them away.
You were kind of...direct.
They're not the only no-show: VILE hasn't reared its head -- not yet. And the test drive's about to start...

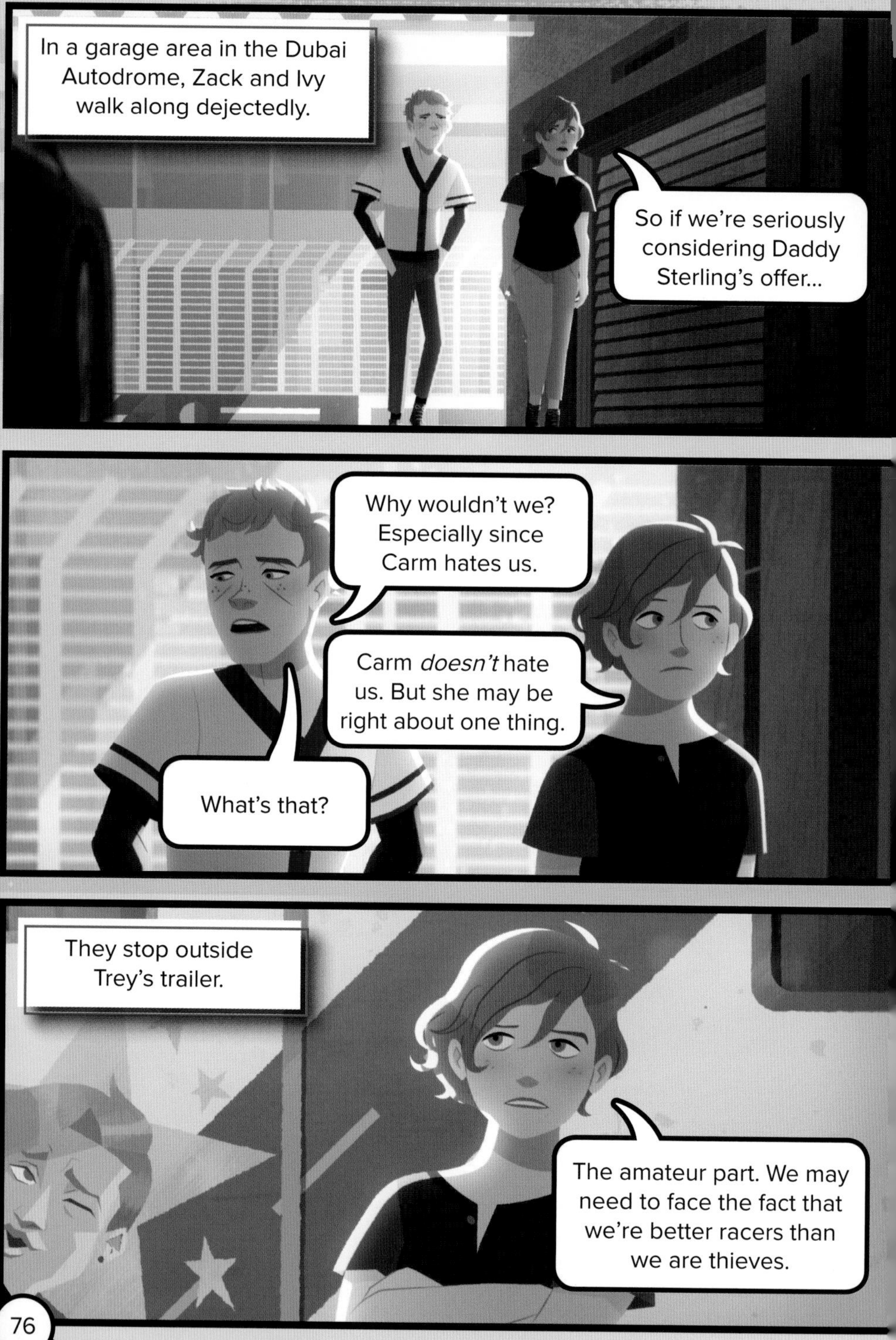
In a garage area in the Dubai Autodrome, Zack and Ivy walk along dejectedly.
So if we're seriously considering Daddy Sterling's offer...
Why wouldn't we? Especially since Carm hates us.
Carm *doesn't* hate us. But she may be right about one thing.
What's that?
They stop outside Trey's trailer.
The amateur part. We may need to face the fact that we're better racers than we are thieves.

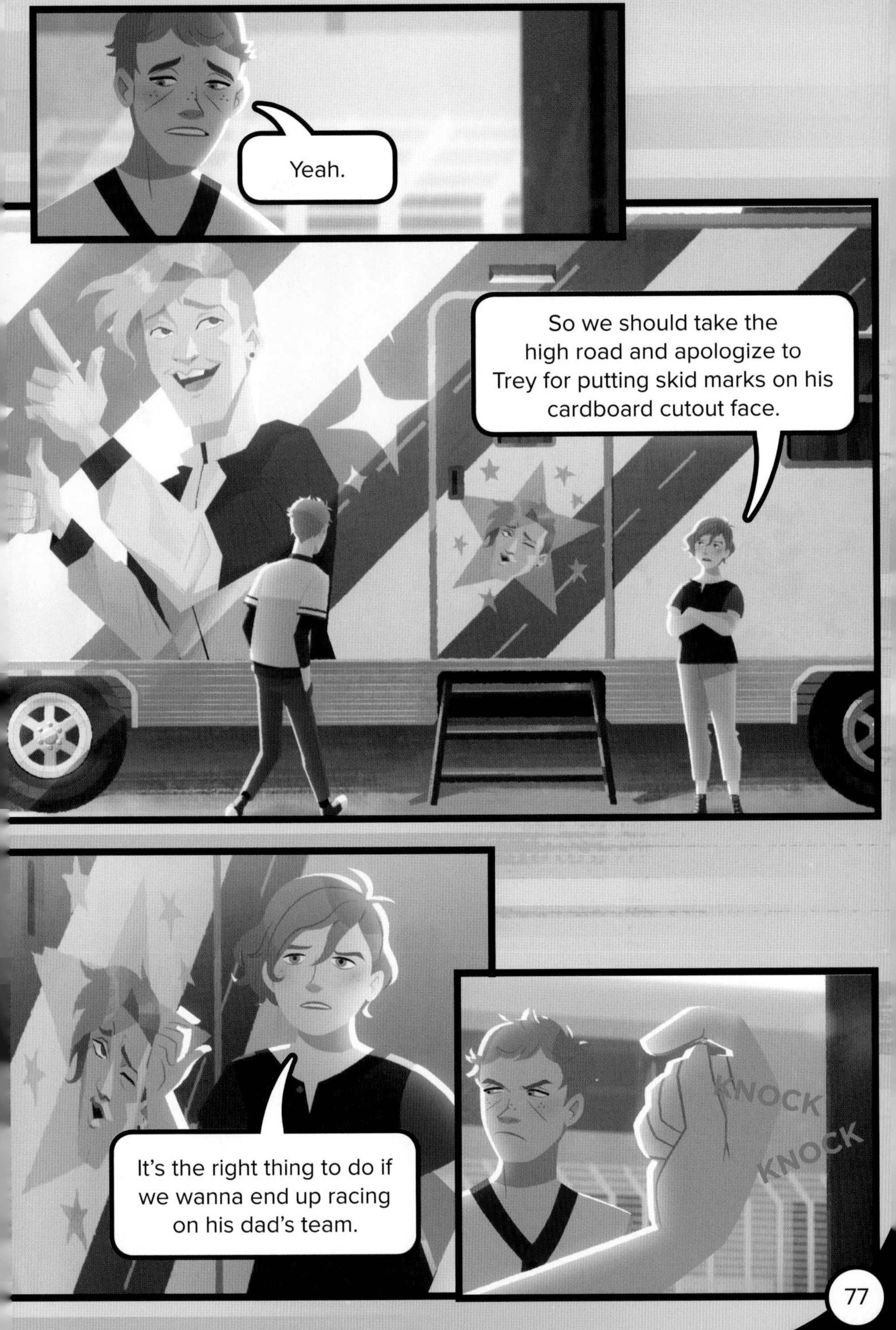

Yeah.
So we should take the high road and apologize to Trey for putting skid marks on his cardboard cutout face.
It's the right thing to do if we wanna end up racing on his dad's team.
KNOCK
KNOCK

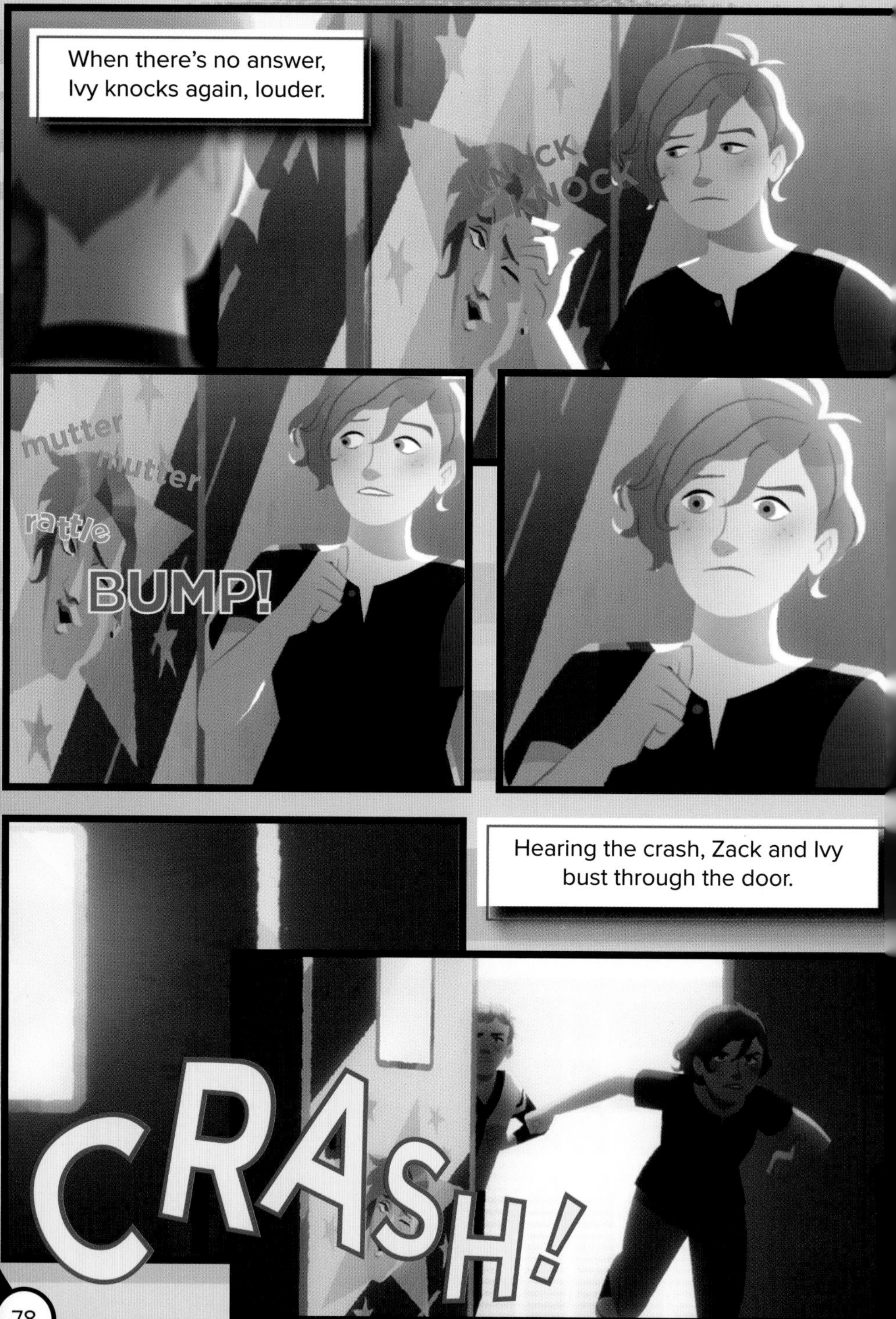
When there's no answer, Ivy knocks again, louder.
KNOCK KNOCK
mutter mutter
rattle
BUMP!
Hearing the crash, Zack and Ivy bust through the door.
CRASH!

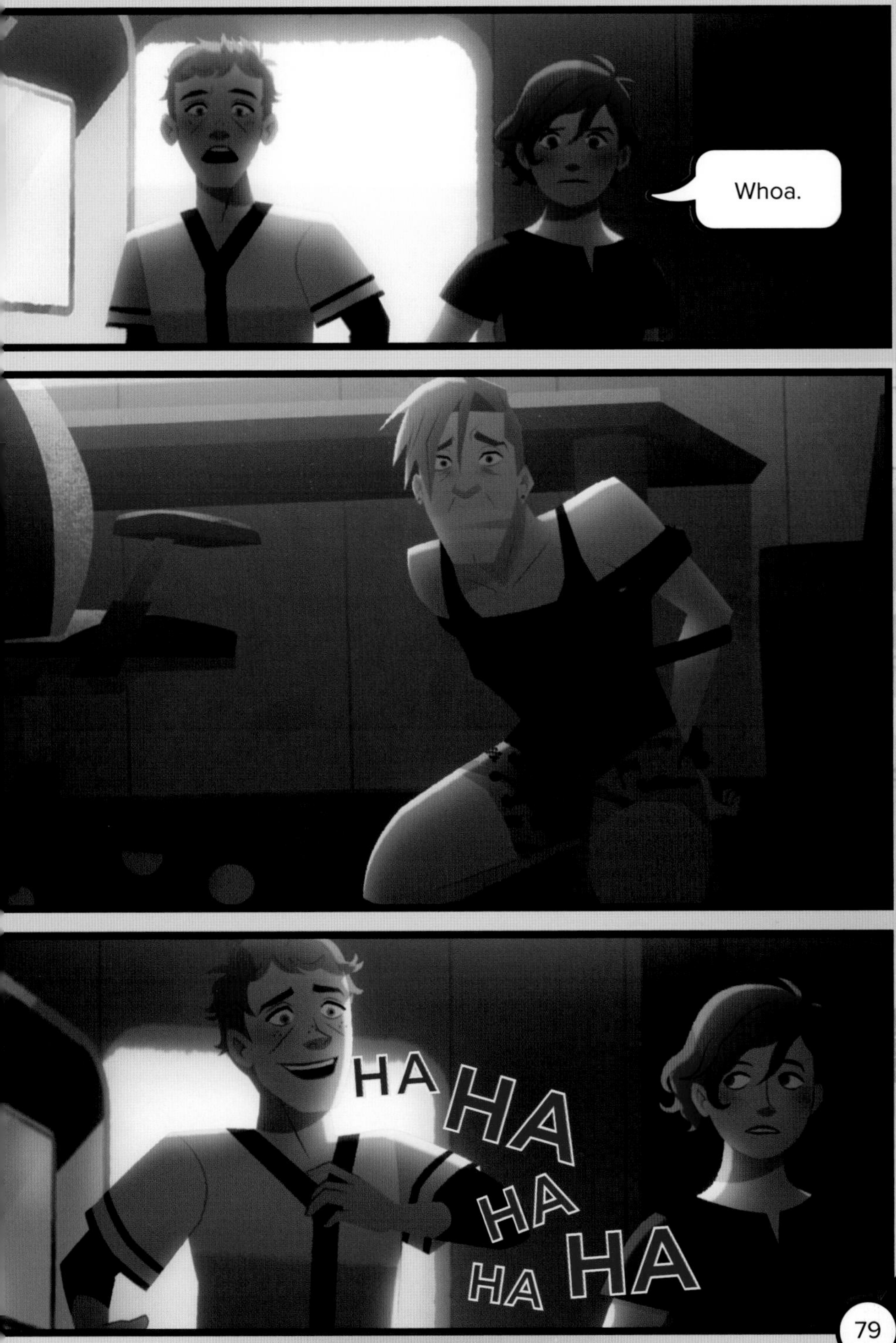
Whoa.
HA HA
HA
HA HA

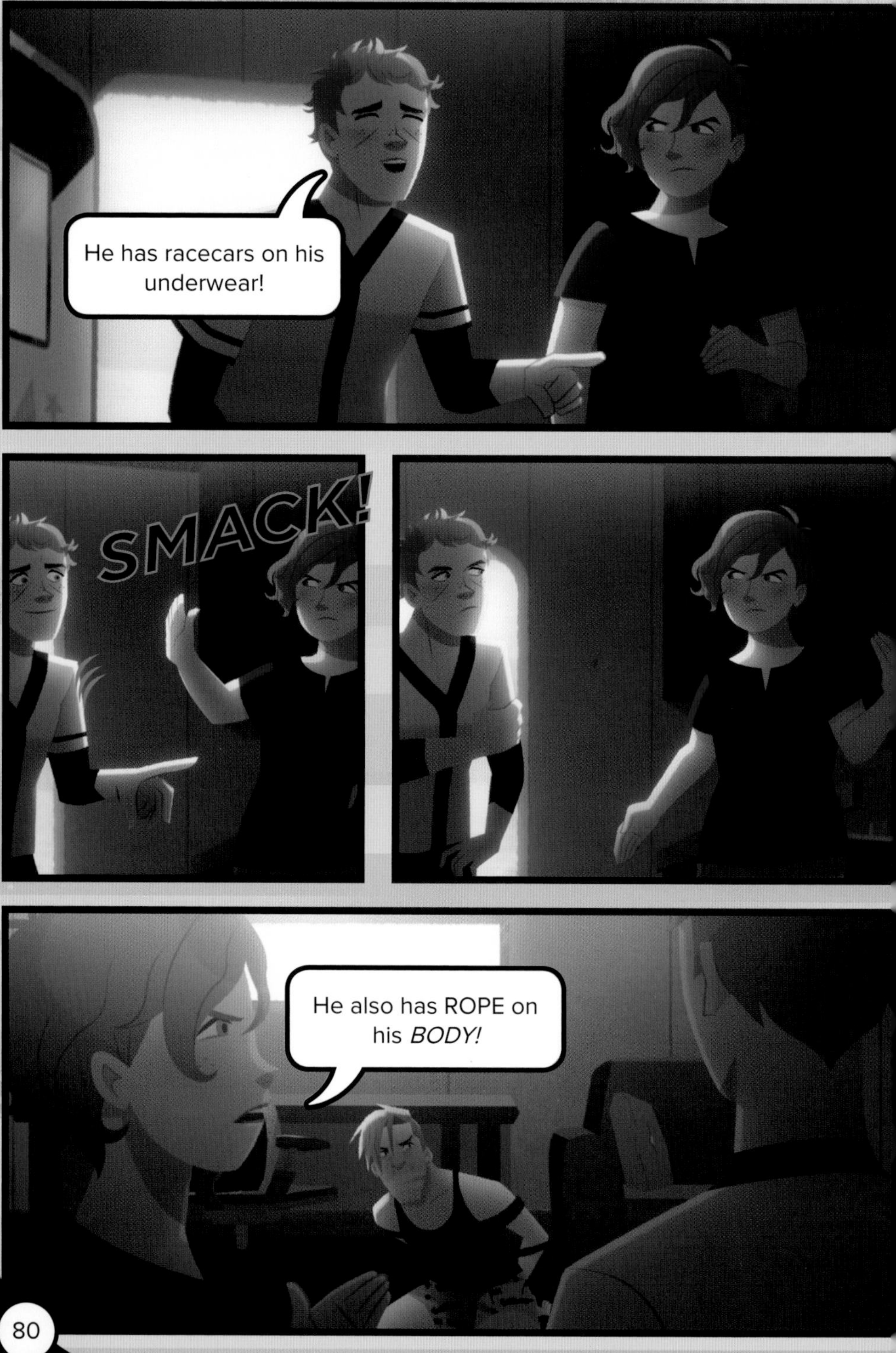
He has racecars on his underwear!
SMACK!
He also has ROPE on his *BODY!*

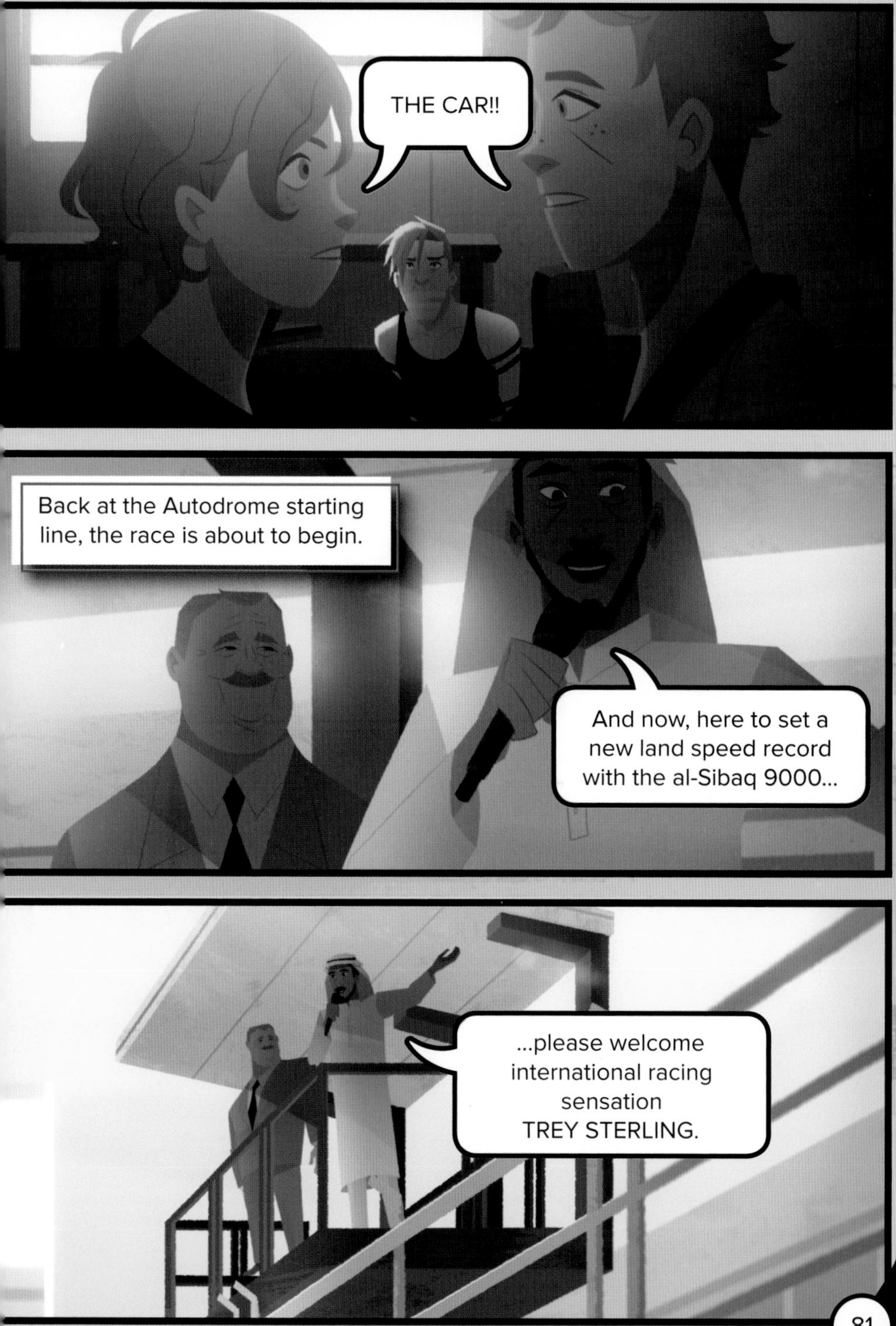
THE CAR!!
Back at the Autodrome starting line, the race is about to begin.
And now, here to set a new land speed record with the al-Sibaq 9000...
...please welcome international racing sensation TREY STERLING.

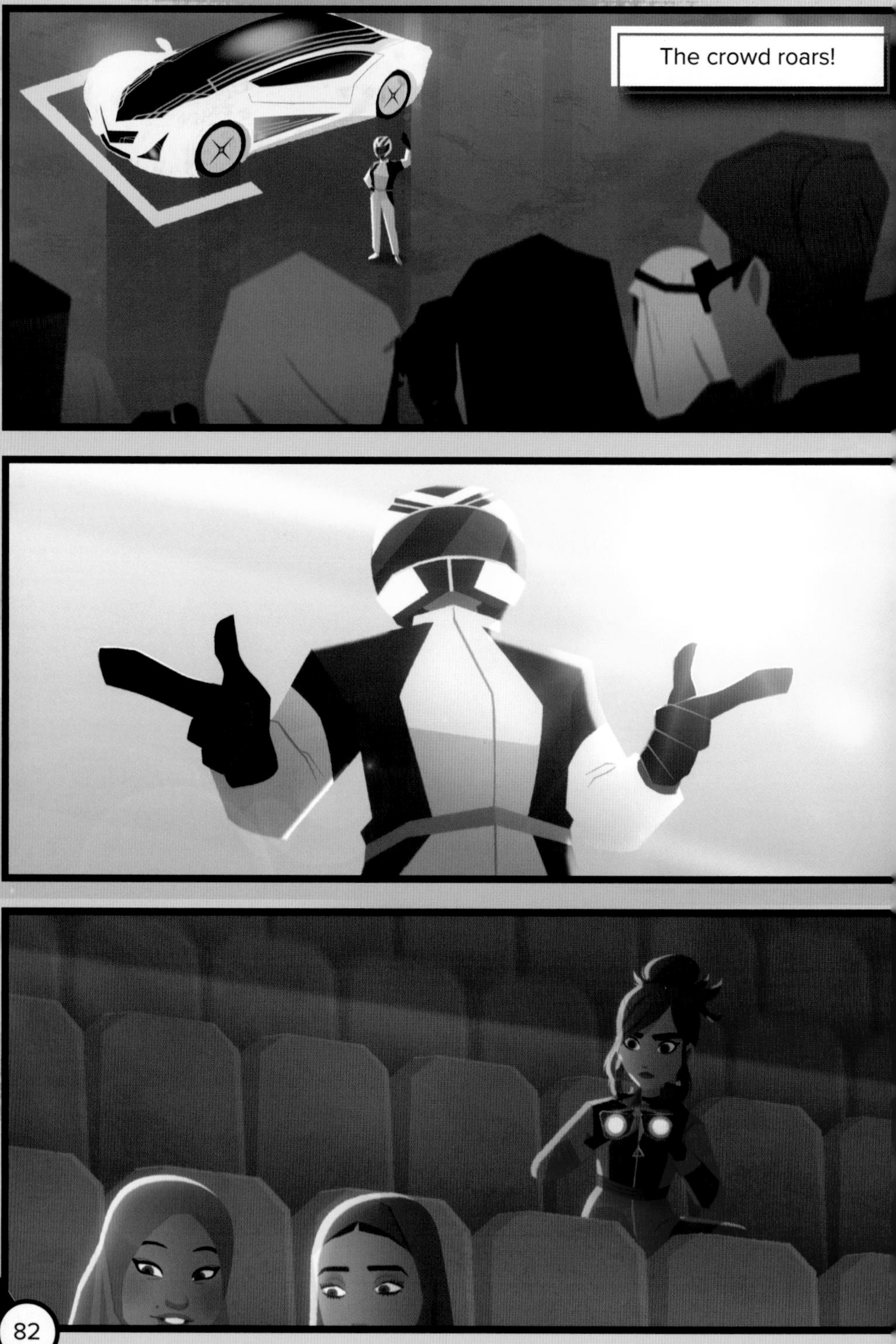
The crowd roars!

The driver enters the vehicle...

...and turns on the engine.

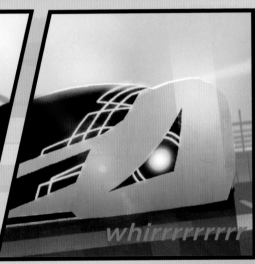

whirrrrrrrrr

BEEP

BEEP

BEEP

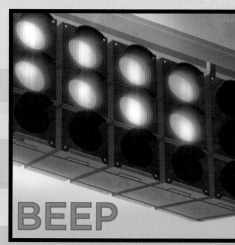

BEEP

BEEP

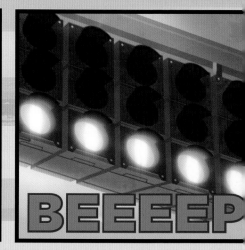

BEEEEP

And the driver takes off!

RRRRrrrrr

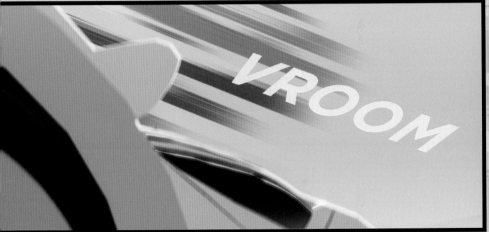

VROOM

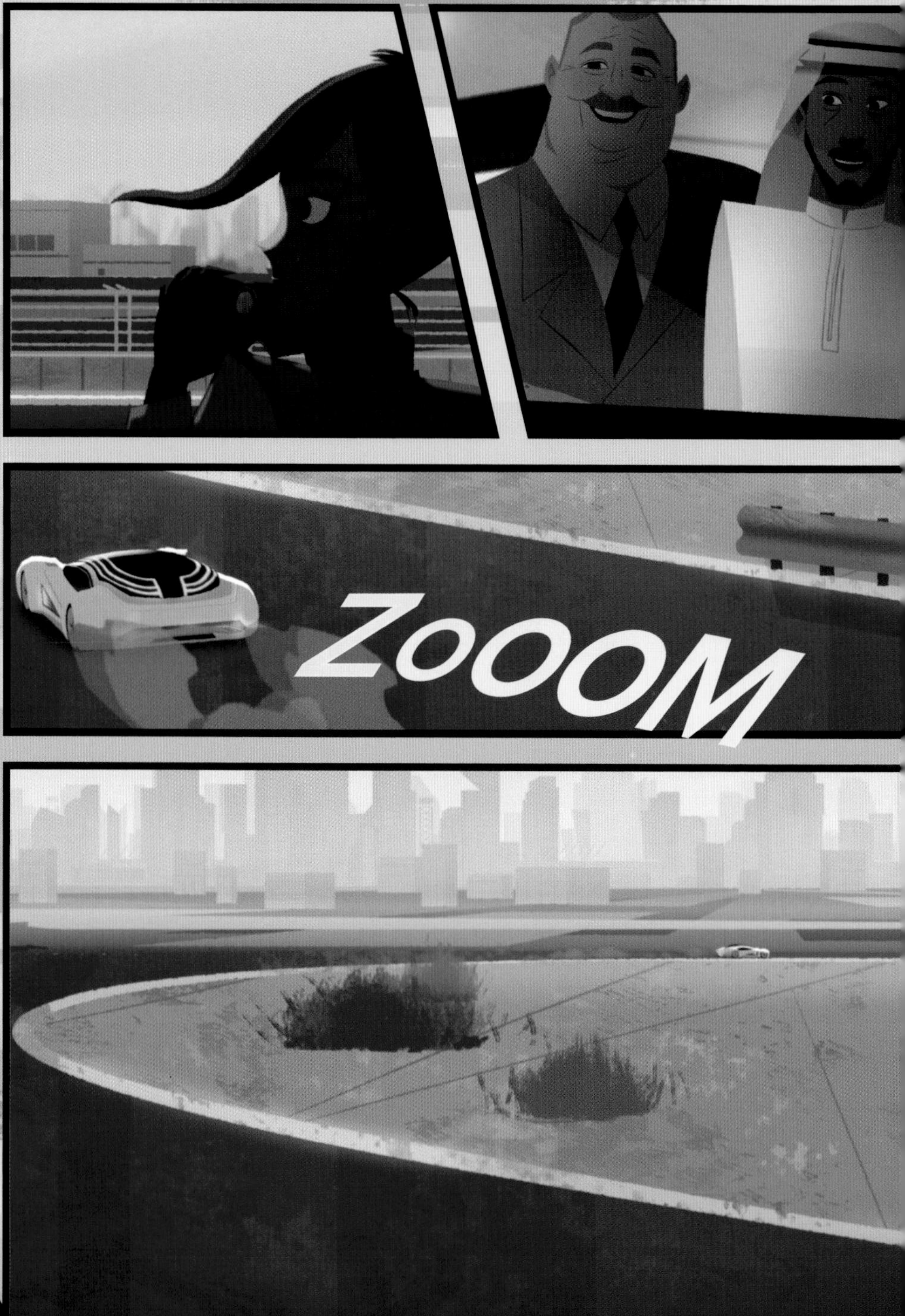
ZoOOM

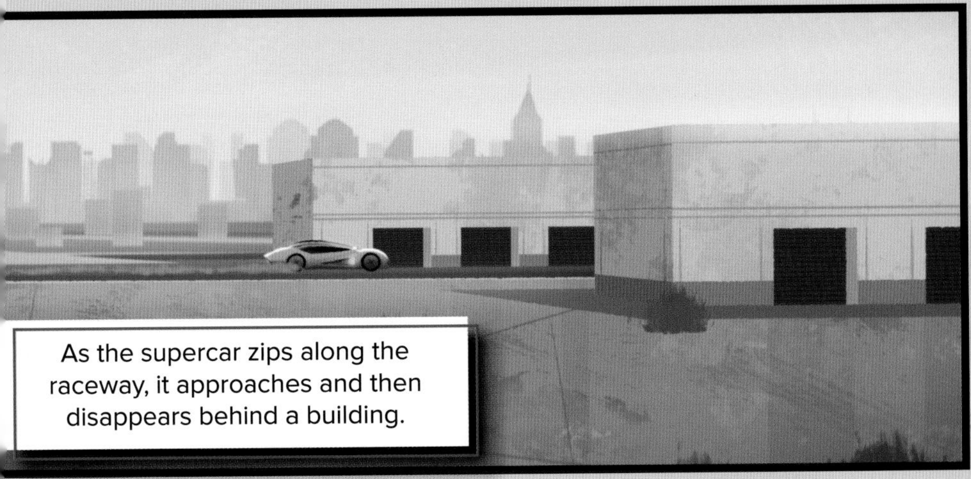
As the supercar zips along the raceway, it approaches and then disappears behind a building.

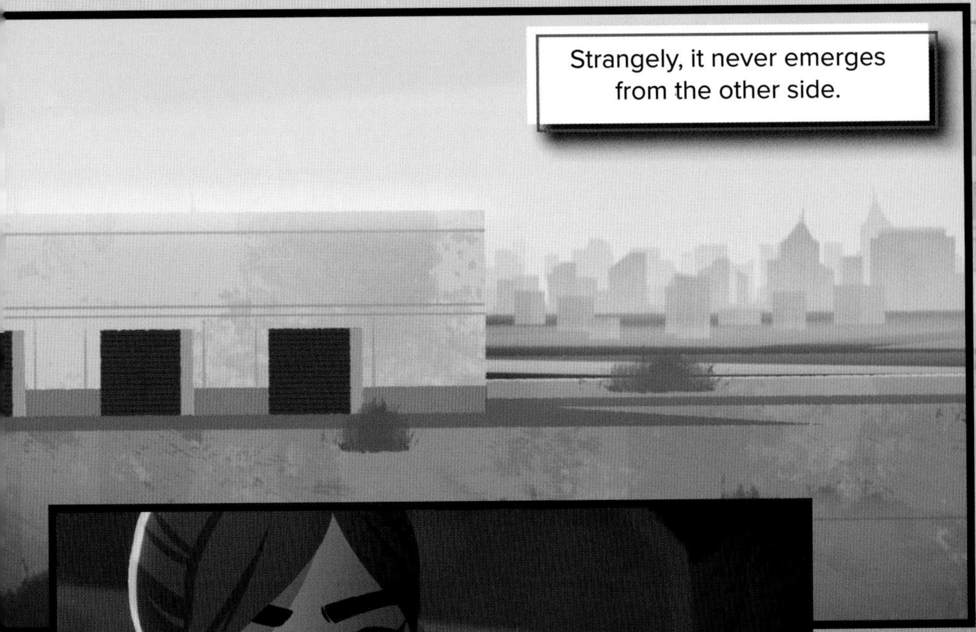
Strangely, it never emerges from the other side.

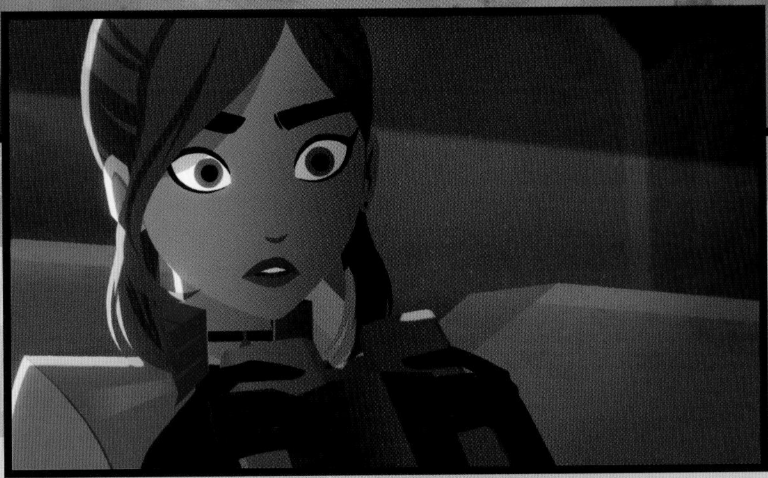

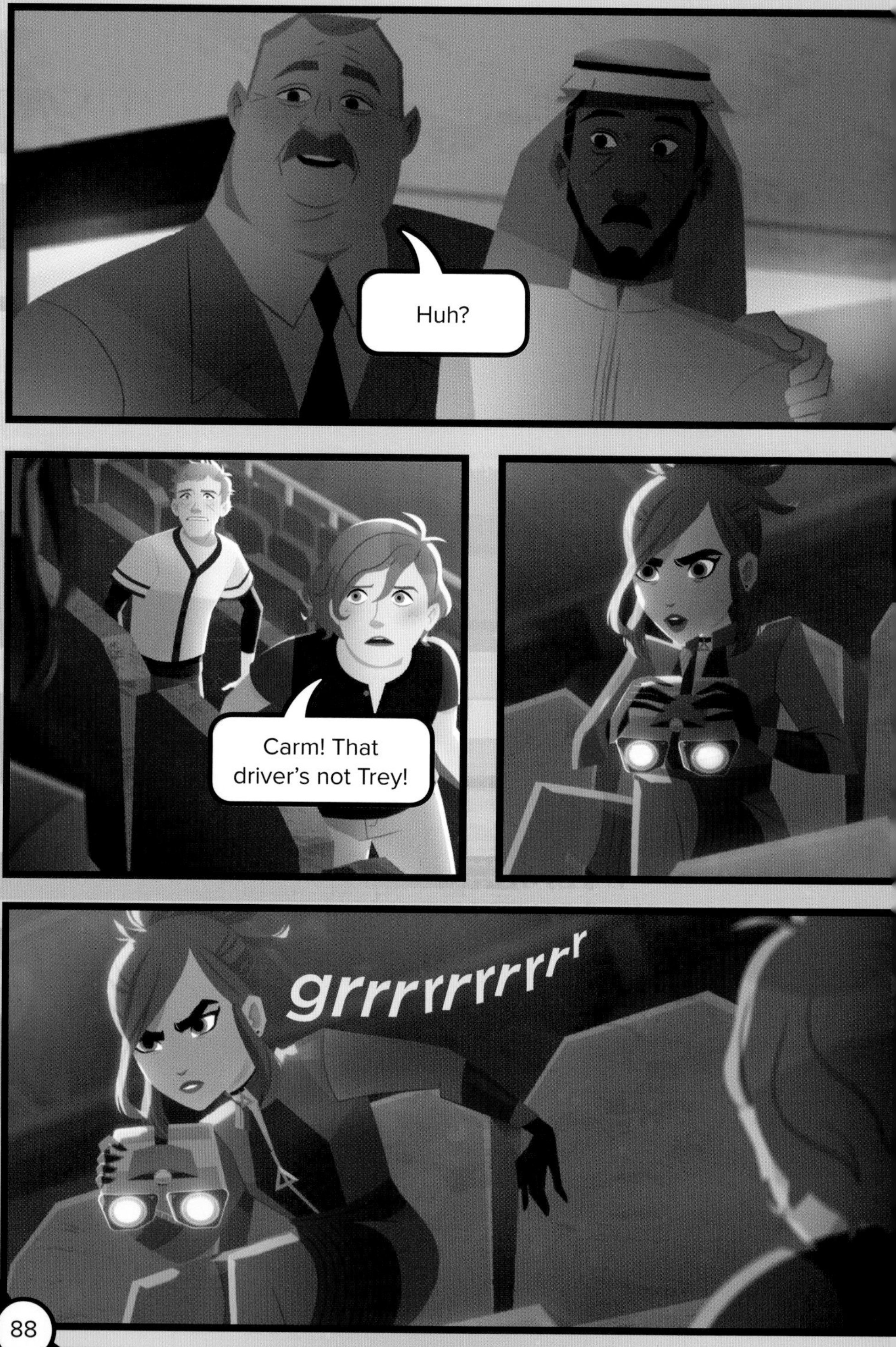
Huh?
Carm! That driver's not Trey!
grrrrrrrrr

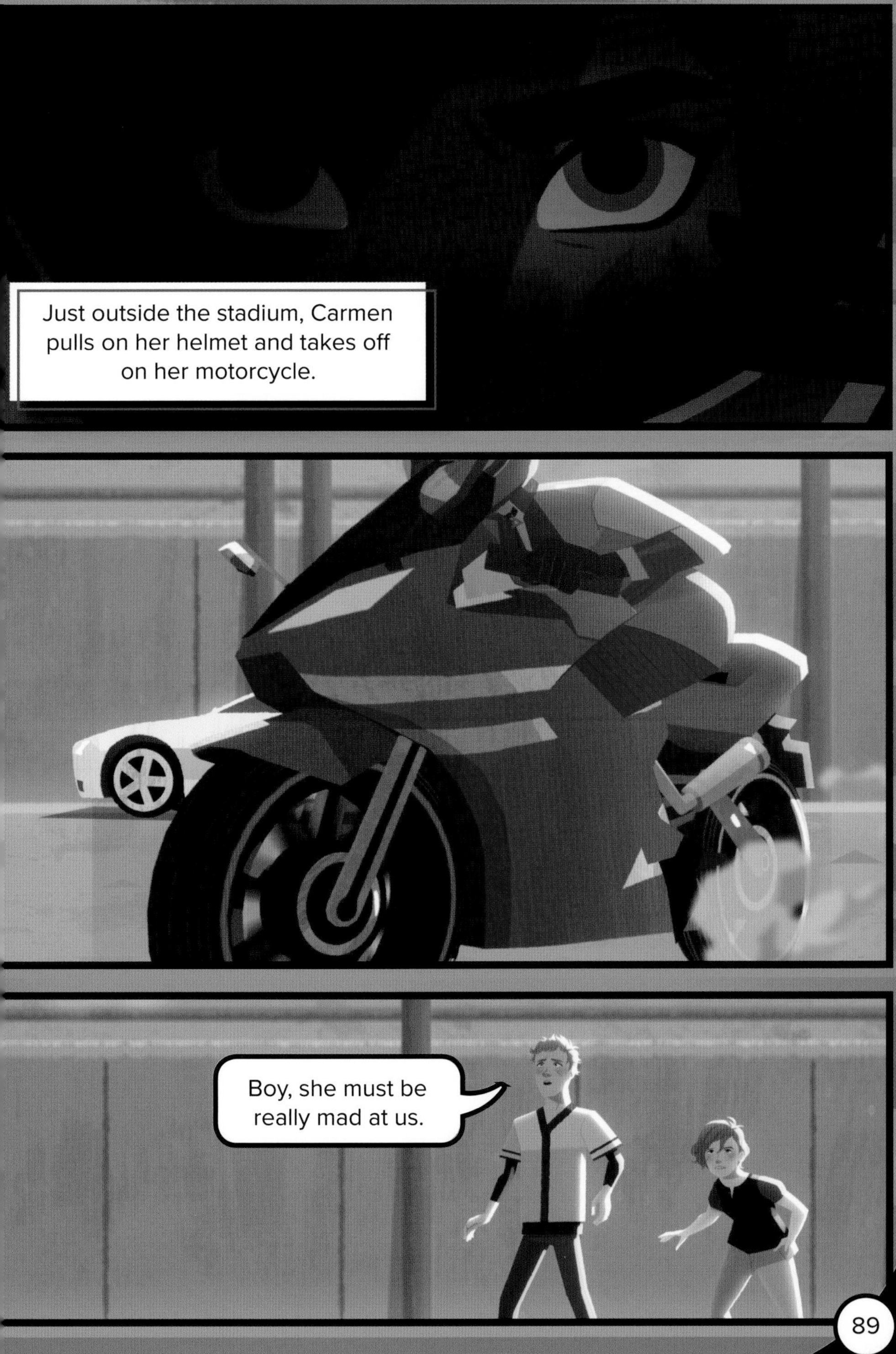
Just outside the stadium, Carmen pulls on her helmet and takes off on her motorcycle.
Boy, she must be really mad at us.

What was she gonna do, take us both for a piggyback ride?

C'mon!

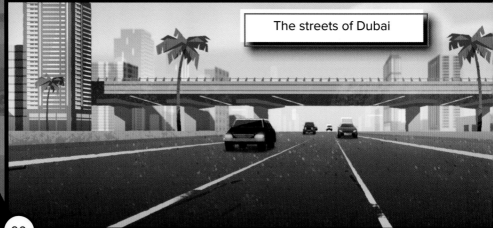

The streets of Dubai

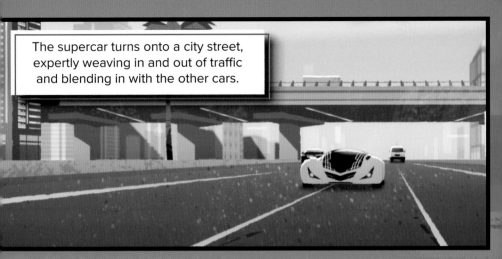

The supercar turns onto a city street, expertly weaving in and out of traffic and blending in with the other cars.

Carmen weaves through obstacles to catch up.

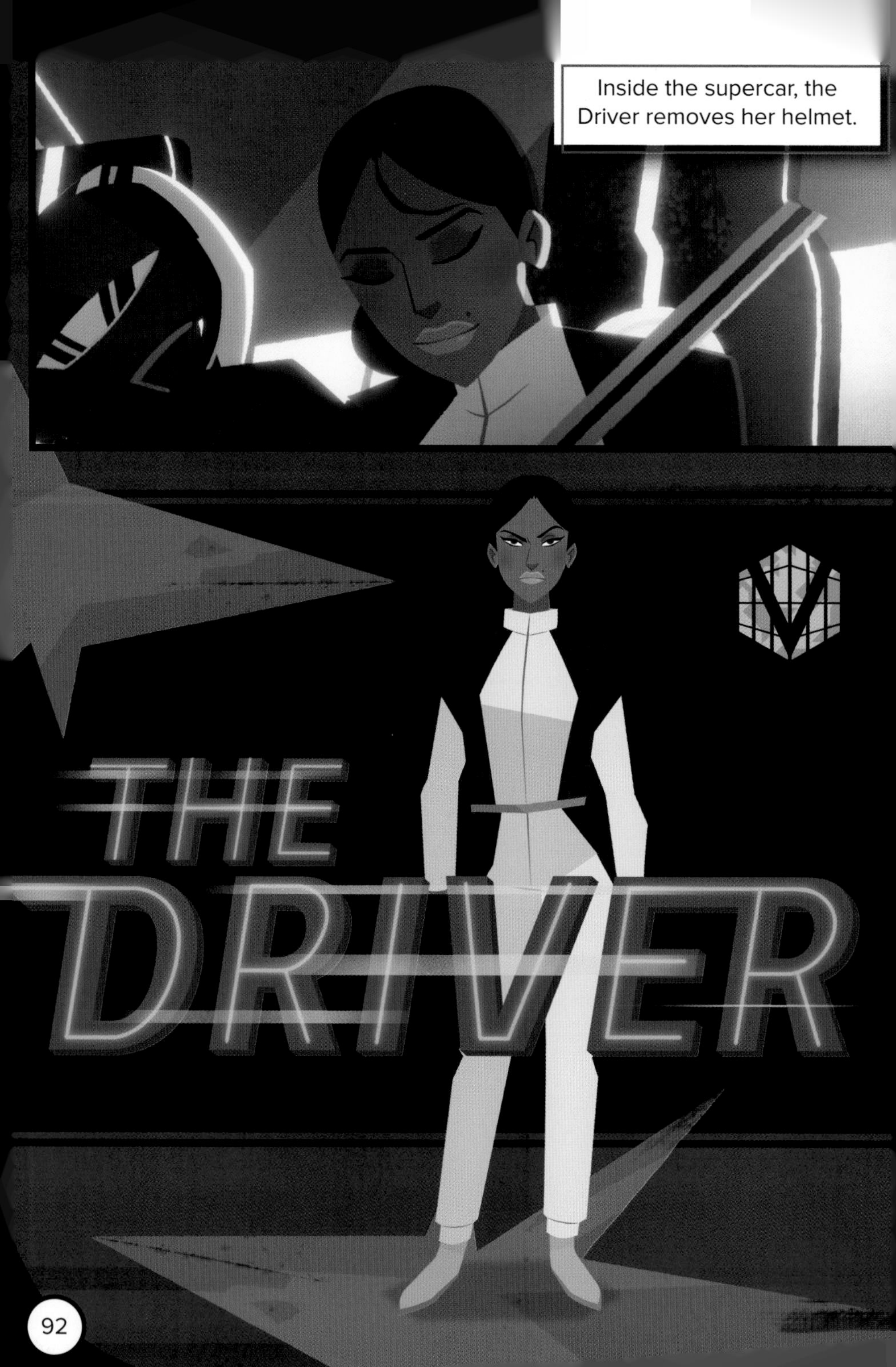
Inside the supercar, the Driver removes her helmet.
THE DRIVER

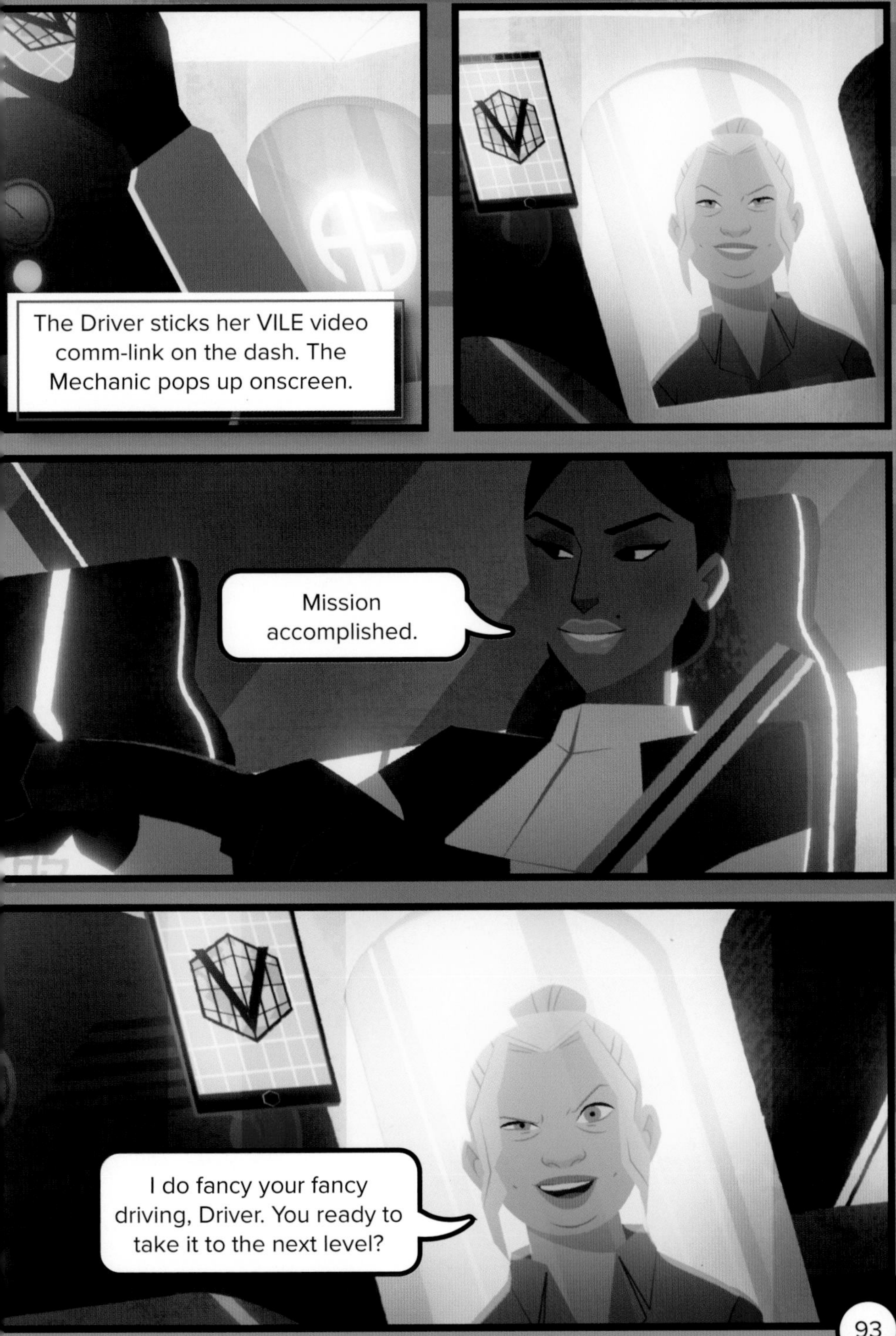
The Driver sticks her VILE video comm-link on the dash. The Mechanic pops up onscreen.
Mission accomplished.
I do fancy your fancy driving, Driver. You ready to take it to the next level?

Ready.

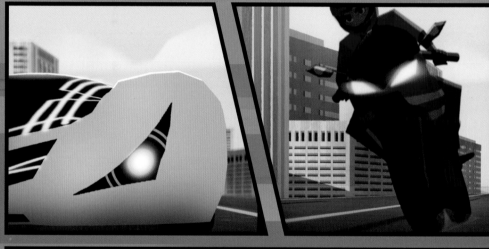

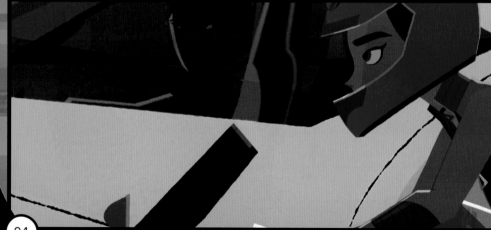

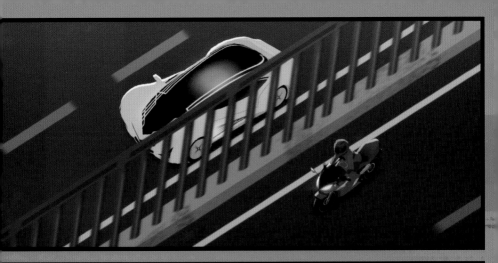

The Driver waves and speeds up a ramp on the highway.

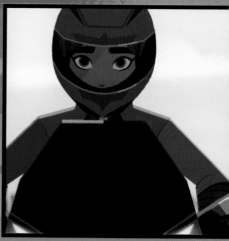

Carmen sees a construction ramp ahead that may be her only chance at catching the supercar.

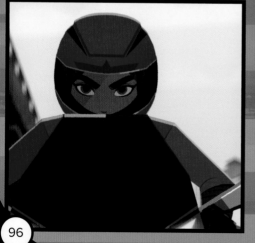

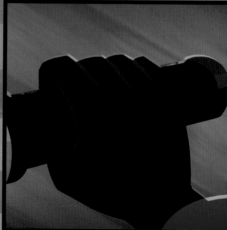

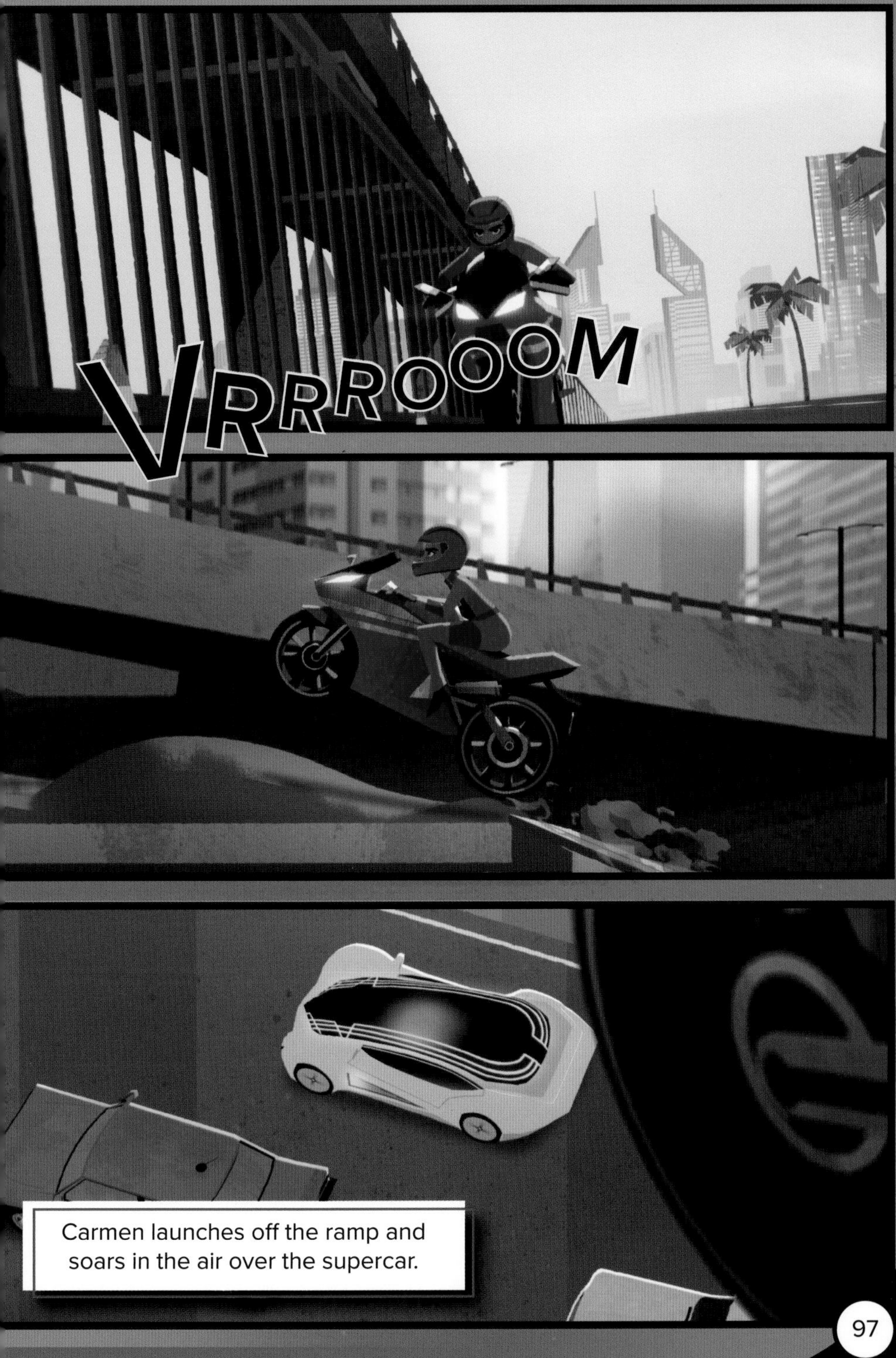
VRRROOOM
Carmen launches off the ramp and soars in the air over the supercar.

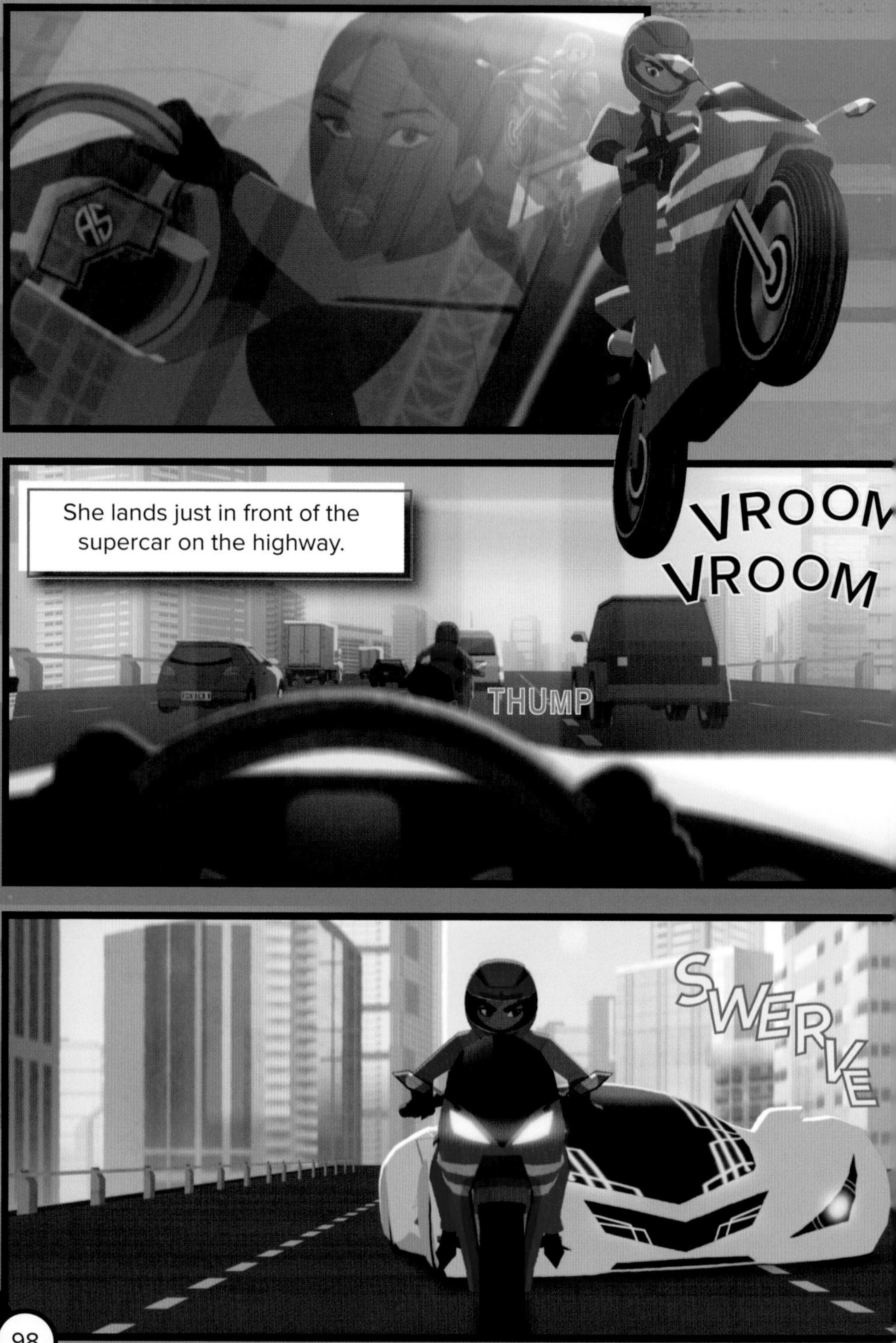

She lands just in front of the supercar on the highway.
VROOM
VROOM
THUMP
SWERVE

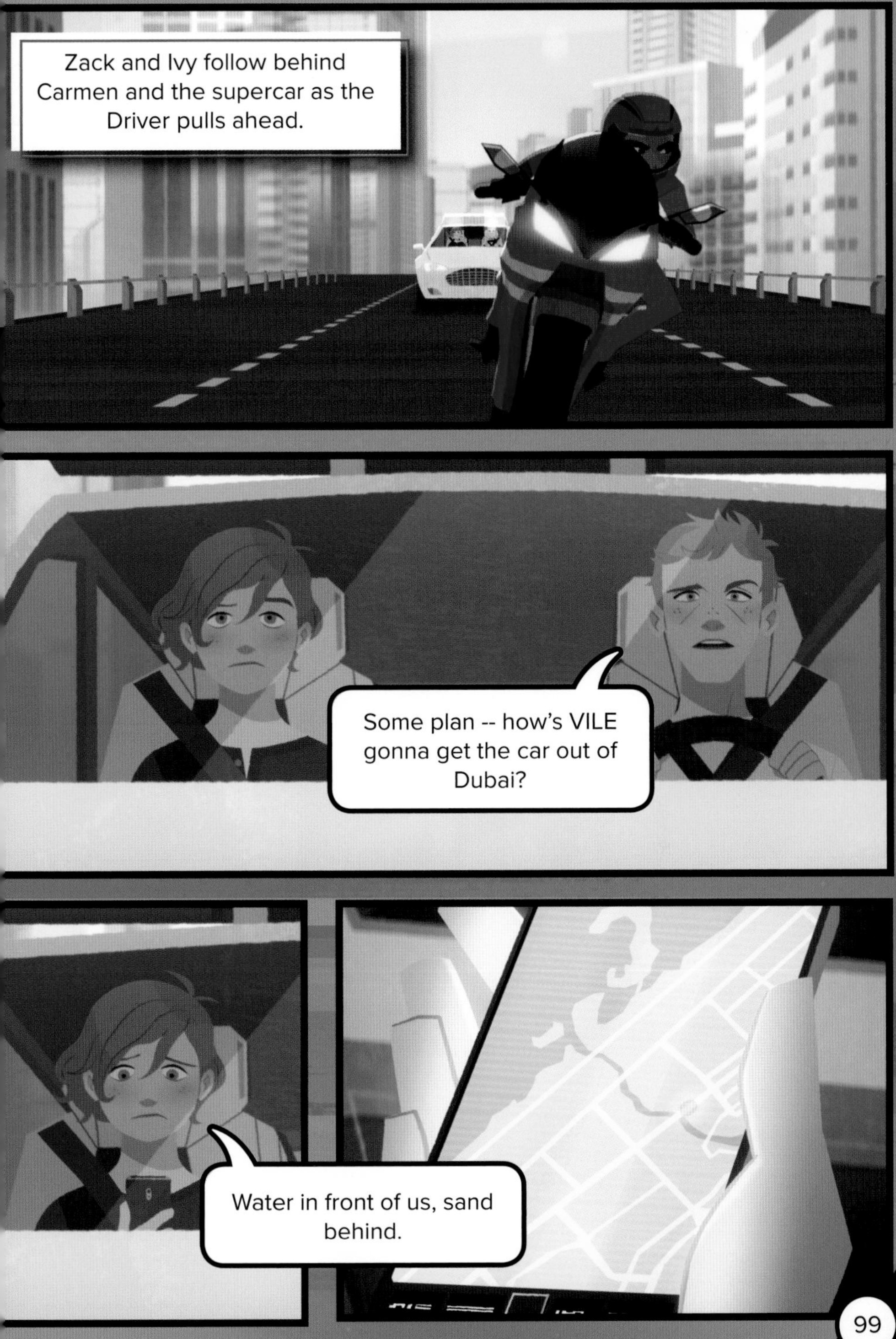
Zack and Ivy follow behind Carmen and the supercar as the Driver pulls ahead.
Some plan -- how's VILE gonna get the car out of Dubai?
Water in front of us, sand behind.

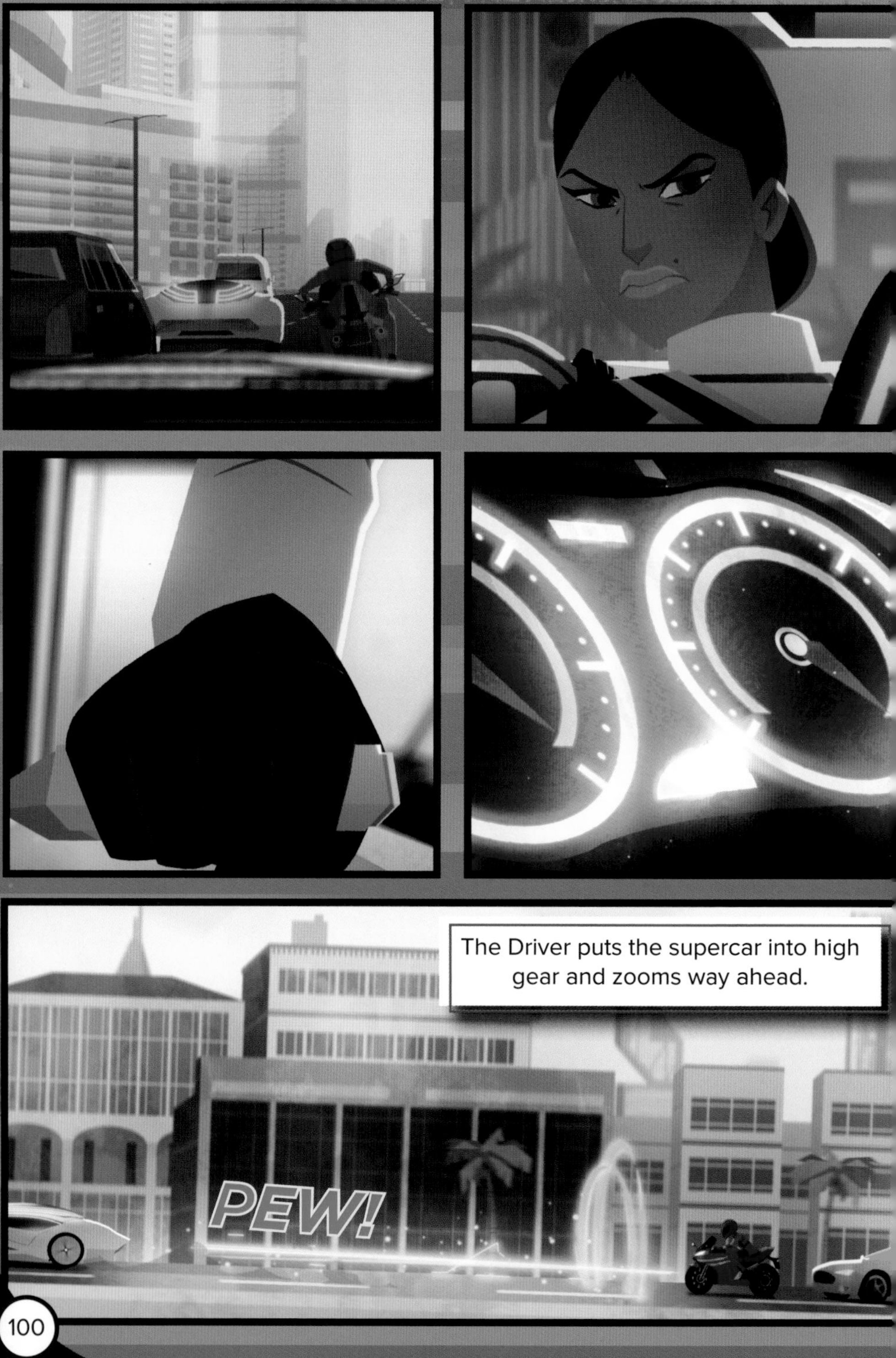
The Driver puts the supercar into high gear and zooms way ahead.
PEW!

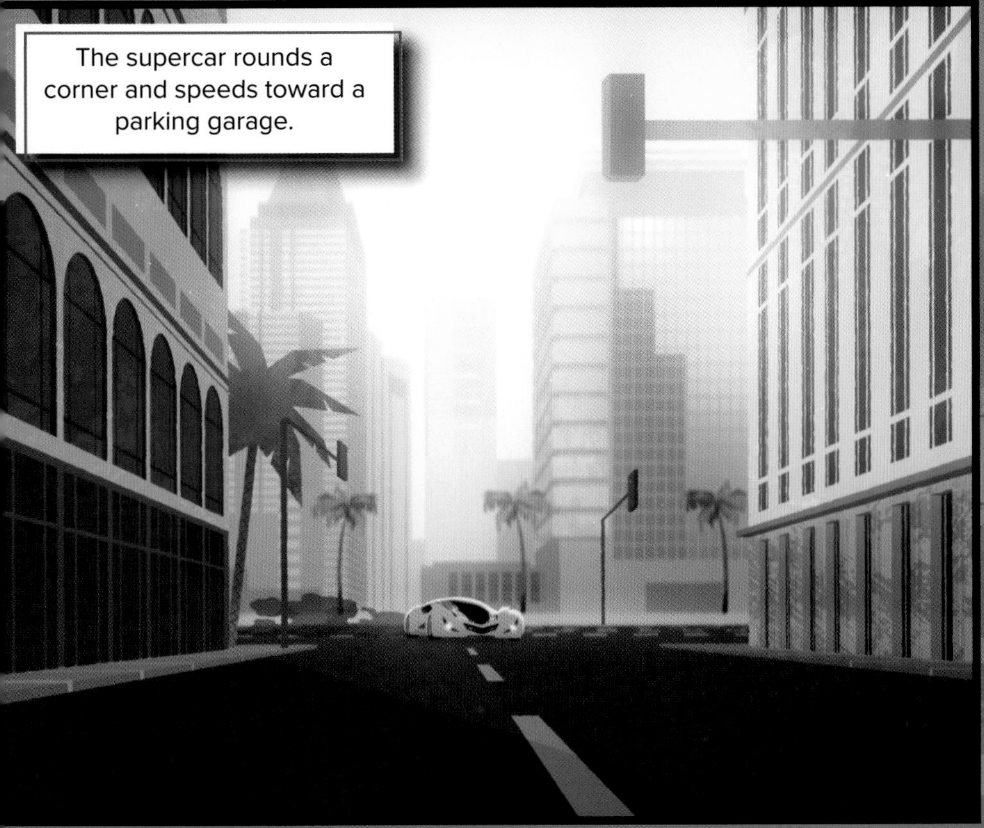
The supercar rounds a corner and speeds toward a parking garage.

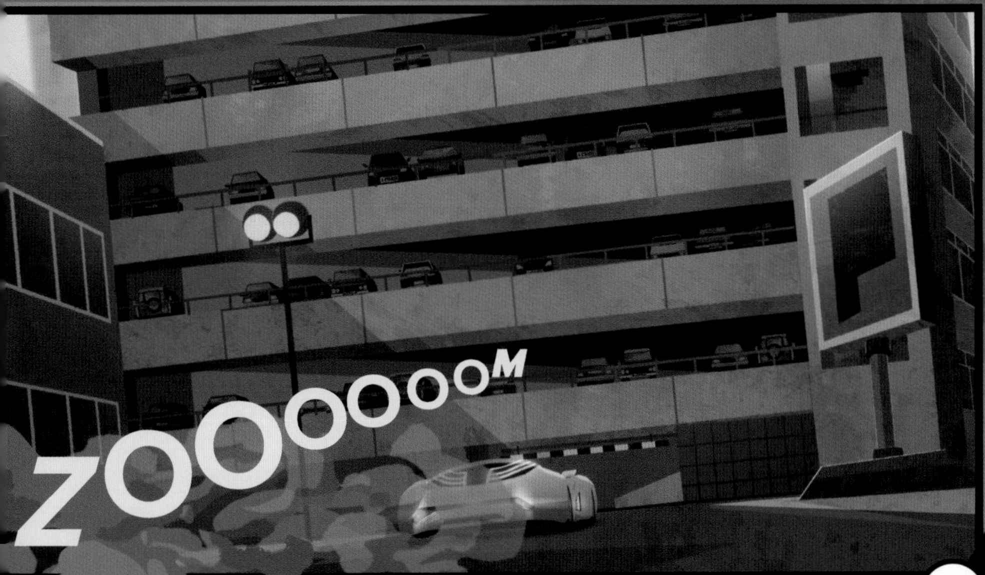
ZOOOOOOOM

Carmen, Zack, and Ivy follow, not far behind.

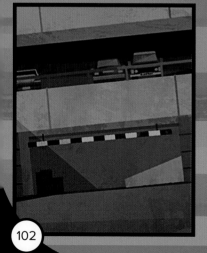

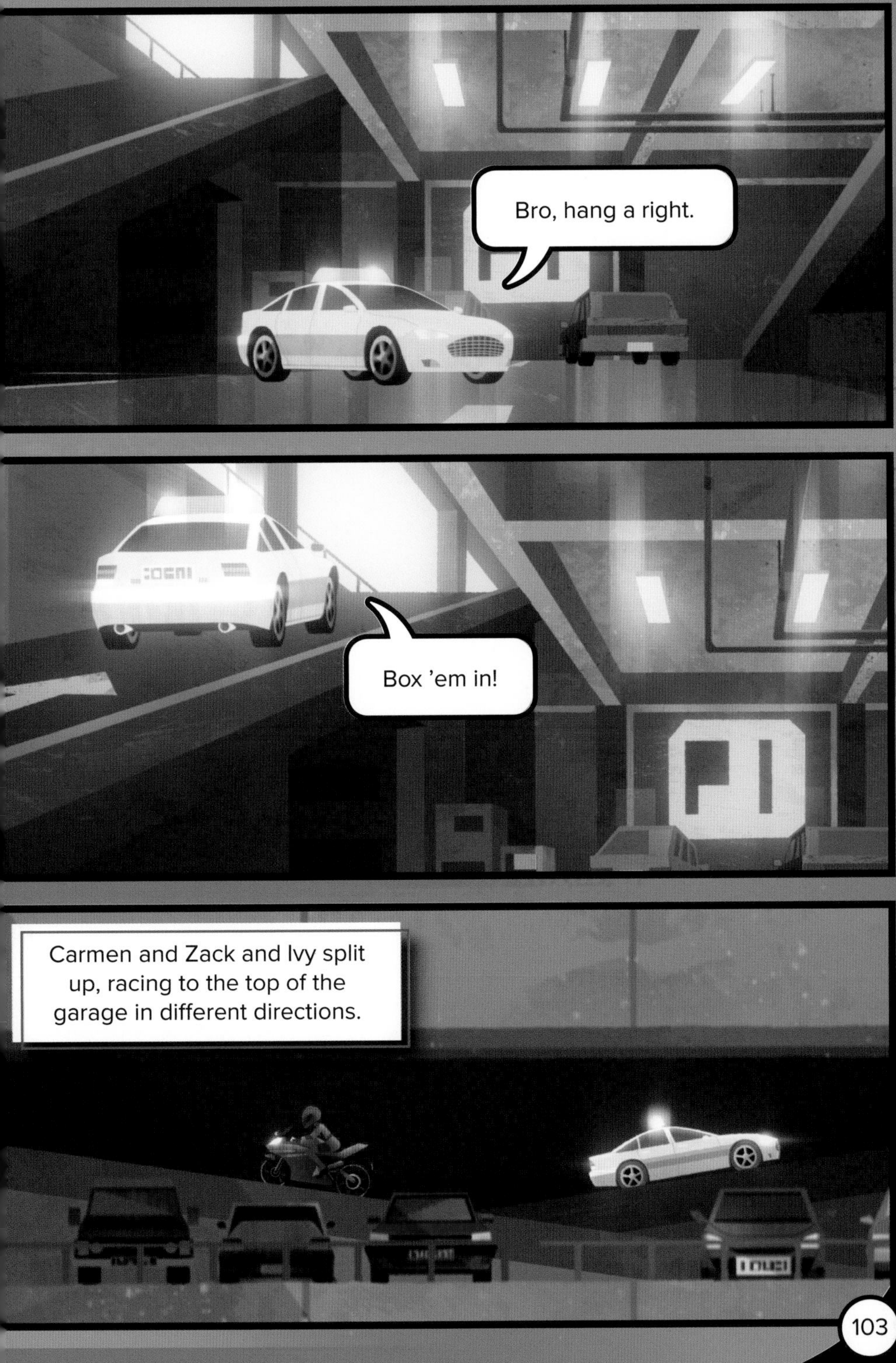
Bro, hang a right.
Box 'em in!
Carmen and Zack and Ivy split up, racing to the top of the garage in different directions.

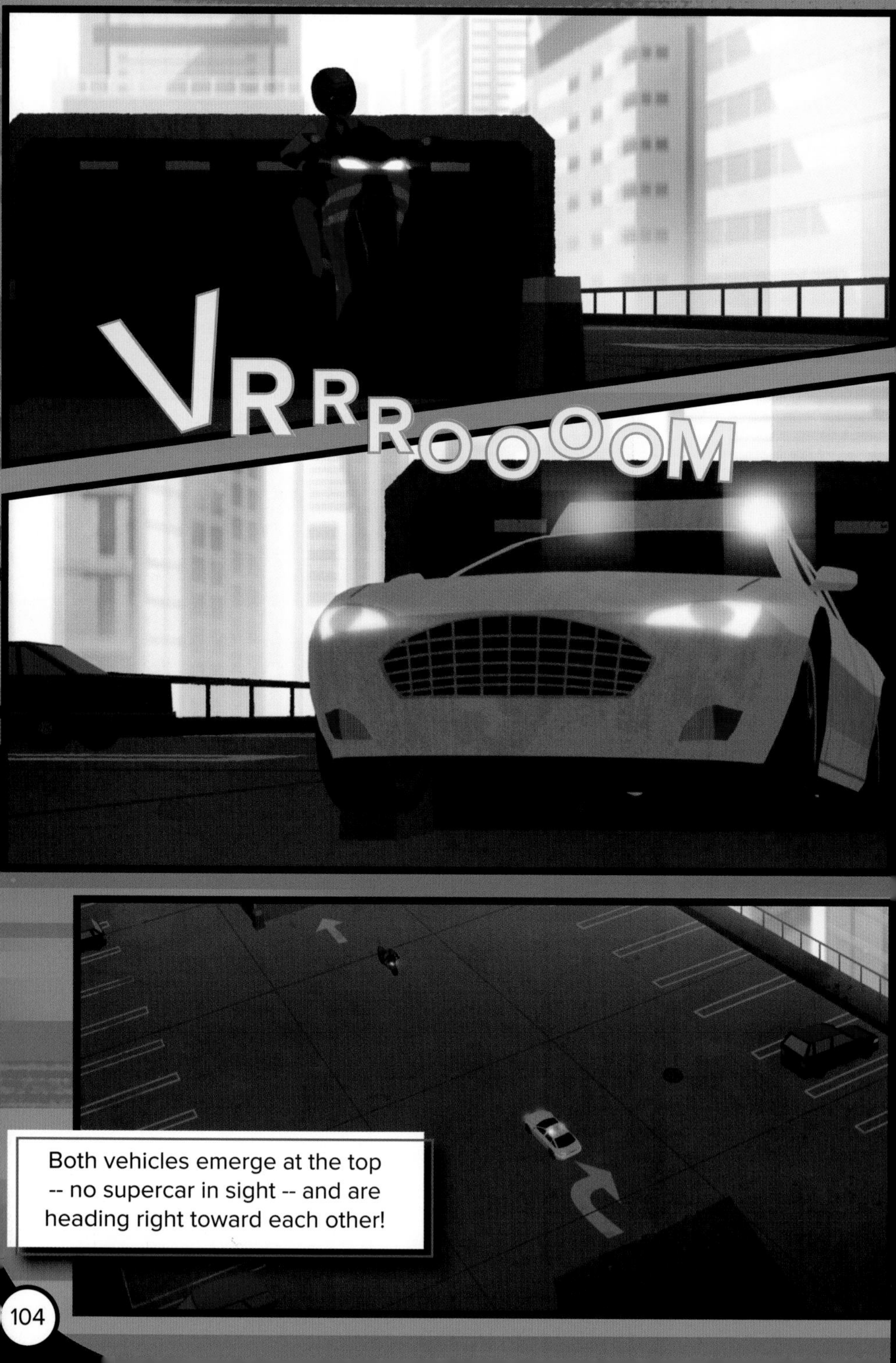
VRRROOOOM
Both vehicles emerge at the top -- no supercar in sight -- and are heading right toward each other!

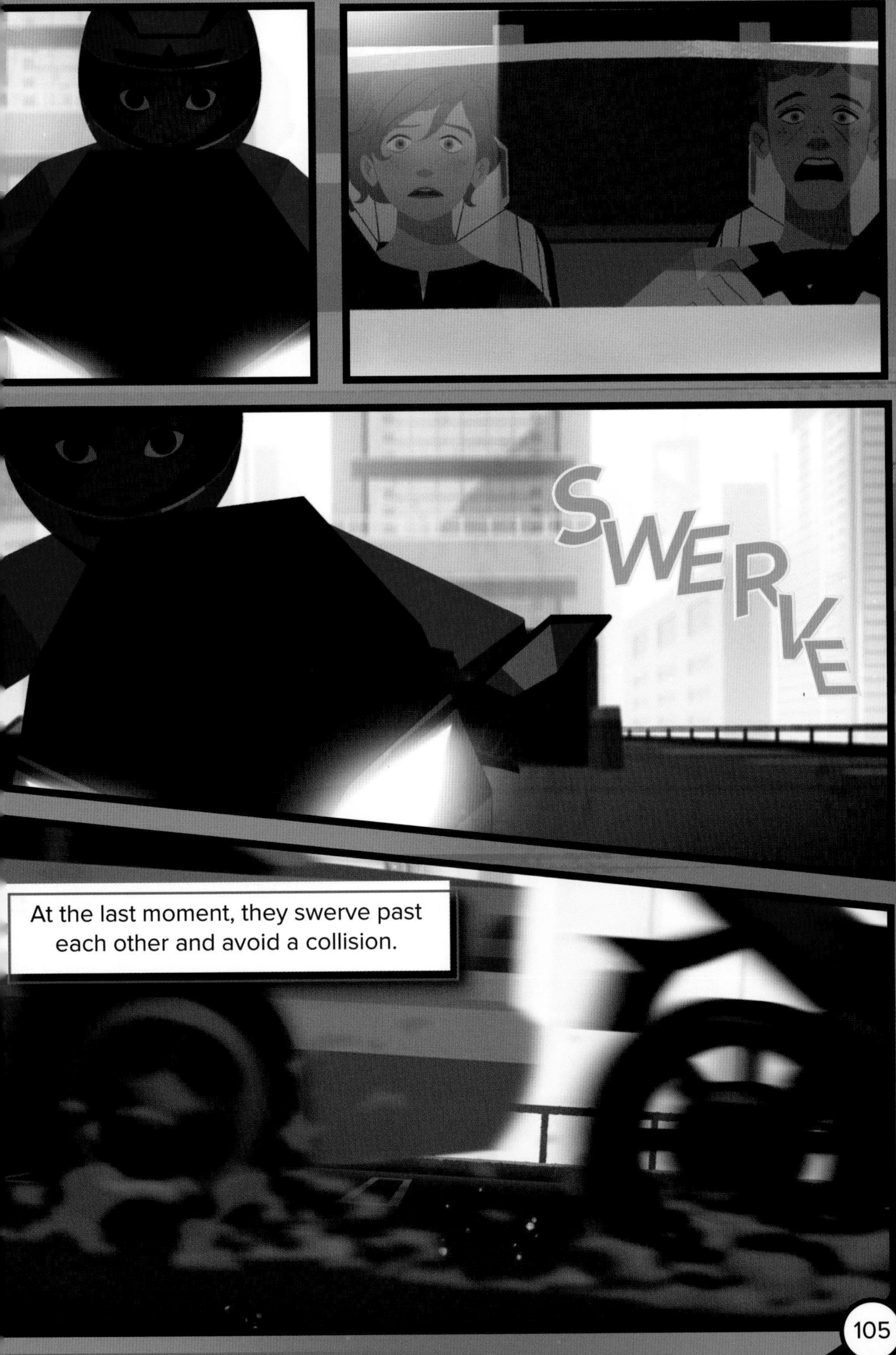
SWERVE
At the last moment, they swerve past each other and avoid a collision.

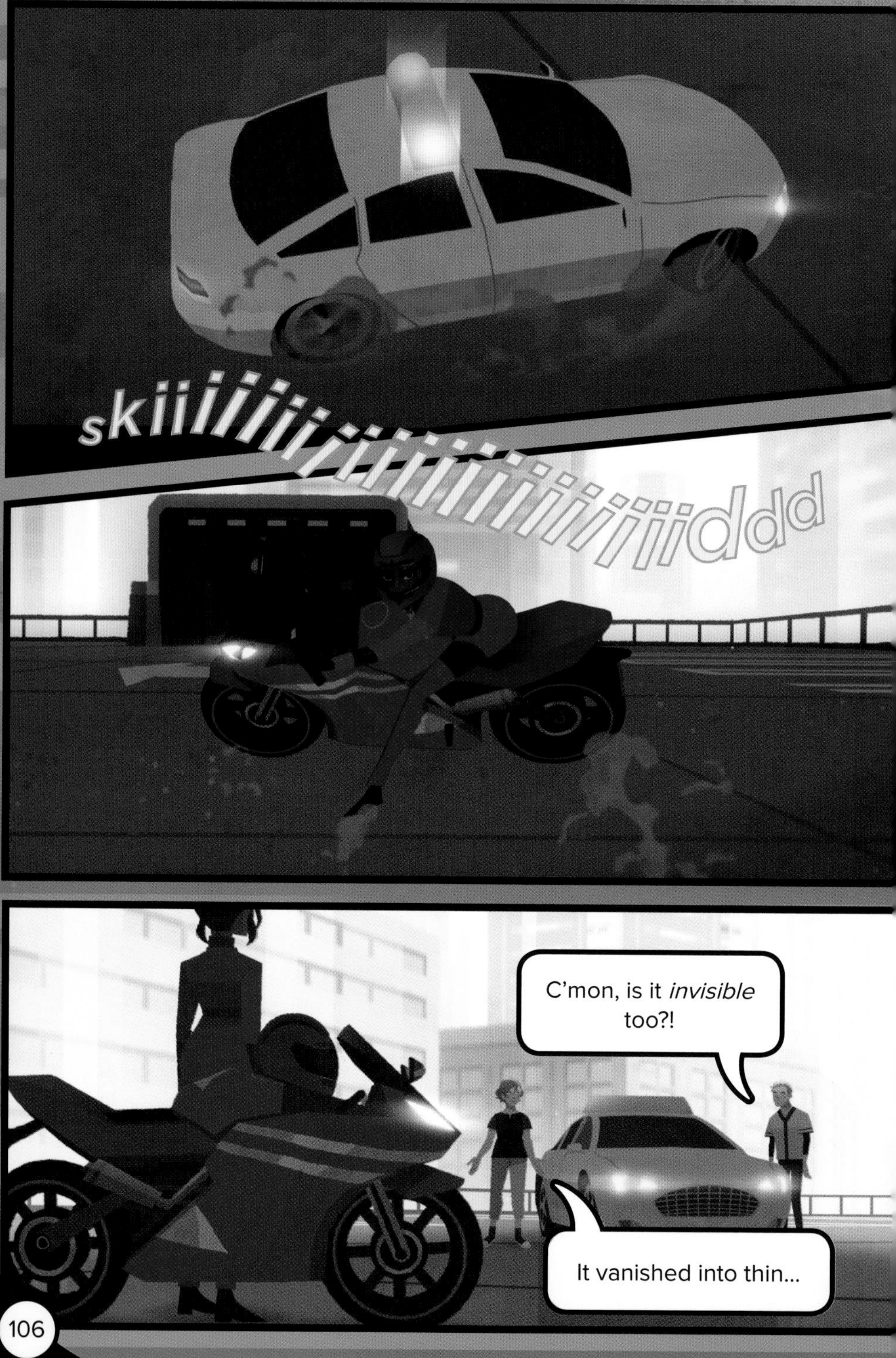
skiiiiiiiiiiiiiiiiiiiiiiddd
C'mon, is it *invisible* too?!
It vanished into thin...

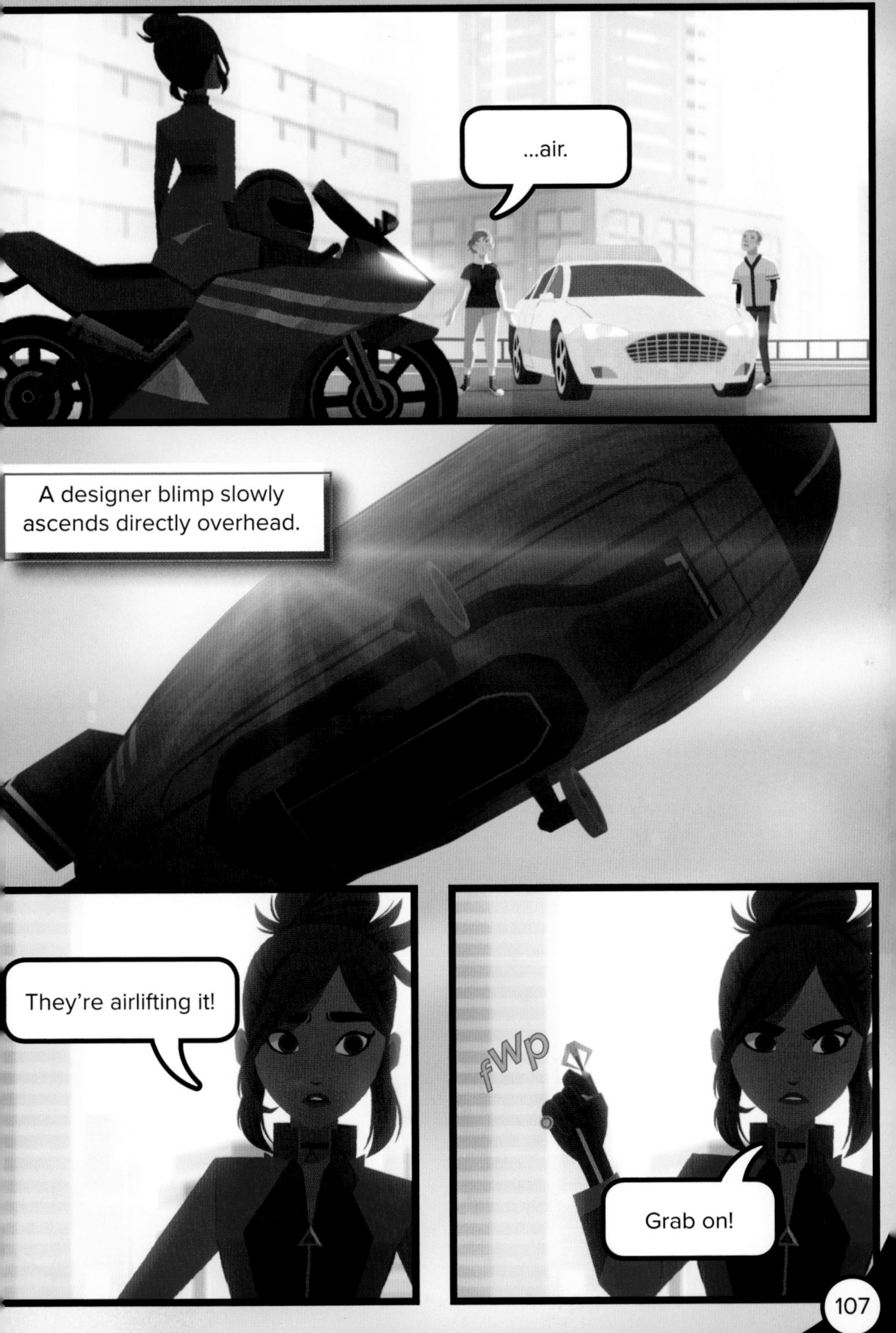

...air.
A designer blimp slowly ascends directly overhead.
They're airlifting it!
fWp
Grab on!

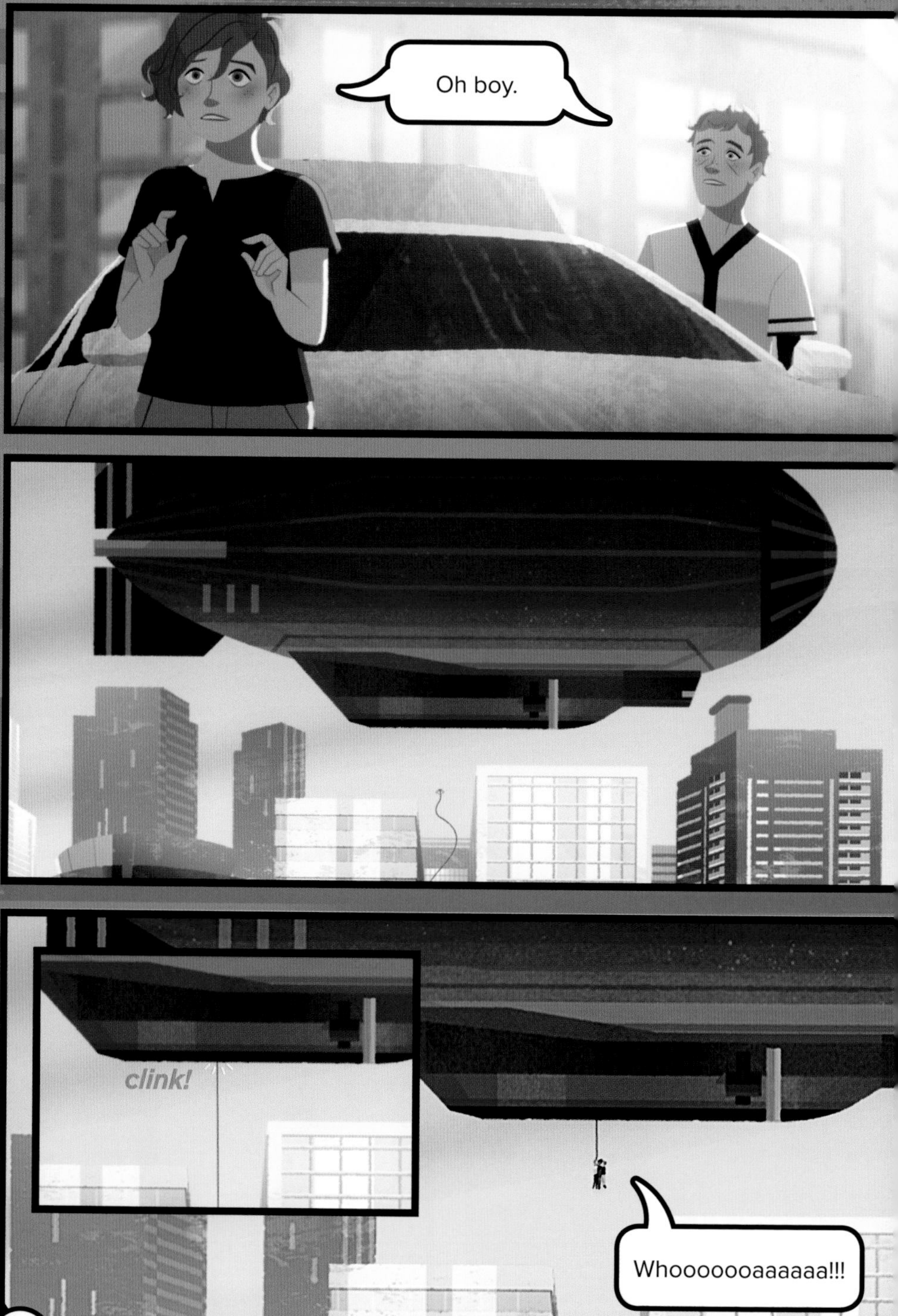
Oh boy.
clink!
Whoooooaaaaaa!!!

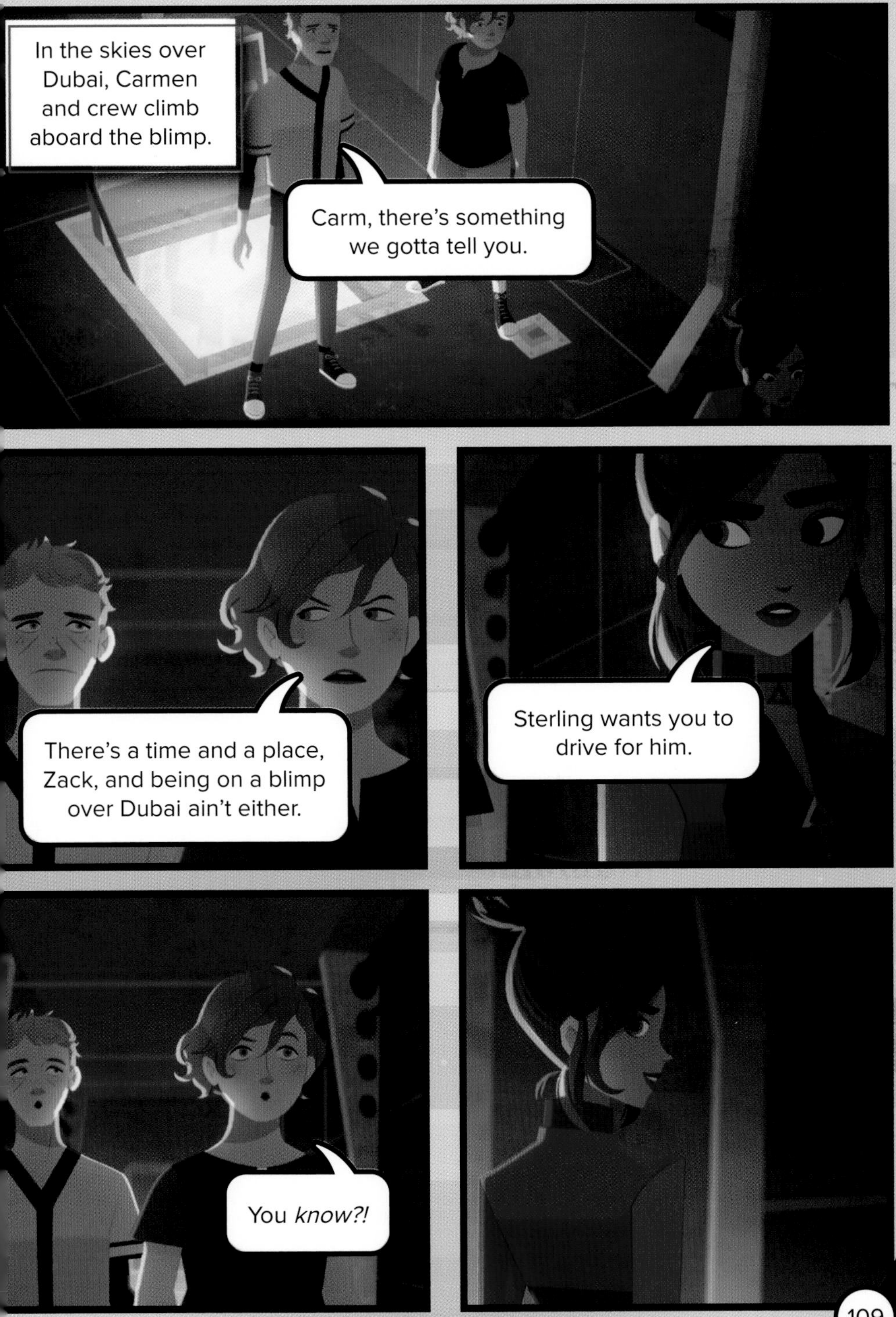
In the skies over Dubai, Carmen and crew climb aboard the blimp.
Carm, there's something we gotta tell you.
There's a time and a place, Zack, and being on a blimp over Dubai ain't either.
Sterling wants you to drive for him.
You *know?!*

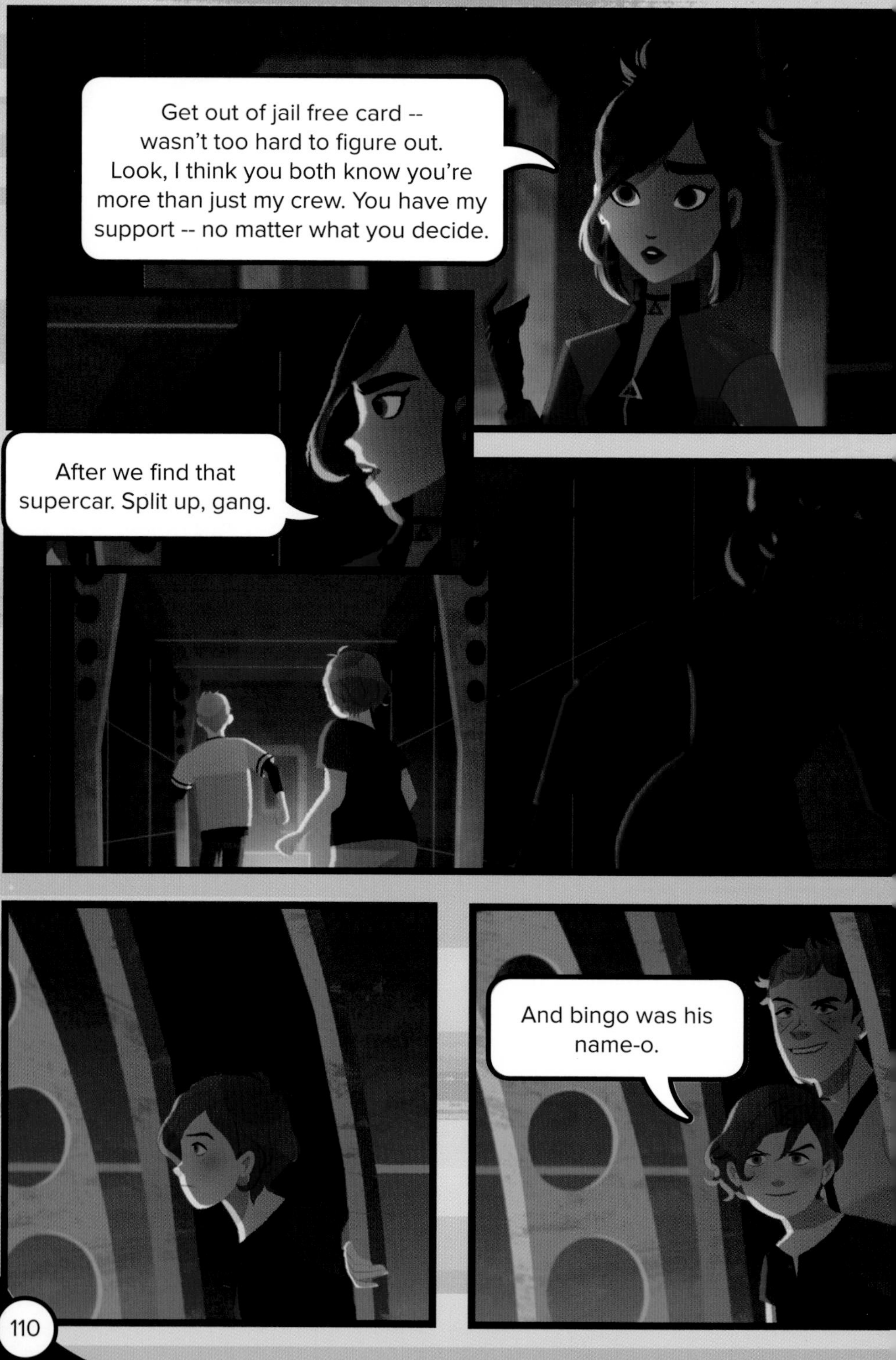
Get out of jail free card -- wasn't too hard to figure out. Look, I think you both know you're more than just my crew. You have my support -- no matter what you decide.
After we find that supercar. Split up, gang.
And bingo was his name-o.

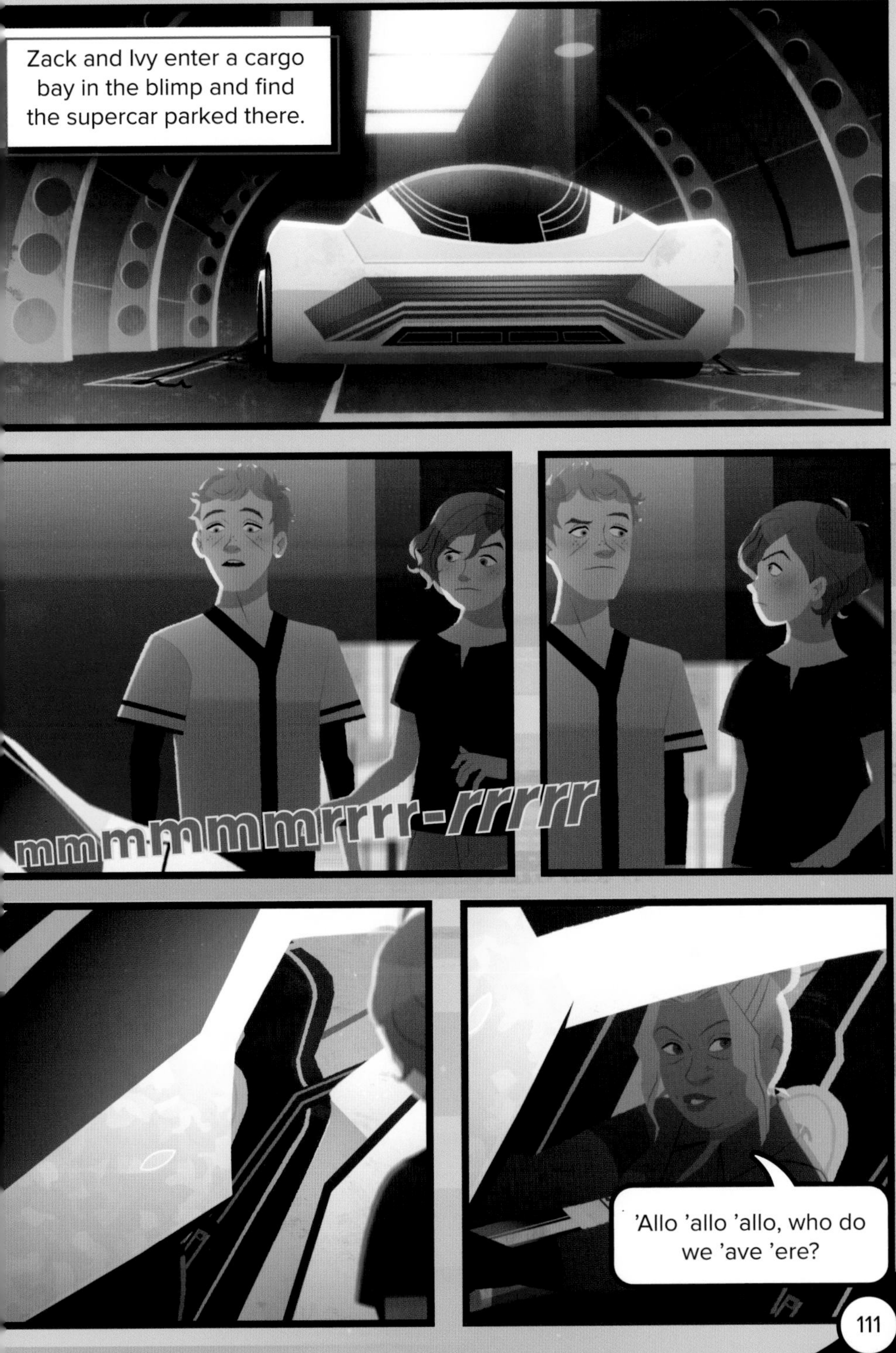
Zack and Ivy enter a cargo bay in the blimp and find the supercar parked there.
mmmmmmmmrrrr-rrrrr
'Allo 'allo 'allo, who do we 'ave 'ere?

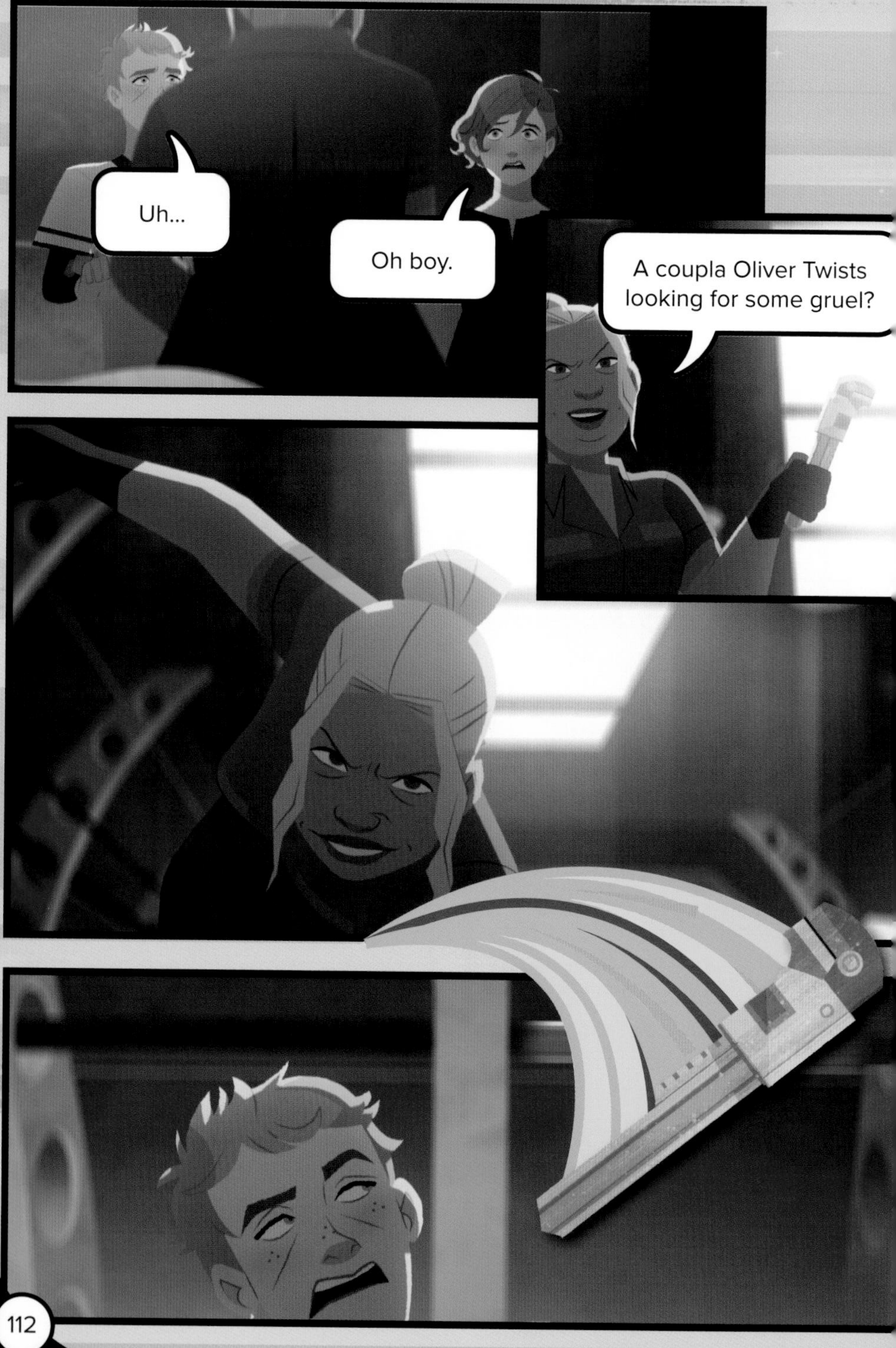
Uh...
Oh boy.
A coupla Oliver Twists looking for some gruel?

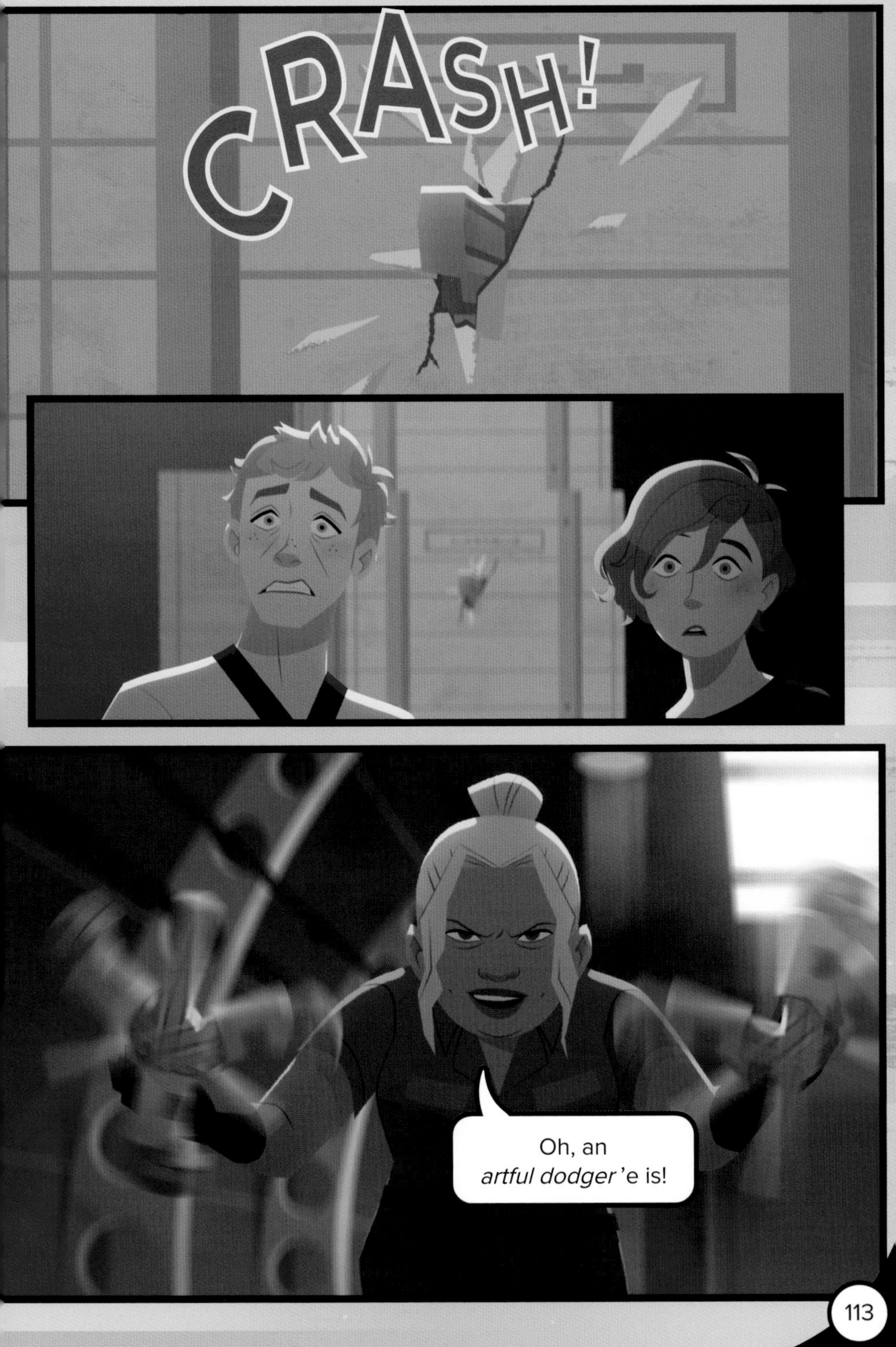
CRASH!
Oh, an *artful dodger* 'e is!

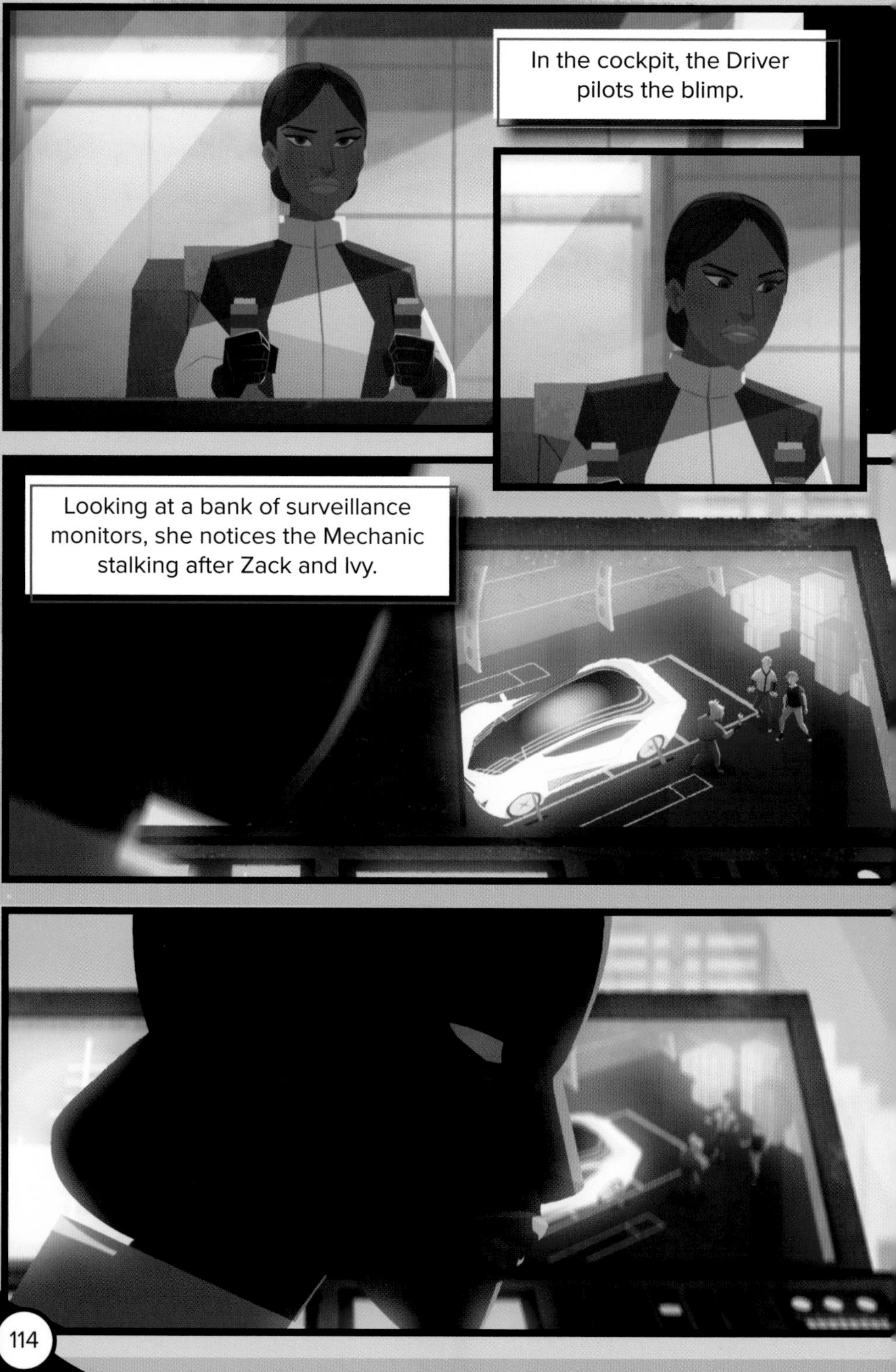
In the cockpit, the Driver pilots the blimp.
Looking at a bank of surveillance monitors, she notices the Mechanic stalking after Zack and Ivy.

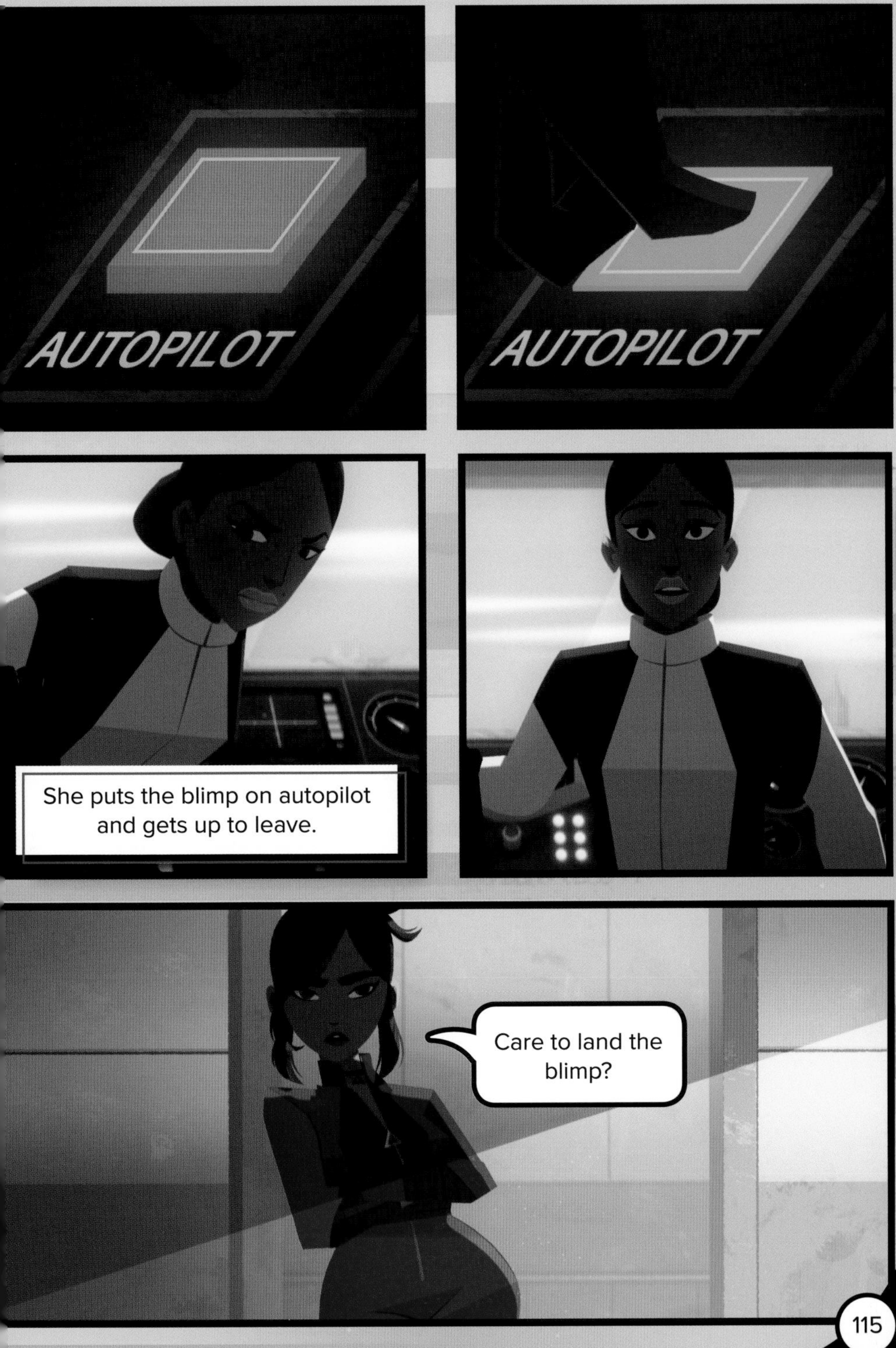
AUTOPILOT
AUTOPILOT
She puts the blimp on autopilot and gets up to leave.
Care to land the blimp?

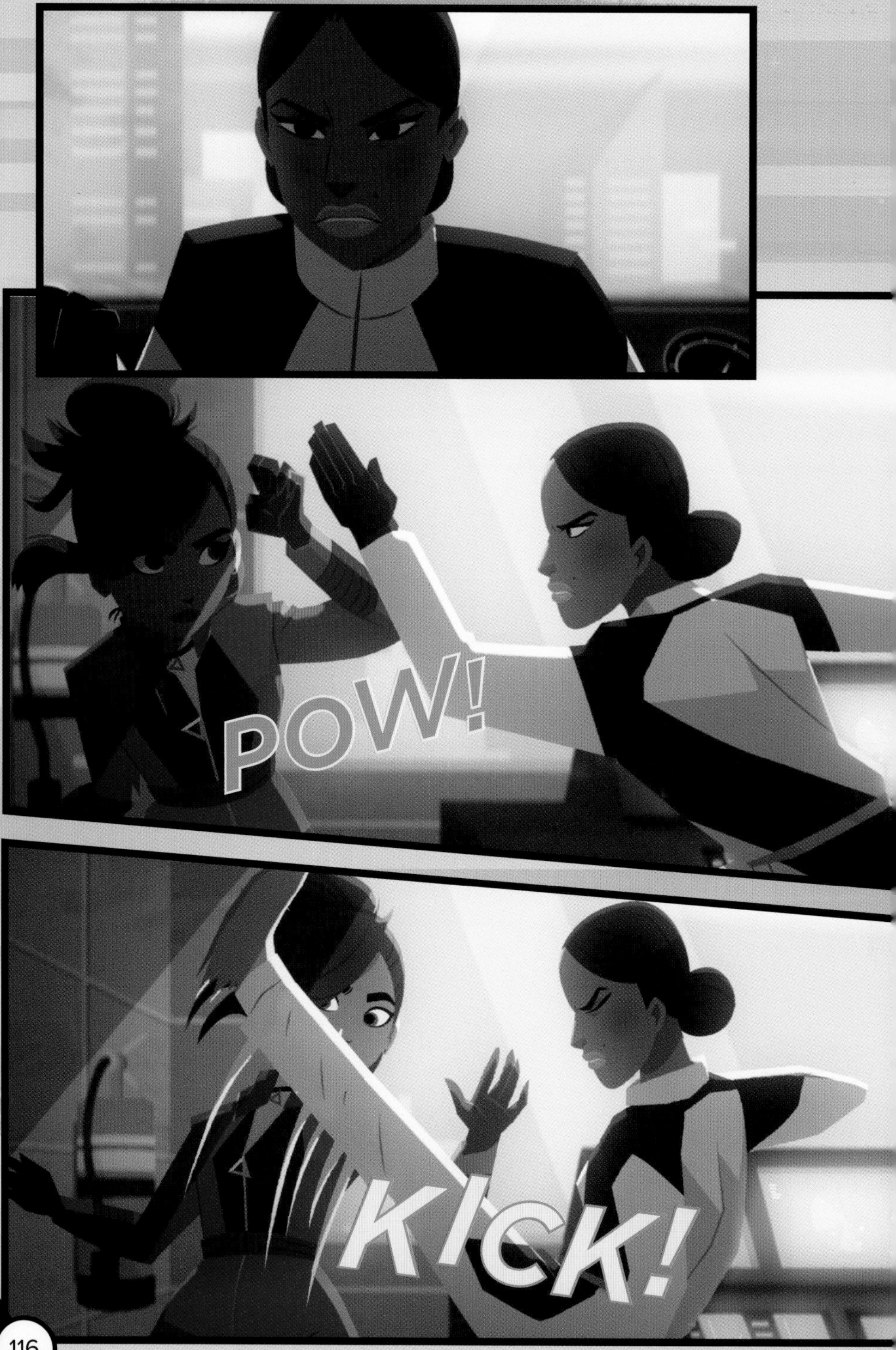
POW!
KICK!

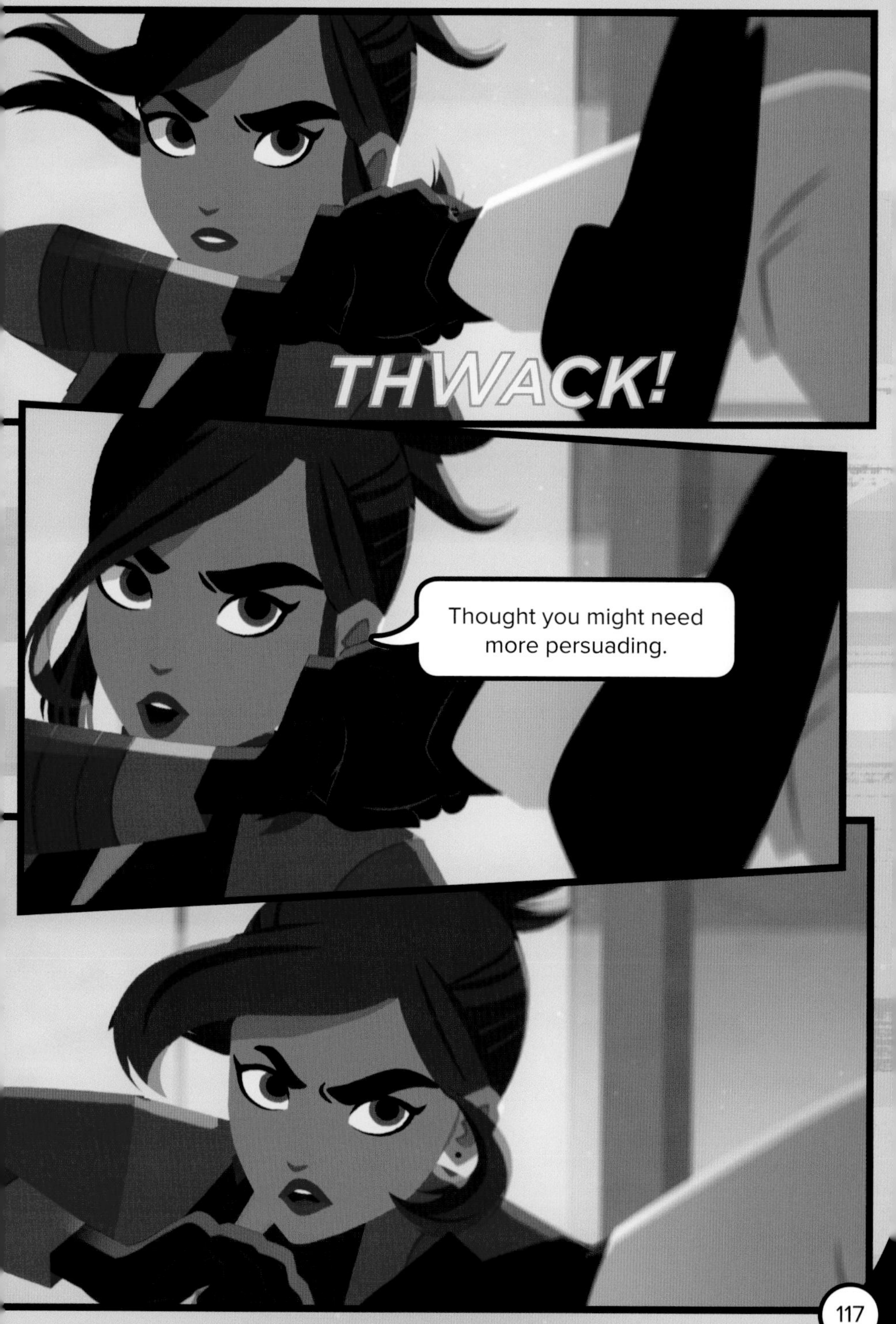
THWACK!
Thought you might need more persuading.

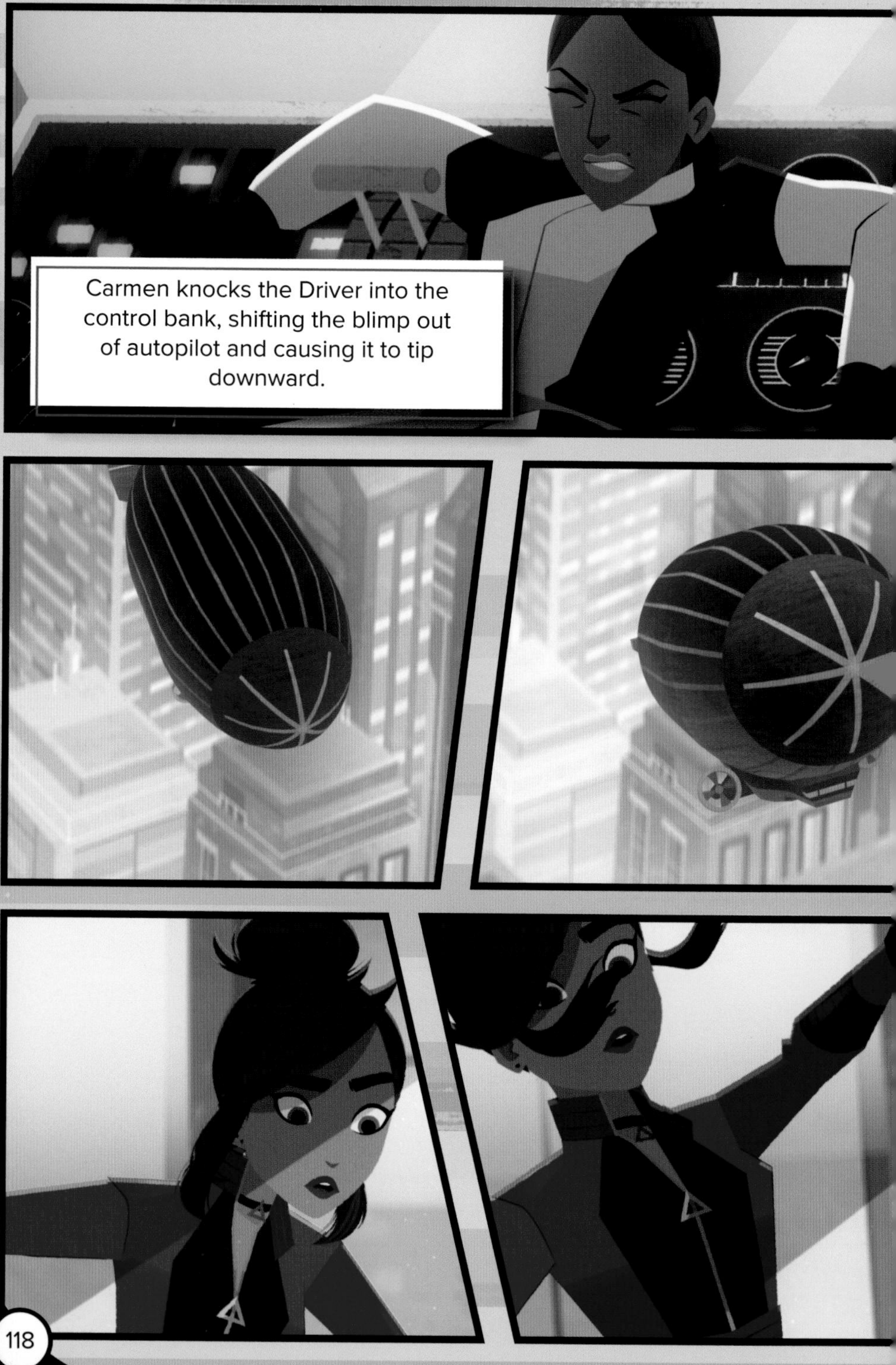
Carmen knocks the Driver into the control bank, shifting the blimp out of autopilot and causing it to tip downward.

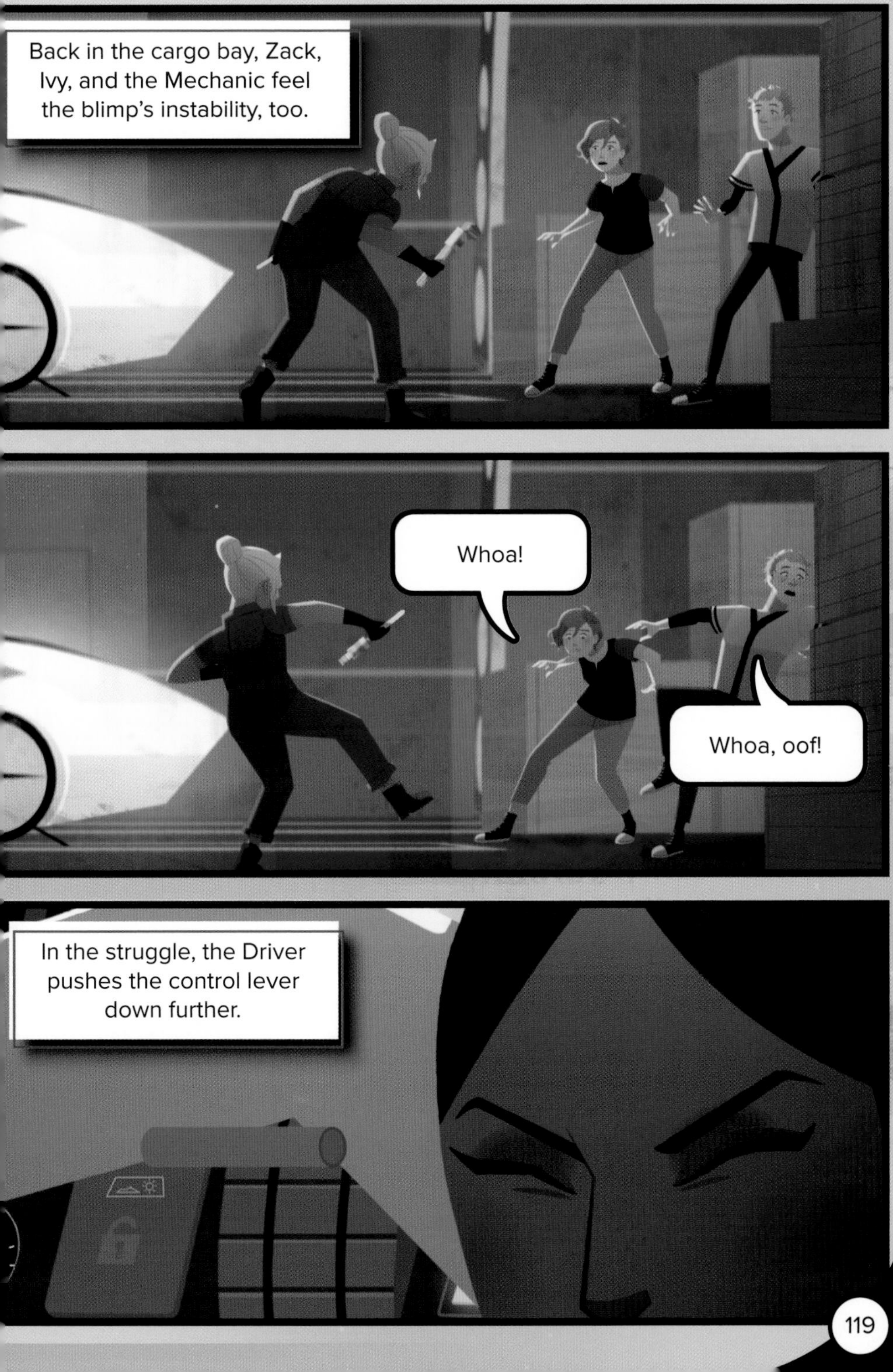
Back in the cargo bay, Zack, Ivy, and the Mechanic feel the blimp's instability, too.
Whoa!
Whoa, oof!
In the struggle, the Driver pushes the control lever down further.

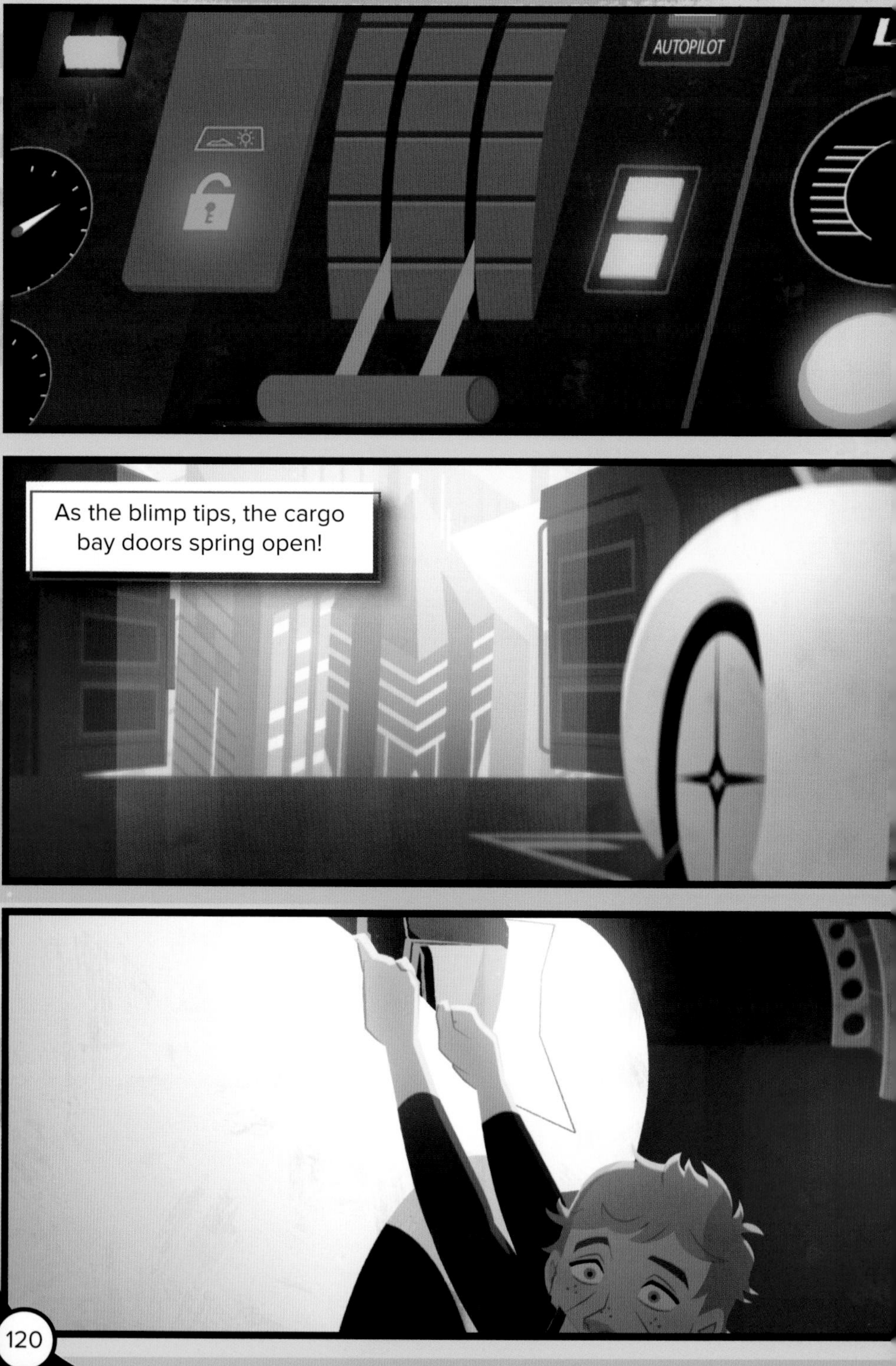
AUTOPILOT
As the blimp tips, the cargo bay doors spring open!

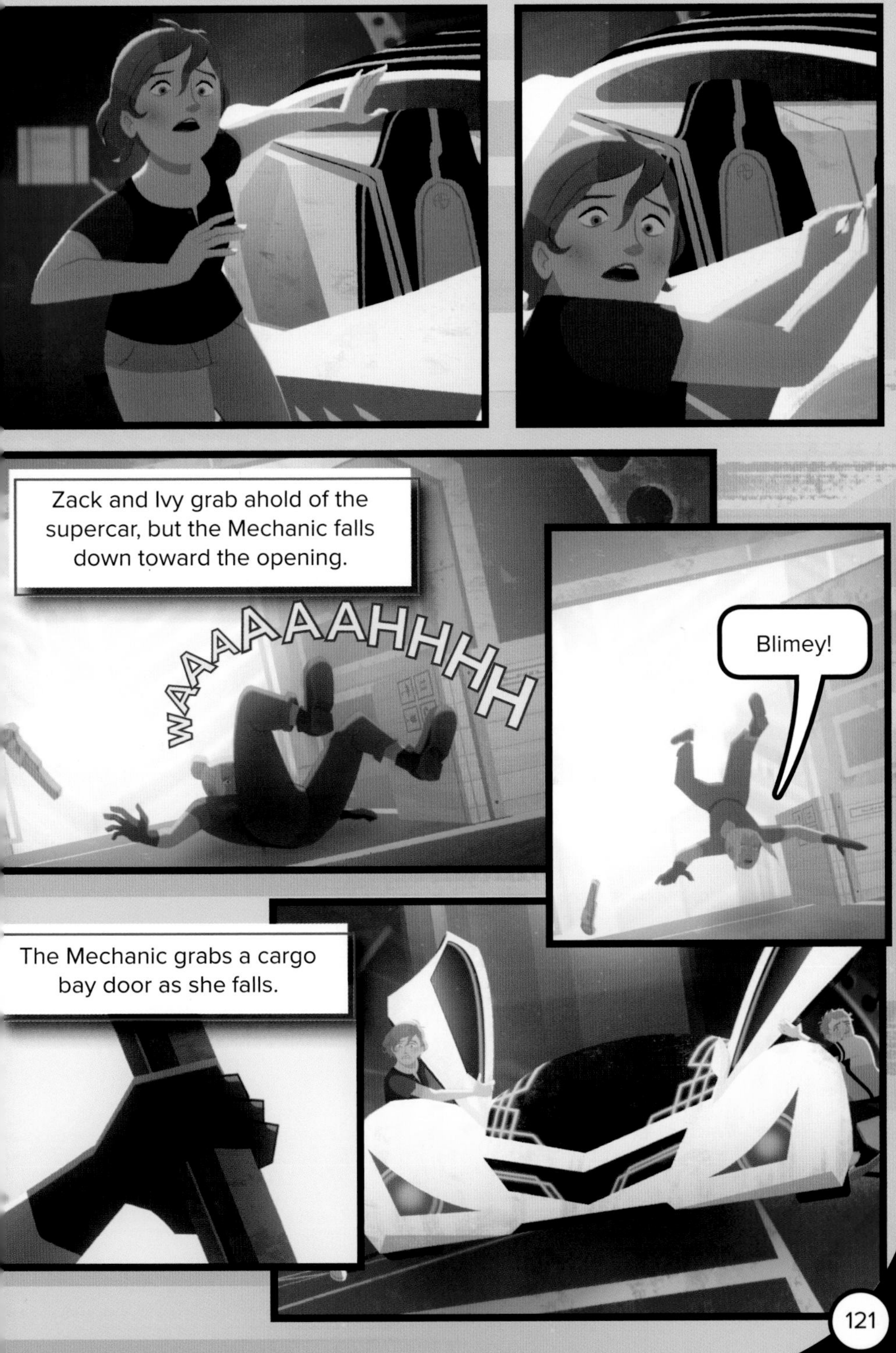
Zack and Ivy grab ahold of the supercar, but the Mechanic falls down toward the opening.
WAAAAAAHHHHH
Blimey!
The Mechanic grabs a cargo bay door as she falls.

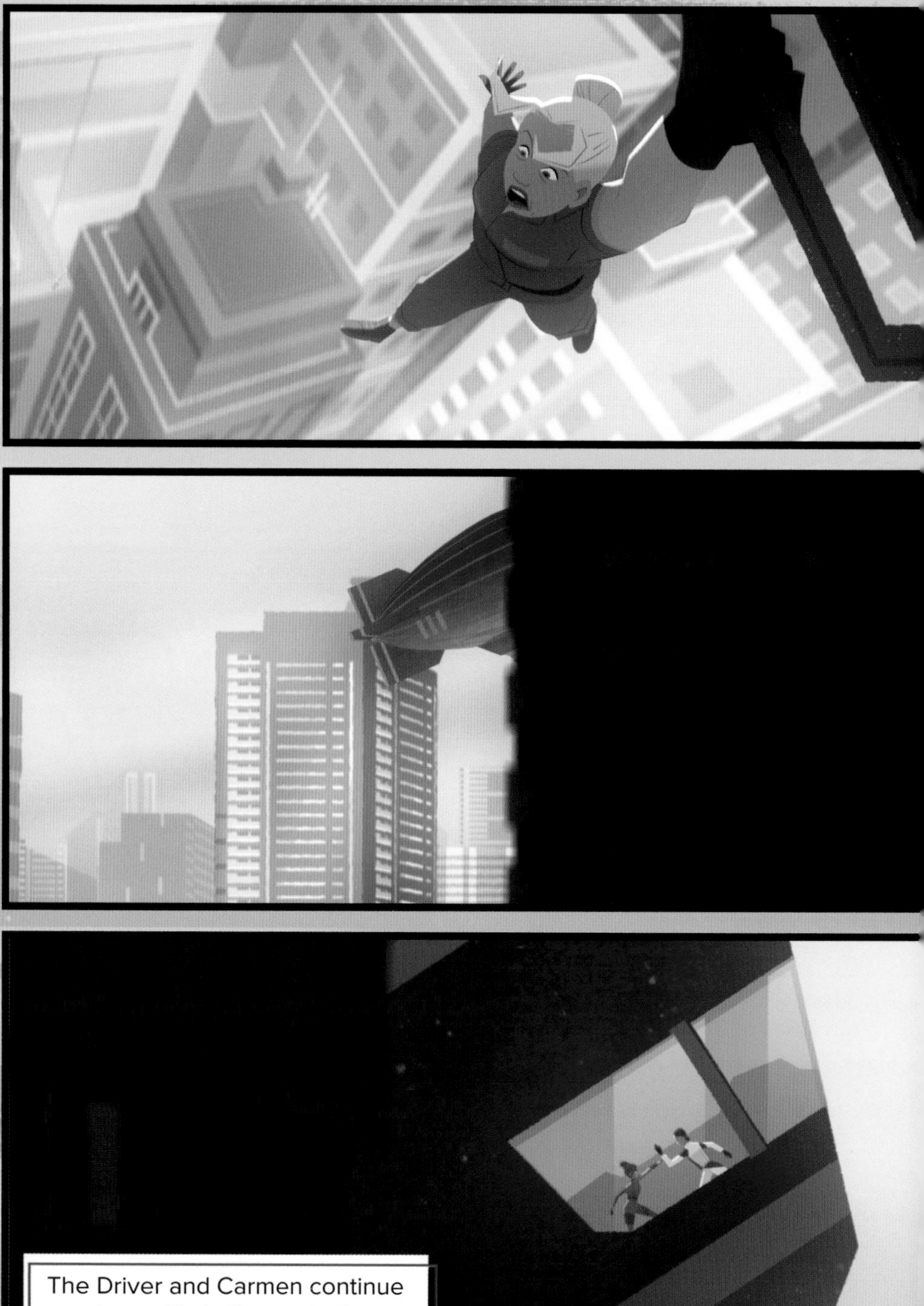
The Driver and Carmen continue to scuffle in the cockpit.

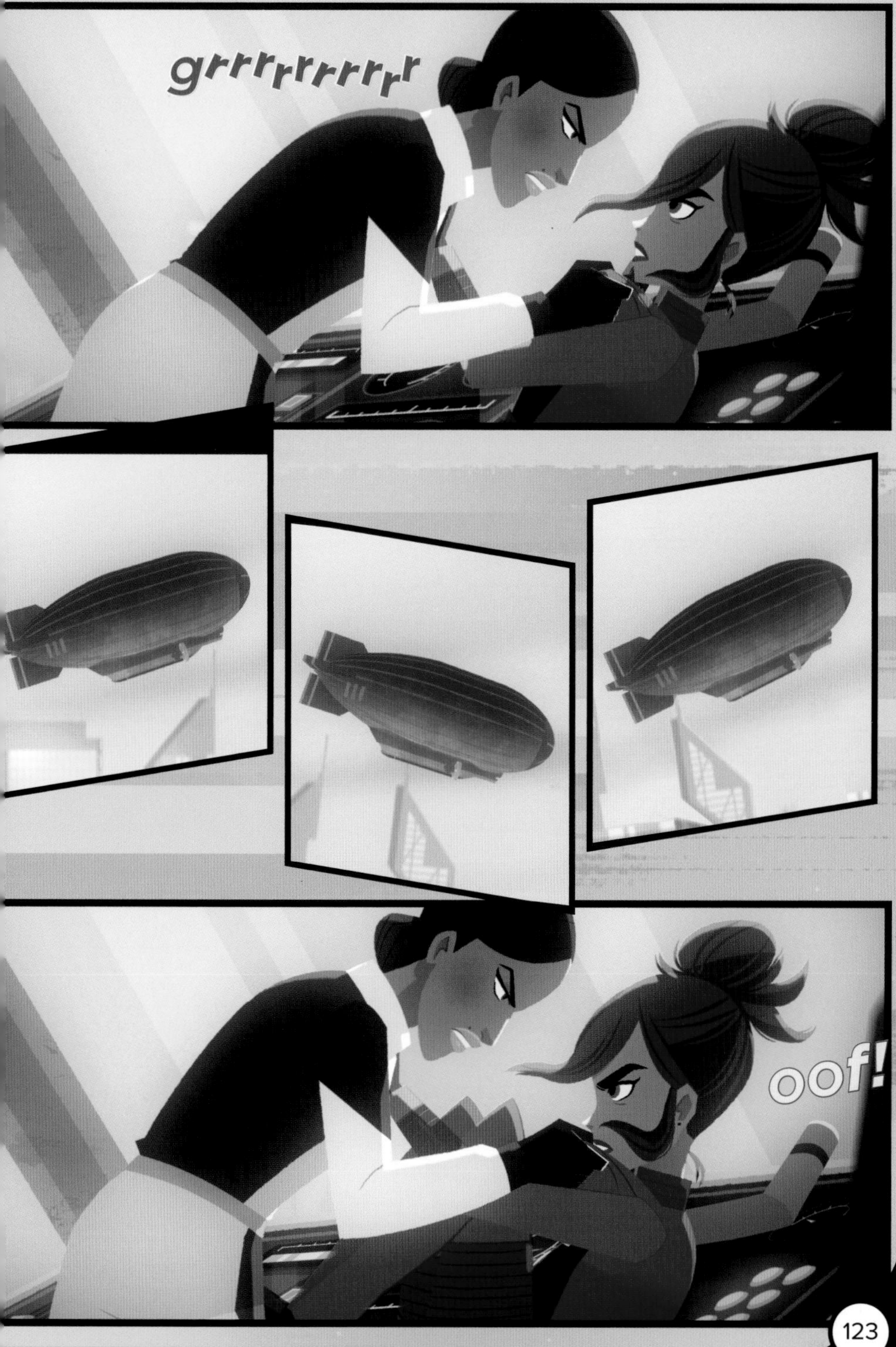
grrrrrrrrr
oof!

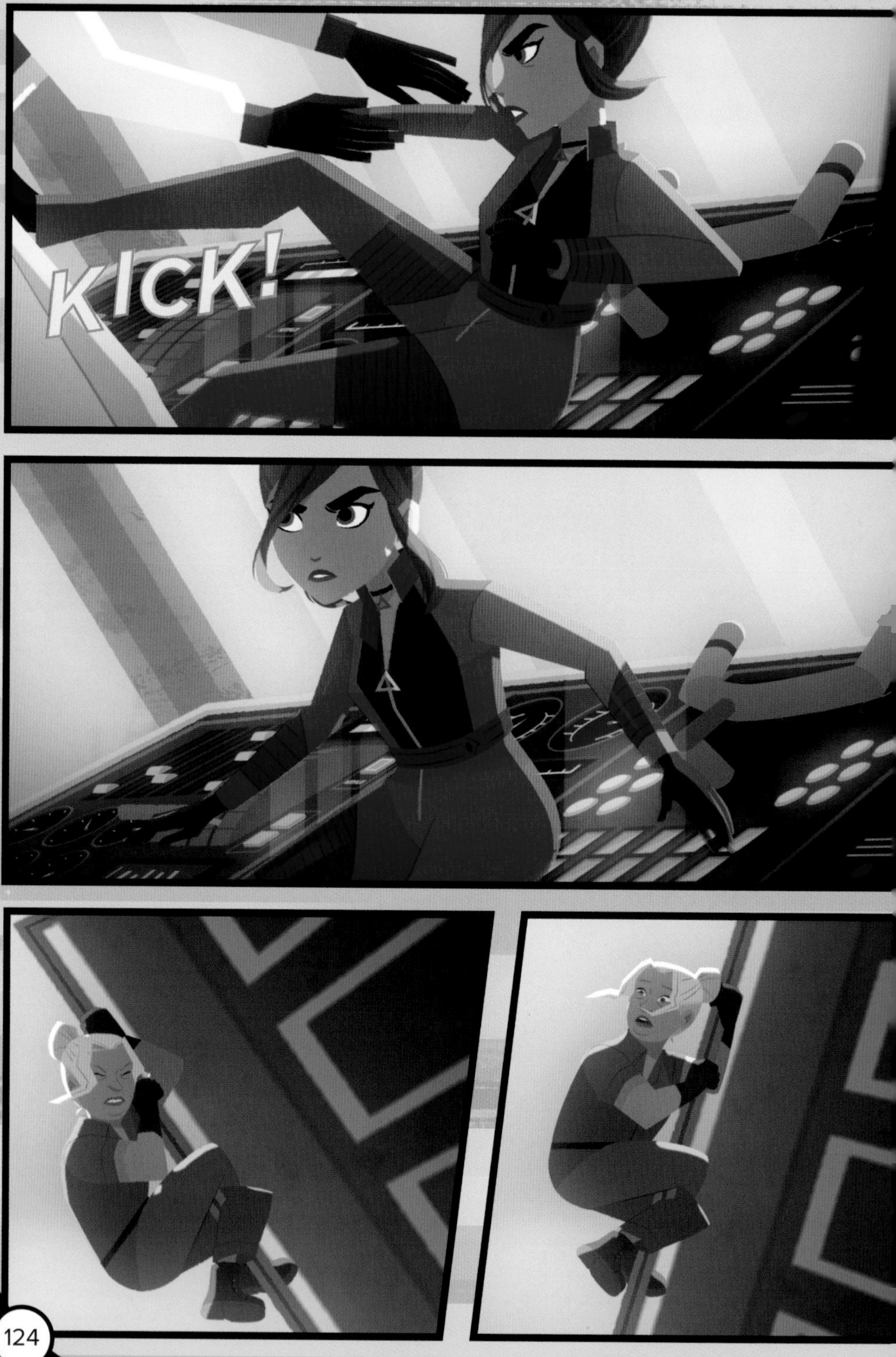
KICK!

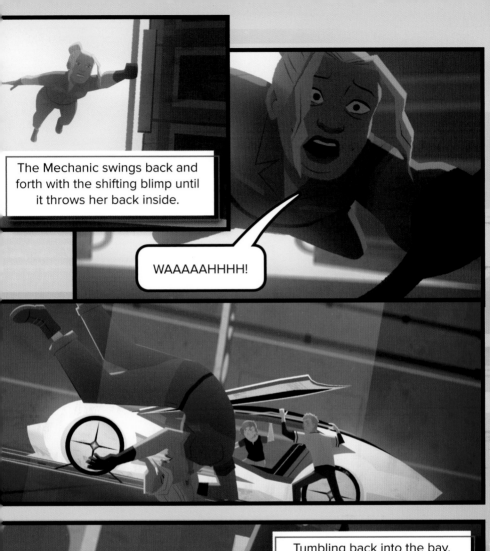

The Mechanic swings back and forth with the shifting blimp until it throws her back inside.

WAAAAAHHHH!

Tumbling back into the bay, she lands in a dazed heap.

Ugh.

The blimp approaches a flat hotel rooftop bar.

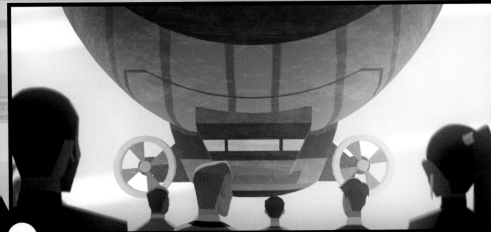

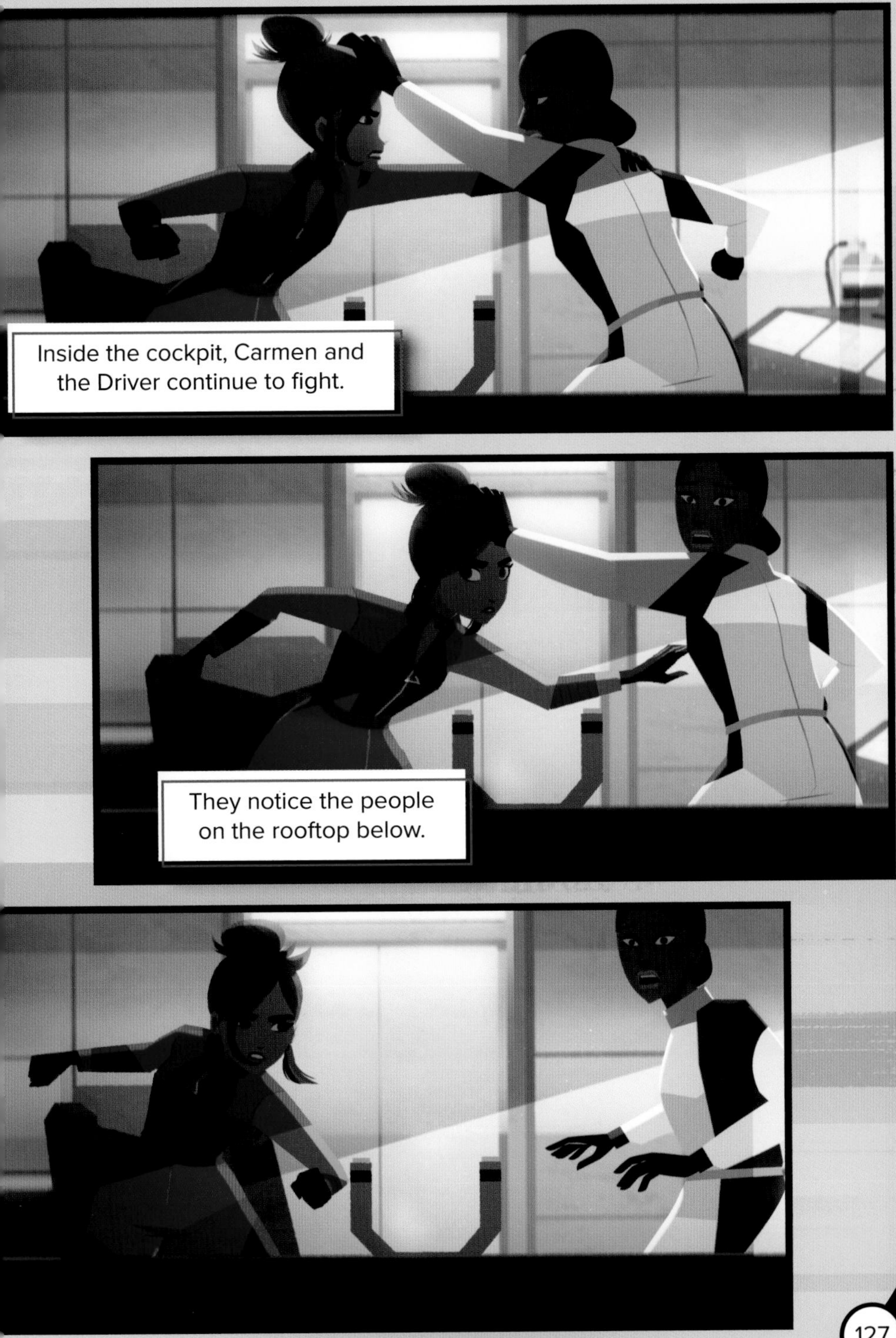
Inside the cockpit, Carmen and the Driver continue to fight.
They notice the people on the rooftop below.

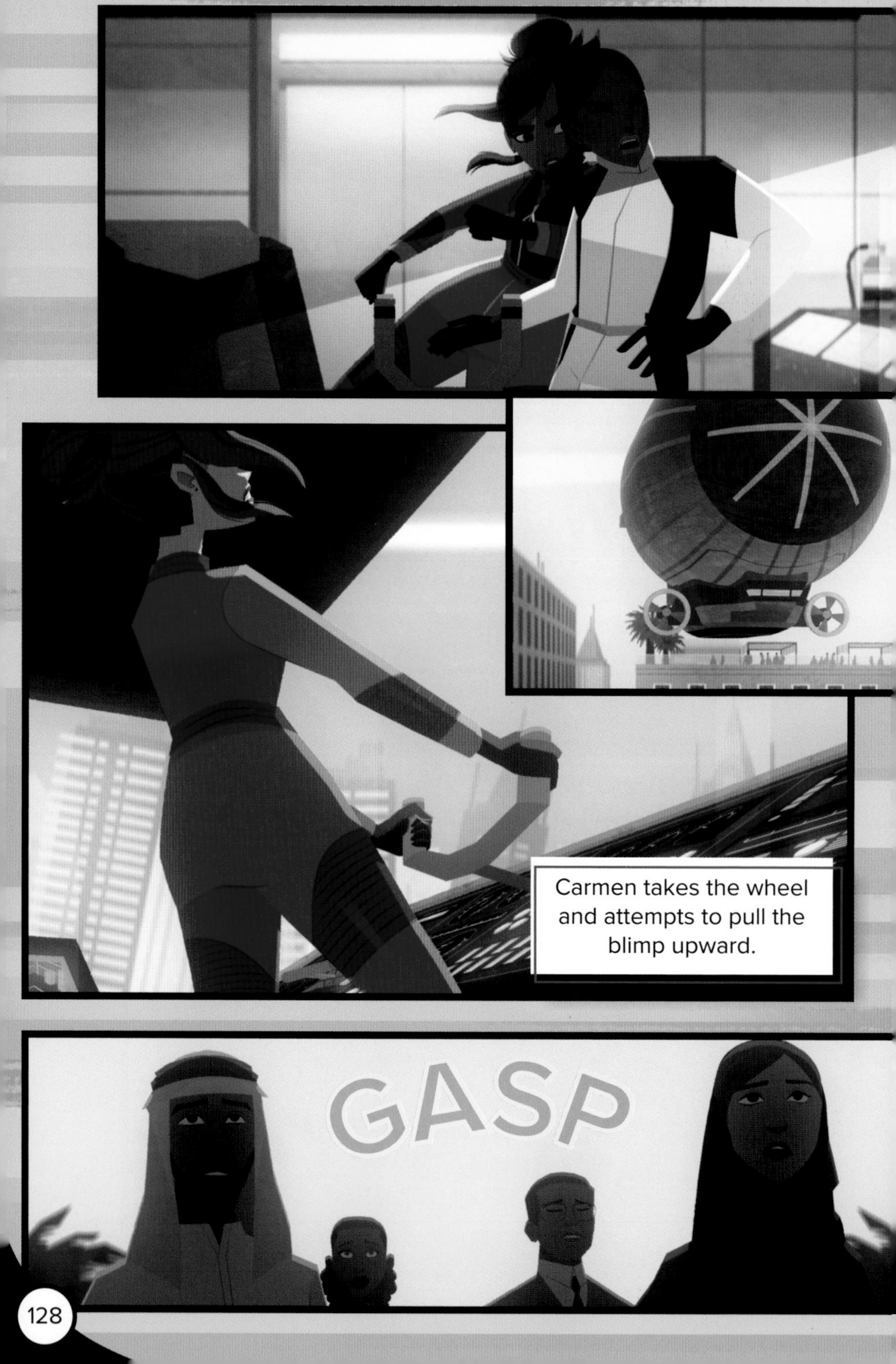
Carmen takes the wheel and attempts to pull the blimp upward.
GASP

The people on the rooftop cower as the blimp shifts back upward just in time.

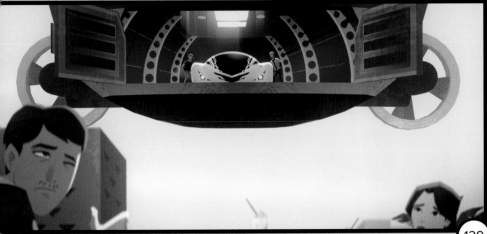

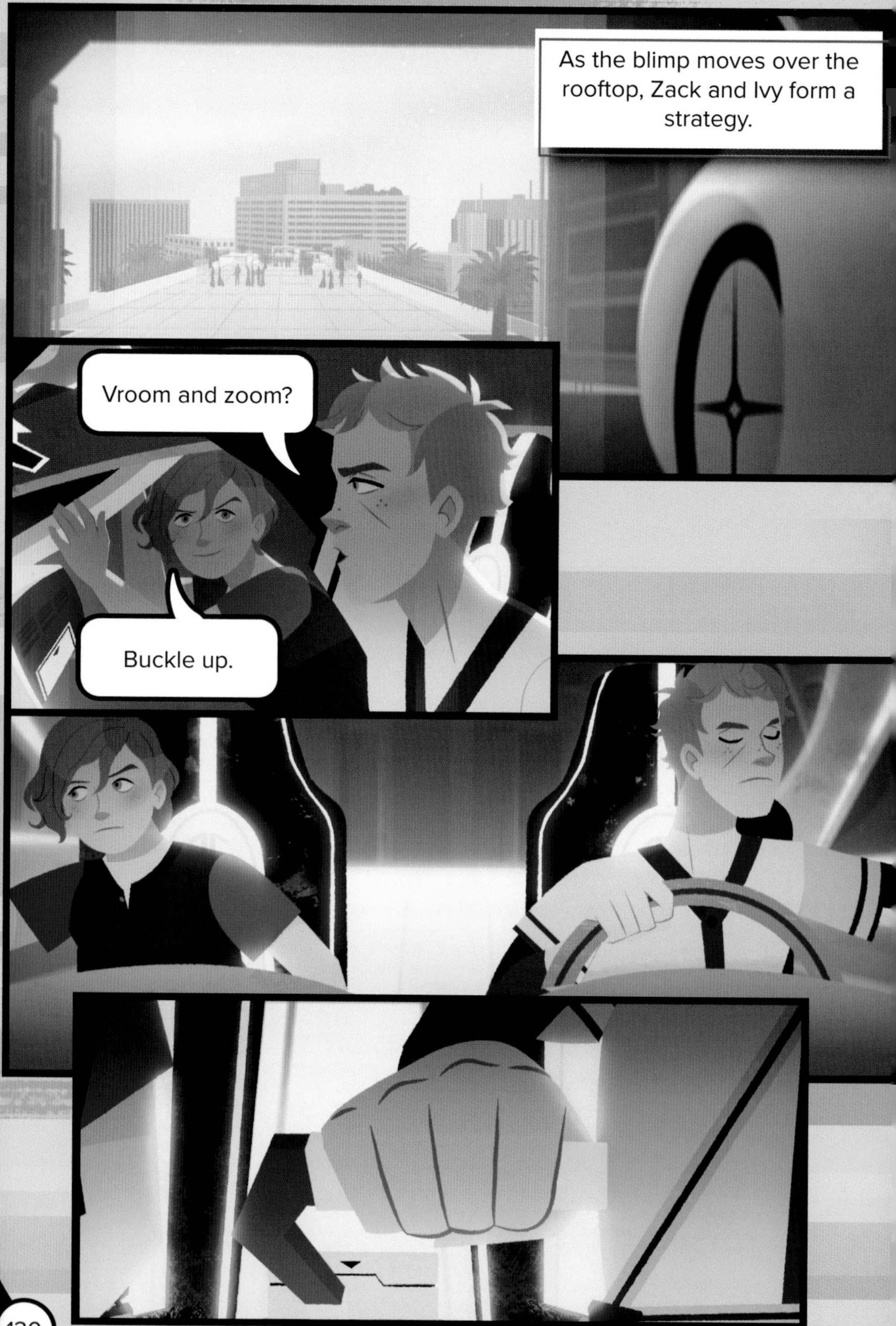

As the blimp moves over the rooftop, Zack and Ivy form a strategy.
Vroom and zoom?
Buckle up.

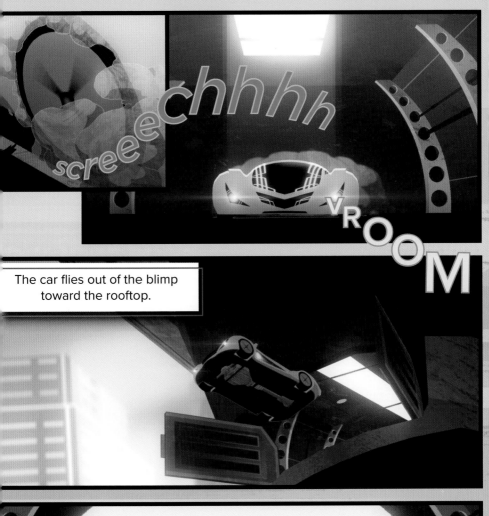

The car flies out of the blimp toward the rooftop.

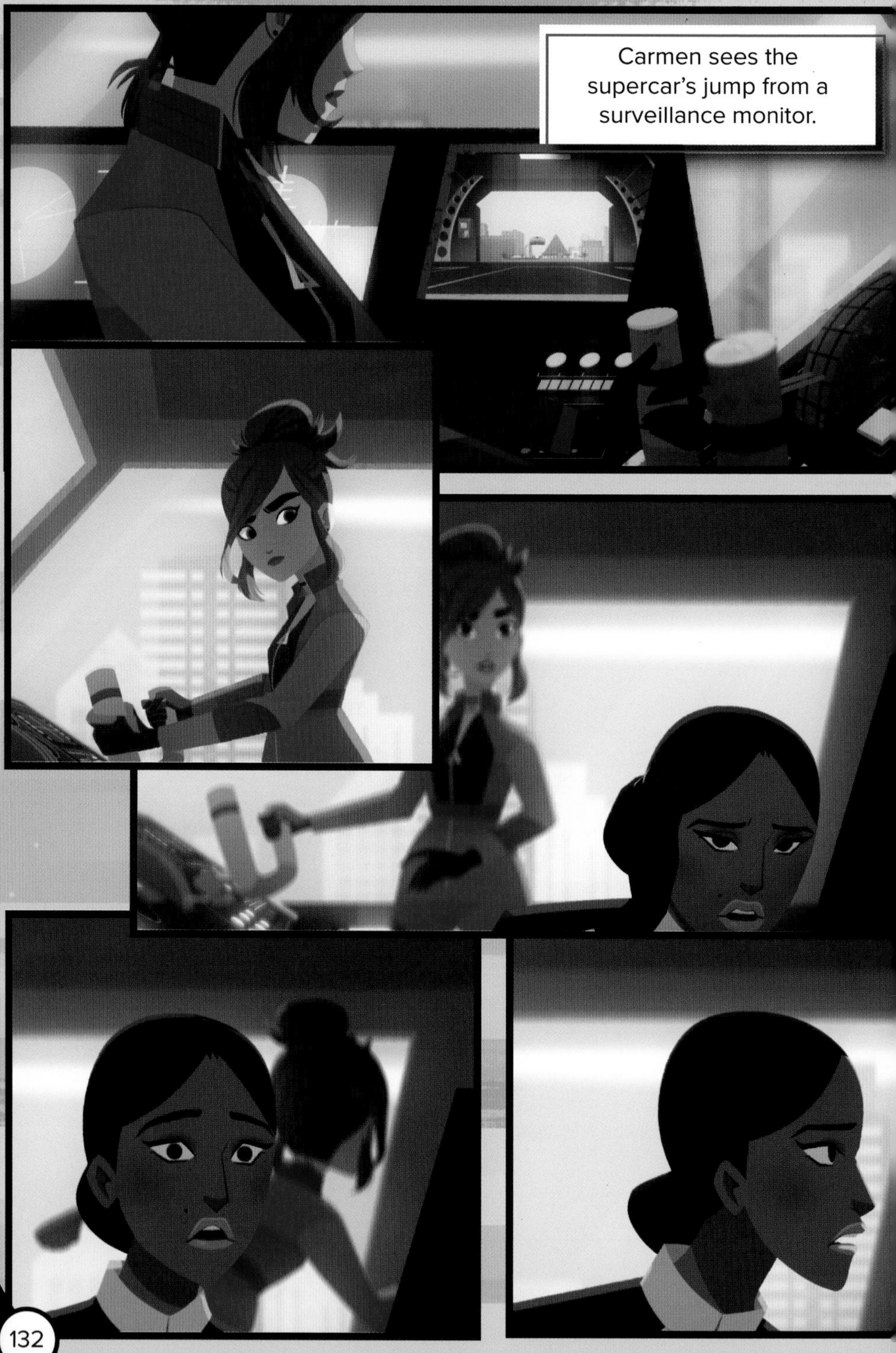
Carmen sees the supercar's jump from a surveillance monitor.

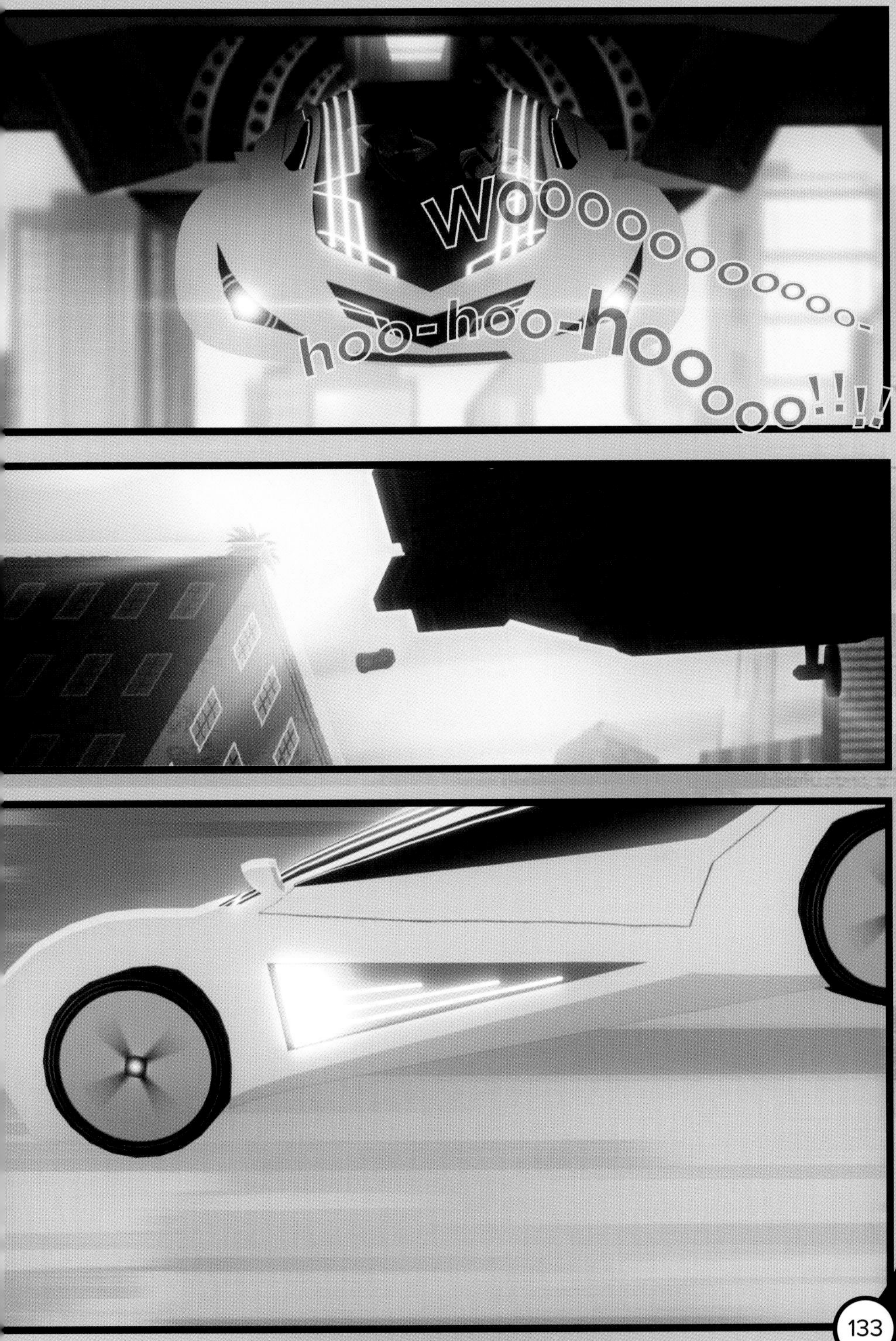
Wooooooooooooo-
hoo-hoo-hoooooo!!!!

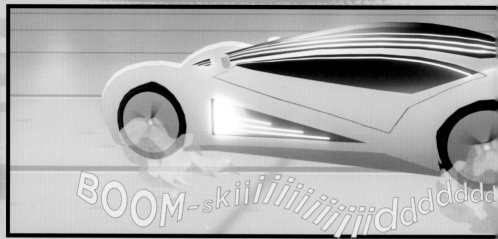

BOOM-skiiiiiiiiiiijjjjidddddd

Aaaaahhhh!!!

screeeeeeeech

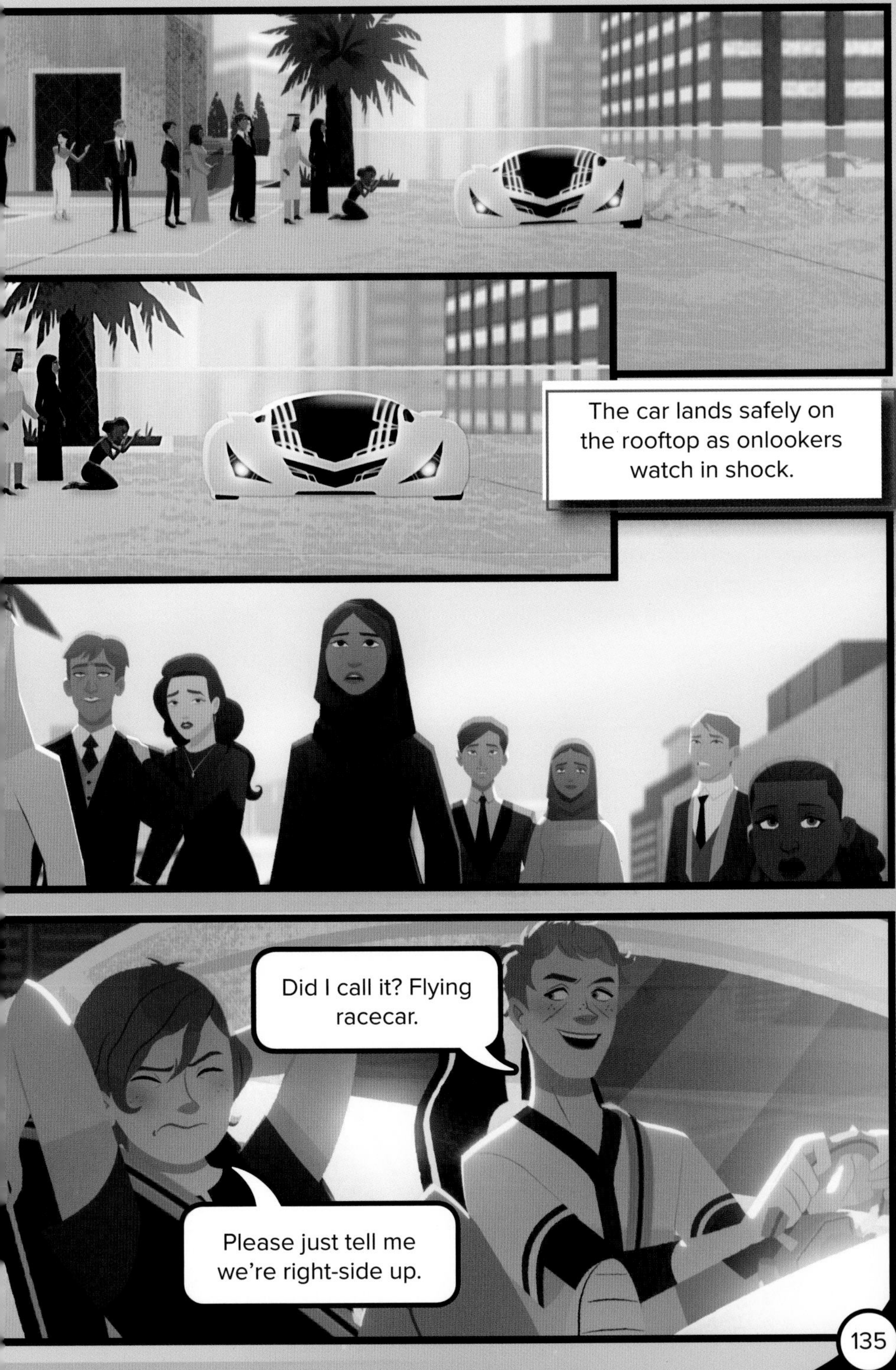
The car lands safely on the rooftop as onlookers watch in shock.
Did I call it? Flying racecar.
Please just tell me we're right-side up.

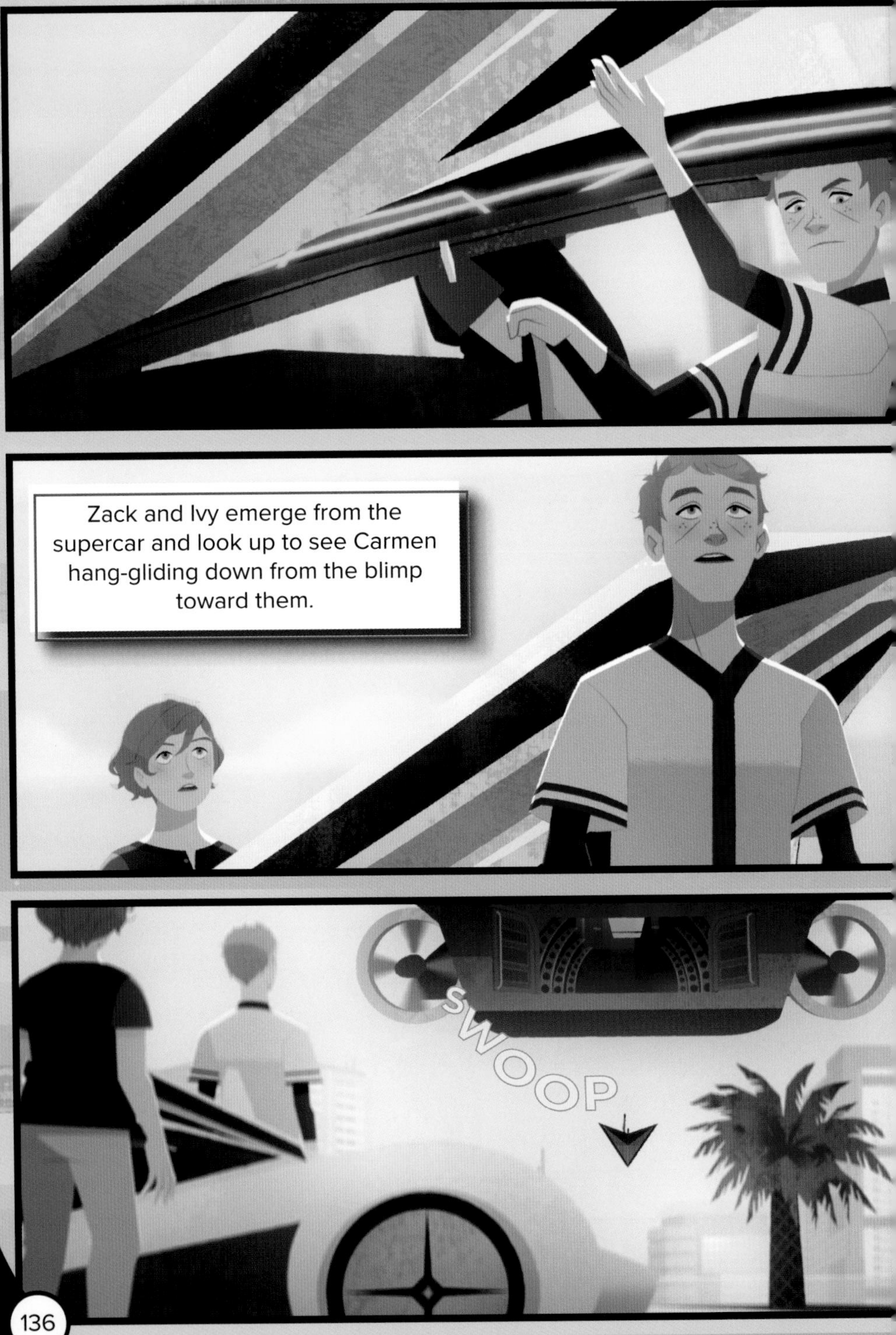
Zack and Ivy emerge from the supercar and look up to see Carmen hang-gliding down from the blimp toward them.
SWOOP

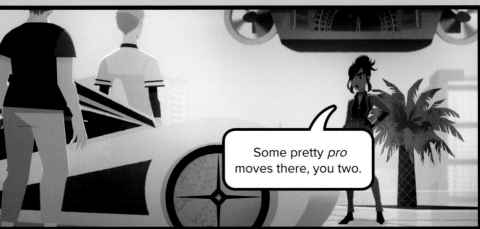

Some pretty *pro* moves there, you two.

In the cargo bay, the dazed Mechanic climbs to her feet as the Driver enters and joins her.

Now, 'oo in Dickens's ghost were *they??*

Some rocket scientist *...and a duke.*

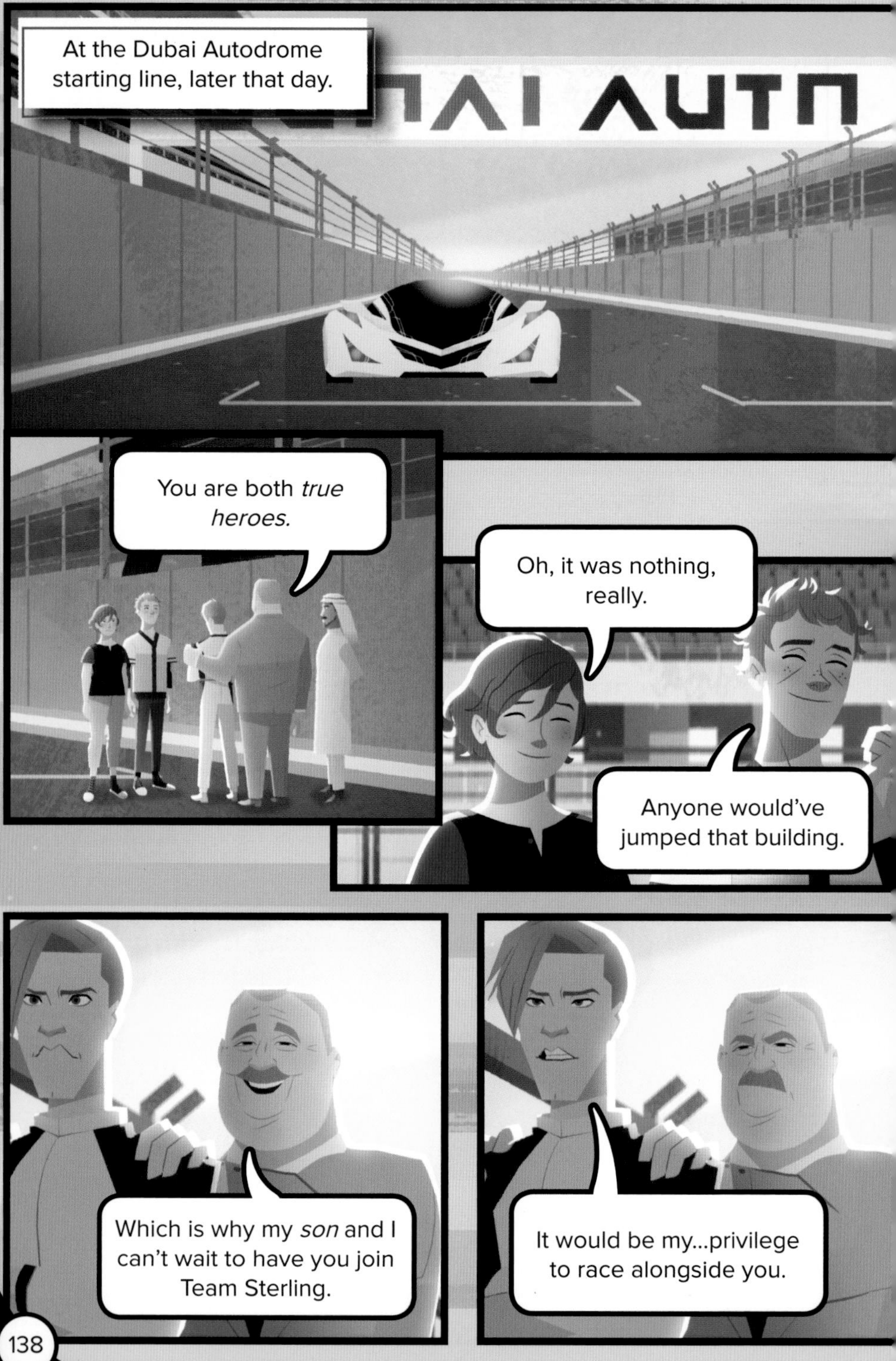
At the Dubai Autodrome starting line, later that day.
You are both *true heroes.*
Oh, it was nothing, really.
Anyone would've jumped that building.
Which is why my *son* and I can't wait to have you join Team Sterling.
It would be my...privilege to race alongside you.

I assume you two've had a chance to consider my offer?

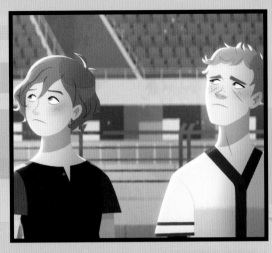

We'd be honored to have you in our family.

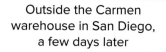

Outside the Carmen warehouse in San Diego, a few days later

You make it to the warehouse, Carmen?

Yes, Player. I'm here. Funny, in a way it all began with Carmen Brand Outerwear. Not sure there's a better place to hang my hat.

Carmen Brand Outerwear

FOR SALE

I'm really going to miss --

Oh man, it looks even BIGGER the second time...you can totally park a BLIMP in there!

FOR S SOLD

-- our midnight calls to room service. But Zack and Ivy chose family over career. Throwing down roots for them is the least I can do.

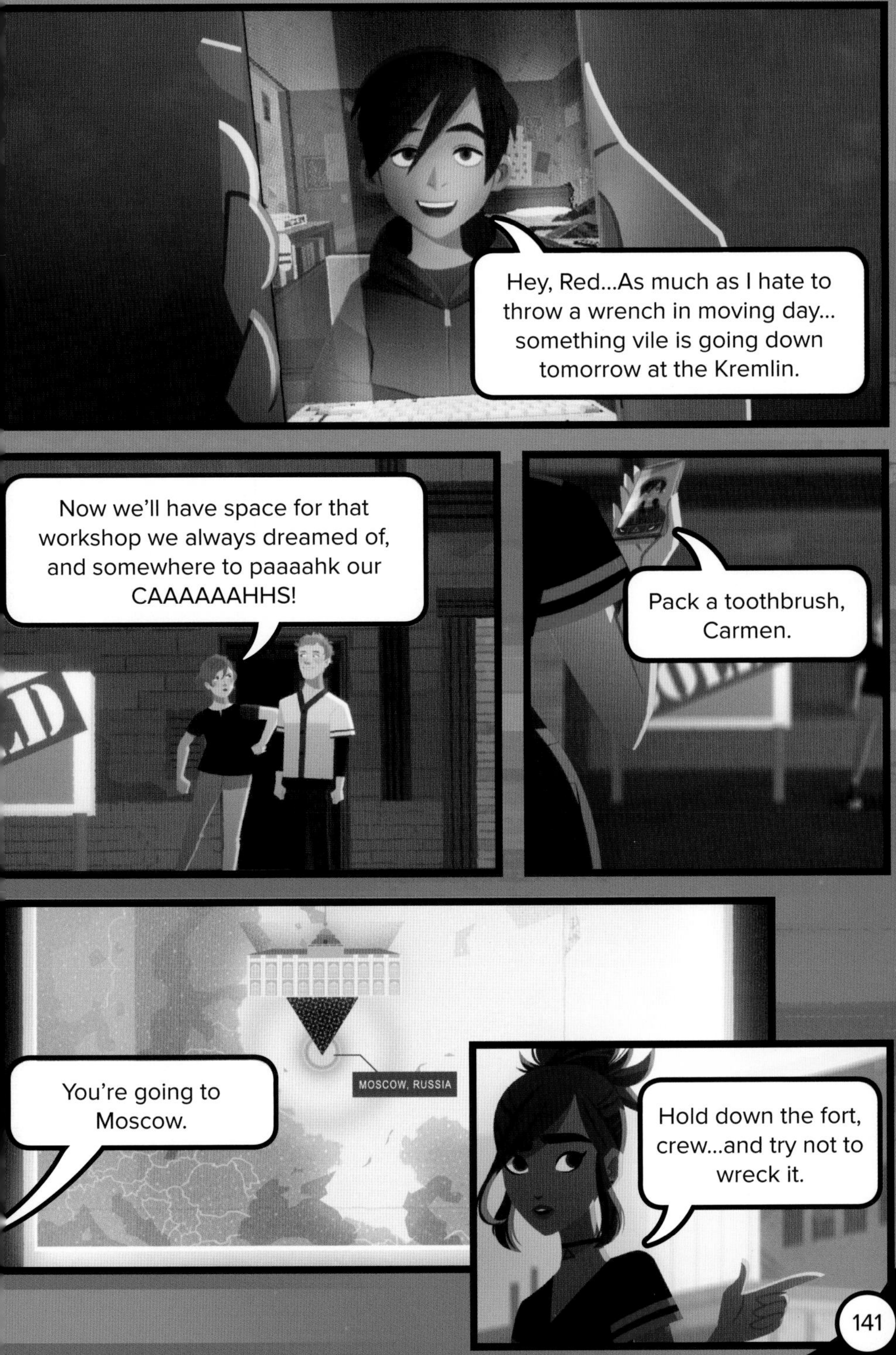
Hey, Red...As much as I hate to throw a wrench in moving day... something vile is going down tomorrow at the Kremlin.
Now we'll have space for that workshop we always dreamed of, and somewhere to paaaahk our CAAAAAAHHS!
Pack a toothbrush, Carmen.
MOSCOW, RUSSIA
You're going to Moscow.
Hold down the fort, crew...and try not to wreck it.

UNITED ARAB EMIRATES

DID YOU KNOW . . .

Capital: Abu Dhabi

Population: 9.9 million people

Official Language: Arabic

Currency: Dirham (AED)

Government: Federation of seven emirates with one advisory body

Flag:

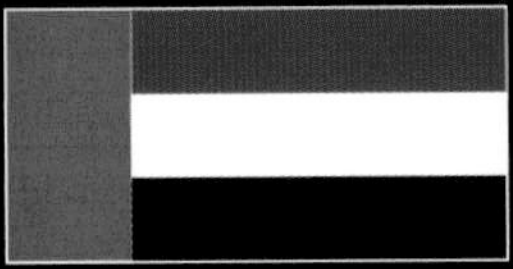

Climate: The UAE has a desert climate; it's hot and humid along the coast and hot and dry in the interior. It gets cooler in the eastern mountains. The UAE does not get a lot of rain, but it does get midwinter and early summer winds known as the shamal that blow in dust and sand.

History: The UAE's history is strongly rooted in traditions of Islam, which came to the region in 630 CE. Its location made it a trading hub between the East and the West for much of its history. In the nineteenth century, the Trucial States were formed under an alliance with the British. In 1969, the Emirate of Dubai began exporting oil, which has become a mainstay of the UAE's economy. In December 1971, the six emirates (Abu Dhabi, Dubai, Sharjah, Umm al-Qaiwain, Fujairah, and Ajman) agreed to establish the federation known as the United Arab Emirates. The seventh emirate, Ras al-Khaimah, was added to the new federation the following year. The emirates have forged a distinct national identity, combining the country's heritage with a modern administrative structure.

FUN FACTS:

The falcon is the UAE's national symbol, and falconry is a popular pastime as well as the heart of Emirati culture.

More than twelve million tourists visit the UAE each year.

The UAE has a literacy rate of 93.8 percent.

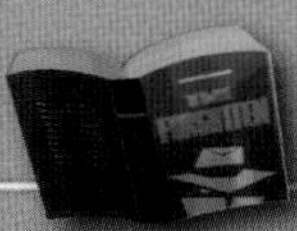

Pearling was Abu Dhabi's most important industry prior to the 1930s.

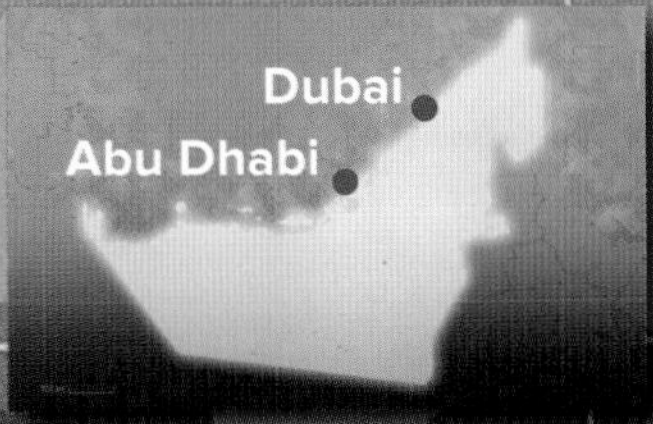
Dubai
Abu Dhabi

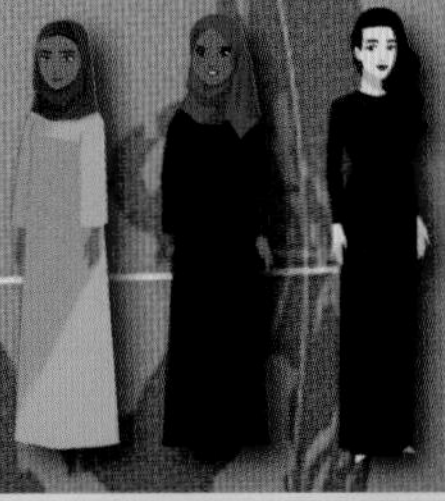

Seventy percent of university graduates and two-thirds of the government workforce are women.

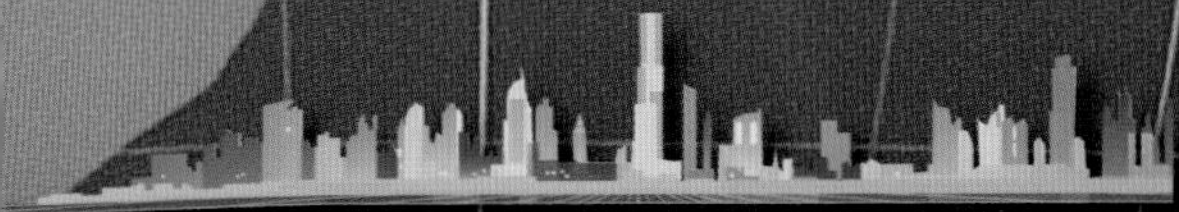

Masdar City, Abu Dhabi, is the world's first zero-carbon, zero-waste, car-free city.

The UAE hosts leading international film festivals, such as the annual Dubai International Film Festival and Abu Dhabi Film Festival.

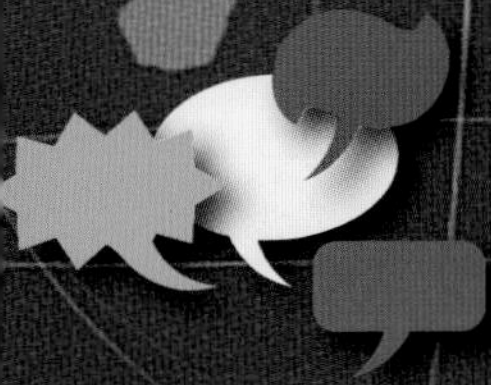

While Arabic is the official language of the UAE, other commonly spoken languages include English, Farsi, Hindi, and Urdu.

LOOK FOR MORE ADVENTURES WITH THE WORLD'S GREATEST THIEF!

NETFLIX
NOW A NETFLIX ORIGINAL SERIES
WHO IN THE WORLD IS
CARMEN SANDIEGO?
Foreword by Gina Rodriguez

CARMEN SANDIEGO
CLUE BY CLUE
NETFLIX
NOW A NETFLIX ORIGINAL SERIES

A CARMEN SANDIEGO Novel
Secrets of the Silver Lion
NETFLIX
A NETFLIX ORIGINAL SERIES
Emma Otheguy

CARMEN SANDIEGO
THE STICKY RICE CAPER
A GRAPHIC NOVEL
NETFLIX
NOW A NETFLIX ORIGINAL SERIES

CARMEN SANDIEGO
THE FISHY TREASURE CAPER
A GRAPHIC NOVEL
NETFLIX
NOW A NETFLIX ORIGINAL SERIES

CARMEN SANDIEGO
THE CHASING PAPER CAPER
A GRAPHIC NOVEL
NETFLIX
A NETFLIX ORIGINAL SERIES

CHASE YOUR OWN CAPER
CARMEN SANDIEGO
ENDANGERED OPERATION
NETFLIX
NOW A NETFLIX ORIGINAL SERIES

CHASE YOUR OWN CAPER
CARMEN SANDIEGO
JETPACK ATTACK
NETFLIX
NOW A NETFLIX ORIGINAL SERIES

WHERE IN THE WORLD IS
CARMEN SANDIEGO?
Fun facts, cool maps, and seek-and finds for 10 locations around the world
NETFLIX
NOW A NETFLIX ORIGINAL SERIES

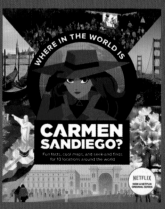